XD

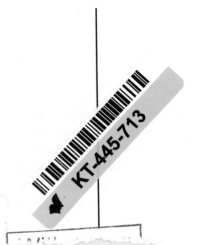

KT-445-713

VICTORI
crossing t
now lives
daughters
of coffee i
had a pass
courses be

Also by Victoria Cooke

The Single Mums' Book Club

VICTORIA COOKE

ONE PLACE. MANY STORIES

HQ
An imprint of HarperCollins*Publishers* Ltd
1 London Bridge Street
London SE1 9GF

www.harpercollins.co.uk

HarperCollins*Publishers*
1st Floor, Watermarque Building, Ringsend Road
Dublin 4, Ireland

This paperback edition 2021

First published in Great Britain by
HQ, an imprint of HarperCollins*Publishers* Ltd 2021

ISBN: 9780008376239

For my children, Scarlett and Amelie, who were not utter horrors during the lockdown of 2020 xxx

Chapter 1

'Ava, are your teeth brushed yet?' I yell up the stairs in vain. When I scoop Henry out of the baby chair, I notice his nappy is swollen and damp. 'Bugger.'

'Coming, Mummy.' The light thud of Ava's feet travels down the stairs. I look her over in horror.

'It's half past eight and you're not even dressed!' I sound like a banshee as I do most mornings because most mornings, Ava really likes to test my patience and after another sleepless night, I'm on the edge.

'I had a cut on my knee so I put some wet tissue on it and—'

'And nothing. Get your uniform on now!'

'But, Mummy!'

Give me strength.

Henry starts to scream. 'Ava, you have one minute to get dressed or I'm taking you to school in your vest and knickers. I mean it.'

'Mum, where are my football boots?'

'Oh, Ralph, I don't know – you had them on in the garden the other day. Try the utility room.'

Henry is still screaming. It's now eight-forty. 'Ava?'

'Coming, Mummy.' She appears in the kitchen, thankfully, for

1

the most part, dressed bar her tie but I'll tolerate the disapproving looks at the school gate for one day.

Otis, our dog, is doing supersonic circles at the prospect of a walk to school.

'Sorry, Otis, we're running late today.' He doesn't get it; instead, he's the only one sitting nicely by the door ready to go. 'Okay, let's get to the car,' I say, thrusting a banana in Ava's little hand.

'But I haven't got my shoes on.'

'Put them on in the car,' I say, shepherding her to the front door. Henry is still screaming – his cheeks red and puffy – but I haven't got time to change him now.

'Ralph?'

'I'm here,' he says, banging his football boots so big clumps of mud fall all over the hallway floor. I sigh but say nothing because I don't have time to argue.

'Take your brother,' I say, pushing Henry into his arms and scooping Ava into my own. 'Right, let's go!'

The school bell rings as we pull up outside. 'Ralph, take Ava to her teacher and run – I'll watch you from here.'

'Okay, Mum.'

'Love you both,' I say as they climb out.

There's a moment of silence whilst Henry looks out of the window. I sit and breathe for a moment, relishing the tiny slice of tranquillity before the torture of Monday supermarket shopping begins. As I put the car into gear, Henry wails again, prompting me to realise I've forgotten the changing bag.

'Buggering hell!' I do a U-turn and a car honks at me because there's an unwritten rule about not reversing near the school gate. I wave apologetically hoping it's another bedraggled mother who'll give me a sympathetic smile. It isn't. It's a smart-looking lady in a flashy BMW who looks less than impressed at having to stop and wait for my U-turn (okay, three, maybe five-point turn).

When I've retrieved the changing bag and Henry is changed

and happy, I make it to the supermarket. It's a small victory that I've remembered my carrier bags and I'm feeling ready for the challenge of battling with the trolley. As I'm unbuckling Henry's car seat, my phone pings. It's a message from school. Hoping there isn't another outbreak of nits, I open it.

URGENT REMINDERS
Please could all parents / carers remember that children must be accompanied onto the school grounds by an adult as per our safeguarding policy. We'd also like to remind you that as part of our commitment to keeping your children safe, cars are not permitted to turn around outside the school gates.

I chuck my phone into the footwell. 'Oh bugger off!'

Chapter 2

Before I take a trolley, I glance in my purse. I've always been careful with spending but there's so-we-can-have-a-holiday careful and there's so-we-can-afford-to-pay-the-bills careful. We're now in the latter stages of careful and have been since Mike left, but whilst my budget is a lot less than it used to be, I can make this work! I take a small trolley so I'm not tempted to over-buy but realise there's nowhere to put Henry, so I swap for a bigger one and thrust it through the doors, promising myself I won't shove a giant multipack of Walkers crisps in.

You can get some good bargains if you look hard enough. I make a few sacrifices and choose all the low-budget supermarket stuff but it's mostly fine and half the time it's the same as the more expensive stuff. As I'm browsing the toilet paper, a familiar voice stops me dead in my tracks.

'Stephanie, is that you?'

'Emily?' The sight of her perfectly coiffured blonde hair floods me with emotion. Since the divorce, I've hardly seen any of my friends. I assumed they'd rally round me with giant tubs of ice cream and talk of what a loser Mike was anyway, but they all got sort of distant and quiet. They probably wanted to give me time.

I walk over, arms wide, and hug her. She doesn't respond;

instead, she goes rigid and I end up awkwardly clutching her expensive-looking, blazer-clad torso. She smells of something posh and likely unpronounceable. I pull back.

'Is everything okay?' I ask, taking in her twisted expression, her microbladed eyebrows pinned into two sharp points by her Botox.

'Yeah, it's good to see you, Stephanie.' She hitches her bag up her shoulder and clutches the strap like she's ready to leave.

'Do you want to go in the café and get a cup of tea?' I blurt before she has chance to. I know I sound a bit desperate and she never really was the supermarket café and tea type. Thinking back, it was always a macchiato in some fancy coffee place. I'd never realised before but perhaps I wasn't the supermarket café type either. I suppose having a husband with a generous income meant I could afford for Ocado to bring my shopping and I at least had time to shower before venturing out so the idea of going somewhere nice didn't make me feel prickly and uncomfortable as it does now.

She glances at her watch. 'Sorry, Steph, my two hours parking will be up soon. It's been great to see you though. We'll catch up soon.'

She turns to leave again and there's no way she's been in here for two hours. She has a basket with a solitary pack of smoked salmon in. She might be a picky eater but unless she's brought in sniffer dogs and examined every pack with a magnifying glass several times before searching the warehouse for the most exquisite salmon on offer, she's lying to me.

'When?' I ask after her. When she turns, she pouts a little in a faux sympathetic way.

'Soon.'

I'm about to say okay when something inside me snaps. 'Are you ghosting me?'

'What are you talking about?' She lets out a small puff of humour.

5

'That's what it's called, isn't it? When someone you thought you were close to vanishes without a trace, ignores your texts and makes you feel like you don't exist and stuff. It's the modern name for ignoring someone.'

Her features soften. 'No, hon, nothing like that. I'm not *ghosting* you. It's just ...'

'What?'

Her body sags but her Pilates-conditioned frame soon pulls taut again. 'Since your divorce, Bradley and I have felt a bit in the middle of you and Mike. I wanted to comfort you and he wanted to go and spend time with Mike. It was awkward so we just decided to stay out of it all – y'know, take a step back. You understand, don't you?'

I go to nod but catch myself and shake my head. 'You mean that because *you* feel a little bit awkward, you're ditching me? At the time when I need my friends the most?'

She looks around. My high-pitched squeak must have attracted some attention but I'm too furious to care. 'Not *ditching* you,' she whispers, 'just giving you time and staying impartial.'

'Mike wanted to divorce *me*! Some kind of midlife crisis or whatever. I was happy. If anything, you should be ditching him. Not that I want you to ditch anyone, just, someone to have a glass of wine every now and then with would have been nice.'

She shakes her head. 'This is exactly what we didn't want.'

'We? We as in you and Bradley or we as in all of you – the whole gang?'

Silence.

'I see.' My voice falters. I'm vaguely aware that Henry seems to have picked something up off the shelf nearby. 'In that case, enjoy your smaller group size. In fact, invite Mike back into your dinner party gang. I don't want to be part of your pretentious circle anyway. There, your difficult decision has been made.' I shove the trolley but it's heavy and stiff. Now that I've lost

6

momentum, it takes much more effort to move it than I'd prepared for.

'Steph, don't be like that,' she says as I shove the trolley one more time, and mercifully it starts to move but not before Henry squirts a tube of something all over me. I recognise the torn. yellow and blue box from my pregnancy days. Preparation H. I'm not quick enough to miss Emily's look of disgust.

Hot needles stab my eyeballs as I walk away. I don't look back and Emily doesn't call after me. I make my way through the checkout as quickly as possible, for once thankful for the checkout lady's super speed. When I leave the shop, I let out a heavy breath.

When I'm home and the shopping is put away, I stick the kettle on. I've got a life to sort out, children to raise and a house to run. I haven't got time to worry about Emily and the rest of my so-called friends. If they're uncomfortable staying friends with me, sod them all. Henry is asleep in his crib and my tea is hot and brewed to perfection. The washing machine has finished but emptying it can wait. I have to take these moments of bliss as and when I can because I never quite know when the next one will be.

After my tea, I take the opportunity to use the loo in peace. One thing they don't tell you about having kids is that the toilet becomes a sort of sanctuary of bliss. A few minutes of self-preserving loo-time can do wonders for your sanity and can mean the difference between being able to take a few deep breaths and get on with things, versus completely losing your composure and letting all hell break lose. Unfortunately, as most parents are aware – the little buggers nearly always find you in there. With Ralph and Ava at school, and Henry asleep, this is my perfect moment – I even have a game of Candy Crush. I'm in heaven. That is until I finish, and realise there's no loo roll.

'Shit!' Pardon the pun. 'Bloody Emily!' Thanks to her catching me off-guard, I didn't pick any up!

I waddle, with my jeans around my ankles, to the changing bag in the hall and then back to the downstairs loo where I clean up and bag the baby wipes because the last thing I need is a blocked soil pipe (that isn't a euphemism).

When Henry wakes up, I change and feed him and pop him into the pram.

'We're going for a walk,' I say, smiling at his podgy face.

As I'm wrestling the pram down the steps to the pavement, my phone rings.

'Mike?' My heart plummets. He'll be welching on father duties, no doubt – he never calls otherwise.

'Hi, Stephanie, listen do you think the kids would be okay with me picking them up from yours on Saturday morning instead of from school on Friday?' Almost!

Yes, they'll mind – their entire week revolves around the exciting things that Daddy will do with them on the weekend. It's their break away from boring Mummy and her homework schedule and reading routine.

'They'll be disappointed,' I say, not wanting to lay on a guilt trip just in case his mother is dying or something. Side note – the best thing about divorce is that you also get rid of the mother-in-law, not that I hope she's dying. The physical distance and absence of obligation is enough.

He sighs dramatically. 'I can get them, it's just that I've had this awful week at work and it's only going to get worse over the next few days. I'll probably have to work late Friday and then there will be team drinks after ...'

Ding ding ding. There we have it. Twenty-one-year-old wannabe Mike fancies a night out with his work friends. Poor cherub!

'Whatever you think is best,' I say. Yes, I'm being passive-aggressive (one of the things he threw against me in the divorce – he just couldn't take it anymore) but, well, I don't care because ninety-nine per cent of my passive-aggressive instances would never have occurred if he wasn't being such a twat in the first place.

'Stephanie, don't make me feel worse than I already do. It's hard juggling a job like mine and, well, you don't work.'

And there it is. I. Don't. Work. Another reason for his emotional stress even though he was the one who told me to give up my job and be a stay-at-home mum because he earns a bloody fortune and the kids need a parent around. Turns out that's not at all true in Mikelandia where kids raise themselves.

'Yet,' I say, and he laughs nervously. I could rant about how being a one-woman feeding, cleaning, bathing, clothing, emotional support machine is a full-time job. I don't because he'll come back with some retort about how he has to fund us all, then things could get quite nasty – I've been there before. I know plenty of single mothers work but we've built a life this way and unpicking it is a process.

'So, you are looking for work?' He sounds hopeful.

'Of course I am,' I say, and it's true. I am, but who wants to hire a bookkeeper whose only bookkeeping experience in the last ten years has been neatly stacking nursery rhyme books and filling in reading logs?

'That's great, Stephanie.' His voice tinkles like a fruit machine dispensing pound coins.

'Is that everything? I'm sort of busy.'

'Henry running rings around you is he? That's my boy.'

Oh fuck off! 'Something like that.'

'See you Saturday morning then, about elevenish?'

Because we can't do without a proper lie-in on a Saturday, can we?

'Fine, see you then.' I end the call and stare at my phone. I don't even know why I have the thing because all it does is bring misery.

When Henry and I get to the Tesco local, I grab a packet of toilet roll but before I get to the till, I panic and check my purse.

I paid cash at the supermarket earlier and I gave the cashier everything I had in note form. I rummage through the coins. There's a queue behind me but I just need ten more pence. I dig deep and catch a large coin between two of my fingers. Yes! A small victory. But the victory is short-lived when I pull it out and it's a murky brown two-pence piece.

'Sorry,' I say, coming out of the queue. I walk back to the toilet paper section hoping for a budget version of the normal own-brand stuff I'd picked but the only alternative is Andrex and I'm not exactly made of money. As I stare at the toilet paper that I'm eight pence away from, everything comes crashing down on me. The divorce, going it alone, juggling the kids, budgeting, my deserting friends, the fact I can't get to sleep at night, and everything knots together in my stomach before propelling itself into my throat like a grenade. My eyes water and my chest heaves. A loud sob escapes and before I even realise it's me making that awful wailing sound, a firm hand lands on my shoulder.

'Stephanie?'

I turn my head and, through watery eyes, see a lady who I recognise as a neighbour from across the street. She's a little shorter than me with frizzy brown hair that she always has tied back. She bears all the hallmarks of a frazzled mum; for starters, her white and navy striped top is inside out.

'Janey?' I say uncertainly. She nods and smiles warmly.

'Are you okay?'

I nod to give myself time to recompose. 'I'm just having one of those days and now I've come here for loo roll and I'm eight pence short – I should have checked my purse before I left but—'

'Shh, hon, listen, we'll go and pay for this and then I'm taking you home for a cup of tea.'

I don't know what it is about the warmth and kindness of this woman who hardly knows me, but it sets me off crying again.

'Why don't you go and get some fresh air and I'll sort this.' She prises the loo roll out of my hand and I might be mistaken but I think she shoves me a little towards the door. Outside, the cold air hits me like a slap in the face. My head starts to pound like an embarrassed little man is trying to dig himself a hole in my grey matter. I contemplate scurrying off but she knows where I live and I really need that loo roll.

'Here you go,' she says, handing me a carrier bag. 'Right, your place or mine?' Despite living across the road from one another for years, we've never said more than a quick hello, or given knowing glances as we've struggled to get the kids into their impossible car seats, but here she is offering me support. I suppose I was always busy before the divorce, people-pleasing the likes of Emily, and ever since Mike left I've been so frazzled myself, I've barely acknowledged anyone. The fact she's doing this for me sends a warmth so strong through my body, it almost sets me off crying again.

Ten minutes later we're in my kitchen and I'm apologising for the mess whilst cursing myself for not tidying up earlier.

She bats away my comment with her hand. 'Listen, I've always thought there was something suspicious about super tidy people – I mean, where do they find the time to be constantly cleaning? They're missing out on something somewhere.'

I laugh. I like this woman.

'Anyway,' she says as she fills the kettle. 'Do you want to talk about anything? I'm a good listener and have a few hours to kill.'

Something about her round face and soft brown eyes compels me to want to open up. I rarely get to speak to other adults, excluding Mike of course but he doesn't count.

When I try to pinpoint the things that are getting to me, I can't. It's not the divorce – I've had time to come to terms with that. The hardest part of the divorce wasn't losing Mike, it was losing the family unit I'd always yearned for. Growing up without a mum and having a dad who was always away left me longing for a proper family. I never grew up wanting to be a nurse or a pop star. I grew up wanting to be a mum and a wife. The loss of that dream is what I'm mourning for, but the version Mike and I had was far from perfect. Today I think it's just life that's getting to me though. It all sounds so trivial when I try to verbalise it – people struggle with so much more.

'I'm just being daft. I'm having a bad day and too many things got on top of me at once.'

'I know that feeling.' She uses the teapot off the shelf by the window and I daren't tell her it was a gift that I keep for orna-mental purposes because she's being so kind. 'Happens to me at least once a day. The kids run me ragged and my other half is as much use as a marshmallow mallet. I love them and all, but I do cherish the time I get when they're at school.'

When she places the mugs of tea down, she sits opposite me at the kitchen table and takes a sip. 'The kids giving you grief too?' She says the statement like a question.

'Something like that. They're not especially bad; it's just the collective nature of them.'

'Ahh, the many-headed beast, though I only have two – you've got your work cut out with three. Listen, it's not my place to say and tell me to shut up if you wish but I heard about you and Mike splitting up and just wanted to say I'm sorry and I'm here if you need help or fancy a natter.'

The kindness Janey is showing me is almost enough to set me off blubbing again. I can't even remember a time when somebody showed me this level of empathy.

'That's so kind – thank you. Today has just been a special kind of horrendous … I didn't sleep. I never sleep.'

'Oh, honey, I know that feeling. All of life's problems seem to want solving the minute you close your eyes.'

I nod but it isn't that. I can't tell her the real reason I don't sleep well. Instead, I find myself filling Janey in on everything else – right from Ava refusing to get dressed and Emily ditching me. Instead of telling me I'm being a drama queen, like Mike would have, or switching off like my old friends did, she listens and pulls sympathetic faces in all the right places. When I've finished, I feel several pounds lighter.

'And to top it off,' I add, 'I was parent-shamed by the kids' school this morning.' I find myself laughing. It's euphoric and unfamiliar.

'Parent-shamed! We're going to get along well. Tell me more?' She rests her head on one hand, her elbow on the table.

She laughs as I tell her there were no kids about when I entrusted my two to walk in unaccompanied. 'Honestly, I think some jobsworth sits monitoring the CCTV just to try and catch a parent out!' I shake my head. 'More tea?'

As I go to fill the kettle, Henry starts to cry. 'Sorry.'

'I'll do the tea – you see to Henry,' she says.

A few hours pass quickly and before I know it, it's time to pick the kids up.

'Right, I'd better get going. I'm taking the car today as my eldest, Tom, has a friend coming for tea and he's a bit of a whirl-wind, this little guy, so I don't fancy walking, but we totally should try and walk together a few days a week. Great for the bum!' she says, slapping herself on the bottom for emphasis. I laugh.

'And listen, my other half, Jimmy, works away a lot so I know how tough it can be on your own. When he's here he's always too tired to take any notice of me anyway, so if you're ever stuck for someone to take the kids to school or look after them while you go on a hot date, just ask – if I'm free to help I will do,' she says, giving me a pointed look that suggests she means it.

My body fills with warmth. 'Thank you – same here, although with you being married and me being a hot mess, I can't see either of us going on a hot date any time soon.' I chuckle but the reality is, I haven't once considered dating. The thought of going

13

through all of that early relationship stuff terrifies me, and besides, I have three children to think about.

'You never know.' She winks and I can't quite tell if she means that I could be dating one day, or she could. Either way, I like Janey a lot.

Chapter 3

It's one-fifteen when the doorbell rings. The kids' bags have been packed and by the door since ten-thirty. Ava and Ralph have taken it in turns to ask, 'When is Daddy going to be here?' precisely every four minutes since they woke up at seven a.m.

'You're late,' I hiss as Mike steps through the door.

'Oh come on, I said even*ish* not eleven on the dot.'

'Since when has quarter past one been even*ish*?'

He gives me a sideways glance as Ralph comes bounding down the hallway.

'Daddy!'

'My big man!' Mike scoops him up and spins him around. Ralph's trainers scrape the wall leaving a black scuff mark about a foot above the skirting board, which irks me, mostly because Mike did it. As much as he grates on me, he is a good dad when he's actually with the kids. It's part of the problem of course – he gets to be Captain Fun whilst I play the role of the evil villain: Regimental Mum. I know this is common during separation but when we agreed on joint custody, Mike promised to take the rough and the smooth. I could say something but he'd come back with some rubbish about me being better at the discipline side or how he has all that rules and routine stuff to deal with at work and he just wants to chill out on the weekends.

'Daddy, Daddy, look at my dress!' Ava comes running down the hallway in the Monsoon bridesmaid dress that she wore to Mike's friend's wedding a few months ago.

'Why are you wearing that?' I shriek. I had it washed and ready to put on eBay.

'I'm a princess,' she says twirling.

'You sure are.' Mike throws her into the air and catches her. 'And I bet you'll only eat pink bonbons won't you?'

'Don't feed her just bonbons,' I say wearily.

'As if I would,' he says before whispering, 'I totally will,' into her ear. She giggles and thrashes her arms and legs around with excitement.

'Don't let them stay up too late or they'll be horrible tomorrow.'

'Stephanie, relax, I'm their *father*. I know what I'm doing.'

'Okay, and you're aware of everything Henry needs because last week Ava said you let him have cake and he's really too young for cake.'

Mike puts Ava down. 'Ralph, can you take Ava to the car? I won't be a minute.' Ralph takes Ava's hand and when they're down the steps Mike turns to face me.

'You need to stop telling me what to do.'

'Mike, I just want you to be on my side once in a while. Not because I want to boss you around or have some backup or whatever, but because the kids need consistency in their lives. They need to have boundaries. Do you know how hard it is saying no to extra sweets when they come back whining, "Daddy lets us have them"?'

'I'm not here to bend over backwards to improve your life anymore, Stephanie. Don't you think I do enough by providing for you all and paying for this place when I don't even live here?' He sweeps his arm around the hallway like it's a grand palace. It is a very nice house, don't get me wrong, it's a four-bed townhouse in Cheshire, which I'm very lucky to live in but I know what he earns and he's trying to make me feel indebted to him.

'You do. I'm sorry,' I say, reeling inside. 'I'll see you tomorrow.' I want to yell that he should be paying for his kids and what he gives us isn't enough after bills but I don't want to cause a row about it. He can be irrational and hot-headed when he gets angry and he's been even worse lately for some reason. I can't risk him pulling all his money and taking us back through the courts.

I spend the rest of the day binge-watching *The Crown*. By late afternoon I'm missing the kids like crazy and sit flicking through photographs of them on my phone – something I do every weekend when they're at their dad's. As I'm looking at pictures of Ava dressed as Matilda for the last World Book Day, a message comes through. It's Janey.

Hi Steph, I saw the kids go off with Mike. Mine are at a sleepover and Jimmy is working away (again). Fancy a drink in an actual pub like two grown-ups? X

I get a flutter of excitement. A pub! I haven't been out since way before Mike left. Our group did a lot of couples' dinner parties. They weren't really pub people. Suddenly I get the taste for half a lager and some dry-roasted peanuts.

That sounds great. X

Perfect – I'll come over in half an hour. X

I run upstairs, throw on some make-up. I'm not a heavy make-up person but I'm not going to lie and say I'm confident with a naked face. This decade has brought some rather fetching fine lines and reddened dry patches on my face and whilst they don't bother me much on the whole, I'm not exactly keen on flaunting them either. I change my baggy sweater for a fitted denim shirt before squirting on the dregs of perfume from a sample bottle I've had in my drawer for years and brushing my shoulder-length light-brown hair. It's the most effort I've made in a long time. As I'm coming down the stairs, the doorbell rings.

We walk to the local pub, which is near the local Tesco. As a duo they make up the underwhelming 'village centre' of Milden, where we live. It's getting dark and I'm on high alert. My fingers encase the small personal alarm in my pocket and my eyes dart left and right. It's only a five-minute walk to the pub and its welcoming glow is soon in my sights. As we reach the doorway, I exhale, sliding my hand out of my pocket. It's a nice village pub type place and half of it is more of a restaurant. Mike and I sometimes came here when I was too tired to cook. The typical 'pub smell' of stale beer and grilled steak fat is warm and comforting and we find a table by the open fire easily. It's pretty quiet for a Saturday.

'What are you drinking?' Janey asks, rummaging in her bag, presumably for her purse.

'Let me get these. I owe you one after all,' I say before pushing my way to the bar. I don't tell her I took twenty quid out of Ava's money box to come out. Obviously, I'm going to put twenty pounds back in as soon as I get my next payment off Mike tomorrow, but I don't know Janey well enough to be sure she'd see the funny side.

I order my half of Fosters, some peanuts, and Janey's Prosecco and it's over a tenner. It's going to be a short night.

'Ahh, this is nice,' Janey says. 'I love my kids but I love a bit of me-time too if you know what I mean. I feel torn in half most days trying to keep Tom off his silly computer games whilst Seren mithers at me to bake or spills slime all over the carpet.'

'How about Jimmy? Is he much help?'

Janey has a mouth full of peanuts so shakes her head. 'He's got a carpet business and spends more or less every day of the week fitting carpets in the most far-flung places you could find. Honestly, you'd think the people round here didn't have use for carpets.'

'Oh.' I'm not sure what else to say.

She picks at the corner of a beer mat and doesn't look up. I can't see her face but her body looks like it's caved in on itself.

Her confident, broad shoulders stoop like someone is pressing down on them. 'I know I should be grateful. He's making decent money but he's not much use when he is at home.'

I swallow.

'Listen, if the kids are with Mike every weekend, we should do this more often. Mine are always sleeping out, which is something since Jimmy never helps out.' She sounds more upbeat now.

I'd love to but I don't think my bank balance could keep up.

'What's the matter?' Janey says, studying my face. 'You've not touched your drink yet.'

I don't want to tell her I'm making it last. 'Oh, nothing. It's just that things … finances, are a bit tight since the divorce. Regular pub trips are a bit out of my league at the minute.'

'Oh, Steph love, you should have said. I've got a nice bottle of pink Prosecco at home we could have had.'

'No,' I protest. 'I'm glad to be out. This is nice and it's not something I ever do. I just can't do it often. I am job hunting though.'

'What did you do before …' She kinks her head side to side, and I take it to mean kids.

'I was a bookkeeper. So it's not like I gave up a huge salary or anything but any extra would help right now.'

'That should be easy to go back into shouldn't it? Nothing is sure except death and taxes, so they say.'

I shrug. 'I thought so but I haven't even managed to get an interview anywhere. I think I've been out of the game for too long. I'd need training on the latest bookkeeping software, and nobody wants to invest that sort of time in their staff anymore. I might have to ditch taxes and go into funerals at this rate.'

She reaches across the table and puts her hand on mine. 'You'll get something soon.'

'It would be nice to get together more though when you're free,' I say, bravely putting myself forward.

'Yeah, it would. Do you know what I've always fancied doing that wouldn't cost much?'

I have a mouth full of peanuts so shake my head.

'A book club.'

I raise my eyebrows. In my brief time of knowing her, I didn't have Janey down as a bookworm.

'That actually sounds like quite good fun,' I say after swallowing my beer.

'I think so. We could meet, say, once a month and talk about what we'd read over drinks and nibbles. We'd have to set a book each month, of course, and commit to reading it.'

I'm so elated I could cry. The inside of my nose is tingling and everything. This is a commitment to see an adult human on a regular basis. 'That sounds fab.'

'Great. Let's choose a book now and we can start reading asap!' She pronounces asap as a word. 'I'll read anything. Is there a book in particular that you fancy?'

I pause to think. 'Actually, there's been so much hype about *The Handmaid's Tale* that I wouldn't mind seeing what all the fuss is about, if you've not already read it. I haven't watched the show or anything.'

Janey practically jumps out of her seat. 'Perfect. I haven't seen it either but have heard so many good things.'

'I kept meaning to give it a whirl but once the kids are in bed, I just need something light and short, so I tend to binge on *Friends* reruns or *Schitt's Creek*.' I don't say why I need something light to help me sleep.

She pulls out her phone and starts typing. 'I'm just ordering it now. Do you want me to get you a copy whilst I've got it here on Amazon?'

I shake my head. 'I'll sort out a copy.' Perhaps I can raid the local charity shops.

'Fantastic,' Janey says jigging with excitement. 'I'll get the next round in.'

Before I can stop her she's off. I search for a copy of *The Handmaid's Tale* online but once you factor in postage it's the price of a couple of packed lunches. If I can't get a second-hand copy, I'll join the library over in Crinkly.

'Here you go, book buddy!' she says, plonking another beer down in front of me with enough enthusiasm the white foam sloshes over the top.

Chapter 4

Something about going out and being in Janey's company has really spurred me on. I've found an advert for a bookkeeper position at a vet's practice in Crinkly, which is the next village along to ours. Rather than request the application form by email, I decided to drive over and ask for one. Otis could do with a worming tablet and I thought it would be better to meet the staff in person, just to prove I don't have two heads or anything. I've been out of work so long that any employer worth their salt is bound to think there's something wrong with me.

Inside, it's quite dark and dingy. The tall reception desk is panelled in worn, dark wood. There's an empty chair behind it. Otis starts to whimper and tug me back towards the door – he's not a fan of the vet's and the distinctive smell must be prompting some unpleasant memories. I crouch down as best I can whilst balancing Henry, and stroke his head until he calms a little. Still, nobody appears and I don't want to knock on the door that says: 'Consultation Room'. For all I know, the vet could be in there telling someone their beloved pet is dead so I should wait. On the other hand, I could be here hours. The decaying remains of Otis and me could go undiscovered for years. There's an advert for the job on the practice's noticeboard that says, 'Ask at reception for an application form.' Brilliant!

After five long minutes, I go to leave but the door creaks open behind me. It's the one to the consultation room.

A tall man appears. He's on a cordless phone and doesn't seem to have noticed me so I sit patiently.

'Yes, Mrs Pearson, the last time you attended was the seventh. Let me just check that for you.' He balances the phone between his ear and his shoulder before walking behind the reception desk where he starts clicking on the computer.

'Was it cash you thought you'd paid? Hang on, Carly keeps a paper record. I'm just going to put you on hold.'

He starts to flick through a paper file on the desk. Two deep lines form between his eyebrows.

'Buggering bugger.' He slams the file down. 'For God's sake.'

I shrink down into the chair hoping he doesn't notice me, and for once Henry rests quietly against me.

The man turns his attention back to the computer and starts clicking away. 'Bloody hell.'

He eventually picks his phone back up. 'Mrs Pearson, I'll need to double-check with Carly but I think you're up to date. Don't worry. You too.'

He hangs up his phone and slumps in the swivel chair, letting out a sigh that sounds like a slowly deflating hot air balloon. I don't really know what to do. He's never going to give me a job now I've just witnessed his outburst; he'll be too embarrassed to ever want to see me again. I sit silently, hoping he goes back in the other room without spotting me.

Then his eyes lock on mine. I freeze, like it helps with invisibility or something.

'Oh, Jesus. I'm so sorry. Can I help you at all?' he asks, rising to his feet and smoothing down his trousers.

I look away, feeling more than a little awkward but Otis yanks on the lead, desperate to get over to the man for a head pat and before I know it, I'm about a foot away looking up into his mesmerising blue eyes.

'Hi,' I say, plastering on a smile whilst wrestling the lead. 'Sorry, he gets excited.' The vet crouches down and fusses Otis, who, in turn, wags his tail in a state of euphoric glee. Honestly, you would think he was neglected.

'I'm Edward and I'm afraid I don't cope well with chaos.' When he's not cursing, his voice is less harsh. It's richer, deeper and much more smooth. He's wearing tweed. Lots of tweed and looks like he's wandered off the set of *All Creatures Great and Small*. Despite that, I can tell he's a similar age to me; mid (okay, late) thirties. I thought you had to go to university for forty-seven years to train to be a vet but apparently not. He's tall and strong-looking with light brown hair but there's something incredibly warm about him too.

'Did you need me to take a look at him?' He gestures to Otis, who is still ridiculously excited to the point where he seems to have forgotten about his fear of the vet's. This place doesn't have the same feel as the large, modern chain that Mike made us go to in the city centre. It's traditional, homely. Perhaps Otis is picking up on that.

'Oh, no. He's fine. Mental but fine. Sorry, I didn't mean to bother you. You seem really busy. I can come back.' I turn to leave.

'Don't be silly, you're here now and besides, I'm always busy so you'd be hard pushed to find me otherwise.' He smiles and his sodalite eyes crinkle a little in the corners. They're the kind of eyes that are hard to look at. The kind that compel you to look, but when you do, they make you ... feel things. Like their beholder can see deeper into your soul with each glint. I look away. How can someone who shoves his arms in cow bums for a living be so captivating?

I shake my head subtly and focus. 'I just popped in for an application form for the bookkeeping job.'

He sighs and his cheeks flush a blotchy rose. 'Ah. That makes you witnessing my little outburst even more embarrassing. Carly should be on reception but she's always buggering off for a fag when I'm not looking and despite having a doctorate, I can't for the life of me fathom her quirky admin systems. There should be some here.' He rummages through a paper tray on the reception desk and eventually pulls something out.

'Are you a bookkeeper?' he asks, handing me, but not letting go of, the forms.

'I am,' I say, then point to Henry. 'At least I was, before children came along. I'm looking to get back into the workplace.'

'Great. Though I have to warn you, I inherited this practice from my late father and I've not had a chance to update the systems and things yet. I'm afraid our books are paper-based and we still use Roman numerals.'

My forehead crumples, then I realise he's joking and relax. This could be perfect. 'Well, that suits me. I'm a little out of date myself – I have a son who's doing his SATs soon and we've been revising Roman numerals.' I smile and watch as his upper body loosens. 'In all seriousness, when I took time out to have children, the whole sector seemed to take that as their cue to change *everything*!' He smiles again and his eyes catch a stream of dusty sunlight beaming in through the small window in the entrance door.

'So, how long have you had the surgery?' I ask, somehow intrigued by this tweed-clad stranger.

'Eight years.'

'Oh.' I can't hide my surprise.

'I know. I've had plenty of time and I'm a real stickler for being organised normally. It's just that my dad's old bookkeeper stayed on for a while. Mabel, God rest her soul. She was lovely but not exactly the computer whizz I needed to make any efficient or meaningful change. Anyway, Carly came along and has had a bash but, between you and me, she's not exactly up to the job either.' The door opens and a young woman walks in. 'Ahh, Carly!'

'Sorry, Doc, felt faint and needed some fresh air.' She erupts into a quite timely, crackling smoker's cough.

Edward glances at me and raises a humorous eyebrow. I stifle a giggle.

'Can't beat a good old lungful of fresh air. Glad you're feeling better. Anyhow ...' He gestures to me.

'Stephanie,' I supply.

'Steph wishes to apply for the bookkeeper job and I have to wrestle some antibiotics down the throat of a labradoodle, so could you take over?'

''Course,' she says.

When he leaves I sort of hover in his wake. Nobody ever calls me Steph and I quite liked the familiarity of it. Edward seemed to fill the waiting area somehow and now he's gone, the place seems cavernous. I have what I need but it seems rude to just leave now he's introduced me to Carly.

'He's a bit stuffy but he's all right. Anyway, the application deadline is next Tuesday.' She leans forward on the desk, her dry, mousy hair tumbling over the edge. 'I shouldn't be telling you this, but we've not had any applicants yet. Between you and me I don't think he's paying enough.'

I glance at the hourly pay on the advert. If I get the job, I shan't be turning left on an aeroplane any time soon, or indeed stepping onto an aeroplane any time soon but it's enough to top up what I'm short of each month. 'That's good to know. Thanks.'

I leave with a strange feeling. Animals have never really been my thing; Otis was Mike's idea but we decided it was best he stayed with the children and I've grown to love him. I don't dislike animals, but I've never called myself an animal lover. I've never even taken my kids to the zoo, but something about this dated little practice makes me feel like I belong.

Chapter 5

'So,' Janey says, squeezing her shoulders excitedly as she pours us both a glass of Pinot Blush with enough vigour that some sloshes over the edge. She wipes the wine splodge with her finger. '*The Handmaid's Tale*. What did you think? I think we're supposed to discuss plot and characters and stuff.'

'I, er, well. It's eerily realistic at the moment isn't it?' I say. Truth is, I've been so busy with the kids that I didn't get the chance to read past the back cover. I cheated and watched season one on Sky. I really hate lying to Janey, but I can't admit that I fell at the first hurdle.

'Oh my God, yes. The things that are happening are happening somewhere in the world right now,' she says. 'That's why it's so scary and to be honest, the perpetual cycle of thankless cooking and cleaning doesn't seem so far removed from my own life.'

'Oh, Janey, I know things can be like that at times but you have a beautiful family.'

Janey leans forward but her face drops to the floor. 'I know. It's just …' She takes a gulp of her wine. 'It's Jimmy. I just wish he was a proper husband. Honestly, if he's not off working, he's at the pub with his mates all the time whilst I keep the house and everything going without so much as a goodnight kiss. Every now and then he expects his conjugal rights with no sort of lead-up. I feel like bloody Offred at times.'

'Janey, I'm sorry. Have you spoken to him about it?'

She shakes her head. 'Not for a long time. To be honest I'm so knackered most evenings that a hot bath and an early night is enough for me. I suppose I just wish that he wanted to be more present in all our lives. At least the mothers in *The Handmaid's Tale* have all those other women to support them.'

'Well, now you have me.'

She smiles and pulls her knees up onto the sofa, hugging them into her body. 'Thank you.'

'Just don't expect me to wear one of those uncomfortable-looking dresses like Serena does. Teal is not my colour.'

Janey narrows her eyes at me. 'Uncomfortable-*looking* – you didn't read the book, did you?'

I wince. 'No, sorry. I watched season one of the TV show because I didn't get time – the kids have been full-on this week and I had to make Ava a scarecrow costume for the summer show. Goodness knows why they need the costumes so early.'

To my relief, she giggles. 'Oh, thank goodness, me neither. I did at least revise the differences between the book and the show so I wouldn't get caught out – that's how I know the dresses were blue in the book, not teal. Good though isn't it?'

'Brilliant. I'm hooked!'

'How about we get started on season two since we don't have a book to discuss.'

'Sounds good.' She snuggles into the love seat and I curl up on the sofa and press play.

'Jesus,' Janey says as the credits roll at the end of episode one. 'They're not holding back this season, are they?'

I shake my head. 'No! I think I need a cuppa!'

When I return from the kitchen with my teapot (which I've

decided I might as well use now), Janey is flicking through her phone.

'I called into the vet's to ask about that job today,' I say, placing the tray down on the table.

'Brilliant. Good for you.' Janey shuffles forwards, reaches over the table, and pours the steaming-hot tea into two cups. 'And, what did you think?'

'It's a strange little place, very dark and dingy. Seems like there are just the receptionist and vet working there who were like chalk and cheese, but it had a vibe about it that I can't explain. Sort of homely but upbeat I suppose.'

'That sounds positive. Had there been much interest?'

'No, that's the bit that's quite exciting. Nobody has applied yet, and when I did a bit of digging, it seems like they've been after someone for about five weeks now.'

Janey raises an eyebrow in suspicion. 'What's the catch? Dark, dingy, two weirdos—'

'I never said they were weird.'

'Dark, dingy, two people who are complete opposites and one common interest.'

'Animal health and wellbeing?'

'Axe murderers. They must be.' She sits back and punctuates the statement with a sip of her tea.

'What exactly do you read normally?' I tease, shaking my head, and she cackles with laughter.

'In all seriousness, if you liked the vibe go for it.'

'I do and I am. I've already filled in the application form. I'm going to drop it in on Monday.'

'Good for you – well done for putting yourself out there.'

There's sincerity in her face that makes my chest swell. It's been a long time since someone had my back. 'Thank you.'

'So ...' She slurps the last of her tea. 'What's next on our reading list?'

'I've no idea,' I say. 'I've spent the last ten years in a blur of nappies and school homework and I haven't really paid much attention to books. I only thought of *The Handmaid's Tale* because you'd have to be living under a rock not to have heard of it.

'How about something that isn't a movie or TV show?' Janey says. 'At least then we'll have to read it.'

'Sounds wise – we obviously can't be trusted.'

She's already scrolling through her phone but makes noise of agreement. 'How about *Eleanor Oliphant is Completely Fine*? I heard the mums at the school gate talking about it a while back and made a note of it in my phone.'

'Perfect; and we'll do better this time. Much better!'

Chapter 6

After dropping Ava and Ralph at school, I head to the vet's with a sleeping Henry in tow. Once again, Carly is nowhere to be seen, so I take a seat with Henry on my knee and await her appearance. After a few minutes, the vet comes out. He regards me with a furrowed brow before recognition melts his features.

'Ahh, it's the out-of-date bookkeeper.'

'That's me but who cares about expiry dates anyway?' I joke, badly. The vet smiles awkwardly before crouching down to look at Henry.

'I've never seen a case of canine alopecia so bad. Didn't he have a thick black and white coat on Monday?' he says.

I wince.

'Sorry, that was a terrible joke,' he says. 'Sometimes working alone can make you a little bit mad and my nurse, Helen, isn't here today.'

'Perhaps we'll stick to saving animals on your part and number crunching on mine,' I say light-heartedly.

'Anyway, Carly has disappeared again so what can I do for you?'

'I just wanted to hand you this,' I say, thrusting an A4 manila envelope towards him. He raises an eyebrow. 'It's my application form.'

His face seems to illuminate. 'Ahh, that's wonderful. What's your name again?'

'Stephanie.'

He holds out his hand. 'Pleased to meet you again, Steph. I'm Edward.' As I take his hand, a little zap of energy jolts me. I can't help but wonder if he feels it too, as he pulls his hand away quite quickly then takes a step back. I'm being ridiculous.

'Er ... as you are aware we've been inundated with applicants for the position. Particularly museum curators and those with a keen interest in historical artefacts – those people can't wait to get their paws on my computer systems.'

I laugh softly. 'Of course.'

He taps the envelope. 'I'll take a look at this and be in touch soon.'

'I'll look forward to hearing from you.' I struggle to stand. With Henry asleep, he's like a lead weight and when I bend to pick up my bag, I can't quite manage to get low enough to scoop it up.

'Here, let me get that for you.' Edward picks up my bag and hands it to me before opening the door.

'Thank you.'

As I walk out, Carly scurries back in batting a smoke cloud away from herself and I can't help but think they're such an unlikely team.

Chapter 7

After calling in at the vet's, I head to the supermarket. I can't quite believe my luck – Henry is still asleep as I shove his podgy legs into the trolley and place him on the seat. I'm feeling much more positive about shopping today. There's some money in my purse as Mike has paid up for the kids, which instantly puts me in a better position than last week. I get the staples: raisins, Rice Krispie Squares and Petits Filous, or 'silencers' as I prefer to call them and chuck in the least offensive veg I can find. I try my luck with a courgette. If I blend it with tomato, garlic and onion and serve it with pasta, the kids will eat it and it will be one-nil to Mum. As I reach the checkout, Henry stirs.

'No, no, no,' I mutter to him and stroke his head. 'Shh.'

I unload the trolley so quickly, even the cashier is struggling to keep up and by the time I'm putting the last few items into my (brought-from-home) carrier bag, I'm feeling smug. As I pull out my card, Henry stirs again. Just as I'm typing in my PIN, he lets out an almighty wail that attracts glances from the other side of the store.

'He's hungry,' I say apologetically to the cashier who responds with a sympathetic, knowing look.

It's pushing one p.m. by the time I'm done. Henry's hunger has gone past the point of no return and I can't face a screaming car journey so instead, I decide to treat us both to lunch in a nearby café. I get myself a coffee and a toasted currant teacake and Henry a sandwich snack box. He's soon munching away happily and I sit back with my coffee, relishing the silence. Then I remember my book – I'd downloaded an app and bought it for a quid. Henry seems content and there's nothing for me to be doing, so I take out my phone and open it.

I'm just finishing the second chapter when I sense a presence hovering over me.

'Excuse me; sorry to interrupt but is that a book on your phone?'

I look up to see someone I vaguely recognise hovering over me. There's a lane that leads off my road and at the top is this huge house with gates like Buckingham Palace. I walk Otis up there sometimes. I'm sure this is the lady who lives there.

'Er, yes,' I reply a little taken aback. The question was a bit odd.

'Oh that's wonderful. I saw the chapter headings and thought it was. I'm Amanda by the way.' She holds out her hand and I shake it. Her voice is clear like ice. Each word perfectly formed and neatly packaged, like the clack, clack, clack of a typewriter's keys being struck.

'Lovely to meet you,' I say.

'You too. I'm a huge reader. What book is it?'

'*Eleanor Oliphant*,' I say.

'Oh I'm dying to read that. I must get a copy. I've been meaning to for ages now.'

'It's good so far,' I say. I'm not really sure what she wants to know about it. 'It's for a book club,' I add, struggling for something else to say.

'A book club? Around here?'

Oh heck, I think I may have oversold it. 'Er … it's not really

34

a formal one or anything – just me and a neighbour getting together really. It's a new thing.'

'Oh, how wonderful.' She slides into the chair opposite and I have visions of having to tell Janey that I didn't read the book again. 'I'd love to join if you'll have me. I've wanted to do something like that for a while now.'

'Oh ... er ...' My cheeks feel hot. I don't know if our book club is really open to others or just an excuse to drink wine but what am I supposed to say: Let me consult Janey? 'Yes, of course you can join us. The more the merrier.'

The muscles in her face relax, softening her deepened lines. 'I'm sorry. You must think I'm odd.' She puts her shopping bags down with a thud and shuffles her chair in a little more. 'I've been reading a self-help book about putting yourself out there and one of the techniques was to take an interest in something someone is doing. Did I seem a bit too forward?'

'No,' I croak. 'Not at all.'

'My ... my daughter moved away a long time ago so the house feels a little empty. I've been trying to meet new people but it's a lot harder than I imagined.'

She stares through me with despondent eyes. I think back to how I felt in the supermarket all those weeks ago and get a pang of empathy. 'Then you should come along to the book club. It's just me and another lady at the moment but we'd love to have you.'

'Thank you. In that case, I will.' She smiles and her grey eyes sparkle. 'You know, I think we've crossed paths on Stable Lane before.'

'That's right, I live on the road at the top. I walk my dog up the lane most days. Don't you have a spaniel?'

'Yes, Toto.' She smiles. 'A King Charles Cavalier. He's old now and can't walk but he still likes to get out for some fresh air.'

That explains why she has a pushchair for him – I'd always wondered about that.

'Anyway, I shouldn't keep you. I'll give you my details and you can just text me when you arrange the next meeting.'

'Oh yes, perfect.' I smile, taking the glossy business card she hands me.

'I'll go and treat myself to a copy of the book,' she says, easing herself up.

I force a smile as she coos at an uninterested Henry before leaving.

'Oh bugger,' I mutter.

'Bugger,' Henry repeats.

'No, shh. It's buggy, we need your buggy, silly sausage,' I say, tearing open a packet of Pom-Bears and thrusting them into his hands.

God knows how Janey will take the news of our new member. One thing's for sure, we'll no longer be able to just watch the TV show.

This book club just got serious.

Chapter 8

'Do you mind if Amanda comes to our next book club meet?' I ask Janey, who has popped in for a cuppa before the school pick-up.

'Amanda?' Her forehead crumples.

'Yes, you know, the lady who lives in that big house at the top of Stable Lane.'

Janey's eyes goggle. 'Oh, Amanda with an aitch at the end?'

I frown. 'It doesn't have an aitch at the end.'

'Then why does she call herself Amandah then?' She twirls around dramatically throwing her arms in the air.

I roll my eyes. 'Yes, she's a bit posher than we are.'

'And she pushes her dog around in a pram like it's her baby.'

'Toto has walking difficulties; he's old and that is a special dog pushchair. I think it's sweet that she still takes him out. You should try getting to know people before you judge them.' I sound defensive, which makes me realise that on some level, I must feel a bit sorry for Amanda. 'I think she's lonely. Her daughter has moved away, and she just approached me out of the blue when I was in the café the other day and sort of invited herself. I could hardly say no – book clubs rarely have just two people watching TV and drinking wine in them, so I didn't really have an excuse.

When I rang her to tell her about our next meet she was thrilled. She's almost finished *Eleanor* already and had a suggestion for our next read.'

She sighs. 'Fine. What are we reading – *Fifty Shades*?'

I cock my head to the side. '*Jane Eyre*.'

'I might've guessed it would be something fancy.'

'It's a classic, it's not fancy. Just give it a try.'

'Okay – but this was supposed to be a bit of fun. Don't come crying to me when you're writing up an eight-thousand-word thesis comparing the use of English language of the past and present.'

I turn around to run the tap for the dishes and smirk. She's feeling threatened.

The next evening, I'm juggling Henry on one hip whilst making pasta. Ralph is at the kitchen table doing a practice SATs paper that he should have done with his dad at the weekend and Ava is practising her spellings. It might look like a scene of chaos to the untrained eye, but I have everyone doing exactly what they're supposed to be doing – I even chopped up that courgette and got it into the pan without anyone noticing.

As Ralph shouts out for help, my phone rings. 'Just a minute, darling.' I kiss him on the head and answer the unknown number.

'Hello?'

'Hi, is that Stephanie?'

'Yes,' I reply, a little frostily, anticipating the usual cold-caller.

'Hi, Stephanie, this is Carly.' She coughs. 'From the vet's?'

'Oh, hi,' I say, funnelling cheer into my tone.

'We've considered your application and I'm pleased to be able to offer you the job,' she says.

My insides squeeze. I move the phone away from my mouth and fist-pump the air. 'Yes!'

'What is it, Mum?' Ralph asks. 'Not now, sweetie,' I whisper.

'I'd love to accept,' I say, back into the phone.

'Fantastic. We'll need you to come down with some photo ID and we'll go through the contracts, check you're happy with everything and sort out a start date. How does tomorrow sound?'

'Brilliant,' I say. 'Any time after nine-thirty.'

'I'll pencil you in for nine-thirty.'

I hang up the phone. 'Mummy has a job,' I say to three blank faces.

There's a moment of silence and I'm braced for the wows and the praise.

'Does that mean you'll be out all the time, like Daddy used to be when he lived here?'

'Oh no, sweetheart, just whilst you're at school, Ava.'

'What about Henry?' Ralph asks. 'Who'll look after him?'

I glance at Henry, who's in his highchair mashing strawberries with his fist. I'd intended to get him in at a nursery but hadn't got around to it. To be honest, I didn't expect to find a job so soon.

'I'll sort Henry out,' I say. 'Could someone, anyone, just be happy for Mummy?'

Ralph shrugs his shoulders but doesn't even look up.

'Well done, Mummy. Gold star for you.' Ava presses something onto my tummy and wraps her tiny arms around me. For the split second it lasts, I relish the feel of her freakishly strong grasp.

When everyone is happily tucking into 'Mummy's special pasta', I slip into the hallway and ring Mike.

'Stephanie?' His 'why are you ringing me on a weekday' tone irks me but I swallow my annoyance.

'I just wanted to let you know, I've got a job.'

'That's great,' he says, sounding a little happier to hear from me. He's probably running the mental calculations as we speak.

'I have a problem. It's all happened so fast that I've nowhere to take Henry tomorrow morning and I have to go in and have like an introduction type thing.'

'Stephanie, you should have made arrangements like *I* have to at the weekends.'

What, like leaving them with me while you have a lie-in? Is what I want to say, but pissing him off won't help here. 'I know. It's just happened so fast,' I repeat instead.

'I have meetings all morning. Sorry, can't help.'

My blood temperature matches the surface heat of Mercury. 'Mike,' I say evenly, 'you've been desperate for me to get a job. It's all you've talked about for the past few months.'

'Yes, but not at the expense of *my* job. I've five people, two houses, two cars and a dog to pay for. You just need money to get your hair and nails done.'

I bite my tongue. I never get my hair or nails done and he knows that. 'Mike, I struggle to buy food.'

He sighs and the phone's mic amplifies the sound, sending a mini hurricane down my ear canal. I brace for impact. We're about to embark on the type of pointless argument that ended our marriage in the first place.

'If you can't look after Henry for a few hours, that's fine. I'll ask someone else.'

He sighs. 'Who will you ask?'

I stumble. I never know which little things will prompt me to think of my mum. Pink peonies, rowing boats and now babysitters. When I was a kid, I missed having a mum so much. My dad was a long-distance lorry driver so I lived with my gran. She was great, but it wasn't the same as having my mum around. With her arthritic hips she couldn't chase me or play hide-and-seek. Now I'm older, I feel robbed of different experiences. My kids missed out on a wonderful grandparent and I've missed out on all the advice that mothers pass down to their daughters. My dad lives in Cornwall and I hardly ever see him, and Mike's mum will only look after the kids when he has them. Other than Mike, there's only one person I could ask.

'I'll ask a friend.'

'Who?'

'A neighbour, Janey. She won't mind.' At least I hope she won't. 'Otherwise, I'll take Henry with me.'

'Well let me know if you're really stuck. I suppose I could try and move some things around.'

After all that fuss? I'd rather ask the child catcher from *Chitty Chitty Bang Bang*! 'I'll figure it out. See you Saturday.'

'Oh, about that, I've been invited on a golf trip this weekend with some of the guys from work. I can't pick them up until Sunday lunchtime.'

I bite my teeth together so hard I think they'll break. 'Sorry, I have a meeting. You'll have to get them Friday night like you're *supposed* to.'

'Stephanie, come on.'

'Sorry, Mike, it's a two-way street. Either we help each other out or we make each other's lives more difficult.'

He sighs again. On a scale of one to exasperated, he's a full-on, lava-infused ten. Mike often goes straight to ten when he doesn't get his own way. He's like a baby sometimes.

'So, will I see you tomorrow morning or will I see you Friday?'

'Friday,' he huffs. 'I really do have a meeting tomorrow.'

Chapter 9

The next day, I head to the vet's after dropping Henry off at Janey's. At such short notice, I didn't have anything that could be deemed 'proper work wear' so the thin, lemon-coloured merino wool jumper that I wore yesterday teamed with black trousers had to suffice. The jumper passed the sniff test by a hair and a whisker (and a few blasts of Febreze) but there's a newfound snugness to the trousers that doesn't exactly thrill me.

'Morning,' Carly says cheerfully when I arrive. It's the first time she's been sat behind the desk when I've been in, so I'm a little taken aback to see her there.

'Morning, Carly. I've got the documents you asked for.'

'Perfect,' she says with a smile. 'Here is a copy of the contract and terms and whatnot. If you have a read-through, I'll photocopy your ID if that's okay?'

I hand over everything I need and sit down to read through the documents. There's a dog barking behind one of the doors and I wonder if Edward is in there trying to soothe the poorly pooch. I force my eyes to the contract. I should be reading this, not thinking about what my boss is doing.

'Right, here you go.' Carly is standing in front of me holding out my passport.

'Thanks.'

Her eyes drop to my middle and her head tilts to the side a little. I know my waistband is digging into newly grown overhang but that's just rude.

'Is that some sort of emblem? It's so pretty but in such an unusual place.'

What does she mean? It's a plain jumper. A beat passes before I look down, remembering the gold star that Ava put on me. My fingers find it first. Hard, dry and crusty; it's no gold star. My mouth goes dry and I clamp my hand to my stomach.

Heat rises up the back of my neck. 'I … I know. Weird isn't it? It's … French.'

It's French. Talk about making matters worse.

Just as I'm about to make a run for it, the surgery door opens and out walks Edward.

Oh no.

'Hello again and welcome to Prescott's.'

He holds out his right hand. I'm clutching the dried pasta stain with my right hand, which is now clammy with panic. What do I do? Do I come clean and say I wore a dirty jumper to my first work meeting? Ten years out of work and I can't pull it together for one day. I straighten up before I crumble. I can do this. I know what I need to do.

After discreetly wiping my palm on my sweater, I hold it out, locking my eyes on his. If I can just maintain eye contact, he won't notice the stain. The instant his blue diamonds hit me, my skin tingles with discomfort. I hold my breath. Keep the stare going. Just a few. More. Seconds.

Eventually, he lets go and I exhale but before I can clamp my hand back over the offending pasta, Carly opens her big mouth.

'Look at where the French put their emblems.' Carly points towards my middle. 'How funny.'

I freeze. Edward's eyes follow Carly's finger.

'Well, the French don't dominate the catwalks for no reason,' he says breezily. Then, he looks at me and his left eye twitches slightly.

Was that a wink? Did he wink at me?

'Right, I'd better get back to work. Nice to see you again, Steph.'

He disappears before I can say anything. What just happened?

Carly's voice breaks my thoughts. 'So, does everything look okay for you?'

'Hmm?'

She gestures to the contract I'm still clutching in my left hand so I take a moment to skim it. 'The hours, they're not written in.'

'Oh yes, Edward thought you might want to choose your own. He noticed you were juggling a little one and said as long as the work is done and the clients' accounts are up to date each day, he didn't mind when you came in as long as you can do the four hours during our business hours, which are eight a.m. until six p.m.'

My insides glow; a stranger being so thoughtful when my own ex-husband can't manage the smallest of things to help me out.

'That's brilliant. Ten-till-two would probably work best for me.'

'Great! You can cover the phones when I'm on my lunch. They seem to go mental as soon as I step away from the desk.'

Which by my understanding was most of the time. I smile.

'No problem. When do you want me to start?' My eyes land on the examination-room door.

'He's about to operate on a doberman with an infected paw so he won't be back out for a while.' Carly seems to read my mind and warmth floods my cheeks. 'If you had something else to ask him, I can get him to give you a call.'

'Oh, no. I … er. I just wondered about the whimpering.'

'Of course.' She smiles. 'Is Monday a good day for you to start?'

I nod. 'Sounds perfect. See you on Monday.'

Janey looks flustered when I get back. She has Henry in her arms and something orange slopped down her cream T-shirt.

44

'He's a handful this one.' She giggles, handing him over.

I kiss him on his sticky head. 'Sorry. I know. Thank you so much.'

'No problem, I enjoyed having him.' She tickles him under his chin. 'So how did it go?'

'Fine, I guess.'

'Oh? That doesn't sound good.' She rests her head on her hands expectantly, so I fill her in. She winces a little when I talk about Carly pointing out the stain and I pull the bottom of my sweater out so she can have a good look.

She shakes her head slowly. 'Yeah, that's no fashion statement I'm afraid.'

I bury my face in Henry's hair and let out a low grumble. 'Why me?'

'Look, you have three kids. The fact you made it out of the house at all is a bloody feat and it will all be forgotten by Monday. You have nothing to worry about.'

I know she's right, but it doesn't stop the awful crampy feeling in my stomach.

'Fancy a brew?'

'I might as well; if they don't revoke the offer on the grounds of being completely inept at life, I won't be a lady of leisure for much longer.'

Whilst Janey makes the tea, I browse nurseries on my phone. 'Bloody hell.'

'What's wrong?' she calls from the kitchen.

'It's going to cost me more than half my wage to send Henry to nursery part-time.' I look at a few other websites including Mumsnet and MoneySavingExpert and it seems the prices around here are average. How do people afford jobs?

'It's not forever. Just a year and then Henry will be two and you can claim help with childcare costs,' she says, handing me a cuppa.

'I know that. It's just so disheartening to get a job after so many years and still not have financial independence.' Janey sits on the couch next to me and puts her hand on mine.

'Just another year. Once Henry is in nursery you might even be able to pick up some hours elsewhere too – you'll have experience then,' she says.

'You're right. It's a step in the right direction,' I say. 'Anyway, on to better and brighter things. Where are we having our next book club meet-up?'

'There's no way Aman-dah-dee-dah is coming to this dump.' Janey casts her arms in the air. 'I tidied up last night and the kids had wrecked the entire place by breakfast time. I gave up and just sprayed everything with Fabulosa. The toys are a tripping hazard so broken bones are likely but at least nobody will get E. coli on my watch.'

I look at the plastic obstacle course on the floor and smile. 'Oh God, my house is awful too. Even after I've cleaned I find ketchup in the most random of places. I'd hate to ruin her fancy clothes.'

'Could do it at the pub,' Janey says, getting down on her knees to pick up and aimlessly throw some toys at a big plastic tub. Some even go in.

'I suppose but it gets a bit crowded in there. I'm thinking of signing up at the library. I wondered if we could do it there? It's open late on a Thursday.'

'Maybe.' She taps the side of her cup twice. 'But we can't have a glass of wine in the library – at least not openly. We could ask Amanda if she wants to host.'

'That seems unfair since it's her first time. I'll tell you what. I'll host – I'll just tell her to wear dark colours.' I wink and reach for my bag.

'What's that?' Janey asks.

'Amanda's business card. She gave it me so I could get in touch with the book club details.'

'I thought she was a lady of leisure. She's in the salon or down at the butcher's most days. What does it say she does?'

I study the card.

46

Amanda Redgrave
Old Manor Farm
Stable Lane
0772548925

'Nothing. It's just her personal details.'

'Who has a business card for themselves if they don't work in a business?' Janey pulls the card off me and inspects it for herself.

'I don't know, maybe she's just organised or she meets lots of new people.' I shrug.

She raises her eyebrows. 'If she meets lots of new people, would she really be gate-crashing our book club?'

'You have a point but it's none of our concern. Let me send her a message to confirm the venue. I said I'd let her know.'

I send the message and quickly after, she texts back. 'Janey, she wants your number.'

'Nope. No way. I don't know how to talk to someone like her.'

'Well, you'll have to figure it out. I can't tell her you said no.'

'Fine.'

'Oh, and she's setting up a WhatsApp group,' I say, reading her instant reply. A few moments later, both our phones buzz with news of a new message.

'I don't even want to look,' Janey says. I pick up my phone. The new group is called 'Book Clubbers'. And the message reads as follows:

Hello ladies, it's a pleasure to be joining your book club. I've almost finished Eleanor and can't wait to chat about it. I'd also say that it was very kind of Stephanie to offer to hold the next meeting but I thought, since I'm new, it might be nice for you to come to my house. I don't want to step on anybody's toes though, so please let me know if you'd rather stick to the plan. Best wishes, Amanda.

'Blimey, she's a fast reader,' Janey says.

'See, she's sweet,' I say.

'It's a kind gesture,' Janey concedes. 'And it gets us out of tidying up again.'

'That's true. Have you started the book?'

'Yes, but now I feel under pressure to really understand it. We're going to need to revise or something.'

'Okay, Janey, look: Amanda is posh, but she's not a literature professor as far as I'm aware. I'm sure a chat about characters and themes will suffice.' The drama queen in Janey does both amuse and exasperate me at times.

'I suppose. I'll reply to her – be polite.' Janey picks up her phone and starts keying out a message. A part of me is quite glad that Amanda has joined our book club. It gives us a focus and makes it more of a thing. Janey and I will still get together for a cuppa a few times a week but the book club will now be something different. Something more meaningful.

Chapter 10

The distinct sweet, musty smell is something that hits me the moment I step inside. *Tall shelves with infinite paper dreams. An imaginarium. Mum is with me. She squeezes my hand with giddy excitement as we browse the colourful picture books.*

The grey-haired librarian is sat reading a book and doesn't notice me until I place my bag on the desk in front of her, prompting her to look up wearily. I'd seen online that you needed some identification to get a card, so I've come carrying that along with the two-tonne shame of having a ten-year-old son who has never set foot in the village library.

It only takes a few minutes to become a fully-fledged member. The place seems well stocked for such a small building, as I stare in awe at the choice. I'm not sure what I'm looking for but so much is catching my eye that I pick up a few titles, judging solely on their covers, and go and sit on the comfy chair in the back corner. The first one, *Big Little Lies*, I've heard of because I saw the TV show advertised and always fancied reading it. I have an hour to kill before I pick the kids up so I might as well sit here and read a few chapters. It feels indulgent but I never do anything for just me.

An elderly man comes in to browse the James Patterson books.

We exchange smiles before he tucks a few books under his arm and disappears. There's a murmuring hum of voices and the female librarian says something that seems loud and misplaced but I'm so engrossed in this book, I'm not listening. When my eyes start to strain, I check the time and it's just after three. I've been reading for an hour and a half. I close the book and notice the dingy light. When I look up, the bright fluorescent strip-lights are off. How odd. No wonder my eyes feel like they've been pressed with a potato masher.

I make my way to the desk and an ear-piercing beeping stops me in my tracks. My pulse quickens. It sounds like a fire alarm. There must be a fire. I race to the doors and yank the handles. They're locked. I glance around, eyes scanning the walls until I spot the fire escape. The beeping makes it so hard to think straight but as I'm running towards the escape door, I realise I haven't seen the librarian. She could be trapped. I divert to the desk. She isn't there. There's an office behind, so I try the door but it's stuck fast.

'Hello?' I yell, banging frantically on the glass widow. There's no sign of anyone in there. I let my arm drop to my side. A moment passes and I realise I don't smell any smoke. I walk back to the main doors. Through the paper poster that faces outwards, I can see the opening times. They're backwards to me but I can still make out that the library closes at two p.m. on a Friday. I slump against the glass. I'm locked in. Trespassing even. My heart hammers against my ribs. Does this make me a criminal? I try to stay calm, taking slow and steady breaths. I should call someone for help but who? Janey? Mike? As I'm searching for my phone, I hear loud voices outside. Oh God. It's the police.

I stand up, hugging my books to my body. The librarian is with them. Her lips pressed together so firmly the colour has drained from them, like two white slugs. She unlocks the door with exaggerated movements and yanks the key out when she's

50

done it. The police officer at the front puts his arm out in front of her, warning her to stay back as if I'm some kind of armed robber holding all these books hostage.

He takes hold of the door handles with both hands. 'Step away from the door and put your hands out in front where I can see them.'

I drop the books and do as he says, catching a look of disgust on the librarian's face as I do so. My hands are shaking. Is he going to arrest me? My children need picking up in ten minutes, I haven't got time to be arrested. My head starts to feel funny, like a soggy tea towel has taken over. He opens the door slowly, fixing his eyes on me the entire time. Two other police officers appear and flank him as the librarian stands behind them with her arms folded. If she doesn't relax her lips soon, I fear they might turn blue and fall off.

'No sign of forced entry,' says the female officer.

'Can you explain what you're doing trespassing in the community library?' the police officer in front asks when he's opened the doors. My biceps are aching but I daren't drop my arms; his Taser is strapped to his chest and he doesn't look afraid to use it.

'I was just reading a book. It's a really good one,' I say pathetically. He glances at the floor by my feet where the strewn pile of titles I wanted to check out now lie.

'What are those there then?'

I frown. 'Books.'

'Watch your tone. It looks like you were trying to take these books illegally. We'll have to take you down to the station.'

'No!' I yell. 'I was not! I was reading them and she' – I jut my chin in the direction of the librarian – 'locked me in.'

The police officer looks back to the librarian and the other two step towards me.

'She signed me up today! Why would I steal books when I can borrow them for free?' My forehead is pulled into an Oliver

Twist-esque 'please, sir' expression and I've never been more grateful of my fine lines.

'Is this true?' the police officer asks the librarian.

'She did come in to sign up for a library card, but I could have sworn she'd gone. I always shout "We're closing. Final check-outs" five minutes before I'm locking up and today was no different.'

Ahh. That must have been what she was saying just after the old man left. 'I didn't hear you.'

She sighs. 'I had just walked through my front door when I got the call about the alarm going off. This is a massive inconvenience you know.'

Perhaps she should pay more attention to who comes and goes. 'I'm truly sorry.'

'You can drop your arms,' the police officer says. Blood rushes to my fingertips when I do. 'I think we've established this was just a misunderstanding. I trust you'll pay more attention to closing times in future?'

I nod. 'Definitely.'

He sighs, ensuring I understand what a massive pain in the backside I am. 'Then you're free to go.'

'Thank you.' I bend to pick up the books.

'Don't think you're taking those,' the librarian says thrusting her hands onto her hipbones.

'I was just going to check them out.'

'We. Are. Closed.' She enunciates each word.

I sigh and glance at the police officer.

'You'll have to come back tomorrow.' He shrugs.

I gather my belongings and put the books on the nearby 'returns' shelf. It isn't until I'm outside, I notice the crowd of people who've gathered. The scandal of a police car too intriguing to ignore for the residents of sleepy Crinkly. I lower my head as one of the officers escorts me off the premises. When we reach his car he turns to me.

'I trust this won't happen again?'

'Never.' In the unlikely event I ever set a foot back in there, I won't be staying. As they drive off, I notice the librarian walk off in the other direction. A few people from the crowd coo over her. One lady hugs her, for goodness' sake. I'm the one who is traumatised! As I turn to leave, I notice a figure in the doorway of the bakery across the road. The familiar eyes deepen the shame that's already swamping me. Hoping he hasn't realised who I am, I speed-walk to my car.

Chapter 11

The practice is the busiest I've ever seen it when I arrive on Monday morning at ten to ten. There's a lady with a cat in a carrier, an old man with some sort of terrier, a younger man with something in a cage that could be a ferret and a young woman with a black and white puppy curled on her lap.

'Morning, Carly,' I say. She's tapping away at the computer but glances up and gives me a warm smile.

'Sorry, we're running behind today. Edward was late back from delivering a calf at Crookney Farm so he's catching up.'

'No problem.'

'The machine there is the one I started to log all the accounts on. It's just an Excel spreadsheet and these are the client records.' She hands me a hefty file.

'Great. I'll just spend some time getting to grips with it all and see where we can make some improvements.'

'Wonderful,' she says, still typing as she glances over at me.

The door opens to the examination room and Edward emerges with a newly coned golden retriever on a lead. His eyes are dark, wide saucers. He does look sorry for himself, I have to say. The dog that is, although Edward doesn't exactly look like he's full of the joys of spring either. His face is red and his hair dishevelled.

He must sense me looking his way as he glances over and gives me a quick nod of hello before handing the self-pitying pooch over to its owner and calling in the ferret. On second glance, it could be a rat.

By the time Carly goes for lunch, I almost have my head around the messy accounts. There are quite a few unpaid bills that I could offer to chase and as much as I didn't want to face him today, I could do with catching Edward for a chat to see if he's willing to invest in some proper software. I've had a look online and found one that looks pretty good and the monthly fee seems reasonable. I wait for a quiet spell and catch him the next time he emerges.

He still looks flustered and I'm hoping that means he'll have forgotten about library-gate and indeed the pasta emblem. 'Edward, sorry to be a nuisance – do you have a second?'

His face melts a little into something quite affable. 'Of course. How is our resident trespasser getting on?'

I cringe so hard I think my stomach turns inside out but I have to laugh it off and move on. After all, I did nothing wrong.

'It's not nearly as much fun entering a property when you're actually allowed to.'

To my relief, he laughs softly. 'I heard it was all just a misunderstanding. Apparently, Maggie the librarian was a bit naffed off because she missed her poetry club meeting.'

I wince. 'I've never felt so terrible and embarrassed all at the same time.'

'I wouldn't worry. It doesn't take much to rattle her cage. I dared to crunch a Polo mint in there once – you should have seen the look she gave me. Anyway, enough about Miserable Maggie, are you finding everything okay here?'

'I think I know where I'm up to now. There are quite a few invoices outstanding if you'd like me to start chasing them up?'

He frowns. 'Ahh, I suspected that might be the case. If you

wouldn't mind, it makes sense for you to do it as you'll be able to explain what the amount relates to. I dread to think what Carly would say.'

'It's no problem. I think the hours will allow for that now that I've got my head around the systems here. There was another thing.'

'Fire away,' he says.

'I've found an online accounts package that would really help us to keep on top of things but there's a monthly fee and we'd probably need better internet.'

He ponders this. 'Okay, I'm about to anesthetise a Dentastix-dodging beagle so I can clean his teeth but if you leave me the details, I'll weigh it all up tonight.'

As he goes back behind the door, my mouth curls at the image of him brushing a dog's teeth. I'm not sure if I should feel bad as I've never once brushed Otis's.

The childminder I got at short notice says Henry was a little unsettled. I get a pang of guilt because he was just chucked in at short notice instead of having the recommended taster sessions. I'm almost sure the emotional damage won't scar him for life.

'Mum, are you unwell?' Ava asks me when we finish her reading homework.

I shake my head. 'I'm fine, honey, why would you ask?'

'Bella Jackson said she heard her mummy telling Lilly's mum that you'd been crying in the supermarket because you're unwell.'

I swallow hard trying to shake off the sinking feeling in my gut. 'Oh, honey, that's not true at all. I'd had a bad day. Do you remember when you cried in the supermarket because they didn't have any Kellogg's Frosties?' She looks at me wide-eyed and nods. 'It was just like that.'

'Okay,' she says, bouncing off her chair.

How dare those bloody women gossip about me. How careless that they've done it in front of the children too. Can't people see I'm doing the best I can? I'm trying to rebuild a life that was torn apart. Why can't people just mind their own business?

Chapter 12

The sun is dipping in the sky, casting its golden glow across the long grass in the fields either side of Stable Lane. It's one of those evenings where you can practically smell the sunshine. It's been a fortnight since Janey and I got together to discuss *The Handmaid's Tale* and the early May weather really has turned for the better.

'I hope she drinks plonk,' Janey says, referring to the bottle of Pinot Blush she'd procured from the off-licence.

'I've only brought Doritos,' I say. 'It will be fine.'

As we near the giant gates, I get my first proper look at the red-brick mansion.

'Jesus, look at this place. I bet her and her husband go days without bumping into one another. They'll be like two marbles rolling around on a footy field,' Janey says. 'Is that pampas grass?'

'I don't know. Maybe.' I shrug taking in the creamy white feathery plumes poking above the tall garden wall.

'Is she a … you know?'

I raise my eyebrows. 'A what?'

'You know. A swinger? Pampas grass is like a beacon in those circles apparently.'

'Is it?' I've never heard of that before.

'Yes! She might as well put a sign up that says, "Swingers Welcome". What if she's invited us here using the book club as a ruse to lure us into her lifestyle?'

'Oh, Janey, stop being daft. I seriously doubt she is. Probably just a keen gardener and it *is* quite pretty. Come on.'

Beside the black iron gate, there's an intercom. A few moments after pressing the button, Amanda's immaculate face appears on the tiny screen.

'Hello, ladies. Just a second, I'll let you in.'

The gates creak open.

'This is how many a horror movie starts,' Janey whispers as we walk through.

'You're obsessed,' I whisper.

The golden gravel crunches beneath our feet as we approach the dark oak double-front door.

'She's probably spent more on these tiny yellow rocks than I spent on my whole house. I've seen them on *Grand Designs* – they're a fortune.'

'That's her business.' As I speak, the door opens.

'Stephanie, Janey, how lovely to see you both. Come through to the orangery. I've got drinks and nibbles out.' She waves us in and we follow her down the excessively wide hallway to a door at the end, which leads into a pristine sitting room. I wonder how long it would take my three to turn this place upside down. There are some French doors, which are propped open giving way to the glass orangery and the lush greenery of the garden beyond.

'You have a beautiful home,' I say as we walk in and sit down on the heavily cushioned wicker chairs. For once, Janey seems lost for words. Perhaps she really was expecting to walk in to a rampant swingers' party.

'Help yourself to nibbles.' Amanda gestures to the spread on the matching coffee table. There are smoked salmon blinis, mini tomato bruschettas, devilled eggs, tempura bites and some other things I couldn't identify if I wanted to. It all smells delicious and my bag of Doritos is cowering in shame – I'm sure it would throw its own self into a bin if it had the legs to reach one. Janey is already tucking in. She hands Amanda the wine and Amanda accepts it graciously so I brave the ceremonial handing over of my offering.

'Sorry,' I say, 'I was in such a rush.'

'Oh don't be silly, I love these. Very moreish. I'll get a bowl.' Amanda returns a few moments later with an ornate pearlescent serving dish that looks like it should be in a museum, not serving the likes of Janey and me. Furnishing it with Doritos is sacrilege.

'Grab a drink from the bar and we'll start talking books,' she says, gesturing to a dark wood sideboard with a built-in wine fridge. There are some champagne flutes out and an open bottle of Prosecco chilling in a bucket. I pour three glasses.

'So, would you two like to start, since I'm the newcomer?' Amanda says, sipping her fizz. Her voice trembles slightly with nerves whilst Janey shoots me a look of panic.

'How about we start with what we thought about the book. What we liked and what we disliked,' I say, registering both of their apprehension.

'I loved it,' Amanda says. 'I liked the complex nature of Eleanor's character and her inner monologue was delightful.'

'Oh I liked her snarky observations, definitely,' Janey says. I share my opinions and we dig a bit deeper. This is good; we're actually talking about the book and all is going well.

'So, what about the central themes?' Amanda says. Janey takes a sip of her second glass of Prosecco. A ploy to occupy her lips, I'm sure of it.

'I thought the theme of loneliness was quite poignant. She likens modern-day loneliness to a cancer – fearful and incurable,' I say. It's the most obvious theme but at least it has plenty of meat to it.

'Yes!' Janey sounds excited. 'It was so interesting on so many levels. The reasons for her isolation were more than just circumstantial. She was socially awkward, but also her physical appearance worked in some way to keep others away. It wasn't really until she helped the old man, Sammy, that a sliver of her inner beauty came through. But it was so profoundly sad.'

'It struck a chord,' Amanda says, her throat contracting like the words are difficult to swallow. It's hard to imagine why. On the surface, this is the woman who has it all. She must be in her late fifties now and in life has acquired more than most people dream of.

Except for friends perhaps?

'Are you all right, Amanda?' I ask softly.

She stares at the rising bubbles in her glass. Then, her mouth opens but instead of speaking, she bites down on her bottom lip.

'Do *you* feel isolated sometimes? Like Eleanor?' The fizz gives me the balls to ask. Janey's eyes are wide open and the rest of her body is frozen. It makes me realise that people don't talk about loneliness. People on the whole are so busy, they don't want to hear about it and admitting you're lonely is hard. There's a photograph on the wall of her and a man I assume to be her husband. It looks fairly recent. Perhaps he's away a lot.

Amanda places her glass on the table slowly then centres it on the coaster. 'It *can* get a little lonely up here. My only daughter works as a doctor in Africa. I haven't seen her in over three years. She keeps telling me to go on Zoom or something and when she has a signal we can chat face-to-face but I have no idea what I'm doing.'

My throat is thick. I've spent more time judging Amanda than seeing if she's okay. 'I know how it is to feel alone. I live in a madhouse. I'm not *technically* on my own, but before Janey took me under her wing, I was completely devoid of adult company. The children are there and they need me, but I'm just a utility to them, to be used at their disposal.'

Amanda and Janey smile sympathetically. At some point they'll have both felt the same. 'I'm completely fine,' I add.

'That's what Eleanor said.' Janey winks.

'At least we have our book club now,' Amanda says. 'Once a month, or a fortnight or however often we meet, we'll have something to look forward to.'

'Definitely,' I say, raising my glass.

'Yeah, definitely,' Janey says, following suit and lifting her glass.

'Cheers, ladies.' Amanda clinks her glass against each of ours. 'Here's to books.'

'To books,' Janey and I chime.

We discuss a few other themes through with an excited buzz. As the evening draws to an end, I'm quite merry. Merry with the Prosecco but also giddy with the exciting warmth of new friendships.

As we're getting ready to leave, I tell Amanda my library story to give her a giggle. 'I'm going to need a disguise to get past the librarian to borrow a copy of *Jane Eyre*.'

'Oh don't worry about that. I have several,' Amanda says. 'I can't resist the different covers. Hang on, I'll get you both a copy from the study.'

'The study?' Janey mouths when Amanda leaves the room.

I shrug.

'My study consists of the kids' iPad on the kitchen table. Oh, and I have a shelf in the loo with a copy of *The Subtle Art of Not Giving A Fuck* on it,' she continues and I can't help but think it's one self-help book that she doesn't need.

'Here you go.' Amanda reappears with two pristine copies of *Jane Eyre*.

We thank Amanda for the books and for our wonderful evening and make our way home.

'She's all right really,' Janey says.

'I told you.'

'I felt a bit sorry for her when she was talking about her

daughter being away. We should help sort her out on Zoom,' Janey says.

I smile. Despite Janey's big overactive mouth, she's got a big overactive heart to match. 'That would be a nice thing to do.'

As we get to where the lane meets our road, both of our phones buzz.

Thank you so much for tonight. I needed it. A x

'I think we all did,' I whisper under my breath.

Chapter 13

The next few weeks are a blur of regimented routine. Like a cheaply oiled machine, I get up and ensure the kids are ready for the day, deliver them to their assigned institutions and head to work. Every now and then we groan as our pace becomes stiff and rusty.

This particular morning, the low-viscosity oil has run out and our machine is grinding to an end-of-term halt. Ralph has lost his PE kit, Ava can't find her school shoes and we're out of bread, which on a normal day wouldn't be an issue, but for the past few days, all Henry will eat is buttery toast and he's refused the banana I lovingly sliced for him, by mashing it into his hair. It's five to nine and instead of kissing Ava and Ralph at the school gate, I'm rubbing Henry's head with a baby wipe whilst yelling at the other two to 'pack any T-shirt and shorts for PE and wear trainers if you can't find your school shoes'.

As we bundle into the car, my mobile rings. On a manic day like this, I wouldn't normally acknowledge it ringing but some sort of instinct prompts me to see who it is. It's the childminder.

'Chloe, is everything okay?' My voice is breathy and flustered as I'm bent over strapping Henry into his stupid car seat where four silly prongs have to be held together at the right angle whilst simultaneously reciting the Lord's prayer and calling on the genie from *Aladdin* to grant a wish. Seriously, most parents see walking or talking as the major milestones in their child's life, but mine was when they could get in and out of the car by themselves.

'Stephanie, I'm so sorry but I think I've got norovirus. It's an occupational hazard I'm afraid but it means I won't be able to take Henry for a few days. I have to wait until forty-eight hours after my last episode and it's not finished yet. It's like a tsunami; both ends.'

No, no, no, not today! To be fair, she does sound dreadful. 'Oh no, I'm sorry to hear that. Thanks for letting me know. Feel better soon.' My voice comes out all high-pitched.

'Mummy, you sound weird,' Ralph says.

I arrive at work early, which is a miraculous feat. Carly is sitting on the wall outside having her morning cigarette break. She smiles a wide smile that twists into something more bitter when her eyes land on Henry.

'I know. I know. I'm sorry. It's an emergency. The childminder has norovirus. I thought I'd come in and see if I could take some work home for a few days.' After Edward gave the go-ahead, I upgraded the main computer and installed a cloud-based accounts package. I've been transferring the client accounts over for the past week and a half and I'm almost done so hopefully it won't be a problem.

She looks at me like I've asked if I can work upside down wearing a dress made of blancmange, but I don't need her permission, I need Edward's. Kettle and pot springs to mind – she doesn't exactly have her nose to the grindstone throughout the whole working day.

When I go inside, he's handing a ginger cat to an elderly lady.

'No more chicken dinners for this one. Just plain old cat food is what her digestive system needs. You can give her some of the plain turkey but definitely no more Yorkshire pudding.'

'Ooh thank you, vet, you're a good 'un. Come on, Ruby.' She

takes the cat carrier from Edward and hovers at reception, presumably wanting to pay. As if on cue, Carly comes in and takes the payment so I head to the kitchen and put Henry's lunch in the fridge. I hear footsteps behind me.

'Morning, Steph,' Edward says, raising his eyebrows when he spots Henry.

'I'm so sorry. The childminder called last minute to say she's ill and won't be able to have him for a few days. I was wondering if I could work from home. I still have the new invoice templates to set up and there's an online tutorial I need to do.'

'These things happen. He's welcome to stay here with you if he won't cause you too much bother? I have a big softie of a Newfoundland in later who's also called Henry – I think the two of them will get along.' He smiles and ruffles Henry's hair. 'It's up to you.'

If I could finish transferring the accounts, I could start chasing unpaid invoices from home for the next couple of days. I glance at Henry who's looking around the room babbling at random objects. His good nature might last a short while. 'Okay, as long as you don't think it's too unprofessional?'

'Unprofessional? You? I'm not even a real vet!' he says with a wicked glint in his eye before heading back into the examination room.

I go and get Henry's buggy out of the car and strap him in. His changing bag has a few toys and snacks in, so I give him those and log on. He's at the awkward stage where he's too old to nap all the time and too young to amuse himself. His attention won't be held for long, so I get cracking.

Carly glances at me as I struggle to get the buggy through the door. 'You're keeping the baby here?'

'Just whilst he's settled, then I'll take him home.'

'I don't know how you manage with three,' she says. 'I have enough with my Luke – he's such a handful.'

For comparison, Luke is fourteen and currently suspended from school for running some sort of cigarette racket.

'It's hard,' I say politely. 'But we muddle through.'

I know she's just making benign conversation but it irks me and I'm not sure why. Perhaps I've come to feel defined by my children and my divorce and a whole host of other things that surround me but aren't me. Getting this job, the book club and making new friends is part of a new, individual version of me and that independent person with a life is who I want people to see.

'What's that smell? Is that …?' Carly gestures towards Henry. Brilliant.

Chapter 14

After Henry stunk the entire practice out, I decided to work from home on Thursday and Carly came to my rescue on Friday by delivering some much-needed files. Henry still keeps asking for a bear; I think the Newfoundland made quite the impression and I'm not sure he'll ever want to go back to the childminder. Now it's Saturday and Mike is coming to collect the children. He's booked the half-term week off work so they can stay with him all week, which means I'll miss them like crazy but also not have to worry about childcare. Today, he's coming early because he wants to take them to the aquarium so I'm frantically packing clothes, toys and books for the three of them when the doorbell rings.

'Ralph, get the door,' I yell.

A few moments later, it rings again. 'Ralph?'

Nothing.

I run downstairs and pull my dressing gown belt tighter before opening the door.

'Not dressed yet?' Mike says in an annoyingly cheery tone. Honestly, it's like he's read *Riling Steph for Dummies*. He's first-class at it.

'No, it's been quite a busy morning. Come in – the kids are around somewhere.'

As if on cue, Ava screams. 'Lounge,' I say walking towards it.

'What on earth is going on?' I ask. Ava's face is red and tear-stained whilst Ralph wears a guilty expression.

'Ralph pulled my hair,' Ava says with hitched breaths.

'She was annoying me, Mum.'

'I don't care if she was annoying you, you don't resort to violence,' I say, disappointed. 'You're older and you know better.'

'But, Mum!' Ralph whines.

'You're being a bit hard on him. They were both in the wrong,' Mike says.

I grit my teeth. 'I know that, but we have a "no violence" policy and Ralph knows this. As far as I'm concerned, that's the worst offence here so I've dealt with it first.'

Mike holds his hands up defensively. 'I was just saying.'

'Well don't. Don't waltz in here once a week telling me I'm doing everything wrong.' Emotion wells inside me but I can't crack in front of Mike. He's probably already heard about my supermarket meltdown.

'Kids, get your things. I think your mum needs to have a bit of a rest.'

The kids, of course, do exactly as Mike asks of them but I'm too wound up to speak. As they're leaving, Ralph scowls at me for the injustice I've just served him but Ava, true to her sweet nature, runs over and gives me a big hug. As I hold her tight, the strawberry scent of her hair fills my nose and lungs with love and I fight harder than ever to keep tears from rolling down my cheeks.

'See you soon, sweetie,' I whisper into her ear.

When the front door closes behind them, Otis circles the mat whimpering. He seems to have a sixth sense for knowing when they'll be gone for longer than a night. I rub his head to try and calm him down but, instead, seem to do nothing for him and upset myself more. Maybe it's my hormones – I don't know. I just miss them and I hate that Mike always gets to be the good guy. I sink to the floor and bury my face in Otis's soft black and white coat. He settles as though he knows I'm more upset than he is.

'Just me and you this week,' I whisper into his fur.

Janey is away this weekend at Center Parcs with her family and some friends. Jimmy hasn't gone, which I thought was odd, but Janey didn't seem to care and since I'm fully up to date on my old friend's 'not taking sides' policy, I'm at a loose end for the weekend. Still, I need to pull myself together; I can't just sit and wallow.

I get dressed and pick up Otis's lead. He starts running around in circles of excitement. 'Stay still, you daft dog.'

Eventually, he sits and waits patiently and I clip his lead on. We head up towards Amanda's house and cross a stile into a field where we follow an invisible public footpath. Since the fields aren't used to keep livestock in, I let Otis off to have a run. He darts about chasing birds he'll never catch and I take deep lungfuls of fresh air. The view of Amanda's house is quite prominent from here. At this angle, you can see most of the building. The glass lantern roof of the orangery peeps above the wall. On the outside, it looks like she has it all. Money, nice clothes, fancy cars and a huge house, but the one thing she craves, human connection, is missing. That's something I have. Maybe I'm alone this weekend, but I have Ralph, Ava and Henry. I'm on speaking terms with Mike and now I have work and the book club. I've a lot to be thankful for and I need to stop feeling sorry for myself.

'Stephanie?' a voice calls. It's coming from the stile. It looks like Amanda. Her puffy blonde hair is blowing all around her face. I wave and expect her to carry on walking down the lane but when she starts to climb the stile, I realise she's about to join me.

When she gets nearer I notice she's carrying Toto under her arm. 'I thought we could walk together,' she says. Her voice is breathy from the walk across the field. Otis runs over and starts

70

barking at Toto. I think seeing a fellow dog being carried as opposed to bouncing around like a lunatic confuses him.

'Yes, that would be lovely.' I smile. 'Shh, Otis.'

'I really did enjoy our book club get-together the other week. I hope Janey is okay with my choice. She didn't seem over-enamoured with *Jane Eyre*, but it's very close to my heart ...' She tails off but there was an ever-so-subtle crack in her voice.

I wait a beat but when she doesn't say anything more, I don't press her. 'Honestly, it's fine. We all should be trying new things. The whole point is to read more and step out of our comfort zone a bit.'

She smiles. 'Thank you for being so kind.'

'Two people hardly made a book club. You did us a favour.' I pant as we stomp over grassy mounds. 'On another note, when we were walking home, Janey and I were wondering if you'd like us to get you set up on Zoom or something, so you can talk to your daughter?'

'That would be wonderful.' She stops walking. The deep lines on her forehead seem to relax. 'Thank you.'

We head to Amanda's house and she makes tea whilst I sit in her study messing about on her laptop. When she returns, I've already got Zoom set up and ready to roll.

'You hadn't enabled your camera, that's all. Why don't you text your daughter and see if she's free?' I ask. It's midday here and the time difference isn't huge between here and any part of Africa.

She pauses in thought. 'Yes. Thank you, I think I will.'

Her daughter emails back straight away, ecstatic judging by the emojis I accidentally glimpsed. Five minutes later, the videos connect and there's an ear-piercing squeal as mother and daughter speak face-to-face for the first time in a long time. I mouth and gesture to Amanda that I'll see myself out and as I do, she gives me the widest grin. A ball forms in my throat and as the sound of their happy reunion dissipates the further from the study I get, another ball starts to grow in my stomach.

The image of my own mum fills my head. She's holding out her arms to me because I've climbed onto a wall and I can't get down. She's smiling and telling me to jump. I'd give anything to jump into her arms right now. My throat tightens. I'm choking. I swing the front door open and run down the steps gasping for air. Otis is lying in a sunny spot on the driveway and bounds towards me when he sees me.

'Hello, you.' I crouch down and hug him but everything gets too much and forceful tears erupt. It's weird because I was a happy kid. I missed my mum a lot but for the most part, I was okay. Nobody spoke much about Mum but old photographs propped up my fading memories. Perhaps life would be different if she were still here. Would she have liked Mike? Would I even have married him? I have no idea what she was like as a person. I mean, people said such nice things about her, but she was dead. Nobody was going to say otherwise.

She was a good mum though. In my five years of being with her, she never raised her voice and she loved me. She'd have been a wonderful grandma; I know that much.

Chapter 15

After a long, relaxing bath, I slip on a new pair of pink llama-print pyjamas that I've had since Christmas, and pour myself a glass of Malbec, which I hope will help me sleep. Netflix doesn't have anything that takes my fancy so I pick up the copy of *Jane Eyre* that Amanda lent me. I only manage a few chapters before a horrendously guttural noise sounds from the kitchen. I run in and find Otis throwing up everywhere. He's lying down and looks, well, for want of a better expression, as sick as a dog.

'Otis, what's wrong?' I ask, stroking his head. He's warm and doesn't answer, of course. I try to make him stand up to go to his water bowl but he won't budge so I carry his water to him.

'Drink something,' I coax but he turns his head away. Then, he starts to tremble. 'Oh no. This isn't good.' A quick Google search confirms that he's probably quite unwell. Before I even think about what I'm doing, I'm dialling the vet's emergency 'out-of-hours' number.

'Hello. Prescott's Veterinary Practice.' Edward's voice is sleep-thickened.

'Edward, I'm so sorry to call so late. It's Stephanie.'

There's a pause. 'Oh, hi Steph. Is everything all right?'

'Yes, I'm fine. I'm calling about my dog, Otis. He's vomiting and shaking. I don't know what to do.'

'Okay, try to stay calm. How is he in himself? Lethargic? Off his food?'

I take a breath to recalibrate. 'Yes, very lethargic. He won't get up and ...' I look to his food bowl '... he hasn't touched his dinner, which is a world's first.'

'Okay. I think it's best to take a look at him, just to be on the safe side,' Edward says in the same soothing tone he adopts with his clients of the human, feathered, scaly or furry variety.

'Yes, okay.' Relief washes over me.

'Can you get him to the practice?'

I glance at Otis's flaccid body, sprawled across the tiled floor. 'I don't think so.'

'Okay, give me your address. I'll come to you and check him over.'

I mumble my address and Edward says he'll be here in ten minutes.

When I hang up the phone, I dash back to Otis who hasn't moved a muscle. I check he's still breathing and he peels a heavy eyelid open to look at me before clamping it shut. The worst thoughts go through my mind. I'm so glad the kids aren't here. What will I tell them if ...

When the doorbell rings, I race down the hallway before realising I'm still in my llama pyjamas. I glance down at the ridiculous print. There's no time to run up and change. This is an emergency.

I run my fingers through my hair and swing the door open. Words jar in my throat. The tweed I'm so used to seeing Edward in has been replaced by more regular attire: dark-blue jeans, a white T-shirt and a burgundy hoodie. He looks at least ten years younger.

'Hi, thank you for getting here so fast. Come in,' I say eventually.

'No problem. Where's the big guy then?' He steps past me carrying a black leather bag that's the same size and shape as the one favoured by Mary Poppins.

'At the end of the hall, in the kitchen on the left.'

Edward is halfway there before I've even closed the door and when I enter the kitchen, he's already crouched down by Otis.

'Hey there, big guy,' he says, ruffling his fur. 'I'm just going to check you over if that's okay?'

He opens his bag with his other hand and takes out a stethoscope. While he listens to Otis's heartbeat I look on feeling helpless then realise I'm holding my breath. Then he looks at Otis's gums and starts pulling at his skin on his back.

'I don't think he's in any danger but he's definitely feeling unwell. Could he have eaten something he shouldn't have? Chocolate? Grapes? Anything with onion or garlic in? Spaghetti bolognese or those fancy sausages with leek in?'

I shake my head. 'Not that I know of, but we were out on the field earlier and he was off running about. I got distracted talking to someone so I suppose he could have found something there.'

'I'd like to keep an eye on him for an hour or so if that's okay – just to make sure he doesn't get any worse. I can take him to the practice if you like or if you're not doing anything, I could hang around here?'

Suddenly my reasonably spacious kitchen closes in, transforming into something smaller and more intimate. The thought of Edward, my boss, sitting in it, filling the space with his masculine frame gives me a funny sensation.

Bodily responses aside, I can't say no. 'Of course, stay; make yourself comfortable. I was having a glass of red if you want one or I can stick the kettle on?'

He tugs at the stethoscope still hanging round his neck. 'Thanks but I'm on duty so I'd better go with the tea.'

'Of course.'

I put the kettle on and excuse myself before heading into the downstairs loo. When I catch sight of myself in the mirror, I'm horrified. It's so much worse than I thought, the llama pyjamas a meagre introduction to the sight of me; they're the precursor equivalent of warming up an André Rieu audience with a kid playing the triangle. My hair is like the straw in the bottom of a rabbit's hutch and my teeth have gone purple. Oh God. I smiled like a fool when I answered the door. I throw my face into my hands, reeling at the memory. Edward must think I'm such a sad sack, drinking alone in my pyjamas. I run upstairs to brush my teeth and hair before heading back into the kitchen.

'Hope you don't mind but I started making the tea.' Edward is standing by the kettle stirring milk into one of the cups. 'I wasn't sure how you take yours.'

'Just a drop of milk, no sugar, please.'

He places the teacups on the table and turns the handles so they're both facing the same way. I fight the urge to smile. It's something I would have done pre-kids.

'Thanks,' I say, suddenly a little embarrassed at calling Edward over. Otis is sleeping now and if I hadn't heard him be sick earlier, I'd be none the wiser to his plight.

'So, are the children in bed then?' he asks, taking a sip of tea.

I shake my head. 'They're at their dad's, thankfully. I'd have hated them seeing Otis like this.'

'Yes, he'd have given them quite the fright.' He takes another sip of tea and I remember I have some dark chocolate digestives. I keep them in a high cupboard where the kids can't reach them. I pop a few on a saucer and place them down on the table between us.

'Oh, I love these,' he says taking one. 'So, how are you finding working at the practice?'

'I'm enjoying it. I think I've got to grips with everything now and the new software is a dream. It's quite a novelty having random animals passing my desk each day too.'

'That's a bit harsh – I shower every day *and* wear a suit.'

I get a sharp stab of panic before realising he's teasing me. He has such a dry tone that it's hard to tell.

I tilt my head to the side and almost ask him about the tweed before realising it's a bit over-familiar; rude even. Being around children all day can really mess with your social filter. 'Did you work in the practice before you took it over?' I ask instead.

He nods. 'Yes, for thirteen years. My dad used to run it and after Mum passed, I qualified and worked for him until he died.'

'I'm sorry.'

'It's okay. It was a long time ago now. Somehow over time, I got used to living without parents. That was his bag.' He gestures to the black Mary Poppins bag. The *All Creatures Great and Small* look is starting to make sense. 'I guess you're also wondering why a hip and trendy young thing like me wears tweed most days?'

'I wasn't … I never …'

'Relax.' He laughs softly. 'My dad used to wear tweed suits and I thought it would give me more credibility when I took over the practice. I was only in my twenties and some of the old regulars had been seeing my dad for over thirty years. I had some big shoes to fill. It didn't matter that I was probably more up to date than Dad with my knowledge; nobody would have let me operate on their family pet if I looked inexperienced. With my tweed suit on, I could practically run around giving everyone's pet a dose of Calpol if they were off-colour, without anyone raising an eyebrow.'

'To be fair, that's all we parents do,' I joke. Edward laughs and helps himself to another biscuit. I'd take one too, but they're so hard to clear from your mouth quickly and I'm enjoying our conversation.

'Do you have children?' I ask without thinking about how potentially loaded the question can be.

He's just taken a bite of his biscuit so shakes his head.

'So what's your favourite animal?' I ask instead.

'Oh, that's a hard one. I'm a dog person at heart, but it depends

77

on what I'm doing and, I know I shouldn't judge a pet by its owner, but sometimes if I don't like the owner …' he puts his hand by his mouth and stage whispers '… I don't always like their pets.'

'Wow, the secrets are all coming out now,' I say and he laughs. His eyes sparkle under the fluorescent light. 'What did you put in the tea?'

He laughs softly but doesn't answer my question. 'There was this old lady, who sadly expired a few years ago. She hated everyone and everything but had this goldfish.'

'You hated a goldfish?' I clamp my hand over my face to stifle a giggle.

'No, well eventually, yes, I suppose I did. Enid used to bring this stupid fish in at least once a week …'

'Are you allowed to call a fish stupid?' I widen my eyes in faux horror.

'No, not really. I don't know, despite the fees almost plunging my parents into penury, it wasn't covered at vet school. Anyway, the reason for Geoffrey's frequent visits ranged from, "he's not eating or pooing" to "he's eating and pooing too much". She never saw the connection.'

I smile, trying not to laugh.

'Then there was my personal favourite: "he's sad".'

'A sad goldfish called Geoffrey? Crikey.'

'Yes. I tried to explain that perhaps the mini tsunami that occurred in his bowl every time she took him on a bus probably made him feel a little out of sorts.'

'Is that true?' I wonder how all the fish on *Deadliest Catch* must be feeling in those giant waves.

He shakes his head. 'I've no idea. I did try to tell her that the little bowl wasn't the best environment for a fish but she accused me of trying to swindle her out of her pension and sell her a big fancy tank. I wasn't, by the way. My deviance was limited to simply trying to deter her from the practice. Anyway, that sort of verbal delight was a common theme right until she passed. I suppose she was lonely and I did recommend places she could go to socialise and get support but she was adamant I was wrong and it was all about the bloody fish.'

'What happened to Geoffrey?'

Edward pats his stomach animatedly. 'Fish finger sandwich with tartar sauce.'

I almost splutter my tea. 'You didn't!'

He laughs. 'No, I'm kidding. I'm a ketchup man, through and through.'

I nudge him playfully before remembering he's my boss and now my vet, not some old friend. It's so easy to blur the lines with him.

Edward drains his cup, rises to his feet and gestures to Otis. 'He looks like he's through the worst.'

'I hope so. He's given me such a scare.'

'I'll check him over again and if I'm happy he's on the mend, I'll let you get some peace.'

I nod, disappointed that he'll be leaving and a little embarrassed that it may have been my fault for crossing a line. I wasn't trying to be flirty. Oh God, the very idea makes my insides curl up and want to evacuate my body in well under the fire-brigade-recommended two minutes.

'He's stopped shaking and he's not been sick for a while now. I'm going to try and get him to drink some water. Do you have any cooked meat in the fridge?'

I go and look. 'There's some roast chicken – the sort you buy ready-cooked for sandwiches when you're lazy like me.'

'Let's try him with a few small pieces.'

I crouch down and offer Otis a piece. He barely moves at first, but then his nose starts sniffing at the meat and he takes it. I smile at Edward, who nudges the water bowl closer and Otis laps up a few drops. We feed him the rest of the chicken and when he's had another drink, he stands.

'Oh my goodness,' I say, feeling two stones lighter.

'Whatever the matter was – he seems to be over it now.'

'Thank you,' I say.

'I didn't do anything,' Edward says modestly.

'You did. You saved me from having a meltdown.' I smile. 'What shall I do about the bill?'

He waves a dismissive hand. 'It's nothing. You gave me tea and biscuits so call it even.'

I look at him for a moment. I'm uncomfortable about not paying for his time but arguing about it would be awkward too. The best thing I can do is accept gracefully.

'Thank you so much. I didn't expect a freebie.'

'You're part of the Prescott vet family now.'

My chest swells as I see him out and then go and let Otis into the back garden for a wee. When I come back inside, the house is cold and empty again. How can one man have filled it up so much?

Chapter 16

'How was Center Parcs?' I ask Janey, who's decorating a birthday cake for herself, really badly. Tom and Seren keep running in and out with random requests and despite it only being Tuesday teatime, I can sense she's already had enough of half-term.

'Hell. I could have gone to the Caribbean for the price we paid and the kids spent the entire time splashing me in the swimming pool and riding their bikes so fast that I couldn't keep up.'

I chuckle. 'So, no time in the spa then?'

'Not a chance. My friend's husband got sick so ended up in bed for the weekend and Jimmy didn't come so it was a relentless kid fest. The only bit of peace I got was when I snuck outside to neck the leftover crumbs from the Pringles tube.'

'Is everything okay between you two? You and Jimmy, I mean.' I don't mean to pry but I'm sensing something is off.

'Oh, yes. Jimmy is Jimmy.' She bats her hand through the air. 'AWOL Jimmy.'

'Has he always been like that?'

She pauses and looks at the spoon in her hand before shrugging. 'Life changes when you have kids, doesn't it?'

My inner voice is screaming 'no' but who am I to talk? Mike wasn't exactly husband of the year and if he hadn't left, I'd still be with him now. I do want to probe further. Janey is obviously more unhappy than she's letting on, but it doesn't seem like the right time. 'At least your friend's husband managed to get some rest on holiday.'

'I also managed to spend a gazillion pounds on food; hence making my own cake.' She licks icing off the spatula she's brandishing in the general direction of the cake. 'What do you think?'

'Is it the Leaning Tower of Pisa?' I ask, taking in the white slanted monstrosity. Although, I've no idea what the green blob at the top is.

'It's a margarita,' she says drily.

I squint at it. 'Oh yes!'

'Don't lie. It's crap. In hindsight, I should have put a proper margarita glass on top. Cakes are not my forte.'

'You shouldn't be making your own.'

'I don't mind. I wouldn't get one otherwise and the kids expect it.' She puts the spatula down. 'I know what you're thinking. Jimmy is a worthless husband. But he hasn't always been like this. He works really hard so I don't have to and he gets tired. When the kids start secondary school, I'll get a job and maybe he can cut his hours down a bit.'

'Do you ever do things together? As a couple?' I've only known Janey for four weeks or so but she's never mentioned spending time with anyone but the children.

'No, there's never any time for that.'

'Well make some time. I'll have the kids over for a sleepover on Friday and you and Jimmy can go out for dinner.'

She frowns. 'I'm not sure he'd even want to.'

'Well ask him instead of waiting for him to,' I say, surprising myself with how direct I sound. 'For all you know, he could be thinking the exact same thing about you. Maybe he thinks you're happy.'

She looks up, pondering this. 'Maybe I will. Anyway, what did you get up to this weekend?'

'Not much. I bumped into Amanda on the field when I was walking Otis the other day.'

'Oh right. Did she have much to say?'

'She was just really grateful for the book club. She thought maybe you were a bit miffed at her book choice so she was worried about that.'

'I'm quite into it now.'

'Good, maybe you can put her mind at rest when we meet next week.'

'I will! So was that the highlight of your weekend then?'

'I had an episode with Otis on Saturday night. He ate something and got sick so I had to call Edward.'

'He's the vet?' she says, still trying to smooth the buttercream icing near the base of the leaning tower of margarita.

I nod. 'He came out and checked Otis over.'

She stops icing to look up and wiggle her eyebrows at me. 'On Saturday night?'

'Yes. It's nothing *strange*, just an out-of-hours service.'

'What's he like – this vet?'

'He's really nice. Couldn't ask for a better boss really.'

'Is he older, younger, gorgeous, Shrek-like? Come on!'

'I think he's a similar age to me. It's hard to tell because he dresses like he's from *All Creatures Great and Small*.'

She snorts.

'He's caring with the animals and has a good sense of humour.'

'He sounds great. Is he single?'

'I don't know but *you're* not.'

Janey gives me a sideways glance and then bursts out laughing. 'I meant for you, you numpty.'

'For me? I don't want to date anyone.'

'Why not?'

'Because ...'

Janey folds her arms. 'Hmm? You've just sorted my love life out so don't shy away now.'

'Because I've just got over a divorce and I'm adjusting.'

'I was going to make a crude comment then, but I suppose you're right.'

'I just need to keep things stable for the kids before I think about who is or isn't single. Besides that, I'm not sure how Mike would react to me meeting someone else. If he started being arsey, it would be a nightmare. Things are only just civil as it is.'

'I get it. So anyway, what do you think?' She presents the finished cake with her hands. Aesthetically speaking, it's terrible.

'Looks delicious,' I say.

Chapter 17

A few days later, I'm at work plodding through. I miss the kids even though they FaceTime me every day. I still find it hard to understand how it all came to this. Passing the children back and forth between myself and the man I vowed to spend my entire life with. I'm not sad about it anymore. All my tears have been shed on the matter. I just don't quite know how I got here. The shrill of the phone breaks my thoughts. Carly isn't here, *obviously*, so I answer.

'Hello, Prescott's Veterinary Surgery.'

'Hi … I have an emergency … it's my dog …' The female caller's voice is broken by hitched breathing and sobs.

'Okay, please take a deep breath and try to remain calm,' I say, copying what Edward said to me – it's my first emergency call. 'Please can you tell me what seems to be wrong?'

She draws deep breath. 'She's in labour and the first pup was born about two hours ago. She seemed fine for a while after and we just thought she had a natural delay between pups but after an hour, she started to seem distressed. We've tried to keep her calm and look for an obstruction or something but she's bleeding heavily now and I don't want to move her to bring her in. Can the vet come out soon?'

85

I check the time. Edward is operating on a dog with a tumour but he's been in there a while and I'm sure he's finished. 'I will go and check. I'll call you back in a few minutes.'

I take the lady's name and number down and end the call. As I do so, Carly comes in. 'That was an emergency. I need to see if Edward can make an urgent home visit. Can you man the phone?' I say, handing her the note. I don't wait for her reply as I head through the examination room towards the operating room.

'Edward, I'm so sorry to barge in. There's an emergency. It's …' As my eyes home in on him, I notice the blood. It's all over his apron and gloves and the nurse, Helen, who is holding a bloody mass of tissue or flesh. I retch and my head starts to spin but I'm not sick; instead my knees wobble and my brain tingles and then everything turns to black.

The light is bright white.

My eyes flicker, trying to open, but the light just burns them. It's like when my science teacher used to ignite magnesium and warn us not to look. The warning served only to compel us to peek despite the risk of irreversible retina damage. I'm sure this light is much less dangerous to the eyes.

'You're awake,' a male voice soothes.

'Edward?' I blink a few times as he comes into focus. For some reason, I'm on the floor in the operating room. 'Did I faint?'

'A little bit,' he says.

I look at my arms and scream. They're stained with something sticky and crimson and a wave of nausea attacks me once more.

'I'm sorry about that. I reached out and grabbed you when you started to fall. We were just about to clean up.' He starts to remove his gloves and apron then I remember what I came in for.

'The emergency—'

'It's okay, it's in hand. Carly called back to say I'm on my way. You've only been out a few minutes.' He stands by the sink and

86

scrubs his hands and arms as Helen tends to the dog on the operating table, who is just coming around. 'You came in as I'd finished stitching her up – Helen was disposing of the tumour.'

The word makes me retch again. 'Sorry, here I'll help you up.' His shirtsleeves are rolled up exposing some strong-looking forearms. Without his usual tweed jacket on, I notice how the cotton fabric of his shirt strains a little around his bicep and for a moment, I can't tear my eyes away. I expect him to offer me a hand, but instead, he scoops me up in his arms. My head whirls around a myriad of feelings. Fear and nausea; the metallic scent of blood still lingering in my nostrils, excitement – I've been swept up in the strong arms of a man – and extreme self-consciousness; I'm wearing a skirt and it's been a week since I last considered shaving my legs – even then I don't think I actually did. Aside from all of that is the uncomfortable, tingly heat that's spreading from each of the points where Edward's body touches mine. A few awkward moments later, he places me on the steel table in the examination room. I flinch at the coldness.

'Sorry,' he says again but he's distracted because he's studying my face. 'How are you feeling now?'

'Like a prize idiot,' I say, adding a small laugh at the end.

'Don't be embarrassed. It happens to us all.'

'Does it?' I imagine so. All that blood and gore must turn a fair few trainee vets faint.

'Not really.' He gives a mischievous wink. 'If you're sure you're okay, I need to dash.'

'Of course – you go!'

His eyes linger on mine for a moment then he gives a small nod, grabs his jacket and bag then disappears out of the door. I sit for a while just looking around the room and down at the table I'm sitting on in a state of disbelief. I've never liked blood but I haven't fainted before, nor has a man ever had to carry me like a newborn baby. Helen interrupts my live stream of shame when she comes in with a cup of tea and plate of biscuits.

'This will make you feel better,' she says, handing me the steaming mug. 'The operating theatre isn't for everyone.'

'Evidently,' I say before taking a sip of the tea. I wince at the sweetness.

'The sugar will help,' Helen says, picking up on my reaction. She natters on about the first operation she ever witnessed and tells me I can go home if I like but once I've had a biscuit and the tea is half drunk, I feel fine and to be honest, I'm sort of hoping Edward comes back. I want to apologise for bursting into theatre – I really don't think I'm allowed to do that. I just panicked.

For some reason, my mind drifts to Edward a lot throughout the afternoon. I can't stop thinking about him: how calm he was in a crisis, how safe I felt in his arms and the concern in his eyes. I catch myself wondering if he's married and what he does in his spare time. Things I shouldn't even care about. When I asked him if he has kids, it was spontaneous. Whether he had them or not didn't matter, I just wondered because I'd been yapping on about mine. If he did, we could have talked about the usual problems or funny stories; if he didn't, I knew to shut up. Now here I am wondering whether he's single. It's partly Janey's fault but also his for picking me up in those arms of his.

'So …' I turn to Carly who is reading something on her phone. 'I feel like I don't know you very well. Tell me about yourself.'

She looks at me like I've asked in a foreign language and it occurs to me that I haven't really spoken to her much, other than to ask where something is on the computer. Oh well, it's done now, even if the words are hanging in the air like burning sage.

'Er, I live with my boyfriend in those flats near the Co-op,' she starts. I rest my head on my hand, nodding along like she's doing a dramatised retelling of *Gone Girl* or something.

I'm still nodding when I realise she's stopped talking. 'Oh, great,' I say.

'We have a teenager, as you know and we're going to Málaga in the summer.'

'Wonderful,' I say smiling. 'I just feel like I've been here weeks now and don't know anything about you and Helen, or Edward for that matter.'

I think that came across as nonchalant.

'Er, well Helen wears her heart on her sleeve and Edward is one of those *what you see is what you get* sort of people. He's a workaholic. I'm pretty sure when he goes home he just carries on doing vet stuff.'

'Vet stuff,' I repeat like it fascinates me.

'Yeah, well, I'm not sure. He doesn't talk about his home life unless he's had a call-out. Like when he came to you on Saturday.'

I tense. Is it weird that she knows about our Saturday tea and biscuit session? 'Ahh, yes. He was great with Otis.'

'I don't think he has anyone really, like friends and stuff. He never seems to go out.'

'Isn't he married?' I do 'flippantly' really well here, so well, in fact, I'll be expecting my shiny golden man trophy in the post sometime soon.

She shakes her head. 'No, I don't think so. He goes out with a woman in the village called Stacy. I don't know how serious things are but if he's ever going out, it's usually with her.'

'Hmm.' I have nothing to say really. I have the information I somehow craved, I just need to move on. 'So, does your teenager like school?'

I wince as soon as I realise I've put my foot in it.

I thought my curiosity was satisfied, but it seems that now I have this burning desire to find out more about Stacy from the village. Because the town where Prescott's vet's is located is tiny, I keep my ear to the ground every time I'm popping into the Co-op or the newsagent's but by the time I leave work on Friday, I'm none the wiser. I treat myself to a Chinese takeaway and plate it up at home. As the smell of soy sauce fills my nostrils, my stomach groans in anticipation.

Removing my phone from my pocket, I open the Facebook app where I go onto the vet's page. There are over eight hundred people, who 'like' it, including Janey, who I know is just trying to check Edward out. Facebook should let you filter the list of 'likers' so the Facebook stalkers can get on with things but of course, they don't, so I have to scroll through all eight hundred plus names.

The first photograph is of a dalmatian with thirty-three likes. I click the blue circle with the white 'thumbs up'.

'Bingo!' A list of people who liked the photograph comes up so I scroll through. No Stacy unfortunately. As I'm scrolling, a message pops up on the screen. It's Janey.

Hi hon, thanks for the offer but no need to babysit tonight. X

That's odd, she seemed up for it yesterday. I text her back asking if she's okay and when she doesn't reply, make a mental note to ask again when she comes over tomorrow for our book club meeting.

I try a few more doggy pics that produce nothing of interest but then, I come across a photo of Edward. He's standing proudly outside his practice holding a red cocker spaniel and the photo has eighty 'likes'. If she asks him out every week as Janey says, she's bound to be one of them unless she lives in a cave and doesn't have Facebook of course.

'Yes!' I fist-pump the air. I've found her. I click the tiny thumbnail of her face, which takes me to her page. It's set to private but I can see her profile picture. She's not at all what I expected. I expected a sophisticated brunette in expensive jodhpurs and a crisp blouse. Without being judgemental or stereotypical, it seems Stacy is a fan of the more revealing outfit and seems quite proud of her ample bosom. Her blonde hair is big and fluffy; it almost reaches her waist and she's doing that pouty face that the boomers missed by a mile, most Gen X avoid like the plague and a lot of millennials are still on the fence about. Picturing her neon skin-tight dress next to Edward's tweed hurts my eyes even through the power of imagination. They'd look quite a sight in real life. Still, if that's his thing, that's his choice.

Curiosity status: Enhanced.

Chapter 18

The kids came home today. Having missed them like crazy, I squeezed them and showered them in kisses and got through a good ten minutes before they completely destroyed the house. Now, I'm running around like a headless chicken trying to tidy up before Janey and Amanda get here. I've entrusted Ava with putting on her own pyjamas and Ralph to have a shower, which just leaves Henry who's a sticky mess and in dire need of a bath but the bath is a whole palaver with toys and bubbles and I usually end up as wet as he does. In the end I fill the sink with warm water and dunk him in there.

With ten minutes to spare, I manage to get everyone in bed. I even get the chance to run around with a hoover and pour myself a glass of Sauvignon Blanc.

'Hi,' I say, hugging Janey when she arrives.

'Read the book so I think I deserve one of them,' she says, gesturing towards my glass of wine.

'In the kitchen,' I say, and she makes her way down the hall.

'Amanda not here yet?' Janey is already taking a glass out of the cupboard when our phones buzz in unison. It's Amanda in the WhatsApp group.

'She's on her way,' I say. 'Anyway, how were your last few days of half-term?'

'I haven't murdered the kids, if that's what you mean?'

I give her a knowing look.

'To be honest, it's been nice. We went on a walk and I even got my two playing Monopoly – I think they've finally had enough of computer games.'

I smile but I get a pang. Since Mike and I split up, he's had the kids during the holidays and I've missed that family holiday time so much. There's nothing I can do about it though. I'm the one who lives near the school and can drop them off and pick them up each day.

'Mine only got home today and I've resumed my position of chief nag.'

'Oh, love, I know it's not easy. Sorry, I didn't mean to bang on about how much fun we've had.'

I wave my hand dismissively, 'No, don't apologise. It is what it is and the kids had a great time with their dad – that's what matters in all of this. Anyway, I wanted to ask about you and Jimmy. Why didn't you go out last night?'

She looks at her hands, which are both gripping the stem of the wine glass. 'Is everything okay?' I press gently.

She shrugs but doesn't look up so I move closer and put my arm around her. 'What is it? You can talk to me.'

'He didn't want to go.' Her voice wobbles as she struggles with the words.

'Oh, Janey. Why? Was it bad timing? It was short notice.'

She shakes her head. 'He just said it wasn't *us* and went off to the pub.'

The emotion in her voice sends pain through the depths of my stomach. I've never seen her so vulnerable before and it shows how we all have our weak spots. 'Well, that's not good enough.'

'I don't know what to do, Steph.' She sniffs then whispers. 'It doesn't feel like a marriage anymore.'

'Oh, honey.' I squeeze her tightly and we stay like that for a good few minutes.

'You need a frank chat with Jimmy. Tell him exactly what you want from him. Actually, tell him how you deserve to be treated.'

She goes to say something but the doorbell shrills and she wipes her eyes and heads to answer it.

'Hello, book clubbers.' Amanda breezes in like a rainbow in a thunderstorm, waving a bottle of Prosecco and a bag of posh crisps. She has her copy of *Jane Eyre* tucked under her arm and what looks like a sheet of notes stuffed in the pages.

'You've come prepared,' I say.

Her cheeks flush. 'If I'm doing it, I want to do it properly.'

'Right then.' Janey gestures animatedly towards the lounge like none of that conversation we just had actually happened. 'Shall we get started?'

We go through and take our seats. Amanda starts us off by telling us why she'd chosen the book and what she loves about it. Janey looks as though she's drifted off but I'm too far away to nudge her.

'I think it's truly wonderful. It never fails to surprise me how strong a character Jane was for the era. She was certainly a fine, albeit early example of a strong feminist character, don't you agree?' Amanda's question brings Janey back to the room.

'It was a bit long-winded wasn't it?' Janey says.

'It's an epic love story; of course it was long-winded,' Amanda says, failing to hide her exasperation.

'I get that,' Janey continues. 'The one-night stand we've all had is an epic romance if you start telling the story from ten years old. So, I was ten and loved building dens, then I kissed a boy for a dare when I was fourteen, did my GCSEs and six years later got drunk and—'

'I haven't ever had a one-night stand,' Amanda says.

Janey casts her a look of disbelief before continuing. 'All I'm saying is: did we really need all that stuff about her childhood at the beginning?'

'Yes, firstly, it made her into a stronger woman, and secondly, it all tied up in the end, didn't it?'

I sit back as the debate unfolds. Is this what a book club is supposed to be like? A year eleven rowing with their English teacher about how the book is nonsense. It reminds me of that funny meme that went around the internet a few years ago – the one that said something like this:

Teacher: Why were the curtains blue?

Student: Don't know.

Teacher: Blue represents sadness. The fact the curtains are closed means they're preventing the light from coming in. Therefore suggesting an impenetrable sadness hangs in the room.

Author: The curtains were effing blue.

I giggle to myself.

'How about something with a bit of grit next time?' Janey says, unconvinced by Amanda's gushing about *Jane Eyre*.

'I really enjoyed it.' I shrug. 'I agree with Amanda but how about you choose the next one?'

'Okay, but first, wine.' Janey jumps out of her seat and heads to the kitchen.

When Janey returns, Amanda draws a loud breath, prompting me to look over. I expect to see her looking impatient, but instead, she's staring at the cover of the book, which is resting in her lap. 'There was another reason I chose this book.'

'Oh?' Janey and I say in unison.

Amanda removes a pristine, white handkerchief from her cardigan pocket and dabs the corner of her eye. It's certainly the night for it.

'I've had this copy for thirty-five years.' She strokes the cover lightly. 'I bought it in Haworth, the day my husband, George, proposed. We'd been on a day trip and walked up to the Brontë parsonage, visited the museum and eaten cake in this beautiful little café. It was the perfect day and after he'd bought me this book, he walked me up to the Brontë waterfall and got down on one knee.'

'How romantic,' I say fondly but Amanda doesn't respond.

'There's something I've needed to talk about and the truth is, I haven't had anyone to talk to in a long while,' Amanda says quietly and I get a pang of sadness.

'You can talk to us,' Janey says softly and I back her up with warm smile.

'I lost George last year and the pain …' She bursts into tears. Immediately after, Janey and I rush to her side.

'I'm so sorry, Amanda.' I thought she was married but her house did feel suspiciously empty – perhaps I should have said something then.

'I suppose I chose this book as a way to remember George, but also as a way to talk about him. I wasn't sure how to bring it up. Talking about it isn't easy.' She blows her nose and I stroke her back. 'I'm sorry you didn't like it, Janey.'

'Oh my goodness. Don't worry about me. I feel terrible now for saying those things. You can talk about anything with us. Tell me what he was like?' Janey soothes.

Amanda talks for a while about how charming George was. He sounds like he had a good sense of humour and treated her like a queen too. It's easy to see why he's left a huge hole in her life.

'Then he had a heart attack. Without warning, it struck him down on the golf course and that was that.' She dries her eyes with the now sodden handkerchief.

My throat constricts. I know how it is to love someone and lose them suddenly. I also find it too hard to talk about.

'It makes you realise how short life is,' Janey says. 'How every day counts.'

I give her a look to say she should take her own advice.

'Anyway, enough about me.' Amanda pulls out a pocket mirror

from her handbag and wipes away the mascara that had smudged around her eyes. 'How's your new job going?' It's a clear attempt to lighten the mood, but I can see how much she needs me to take the bait.

'On the whole, I love it, but it was quite traumatic yesterday. Edward, the vet, had to put an old sheepdog to sleep.'

'Oh, that's sad,' Amanda says.

'*Pet Sematary*,' Janey says, sloshing more wine into each of the glasses on the coffee table. 'That's what we should read next. The sheepdog story gave me the idea – we wanted something with grit.'

I shake my head. '*Pet Sematary* it is.'

Amanda and Janey fall into an agreeable conversation about Stephen King but since telling the sheepdog story, I seem to have Edward on the brain. I keep trying to picture him and Stacy together, but I can't make them fit. Why is it bothering me so much?

'Are you with us?' Janey is looking at me.

'Yes.'

'I was just saying you need to get the book request in at the library if you're going to get a copy in time. You looked as though you'd gone to another planet for a minute.'

'I was just thinking about work.'

Janey turns to Amanda. 'Has she told you about the hunky vet she works with?'

Amanda shakes her head but hunches forward in her seat like she's ready to hear more.

'I knew you'd Facebook-stalked him,' I say. Janey laughs.

'I might have had a little look. If he's single, he'd be quite the catch. Tall, good-looking and he must have a sensitive side, wanting to save animals for a living.'

'He … well … I suppose. He's a nice guy but he's just my boss.'

'Oh yeah.' Janey winks.

'He is.' My voice is a high-pitched squeal. 'He's a very good boss too and I don't want to jeopardise my job so don't go gossiping. You know how things spread in this village.' Janey pretends to zip her lips shut. 'Anyway, I don't think Amanda wants to hear this.'

'Oh I do. When I asked about work I was hoping to lighten the mood, but this has exceeded my expectations ten-fold.' She grins.

'Well, for the benefit of those in the room desperate for something juicy, he's seeing someone.'

Janey's jaw drops. 'Who?'

'A woman called Stacy. I don't know her but Carly at the practice said they go out together from time to time.'

'That's a shame – he's hot as hell,' Janey says, curling her feet up on the sofa.

'So, are you thinking about courting?' Amanda asks as Janey snorts.

'No. Not at all,' I say with the powerful assault of anti-aircraft missile.

'Sorry, I didn't mean to seem nosy.' Amanda clears her throat. 'I'm not very good at the whole girls' chat thing.'

My abdominal muscles tighten. I've made her feel bad. 'Don't apologise, it's just not something I've ever considered. It's a shock to even think about dating again. I'm run ragged by the kids each day and my body is a mess. My stomach is saggy from three kids, I'm covered in cellulite and my pubic hair is trespassing way beyond my knickers' elastic. In *all* directions.'

'Don't worry about your tummy – we all have that and you can get a bikini wax,' Janey says.

'I just don't think I could pull myself together enough to go on a date.'

'Understandable,' Amanda says with a small apologetic smile. 'I'm not sure I could consider dating again.'

'But you've never had a one-night stand,' Janey says, then screws her eyes up. 'I'm sorry, that was insensitive. I've had too much wine.'

Amanda laughs. 'Don't worry. A year has passed – I'm okay. It was a difficult year. My daughter couldn't get back for the funeral and we don't have much family. I'm okay though now. I just felt like I needed to talk about George to bring his memory alive. It was starting to feel a bit like he didn't exist.'

'That's what friends are for,' I say.

'And never say never on the one-night stand.' Amanda winks but I suspect she's just teasing Janey.

'God, I can't imagine going through all that awkward first date stuff now,' Janey says.

I laugh along, but the truth is, as scary as dating seems, a lifetime of being alone is terrifying to me. Perhaps that's why she puts up with Jimmy, because the alternative is more frightening. Yes, right now dating seems too much, especially with Henry being so small, but I'd like to think I'll meet someone in the future. Someone to share meals and walks with, someone to grow old with. Otherwise, when the kids leave home, I'll have nobody.

'Can you pass me the Prosecco?' My voice croaks.

'It's all gone.' Janey shrugs. 'I probably should call it a night. Both kids have swimming in the morning and it's hard enough to drag myself out of bed at the best of times.'

'I should get going too,' Amanda says. 'But thank you, both. As weird as it sounds after all the tears, I had a wonderful evening.'

When I close the door, I don't feel like going to bed, so I open a bottle of rosé from the fridge and flick through Netflix for something that doesn't require too much brainpower. I find it hard to concentrate. I'm too light-headed. If I didn't know better I'd swear I was coming down with something, but I've felt like this since Janey brought Edward up and we had the whole conversation about dating. After a few sips of wine, the unease starts to melt a little. I put on a new comedy series that people have been raving about but find myself flicking through my phone. It buzzes in my hand. It's Amanda on our WhatsApp group.

Thank you for being there xx

Immediately Janey replies:

Any time xx

Then Amanda.

Sorry if I upset you, Stephanie. I won't mention it again xx

There's that pang again.

No, I'm sorry. I was just taken by surprise. I pause before adding, **We're friends now. You can say anything to me xx**

Chapter 19

'Temperamental cat?' I ask a rather flustered Edward. He's emerged from the examination room looking a little red and dishevelled – he's even loosened his tie – things must be bad.

'The little rascal won't let me near her. I need the nurse to hold her still.'

Helen, the nurse, is out on her lunch. 'Is Mrs Pearson not due back to collect Ruby soon?' I'd overheard her telling Carly she'd be back at one and it's five to.

Edward rakes his hands through his hair. 'She'll have given her Yorkshire pudding again, you mark my words, but without examining her abdomen, I can't be certain.'

'If it's just holding her still, I could do it.'

Edward glances around the empty surgery and nods. 'Yes, please. I need to go to the farm soon to check on one of the horses down there so I could do with sorting Ruby and her irritable bowel sharpish.'

I follow him into the small room where he puts the cat on a metal table. She arches her back and hisses. I wonder if she can sense I'm a dog person.

'Relax, Ruby, I just want to feel your tummy. If we don't get to the bottom of this, we could have a much bigger problem on our hands and we don't want that, do we?' he says, looking the cat dead in the eyes. I can't help but smirk at Edward in his slightly rumpled tweed, talking ever so earnestly to a cat.

'Steph, I'm going to lie her down on her side. Could you help restrain her? You'll have to use a bit of force – she's quite feisty.'

He lies the cat in position. 'I need you to put your hands where mine are and whatever you do, don't let her go.'

Slowly, I slide my hands along her glossy fur, until they reach Edward's. He gives me the nod, so I slide my left hand beneath his big, warm hand. Little bolts of electricity zap me as I do and for the few seconds it lasts, I can't focus on anything but his touch – it's strangely pleasurable. I swallow hard before moving my right hand into position. The same thing happens again. I wonder if he felt that too or if it's just my imagination. I study his face. His jaw is set, his eyes are serious, intent and giving nothing away. I get an overwhelming urge to reach out and run my hand over his smooth skin; instead, I look at the wall and try to focus on the job in hand. He listens to the cat's chest or abdomen – it's impossible to tell – then slides the stethoscope off.

'I've already run blood tests and X-rayed her but there is definitely some bloating. I'm just going to apply some pressure to see if she's in any pain.' He looks at me pointedly so I nod even though he's talking to me like I'm the nurse but I really have no idea about anything other than the mild palpitations his proximity is causing me. As he presses her stomach, the cat wriggles and claws at my hands and I reel backwards.

'Sorry,' I say realising I've let her go. I pin her back down.

The bell on reception shrills. 'That will be your mummy,' I say to Ruby. 'Do you still need me or should I go through? Carly was outside when I came in.'

He pauses in thought. 'You go. I had a good feel and she seems okay.' As I place my hand on the door handle, he draws a breath.

'Oh, and thank you for stepping up. You've saved me a lot of apologising and explaining.'

Warmth reaches my cheeks and I allow myself a little smile as I leave the room with a new level of envy for Helen.

'Hi, Mrs Pearson,' I say, donning a huge smile.

'Ruby. I'm here to collect her.' She presses her lips into a hard line. Pleasant as always.

'Take a seat, Mrs Pearson. Edward will bring her out in just a moment.'

I start generating the invoice for Ruby's treatment. As I tap away at the keyboard, I sense Mrs Pearson's eyes weighing heavily upon me. I glance at her and she doesn't even have the decency to look away.

'Is there anything I can help you with whilst you wait?' I ask.

'No.' Thick air hangs around her. Slowly, it makes its way towards me and my throat is constricted. I swallow hard. Suddenly, the door to the examination room opens and Edward waltzes out. I can breathe again.

'Mrs Pearson,' he says cheerfully, 'I have Ruby here for you.'

Mrs Pearson's face lights up as she collects the cat carrier from him. 'Whatever was the matter?' she asks the cat rather than Edward.

'She was a little bloated – I think it was a bit of colic so I've given her antacids and she seems to have settled. I'm going to give you some to take home but, Mrs Pearson, your cat needs to be kept on a strict diet. No more human food – I'm pretty sure she's struggling to digest it.'

Mrs Pearson sighs wearily. 'Yes, vet. She only had a bit of my birthday cake.'

Edward casts me a look and I have to bow my head so she doesn't see me stifling a smile.

'I'm afraid birthday cake is off the table for Ruby. She's getting on a bit now and she's prone to colic – it's the kindest thing to do.'

'Of course.' She smiles. 'Thank you, vet.'

She pays happily and practically skips out of the door. 'How do you do that?' I ask Edward as he's putting his blazer on.

'Do what?'

'Tell her what to do in such a nice way. I think I'd have just screamed at her to stop being such an idiot.'

He laughs softly. 'Bedside manner is part of the job description. Mrs Pearson is lonely. She'll be back soon and no matter what I say, she'll be giving that cat custard creams and gin in no time at all.'

'God I hope not. That would be a terrible waste of gin.'

'What would?' Carly burst in.

'Oh just Mrs P feeding her cat all sorts of extravagant foods again,' I say as the warm fuzzy feeling of sharing a joke with Edward dissipates.

'Should report her,' Carly says with a complete lack of empathy.

'That won't be necessary,' Edward says as he rummages through his vet bag for something. 'The cat hasn't got much mileage in her and she's happy enough. Now she has her antacids she'll be comfortable.'

Carly rolls her eyes but Edward is still digging deep in his bag.

'Have you lost something?' I ask.

'Stethoscope,' he says distractedly.

'You mean the one around your neck?' I say, pointing. He pats his chest, grasping the stethoscope when he finds it.

'I could've sworn I took that off.'

'You did but I suppose you must have slipped it back on subconsciously.'

'Well, it's a good job one of us is on the ball,' he says picking up his bag. 'Right, I better get down to the farm. I'm not back in today so I'll see you both tomorrow.'

Carly's eyes don't leave her computer screen but she waves her hand in acknowledgement.

'See you tomorrow, Edward,' I say and for some reason, my eyes linger on the door long after he's passed through it.

Chapter 20

'Who fancies a picnic for tea?' I ask and I'm greeted with a disharmonic chorus of 'yeses'. There are a few nice river walks near us, but it's a lovely day and I fancy a drive out to somewhere different. After throwing some sandwiches together and stuffing a selection of snacks into a backpack, I buckle the children in the car and set off with a little belly fizz of excitement at the prospect of doing something so spontaneous. Sod the spag bol I was going to make. I'm a woman in charge of her own destiny.

The village where I work, Crinkly, has a little playground just past the pub and I'm sure it has a picnic table with stunning views of the river and countryside. If we eat there, the kids can run off some energy. I scoop up Henry and shepherd Ava and Ralph towards it.

'Steph?' The familiar voice stops me in my tracks.

'Edward, hello.' I freeze for a moment then turn to the children. 'This is Mummy's boss.'

Ava and Ralph mumble a 'hello'.

'Off for a pint?' he says to Ralph, who pulls a face of disgust.

'We're having a bit of an adventure – a picnic in the park,' I say before Ralph goes on to say how it's weird that we've come here or something.

'A picnic in the park,' Edward says full of animation.

Ava beams proudly. 'Yes.'

'I thought since it's a nice day, we could have a bit of an outing and get some fresh air.' I don't know why I'm explaining myself; it isn't like I'm doing anything wrong.

'How exciting! I'd better let you get to it then.'

'You can come and sit with us if you like,' Ava says and my stomach practically folds in half. Edward glances at his watch.

'I'm sure Edward has somewhere important to be, Ava,' I say, wrapping my arm around her.

'I could sit down for ten minutes on one condition.'

'What's that?' Ava asks.

'You let me pinch a crisp.'

'Fine, but only if I can choose it,' she says.

We walk over to the bench and sit down. Edward sits next to me whilst Ralph and Ava sit opposite. Henry is in my lap. I hand out the tinfoil packages and we start to tuck in.

'Here you go.' Ava hands Edward a minuscule crisp.

'Thank you.' He smiles and accepts graciously.

'She washed her hands before we left, I swear,' I whisper as he pops the crisp into his mouth.

'It's all right. I think my germ tolerance is pretty high,' he says. 'You don't want to know where my hands have been today.'

Ralph finds this hilarious whilst Ava looks confused and I can't say I'm not enjoying the dynamic Edward has brought to our little picnic.

Seemingly pleased with their new audience, Ava and Ralph both chat away about school and games they've played. Ava has been learning about the *Titanic* and tells us everything she knows whilst Ralph talks about why he's excited to go to secondary school and it's all news to me – they never utter more than a word about school on any other day. Even Henry is a dream. As the children talk, I keep offering my crisps to Edward who takes one each time. It's so natural and in this setting, it's hard to imagine that he's my boss who I hardly know.

'Oh no,' Edward says, prompting all the eyes from around the table to fall upon him. 'I have to go. I'm supposed to be meeting someone outside the pub any minute now.'

'It's probably going to get chilly soon so I want to get going too.'

'Aww do you have to?' Ava whines.

'Yes. I'm so sorry, but maybe we could do this again.' He's just being polite but the idea of this being something we plan makes me tingly inside.

'We'll get you some crisps of your own.' Ava smiles.

'Count me in,' he says before turning to me. 'I've enjoyed this. Thanks for letting me gate-crash your picnic.' He smiles and I can't help but notice his shoulders do sag a little as he checks his watch.

'Thanks for gate-crashing. These kids have never behaved so well.' I laugh.

I expect him to go but he pivots on his foot and places his hand on my upper arm. I feel like lava has turned me to stone. I'm hot and unable to move. 'I think I needed this, Steph.'

'Oh?' I ask, taking a step closer.

He presses his fist to his chin. 'I suppose I forgot what family life was like.'

My heart twists. Before I can reply, he wishes me goodnight and heads towards the pub. The children run off to play in the playground whilst I stay on the bench with Henry, who is still eating mushed-up handfuls of a Dairylea sandwich. In the seconds since he left, my head seems to have turned the evening into a full-on big romantic love scene from a Hallmark movie. I'm being such a fool. Edward is my boss and he's spoken for.

As he rounds the corner near the pub, I catch the side of his face, which breaks into a wide grin. He greets someone I can't see, then a lady appears from around the corner and kisses him on the lips. There's no mistaking the huge puff of yellow hair and the pink leather jacket. Everything inside me sinks, even though deep down, I knew who he'd be meeting.

'Mummy, Mummy? When can Edward come for tea?' Ava shouts from the roundabout as Ralph spins her around.

I force a smile. 'I don't think it will be any time soon.'

Chapter 21

Work has been hectic today. We've had a dead rabbit brought in alongside a distraught little girl desperate to know if there was anything we could do, a parrot with a bald patch and a constipated dog that won't stop eating socks.

When I eventually stop to make coffee, Edward pops his head around the door in a brief gap between patients. 'Steph, have you got a sec?'

'Of course. What is it?' I fill my cup with hot water.

'I just wanted to say how much I enjoyed spending time with y—'

My phone pings, the volume on full blast. Ava was messing with it in the car this morning. I give Edward an apologetic look. When I look at the screen, I'm surprised to see a text message from Mike.

Need to talk to you. Can I call round later when the kids are in bed?

That's odd.

'Is everything okay?' Edward asks and I realise I'm frowning at the illuminated screen.

'Oh, yes. It's Mike … my ex-husband.' I turn off my phone. 'Sorry, you were saying something.'

He brushes whatever it was away with his hand. 'It was nothing important. It looks as though you have enough on your plate.'

He pulls the door closed and I reread the text. Why would Mike need to talk to me when the kids are in bed? The divorce is done, everything between us is amicable(ish) and I got a job like he wanted. Oh God, perhaps he wants me to sell the house. Maybe money is tighter than he initially let on and he needs to drop the amount he gives us. No, that can't be it – he's spoken about money problems before when the kids are around. He knows as well as I do that it's too boring for them to care about. Plus, he would have said my wages weren't enough when I told him about the job. Maybe he's moving away? A new job? Abroad? Would he do that to the kids? He probably would. I'll be furious if that's it.

The text message plays on my mind all day. So much so, I don't even remember to reply until I've picked the kids up from school. I call Janey to see if she wants to bring the kids over for an early tea. By the time she arrives, I've worked myself into a bit of a state.

'It's chicken nuggets, chips and beans if that's all right?'

'Carbs, protein, veg … all the main food groups covered … 'course it's okay.' She shrugs. 'Anyway, you don't whip up culinary delights for the fun of it. Spill – what's bugging you?'

I smile guiltily. 'I'll pop the kettle on.'

Five minutes later, I'm shooing the kids into the back garden and placing two steaming mugs of tea on the kitchen table.

'It's Mike.'

'Mike? I expected this to be about Edward.' She darts over to the window and bangs on it. It seems Tom has Seren in a head-lock.

'Edward? No, there's nothing to tell.' The image of his face this afternoon pops into my head. He wanted to tell me something earlier. I've been so wrapped up in Mike's message all day, it went over my head completely. I can't deal with that right now. This is about me and the kids.

'Mike wants to *talk* later. Without the kids being there.'

'Oh.' She blows her tea. 'Any ideas what about?'

I shake my head. 'No. The money stuff is already resolved and that's all he's ever wanted to talk about since the divorce.'

'Maybe he's met someone.' Her tone is unusually gentle.

I shake my head. 'I honestly don't think so. He isn't like that. He's slovenly and self-centred. As long as he's in charge of the TV remote, he's happy. Unless he's met someone with terrible taste in men who dreams of a life of servitude, it's unlikely.'

'But men have needs.' She peers over my shoulder to check the children are still occupied. 'Do you think he perhaps wants to get back together?'

I splutter my tea. 'Oh God no. When he told me he wanted a divorce, he said he loved the kids but didn't want to be with anyone. He wanted the freedom to golf and watch what he wanted on TV without having to think about others. He said he felt suffocated because I always wanted to involve him in everything. I honestly think he just prefers being alone. He even said he only married me because it was what he thought he was supposed to do.'

'Sounds like a right charmer. I'm sorry I didn't get to know him,' Janey says drily.

'I know it sounds bad, and it is. It's terrible, but at the time, I sort of agreed with him. He was always grumpy. I felt like I was forever nagging at him to do anything that was remotely family-orientated and all we did was bicker. I was almost relieved when he suggested getting a divorce. To be honest, he's a good dad and that matters so much more to me.'

'He could still have changed his mind,' she says.

'I guess so. I just don't see it.'

'Think about it. He's been on his own now for over a year; you've been divorced over half that time. That's long enough to realise what side your bread is buttered. He may have realised living alone isn't all it's cracked up to be.' She shuffles forward in her seat. 'Think about it – when he lived here, he had you at home full-time. A cook, cleaner, ironing goddess extraordinaire.'

'God, you make me sound like a 1950s housewife.'

'I know it was just what suited you both at the time, but you have to admit, it had its perks from Mike's point of view.'

'So you think he wants me and his old life back because he misses the un-hired help?'

Janey sips her tea. 'Stranger things have happened. You said it yourself – someone who dreams of a life of servitude. Can't be many women like that about.'

The image of Mike begging me to take him back pops into my head. I just can't see it but then, he can be impulsive. What if the divorce was an impulse that he's come to realise was wrong? The oven beeps, bringing me back from a strange place.

'I'll plate this up. Can you shout the kids in?'

Once the children are sitting around the table eating, the kitchen descends into noisy chaos and our conversation is pushed to the wayside. As Janey dollops ketchup on each of the plates, I can't help but wonder if she's right about Mike. We haven't been apart for all that long, really – definitely not long enough to fully get over our relationship breakdown and Mike *is* the sort who'd miss the convenience of having me around. Whilst that should offend me, I can't ignore how convenient it would be to have him back too. I could read in the bath uninterrupted for a start! It's not particularly romantic, but romance isn't really what family life is about. It's about compromise and teamwork and it's that I miss the most. It's that I craved my whole life. Perhaps, in time we could learn to be romantic again – perhaps get couple's counselling. The notion is weird to me, but it doesn't horrify me. There was a time I was attracted to Mike after all.

By half past six, Janey starts rounding up Tom and Seren. 'I want to make sure you've plenty of time to get the kids to bed before Mike comes,' she whispers and I'm grateful. I need a bit of mental preparation time, I think.

As she's going I realise we've spent the whole night talking about me. 'Oh God, Janey, I haven't even asked about you and Jimmy. Did you talk to him?'

'Don't worry about me.' She smiles but I can tell it's forced. I feel terrible.

By seven-thirty, the kids are bathed and in bed. I had to bribe Ralph with some extra iPad time tomorrow but the other two were shattered after all the fresh air. I can't explain why, but I find myself at my dressing table touching up my face with a bit of concealer. I even add some mascara and brush my hair. I forgot what a difference a bit of make-up can make and for a fleeting second, I think about Stacy and all the effort she seems to make. Perhaps I am a bit plain.

At five to eight, I pour myself a glass of red and check myself over in the mirror. For the next few minutes, I can't relax knowing Mike is due to turn up at any time. I sit and stand and wander from the kitchen to the lounge and back. The words I want to say are like alphabet soup in my head. Perhaps I'm overthinking it but these past few months have been hard, really hard in fact, and if there's a chance things could go back to the way they were, I think I'd take it. I'd have the family unit once again and that's worth more to me than anything.

I'm going to take Mike back.

Chapter 22

At eight-twenty, the doorbell rings. I've chewed my nails down to the quick waiting for this.

'Hi,' I say, gesturing for him to come in with my wine glass. A bit of wine sloshes onto the floor. 'Fancy a glass?'

Mike runs a hand through his hair. He only does that when he's nervous. This is a good sign. I think. 'Yes, go on then.'

He heads into the lounge as I go to the kitchen and pour him a glass of merlot. I top my own glass up and run my fingers through my hair before following him through to the lounge. He's sitting in the armchair he always used to sit in. It's weird seeing him there again, I don't think he's stayed long enough to sit down since he left.

He thanks me for the wine and gulps the first mouthful greedily.

'What is it, Mike? What did you want to talk about?'

'You look … different?' he says. My abdomen squeezes tighter.

'Do I?' I try to sound nonchalant.

'Whatever you've done, it suits you.' This is the closest thing to a compliment I've had from Mike in years. Janey was right. We're really doing this. I can see how hard this is for him and I'm about to burst. I just need to hear him say it, I need to hear the words and I'll do it, I'll take him back.

'Just say what you came to say.' My voice is low, almost a whisper. Perhaps you could even consider it *husky*. I'm using all the subliminal tricks to encourage the words out of him.

He draws a deep breath. 'When I left, I thought I needed space, to live alone. I really did. I never felt suited to living as a partnership, or a team for that matter and it was never anything you did wrong. I was so selfish and you'– he sighs – 'well, you know that, don't you?'

Everything loosens inside me and I go over and kneel beside the chair. 'I know but we were in a bad place.'

He puts his face in his hands and rubs the light stubble. Perhaps it's the merlot, but I find myself taking his hand in mine. 'It's okay. Whatever you need to say, say it.'

He raises his eyebrows and curls his fingers into a fist beneath my hand. I get why he's uncomfortable. He ripped apart our family, but he needs to know I'm here to listen – we all make mistakes and I can forgive him.

All of a sudden, he stands up shattering the tension in the air. 'Mike?'

He presses his fingers to his temple. 'Stephanie, I don't quite know how to say this but I knew it had to be in person. I just didn't expect you to be acting all' – he waves his hand in my direction – 'weird. Anyway, I have a girlfriend called Kate and she's moving in with me.'

The air is claggy and thick. I almost choke on it. 'I'm sorry, what?'

My head spins. How could he have a girlfriend without me knowing? The after-work drinks? The rescheduled pick-ups and the missed weekends with the kids all seem to add up now.

'I didn't want to tell you until I knew it was serious.'

'What about the kids? Do they know?'

He shakes his head. 'Of course not, but I'm going to have to tell them.'

I can't speak, so instead, I nod. I can't imagine what this will do to them.

'Wait, you didn't think I came here to—'

I hold my hand up to cut him off. I can't hear him say it.

'Oh, Stephanie. Really?'

I bury my face in the seat cushion of the chair and to my surprise, Mike crouches down beside me.

'Stephanie? And you would have taken me back?' The incredulity in his tone is like a bucket of eggs have been poured over me.

Tears press my eyes and I shake my head. 'I don't know.'

Mike places his hand on my back and rubs. It's too much and the tears erupt. 'Stephanie, I was a rubbish husband to you; why would you even want that?'

I shrug. 'I suppose I thought if you realised you were wrong, you'd make more of an effort. You know that all I ever wanted was a family and I really would do anything to have us all back together again. You know what I went through as a kid.'

'Oh, Stephanie. I know that but surely you want to be happy too? You can't cling on to a bad marriage because of a childhood dream. You still have a family. You still have a friend.' He gestures to himself.

I manage a watery smile and after a few moments, something else occurs to me. 'If you wanted to be on your own, why did you get a girlfriend?'

'Kate understands I need my space because she does too. She is off with her friends all the time and works full-time. Even when we move in together, we won't be living in each other's pockets. You're a homebody and there's nothing wrong with that. You deserve someone who wants the same things as you do.'

I glare at him. 'I … I'm not a *homebody*. Someone had to raise the children. Food doesn't cook itself and the house doesn't stay tidy after the annual spring-clean. I did what I had to do for our family. I would have loved to have a career. I dreamed of after-work cocktails in Manchester but at the time, you were much further on in your career and making a lot more money than me so I made a sacrifice. For us.'

My shoulders are shaking with the force of my tears. I even make a gasping sound as I sob. I can't tell if it's the anger, rejection or humiliation that's causing them.

'I know. I'm sorry – I didn't mean that. Come here.' Mike pulls me into his arms and I let the tears flow. I don't try to stop them because I need the outlet. I've been bottling up my emotions since the divorce and, in an effort to stay strong for the kids, I never actually mourned the loss of Mike.

'You were an awful husband.' I stifle a laugh and Mike does too.

'And you were a wonderful wife. Most men would kill for someone like you.'

I sniff.

'Seriously, I didn't deserve you. You're kind and you always put everyone else before yourself. The fact that you were about to take me back says it all.'

I bury my face in the crook of his arm, his familiar scent a comfort despite everything.

'Maybe it's time to put yourself first. Go out and meet someone.'

The thought makes me wince. 'I don't think I'd have a clue where to start. Maybe I was going to take you back because it's a case of better the devil. I wouldn't know how to go about meeting someone else and I'm not sure I even want to. I'm not *unhappy* as I am.'

'Well, I'm going to do better. I'll be a better dad and I'll pick the kids up on time so you can focus on yourself. I realise now that I've taken you for granted and that needs to stop.'

I nod. 'Yes, you have a bit.'

'I suppose I never felt it was an issue before but whilst I've been out living my life, you've been wading through a muddy rut. I haven't been fair to you.'

I don't say anything. He's said it all and I'm only just realising it now.

'So, where does Kate fit into all of this? Does she know about the children?'

'Yes. She hasn't met them yet but I was hoping to introduce them at the weekend, over an ice cream or something.'

Bile rises in my throat. I've spent the day convincing myself that getting back together with Mike is a good idea and now I've got to get my head around the kids meeting *Kate*.

'Are you sure things are serious enough to introduce her to the kids?'

He nods. 'We're moving in together, Steph, yes it's serious. Plus, they're going to see all her stuff around my apartment so I need to be honest with them. They're resilient kids; they'll cope and Kate's great.'

The last few words are a punch to the gut. 'I don't know. It's a lot to take in all at once. Why didn't you just tell me about Kate when you started seeing her? At least then I could have come around to the idea of her moving in and being stepmum to my kids.'

'She won't be their stepmum and she isn't trying to replace you. She wants a relationship with them as their dad's girlfriend.'

I turn to sit down on my bum, resting my back against the chair. Mike follows me. The two of us must make quite a sight sitting on the floor, me no doubt panda-eyed and him covered in my soggy tears.

'How did it all go so wrong?' I say.

'Did it go wrong or did it just go off track a little? We got three beautiful kids out of our marriage and we had some good times.'

I lean my head on his shoulder. 'I suppose we did. I guess I just expected us to last the course. I thought we'd grow old together and take our grandkids to the park and all that sort of stuff.'

118

'There's nothing to say that won't happen, just in a slightly different way. I know I've been a bit of a tosser. I panicked about money and the way I spoke to you about getting a job was all wrong. I'm sorry.'

'You were a tosser but I'm glad you pushed me. I love my job.' I take a tissue from my pocket and blow my nose.

'Good. Maybe we'll muddle through this and things will be all right. I love those kids, Steph. They're brilliant little cretins and I'll always love you. I guess I see you more like a sister.'

I smile. 'That should horrify me, but do you know what? It makes me happy. I love you, Mike, but I don't want to live with you ever again.' We both start laughing.

'Shall we start this divorce thing over?'

I look at him. Black, soggy mascara splodges mark his shirt. 'Things are going to be weird with another person involved.'

'Listen, you're the mother of my kids. If you're not comfortable with anything, let me know.' He reaches for my hand. 'If you want to meet Kate, you can. If you never want to see her that's fine too.'

'I suppose I'll have to think about it. It's all a lot to process.' I can't picture him with anyone else. I'm not hurt, it just feels weird.

'How about the weekend? Is it okay for her to meet the kids?'

I pause. This weekend feels too soon but I suppose there will never be a time that feels right. 'If you really think there's some mileage in the relationship then yes, I suppose it's best to get it out of the way.'

'If you want to come too, you can do.'

I glance at my slippers. 'No, thanks. I think it's best to let the kids adjust first.'

I need some time to get used to the idea. I am, after all, second best.

'Well, if you change your mind …'

'Yes. I know.'

Chapter 23

'Is everything all right, Steph?'

The words startle me. I've been staring at my cup of coffee for so long it's now the temperature of the North Sea. Edward is hovering over the desk wearing a concerned look.

'I'm fine,' I say.

'Are you sure because I just offered you a Jaffa Cake and you didn't even look up? It's not like you.'

I force a smile. 'Sorry, I've a few things on my mind. Nothing that will affect my work though – just my waistline, in a good way, I suppose if I keep passing up Jaffa Cake offers.'

Edward doesn't smile at my joke; he's still frowning. 'I'm heading to the bakery at lunch, fancy a walk?'

Oh brilliant. A pity scone – but I'll take it.

'Okay.'

'You do know I don't get a lunch break, don't you?' I say as Edward and I walk the short distance to Mother Hopton's bakery in the village.

'What?' He feigns shock. 'Then you should report your boss immediately.'

I laugh. 'He's terrible in many ways but given I only work four hours a day, not giving me a lunch break isn't one of them.' I bite down on my tongue. I don't know what's the matter with me. That was far too familiar.

We walk in silence for a moment and then he asks: 'So what is it that has you turning down Jaffa Cakes?'

'Oh, nothing really.' I hug my arms to my body to try and rid myself of the cramping in my stomach.

'Are you sure? You haven't been yourself since that text message you got yesterday. I'm a good listener if you want to talk?'

I take a breath. 'My ex has met someone else and we're telling the kids about it at the weekend. I'm worried about how they're going to take it.'

'Sorry, I didn't mean to pry. I didn't realise it would be something that personal. If you don't want to talk about it, just say.'

'No, it's fine. It is what it is I suppose. This was bound to happen. I suppose I just didn't expect it to be yet. Mike always said he wanted to be alone, so I didn't think he'd meet someone less than a year after our divorce was finalised.'

'Divorce is never easy,' he says, in a way that makes me think he empathises rather than sympathises.

'Have you ever been married?'

He stops walking and rubs his chin. His expression turns more thoughtful and I'm not sure if I've upset him.

'Sorry, if it's personal, you don't have to say.'

'No, it's okay. We're on the subject. Yes, I was for a time. Only three years. She was a bit younger than me and we wanted different things.'

'I'm sorry.'

'Enough time has passed now that I'm over it. Besides, I'm so busy with the practice, she could still be there, living at my house and I wouldn't know. Perhaps I should have a good look around later, just in case.'

I smile and we carry on without a word until we reach the bakery.

'The Belgian buns here are to die for.' He holds the door open for me, all traces of fleeting emotion gone.

'I don't need to take your word for it, they look it,' I say, clapping eyes on the giant iced treats. 'Fancy sharing one? They're too big for me.'

'Good idea – I've had far too many Jaffa Cakes. I might as well move in with Mrs Pearson and let her overfeed me into an early grave.'

I stifle a laugh. 'Don't let her hear you say that! She'd probably take you up on it.'

'Why? Is she here?' He glances around dramatically. I can't work Edward out; he's verging on the edge of eccentric. Had he been born thirty years earlier, he'd make more sense than a final jigsaw piece. One thing I do know is that he uses humour as a defence mechanism.

We order two sausage rolls, two teas and a giant Belgian bun to share and make our way back towards the practice. It's a pleasant day so when we arrive, Edward suggests we sit on the little wall outside.

'We're making a habit of these impromptu alfresco dining experiences,' he says whilst unwrapping a sausage roll. I'm desperate to ask him what he was going to say the other day when I was making coffee but I don't want to ask. The moment has passed now and it doesn't feel right.

Instead, I say, 'At least today you don't have to decipher the din of three kids who don't belong to you whilst having soggy crisps thrust at you.'

'Yes.' He smiles. 'Well, Ava is a bit stingy with her crisps, but otherwise, it made a refreshing change. I'm more used to TV meals for one or stuffy gala dinners.' I get a pang when I remember what he said about feeling part of family life again.

'You must go out with friends for dinner?'

His mouth is full so he makes a 'sort of' gesture with his hand before taking a sip of tea. 'Ouch. That's bloody hot.' He sloshes some tea on his shirt and rubs it frantically with his napkin.

'I'm not surprised – tea in a polystyrene cup is always served at four thousand degrees. It's common knowledge.'

'You're absolutely right,' he says. 'Anyway, back to the question, I don't really have that many friends. I had loads at uni but we're spread across the country now and hardly find time to get together. Being a vet is unforgiving. If you own your own practice you might as well walk around with it dangling from your neck like an albatross.'

'I see how hard you work and often wonder if you ever take time off.'

'Not really. I mean, I could if I had reason to, but I'd feel guilty. I'm the only vet locally and many of the older customers rely on me – same with the farms. I hate letting people down.'

Is swooning a thing? Because I think I just did it. Either that or there's a tiny nightclub of minuscule teenagers dancing to 'Jump Around' in my tummy. Get a grip, woman!

'When I was married, I was working for my dad and stuck to business hours with one night a week on call. The way he ran things was very old-fashioned. He knew everyone and their pets by name and I suppose, when I took over his legacy, I wanted to preserve it. I did always intend to take on another vet to free myself up, but I didn't ever have a reason.'

He looks down into his tea.

'But the option is there, for the future,' I say, trying to pick out the positive. 'And at least your flaw of being a workaholic makes you some money. Mine just make me wish for a plastic surgeon and a blank cheque.'

'Hey, I hope that's not true. You're perfect.' A soon as he says it, those red blotches appear on his face again. 'I mean, anyone could see that. Nobody needs plastic surgery.'

The fleeting lift in my chest sinks with the grace of a bowling ball when he adds the last bit. I'm so confused. I'm too old to wonder whether someone likes me or not. The whole idea of that high school nonsense is quite frankly icky but he's sending all these mixed signals. I keep having to remind myself he has a girlfriend and he's my boss so clearly there is something between us. Something quite undefined.

'So ...' He breaks my thoughts. 'Have you got a plan for introducing the new girlfriend?'

I pick a piece of pastry off the sausage roll and shake my head. 'Mike is going to do it. I think he's going to take them all for ice cream or something – knowing my lot, they won't notice the new mum once he's distracted them with treats.'

Edward visibly winces.

'Gosh, that sounded much more bitter than I intended it to. It's just all very sudden and to be honest, I thought he'd take longer to realise a fairy didn't wash his socks and cook his meals.'

'Did you think he might come back to you?' The question pierces a raw part of me that's been buried somewhere deep. 'I'm sorry, I was just trying to ask meaningful questions. I didn't mean to stick my nose in. I've upset you.'

I sip my tea. It's still scorching hot but it's a different type of pain; more welcome than reliving the embarrassment of last night. 'Don't apologise. Maybe a subconscious part of me did. I can't say whether thinking he might have come back to us was a deep hope or desire; an expectation perhaps. When I use my head and think about it logically, no, I knew it was a permanent separation. I think ... I maybe ...' Edward covers my hand with his. He's sitting so close to me I can feel the heat radiating from his body. He's rolled back his shirtsleeves, revealing a light tanned forearm. My hand looks tiny beneath his.

'Only tell me this if you want to, not because I asked.'

I want to but Edward is my boss. This is weird. My whole body thinks so. I can tell by the way my inner organs have coiled up and my mouth feels like it's full of cotton wool. Every part

of me knows I should shut up and keep the professional boundaries but there's a stronger part of me that wants to open up to
him. The same part of me that's somersaulting with the gleeful
feel of his hand on mine. The truth is, all my friends ditched me
because having to pick a side was too much bother. Janey would
just say something unhelpful like 'fuck him' and I don't really
have anyone else to talk to.

'He came over last night. The message he sent said he wanted
to talk and could he come over once the kids were in bed, and
somehow, with the help of my friend, I came to the conclusion
he was going to suggest we give things another go. It's utterly
ridiculous when I play it all back over in my mind but that's the
peak I'd reached by eight o'clock last night. I'd made a bit of an
effort with …' I wave a dismissive hand. 'Make-up and I'd poured
wine. I basically embarrassed myself royally.'

'I'm sure you didn't. If I were Mike, I'd have been flattered.'

'Well, you're very kind. And actually, it all worked out in the
end. We sort of made peace with one another. We've been on
reasonable terms since the split but there's been sniping and to
and froing with the kids. I think we've reached a point where
we could actually be friends. Maybe even have family days out
with me, Kate and Mike. I'm not jealous of her by the way –
Kate.'

'I never assumed you were.'

'It's just the natural feeling, isn't it? She's supposed to be the
arch-enemy.'

'I suppose so.'

'I felt rejected by Mike. I felt old and frumpy – a bit like I'd
been tossed on the compost – but not jealous. She's done nothing
wrong.' I laugh. 'She's a bloody fool but she hasn't done anything
wrong. I am worried about the kids though; this is going to be
hard for them.'

'Your kids are wonderful, Steph. They'll adapt.'

I nod. 'Yeah, I know.'

'I guess we have just one more problem to solve ...' Edward raises both eyebrows and I frown, not following. 'How on earth do we cut a Belgian bun without getting sticky hands?'

I pull a packet of wipes out of my bag. 'Tools of the trade.'

Chapter 24

After Mike left last night, I'd sent a text to the book club WhatsApp group in a blind panic. I can't remember what I wrote exactly and the thought of rereading it makes me wince, but it was something along the lines of 'Mike has a girlfriend. I'm the mouldy bread crust at the bottom of the bag'. There was definitely something additional like the kids are going to prefer their new mum and I'll have nobody. Or words to that effect. Needless to say, both Amanda and Janey replied immediately. Amanda with the generic 'Oh no, I'm sorry. Is there anything I can do' and Janey with the predictable 'What a twat'.

So, Janey has called the kids for an emergency sleepover at hers and is leaving Jimmy in charge whilst the three of us go to the pub and, I must admit, I'm sort of glad she's making him take some responsibility. Although, after my lunch with Edward earlier today, I'm not sure I'm in the mood. I have a weird churning in my gut that's making me uneasy. I don't think the lunch was particularly awkward, I actually enjoyed it. It's more of a hindsight thing; a belated acknowledgement of spilling all to my boss as being a bit weird. I haven't processed it and now there's no time because I need to get ready, pack the kids' overnight things and get to the pub to process a different set of feelings. Honestly, if I knew I was going to be juggling all these emotions, I'd have mentally cleared out the 'teenage angst' years to make room.

The doorbell rings right on time. 'Door's open,' I shout. I'm in the middle of putting some diamante studs in my ears that I bought from Claire's accessories about four years ago. I've only just opened them.

'Ooh someone's making an effort! A certain vet isn't going to the pub tonight, is he?'

I frown. 'No. It wouldn't be our pub anyway. He lives over near the practice in Crinkly.'

'You never know, maybe he lives life on the edge and ventures to Milden for spontaneous nights out.'

'Unlikely. However, the kids are ready for their random sleepover,' I say throwing her a big smile. 'Anyway, tell me, did you talk to Jimmy? Is that why he's babysitting? Is he trying to make it up to you?'

'Do you know what, let's talk about it later. Don't want to put a dampener on things.' Before I get a chance to speak, she shouts for Ralph and Ava. 'Right, I'll take them across and get them settled. You give me a shout when you have your glad rags on.' She scoops up Henry.

'Do you need his travel cot?'

She shakes her head. 'No need. We still have ours.'

Half an hour later, Amanda, Janey and I are all walking towards the pub. The fact there are three of us and an excited buzz of chatter helps me relax a little. To be honest, the nights haven't felt as terrifying recently. For weeks, I've gone to bed replaying conversations with Edward in my head and as crazy as it is, it's helped me.

'So, how are you, Stephanie?' Amanda asks.

'I'm okay. It was a shock and I felt a bit like the last green, sprouting potato in the sack when I panic-texted but I think Mike and I will actually be a lot closer now. He's been an idiot really and I can see now it's because he was stressed. It can't be cheap having a family and a girlfriend to pay for.'

Amanda crinkles her eyes like she's in pain.

'It's fine. I'm fine,' I say dismissively. 'We talked and after the initial shock and feelings of rejection, I think we'll be friends. It will be better all round for the kids if we can make that work.'

'I'm sorry, Steph,' Janey says. 'I made you think he wanted to get back with you. That's probably why you were in so much shock. I'm such an idiot.'

'Oh, no. I think, deep down, I suspected the same but got caught up in the idea of being a family again. I definitely didn't expect him to have met someone. I suppose I just don't see Mike as being the type of person to be *noticed*. He sure as hell won't have put himself out there. This Kate woman must have accidentally landed on his lap whilst simultaneously being speared by Cupid's arrow.'

'I'm still sorry. You're a wonderful person, Steph. Why wouldn't he want you back?' Janey says, pulling me into a hug.

We arrive at the pub. The warm air hits us as we walk in out of the dank evening air.

'Right, I'll get 'em in and you find a table,' Janey says.

Amanda and I weave our way through the groups of punters sipping pints and eating peanuts. There's a little snug in the far corner and we manage to score a table right at the back.

'Oh it feels good to be out,' Amanda says, shrugging off her coat. 'I've been stuck in with a cold all week and I'm so glad to be over it.'

We chat for a while and then spot Janey balancing a tray precariously as she fights her way through the throngs of people.

'Over here.' I stand up and wave. She spots me and heads over.

'Busy tonight,' she says, handing out the three glasses of Prosecco.

'Anyway, glad you found a table. Cheers, ladies.' She holds her glass up and we each clink our own against hers.

'Right then. So, where were we?'

The Mike debacle crops up again but if I'm completely truthful, I'm doing very little of the talking. Amanda and Janey seem to be solving my ex problems all by themselves. I don't even think they notice when I slip to the bar and return with another round.

'I actually had this conversation with my boss today. Is that weird?' I say, impinging on their chat about a next-phase plan for me.

'What? Edward? As in your boss, Edward? You told *him* about Mike coming over last night?'

'He saw I was a bit out of sorts so invited me to walk to the bakery with him at lunch and we chatted. He's actually really easy to talk to. It all sort of, fell out.'

'It fell out, did it? What else fell out?' Janey winks and I cock my head sideways to indicate my lack of humour on the matter.

'He's divorced too,' I say, moving on from Janey's sordid mind.

'Perfect. He obviously likes you if he's taking such an interest in you and treating you to baked goods.'

'He doesn't have many friends; he told me as much so I think he's just a bit lonely. The only people he talks to are clients at the practice and the staff. Carly is on a different wavelength and there's the nurse but I have only met her a few times. She's lovely but older and has all her own family stuff going on.'

'If I didn't know better, I'd say you had a *vet*ish.' Janey giggles and I roll my eyes. 'Oh, come on. We can tell you like him.'

The bubbly Prosecco has given me a warm, giddy feeling and the urge to admit it is too strong. 'Okay, yes. I do like him. He's a bit odd but has this genuine kindness and patience that you don't often see in people these days. It's almost like he's from another era. But ...' I give Janey and Amanda a loaded look. 'He's my boss. Neither of us would want to muddy the waters along that definitive line.' I take a sip of my Prosecco to punctuate the finality of the statement.

'Fair enough,' Amanda says.

'You're using some very big words,' Janey says. 'You almost sound believable.'

'I thought we were here to cheer me up? Not railroad me into begging my boss for a date.'

'That's exactly right,' Amanda says. 'So I'll get the next round in.'

'So what happened with Jimmy? I can tell something is wrong,' I ask Janey when we're alone.

'I told him I had a friend in need and he'd have to babysit.' She roots in her bag and when she doesn't produce anything, I suspect she's upset.

'Good for you.' I frown. 'And me.' I nudge her gently. 'But that's not everything, is it?'

'I haven't spoken to him since he turned down a meal out with his wife.'

'Oh, Janey.' I notice her eyes welling up and it breaks my heart.

'I'm going to give him an ultimatum. I hate the idea of it but I don't want to bring the kids up in a house filled with arguments and frosty silences and at the moment I have a closer bond with Donald Trump's toupee than Jimmy.'

'That's a lot to go through. Remember I'm here for you.'

When Amanda returns, the conversation moves away from ex-husbands and intriguing bosses and we have a real laugh discussing our wildly different school years. Janey was one of the cool kids, the sort you wanted on your side. Amanda went to a private boarding school and her idea of shenanigans was sneaking out of bed for a midnight feast. Mine was the most beige. I was just one of those kids who coasted through in the middle, both academically and socially. It's weird how we're all sitting here on a relatively level playing field now. Granted, I'm out of cash and need to leave before we start on second rounds and Amanda probably has a black American Express card in her purse with a credit limit that would buy the entire pub but none of that matters, we're just three women having a great time.

'So, Amanda, what do you do for fun?'

'Well, you already know I love to read and I do a bit of gardening, but only the flower beds because the rest is too big for me to manage. I bake a bit and—'

'Boring,' Janey shouts and I wince. 'Real fun. I know we're all a bit past it, but I mean going out and doing things exciting.'

'What do you do that's exciting?' Amanda flips the question back to Janey who drops her head onto her resting arms and sighs.

'Not much. Up until a few years ago, I'd have the odd night out in Manchester with a few of my old friends. We didn't do clubbing but we'd have cocktails in nice bars and that sort of thing. It sort of tailed off when everyone had kids and now I hardly see them.'

'Maybe we should plan something fun to do together,' Amanda suggests. 'I'm not sure what. Maybe one of those escape room things and a cocktail after or a shopping trip and champers lunch.'

My mouth feels dry; this is starting to sound expensive.

'All right, you're on!' Janey says. 'Hey, didn't you say you'd never had a one-night stand, Amanda?'

'No. Not a chance is that ever going to happen,' she says, crossing her legs as though Janey meant right here, now.

Since it's my 'big day' tomorrow, I have a good excuse to call time on the evening before Janey heads to the bar to start the second lot of rounds. We walk home and Janey agrees to drop the kids off at eight in the morning so I have a few hours with them before Mike comes. We walk Amanda up the lane and when we get back to our road Janey turns to me.

'Are you sure you're going to be okay?'

'I nod. Yes, I think so. It's just very new but I'll adjust and so will the kids. Are you going to be okay?'

'Always.' She hugs me tightly and wishes me goodnight. 'I've got my gal pals now, haven't I?'

When I get inside the house, the air is thick and still.

Tomorrow my family is going to change forever.

I've never felt more alone.

Chapter 25

We're all buzzing around waiting for Mike. Ralph can't find the charger to his DS, Ava has lost her favourite doll (today's favourite I might add) and Henry is wailing for no apparent reason. My carefully laid plan was to sit Ralph and Ava down and explain that Daddy would be introducing someone special to them today. I was going to warn them about being kind and having good manners and all the normal stuff you go over with kids when you don't want them to reflect badly on you as a mother. As the morning descended into chaos, there was no chance of sitting down for a heartfelt chat. Instead, much to my shame, I ended up screaming up the stairs that Ralph wouldn't need his DS and Ava wouldn't need her doll because Daddy has something important to tell them. When they come home tomorrow and things are a little calmer, I'll be here with hot chocolate and cuddles instead.

The doorbell rings bang on time (for once) and whilst Ralph is still hunting the precious charger cable, I answer it.

'Hi,' Mike says sheepishly.

'Hi,' I reply, opening the door wide enough so he can step inside. There's a moment of awkward tension as we both (or at least I) replay the events of Thursday night.

'The kids are almost ready. Can I get you a drink or do you need to dash off?'

He checks his watch. 'I should get going really.'

I nod. 'Listen, I haven't had the chance to tell the kids what today is all about. They're in a fractious mood. I think they're restless.'

'That's fine. I'm going to take them to the park, let them burn off some energy and then tell them about Kate. All being well, we'll meet her at the ice-cream parlour by the river.'

'Good thinking,' I say as Ralph comes hurtling down the stairs. 'Found it.'

'Good, now grab your overnight bag,' I say walking into the lounge to scoop Henry out of his playpen.

'Henry hasn't eaten much so be warned – a tantrum could brew at any second. I've put some rice cakes in the changing bag just in case.'

'Daddy!' Ava squeals as she does her usual run up to him and Mike fakes having the wind knocked out of him. I have to look away because this is the last time they're going to see their father in the same innocent light. Whatever they think of Kate, our family dynamic is about to change.

They leave shortly after and I get stuck into a deep clean of the kitchen. When that's done, I take Otis on a long walk. We both return muddy and after I've hosed him down, I run myself a bath. It seems odd to have a bath in the afternoon but I've nothing better to do and I want to keep myself occupied. When I get out, I notice several missed calls from Edward. My first thought is that there's been an emergency. I wrap my hair in a towel and call him back.

'Is everything okay?' I ask before he has time to say hello.

'Yes. I mean no. It's Mrs Pearson. Ruby has gone missing and she's beside herself. I wouldn't have called, it's just … well, I thought you might be glad of the distraction today so wondered if you wanted to help me search for her? There's absolutely no obligation though.'

I deliberate. On one hand, I'm all warm and cosy after my bath and I could just curl up with a movie and a glass of wine but on the other, there's a good chance I'll be on tenterhooks worrying about the kids and I sort of feel for Mrs Pearson. 'Give me fifteen minutes and I'll set off.'

'Fantastic, meet me at the practice in half an hour.'

I put the phone down and glance at Otis. 'It's your lucky day, buddy, we're going on a cat hunt.' His ears prick at the word cat. 'We're not going to eat the cat,' I say sternly. God, is this what I have to look forward to, conversations with the dog?

'So, what's happened?' I ask Edward when I get to the practice. He greets Otis by ruffling the fur around his neck.

'Mrs Pearson opened the door to the postman and Ruby shot out. She said she's never done anything like that before. She's a house cat.'

'Oh, maybe it's your fault. That poor cat has probably gone off searching for better food since you damned her to an eternity of cat food.'

'It's funny you should mention that because Mrs P said exactly the same thing.'

I can't help but laugh at that. 'Okay, so where have you searched so far?'

'I've just had a walk around, looking over walls and fences into people's gardens. I think we need to knock on some doors to ask if anyone has seen her. We should also ask people to check sheds and garages in case she's been locked in accidentally.'

'Good thinking. Should we split up to cover more ground?' I say. Edward looks at me and pauses.

'Er, yes. Good idea.'

I nod. 'Come on then, Otis, show me what you're made of,' I say yanking his lead. After all the attention he got off Edward, he doesn't want to leave and, weirdly, I know exactly how he feels.

Otis and I walk down the street closest to the practice and

make our way down, knocking on each door as we do. Nobody has seen a cat matching Ruby's description, but when I mention I work at Prescott's vet's I get a wide variety of animal health-related questions. Most don't even seem to care that I'm only the bookkeeper and would quite happily take my free advice on worming and inoculations.

When I'm nearing the last few houses, I come across a pretty little cottage. All the houses around here are well kept but this one meticulously so. The paved path leading to the front door looks recently swept and weeded. Mine hasn't been done since Mike moved out; a realisation that makes my neck prickle with shame. The pale-green front door has two newly planted hanging baskets on either side. Each one bursting with a colourful array of flowering plants. There are also a few planters dotted around the small front garden adding colour and a sense of pride. I think of my own, the small rectangle of flagstones with grass and dandelions sprouting between the cracks and the pot that houses cobwebs and the brown, slimy leaves of an ex-cordyline plant. I make a mental note to have a bit of a spruce-up. Seeing something like this every day would really cheer me up.

I stop admiring the garden so I can actually knock on the door. Otis sits patiently beside me. A few seconds later, the door opens and the sight of the woman standing before me takes the wind out of my sails.

'Hi, can I help you?' She smiles. If the fluffy waist-length hair wasn't giveaway enough, the pink dress might as well have had her name embroidered on it. To give her credit, she's still smiling at me even though I've taken far too long to say anything.

'Er,' I falter. There's something about meeting someone for the first time after a Facebook-stalking binge that quite rightly makes you squirm with discomfort. 'A cat. I wondered if you'd seen a cat. Mrs Pearson from down the way has lost one. Ruby it's called. Ginger thing, vomits a lot … Some of us from Prescott's have been out looking for it but we're having no luck.'

'Aw poor Mrs P. I haven't seen anything but I'll check the shed out back and give Eddy a call if I find anything.'

Eddy? The familiarity with which she says the word makes my skin prickle. I don't see Edward as an *Eddy* at all but then, why would I? He's my boss not my mate from down the pub.

'Thanks, that's great. Yes, just let … *Eddy* know.' I cringe when I say it.

'Will do.' She smiles and does a little shoulder hitch. 'Take care, lovey, and I hope you find Ruby.'

I smile and wave my hand as Otis bounces to his feet. Nobody else on the street has seen the cat so I head back to the little junction near the practice and start on the next one. A woman at the third house thinks she saw her about half an hour ago, hiding in her garden. She lets me go in and check and it dawns on me that the last time I saw this bloody cat, I was pinning her down against her will. I hope the rumour that cats hold grudges isn't true. As I forage under the shrubs, I get the uneasy feeling that I'm being watched. What if Ruby pounces on me? I glance at Otis who's lounging around on a sunny patch of grass. Surely if I was in imminent danger, he'd be poised to help?

I crawl a bit further into the thick shrubbery. Something is rustling to my right. I freeze and it stops.

'Ruby?' I call. I have no idea if cats respond to hearing their names being called but I have nothing else. 'Here, Ruby.'

All of a sudden, a flash of ginger whizzes past me, causing a prickly branch to hit me in the face. 'Ouch.' The bloody thing nearly took my eye out. Otis is going mad, barking his head off in giddy exhilaration. By the time I crawl out from the under-growth, there's no sign of the cat anywhere. I take out my phone and dial Edward.

'Hi, I found the cat but—'

'That's brilliant. Where are you?' he says.

'I'm at number 3 Rose Terrace but listen, I've lost her again. If you come quickly we might be able to find her.'

'On my way.'

I plonk myself down next to Otis, who seems to have calmed down.

'We make a crap team,' I say, stroking his head. He looks up at me like he couldn't care less. He made a big row on sighting the cat – his work here is done.

'God. Stephanie, are you all right?' I turn to see Edward running out from the lady's kitchen.

'I'm fine. Listen, based on Otis's barking I think she went over the back fence. It leads to the path by the river. You go. I've scared her half to death and Otis tried his damnedest to scare the other half of her into an early grave. I think she'll run away as soon as she catches sight of us.'

'Okay, but I want you to go and wait for me at the practice.' He reaches in his pocket and takes something out. 'Here's the key. Let yourself in and grab a cuppa. I want to take a look at that cut on your head.'

What cut? I raise my hand to the smarting part of my forehead. It's moist. When I glance at my fingertips, they're bright red. 'Okay. Let me know if you have any bother. As you can see, I'm a complete pro at this.'

He smiles before darting off. I thank the lady who owns the garden and apologise for my plant ruffling. She wishes me well and I make my way towards the practice.

I head into the toilet to assess the damage. Injury wise, I'll live. Aesthetically, it's a travesty. My forehead looks a real mess and I'm filthy. My pale-yellow sweater is grass-stained and my light blue jeans have damp mud ground into the knees – I look like one of those kids in a Persil advert in the Nineties. I wet some loo roll and start to dab at the cuts and grazes, taking particular care around the deeper cut on my head that's still oozing blood. I repeat the process a few times and when the wounds look clean,

I go and sit in the waiting area, holding a clean tissue to the nastier wound. I scroll my phone to pass the time and I'm not sure how long has passed when the door tinkles and opens.

'Sorry, that took longer than I imagined. I swear that bloody cat has an axe to grind with me. She certainly got her revenge for all the times I've had to inject her,' he says, pointing to a tear in his T-shirt.

I laugh softly. 'In hindsight, we were probably the worst two people to be searching for that cat.'

'Well, a tin of tuna did the trick and now Ruby has been reunited with Mrs Pearson and all is right with the world.' He catches sight of me. 'Apart from your head. I need to take a look at that.'

'Honestly, it's just a cut.'

'It's still bleeding. Let me have a look to see if you're going to need a stitch or two.'

Edward kneels in front of me. I remove the tissue and immediately after, warm liquid trickles down my forehead.

'Hang on.' Edward rises to his feet and heads through to the examination area. Beyond that is the operating room and a little storeroom where all the supplies are kept. He returns moments later with some sterile wipes and cotton wool.

'You don't mind if I …' He gestures towards the pack of wipes and I nod for him to go ahead. 'It might sting a little.'

He dabs at the cut with the wipe and despite his gentle touch, a burning pain sears my entire forehead and I wince.

Edward flinches. 'I'm so sorry.'

'No, it's me being a baby. I'm okay, I promise.'

When he gets to work the second time, the area has numbed a little and it isn't so bad. I'm more taken with how gentle, yet diligent Edward is. I suppose some of the animals he treats are tiny; like little mice and hamsters and things, so he has to be. His hands are soft and his fingers long. I wonder if he ever played the piano. I'd heard doctors often take up hobbies that require good dexterity; like knitting or piano because it helps keep their fingers nimble. I'd ask him but it seems a bit weird.

'I think you'll get away without a trip to A & E,' he says looking me in the eyes. He's so close, his cool, minty breath tickles my skin. I swallow and nod. I don't trust my voice to work. 'I'll pop a couple of steri-strips on though, just to make sure it heals well.'

'Okay, thank you.' I glance at Otis who's unaccustomed to so many walks in one day and is sleeping his doggy head off.

'Just call me Florence.' He smiles. 'You'll have to keep the area dry and make sure you don't scratch them or I will have to cone you.'

'I'll try,' I say, smiling back.

I think I understand Edward now. His thoughtful, kind and caring nature confused me. I mistook his good nature as attraction, but I think that was wishful thinking on my part. If I remove the rose-tinted glasses, he's like this with everyone. Today, he's given up his day off for Mrs Pearson and I'm pretty sure he doesn't challenge Carly on all the smoking breaks because he knows she is finding parenting stressful and needs that quiet time.

'How about a celebratory drink at the pub?' he asks. 'There are no dogs allowed in but it's a nice enough day to sit in the beer garden.'

I glance at my watch for no reason other than to stall my answer and stop myself from shouting 'yes' too quickly. It's just gone four. The kids will have spent hours with Kate now. Is it awful that I haven't thought about it once since joining Edward's cat hunt?

'That sounds wonderful.'

'Okay, give me a few minutes to clear all this away and tidy myself up,' he says, scooping up the empty steri-strip wrappers and wipe packets.

Ten minutes later, we're walking along the riverbank to the

pub. I get a pang in my stomach. 'My kids are just a few miles along this river having ice cream and meeting their dad's new girlfriend.'

Edward stops walking. 'Are you okay about it?'

I shrug. 'I thought so, and to be honest, my new career as a cat-catcher has taken precedence. I haven't thought about it once until now. I just hope they're okay. I honestly have no idea how they're going to react to it. Obviously, Henry will be none the wiser, but Ava and Ralph …'

Edward puts his hand on my shoulder. Heat radiates through me. 'Whatever they feel, they will always have you. That won't change regardless of who enters or leaves their lives.'

'I hope so,' I say. 'I thought I'd always have my mum but I lost her when I was five.' That comes from somewhere so deep inside me, I don't think anyone other than Edward could have unlocked it.

'Oh, Stephanie, I'm so sorry, I can't imagine how hard that must have been.'

'I can hardly remember her really and that's the saddest part.' I coil Otis's lead around my hand.

'Was she poorly?'

'No.' I swallow hard. 'She was … attacked.'

'Oh my God.' He clutches his hand to his mouth.

I stop walking to watch the steady flow of the river. The memory is still so vivid despite the thirty-something years that have passed.

'Be quiet, the witches will hear us.'

I can still picture myself in that pink tutu; two of my steps to every one of hers. My eyes fall closed as I'm taken back to that night.

I squeeze Mummy's hand tighter. I never know whether to believe her when she talks about the witches in the park. I thought they were made up but Mummy wouldn't lie, would she? It's pitch-black and the park doesn't seem as fun as it normally does; nobody is laughing on the swings or zipping down the slide. We walk through this same park every week to get to my dance class but since the winter nights have started to draw in, it's become darker and I wish Mummy would drive us instead. I glance around, looking for signs of witches, straining my ears for a cackle. Warm yellow lights from the houses around the park add to the spooky effect. I'll be glad when this short walk is over.

As we near the end of the path, there's a shelter where the Sunday morning football players can sit and put their boots on. The air is filled with a weird, sour smoky smell and there are people talking in the distance. Witches? My heart starts beating fast but Mummy keeps walking towards them. I try to pull her back but she just pulls me forwards with ten times my strength.

'Almost there,' she whispers.

The voices don't sound like witches and I start to relax. It's just some teenagers.

'Nice bag you got.' It's a male voice but I can't see his face. I glance at Mummy's handbag. She hates me playing with it but sometimes when I'm playing dress-up, she puts it on me for a minute. He's right, it is nice.

Mum doesn't reply, which seems rude. Instead, she speeds up towards the alleyway that leads to the dance school. She's pulling me faster than I can walk.

'Slow down, Mummy,' I whine but she doesn't speak. All of a sudden, she stops. When I look up, a teenager is blocking the alleyway. There are walls either side of us, making it impossible to walk around him.

'Excuse me,' Mummy says in her stern voice. She's probably mad that I'm going to be late for class again.

'Said I like your bag, didn't I?'

He must be annoyed that Mummy didn't say thank you.

'Sorry, I didn't hear you. Can I get by? We're late,' she says politely.

'Gimme your bag and I'll move.'

Mummy steps backwards and turns, yanking my arm. Two more

teenagers are blocking the other direction. Why would they want a handbag? They're boys.

'Do your mothers know you're out, harassing folk? I'll report you to the police,' she says. She uses her stern voice again but it wobbles a little.

One of the boys laughs. Another lunges forwards and grabs the strap of Mummy's bag. Something silver glints in the moonlight but it's so quick, I don't see what it is. Mummy gasps, like the time I was winded on the bouncy castle. The boys run off.

'Stephanie, run to dance. Don't stop … running … until you're inside. Tell them … Mummy is in the park … in trouble … ambulance.' Her eyes are wide as she falls to the ground. She looks worried so I do as she says. I run and I don't stop until I reach the dance school and tell my teacher everything.

'Steph?'

I snap back to where I am, by the river. 'I haven't thought about it for a long time.'

'I'm so sorry. What an incredibly awful thing to have gone through. I hope you had the help and support you needed.'

'Well, it was a long time ago now.' The familiar swell of sadness threatens my composure so I bend down and kiss Otis on his head. I never tell people this story. Even at secondary school, I kept it to myself because I didn't want to be known as the kid whose mum was killed.

'She was stabbed by some mindless thugs who tried to mug her. I was there but I didn't really see anything … The worst part is how senseless it was. I didn't get it at the time, I was too distraught, but the more I grew up, the more angry I got.'

'I can't imagine how terrible that must have been for you and your family,' Edward says softly.

'I don't remember the aftermath much. I know they were caught and sentenced but it didn't help our family. All the grown-ups tried to shield me from their conversations. I remember my dad's face. All slack and hollow. He lost loads of weight and never really seemed like my dad after. I guess his spark had died with Mum.'

'I'm so sorry,' Edward says. 'You don't have to tell me any of this if it's too difficult but I'm here to listen if you want to.'

'It's sort of relevant to how I'm feeling today, you see. I'd made this pact to be the best mum I could in honour of her because that's what she was to me. From what I remember, she was wonderful, so you're right, I will be there for those kids but I can't take it for granted either. I should be making every minute with them count but the reality is I spend most of my time yelling or barking orders at them.'

'You're a great mum and a strong woman, Stephanie,' Edward says but the truth is, I don't feel like either of those things. When something awful happens in your life, you have no option but to carry on.

There's a table in the beer garden overlooking the river and Edward asks me to grab it while he gets the drinks in. He's insisted on buying since I came to help him catch Ruby. I know he's just trying to cheer me up but it's working.

'Here you are,' he says, placing half a lager and some dry-roasted peanuts in front of me. He has a pint and some of those posh salt and vinegar crisps. 'I love it here,' he says, tearing open his packet. A family of ducks waddle along the riverbank and a heron swoops down to the water.

'I've never been here. The pub in our village is pretty decent too so on the rare occasion I go to a pub, I tend to go there. I'm surprised you ever get the chance; you always seem so busy with work. Look at you here, on a Saturday, drinking with an employee after hunting for a client's cat.'

'I do work a lot but I tend to pop in here at least once a week.'

'Who with?' I blurt the words out and immediately want to claw them back. A flicker of surprise runs across his face. 'Sorry, it's just that you said your friends all lived away but obviously, you could still have *some* friends here or a date or you could come by yourself and all of those things are okay.' I can't seem to shut up. The corners of Edward's eyes crinkle and I'm glad I haven't offended him.

'Sometimes I come for a quiet pint after work, especially if it's been a stressful day. I'm on first-name terms with most of the bar staff so there's always someone to chat to and there's a woman in the village who I meet here sometimes.'

There's a heaviness inside me at the thought of him and Stacy here, laughing away over Blue Lagoons with bright paper umbrellas in or whatever it is she drinks. 'That's nice,' I manage.

'It's not *like that*; she's just a friend.'

I don't know what he thinks I was implying. I didn't imply anything. My heart rate picks up. Oh God, now he thinks I'm sad because he has a girlfriend. 'Hey, you're the boss. I'm not paid to judge; it's your personal time you can do whatever you want.'

Hang on. Why did he want me to understand it's not *like that*? I need to change the subject before things get any more awkward. 'So, where did you study to be a vet?'

Thankfully, the conversation moves into a more comfortable zone and we chat and laugh about our uni years.

'Can I get you another drink?' Edward asks, gesturing to my empty glass.

'I'd better not. I'm driving and Otis needs his dinner. I should get home.'

His features drop a little but he pulls them back up and into a smile. 'Of course. Thank you for your help today.'

'It was no problem,' I say, gathering my bag and unclipping Otis's lead from the bench leg.

'I'll check on your cut first thing Monday, but try to keep it dry. If it does get wet, pat it gently with a towel.'

'Will do. Enjoy the rest of your weekend,' I say.

Chapter 26

The house has had the soul sucked out of it. I thought the kids might have FaceTimed me tonight but I've heard nothing from them and I don't know if that's a good or bad thing really. My mind flits between imagining them having a fun evening with movies, popcorn and lots of laughing with Kate, versus them in floods of tears and Mike trying to console them unsuccessfully. Neither scenario sits well with me.

I try to phone Janey. She's been AWOL recently and I know she's having a rough time with Jimmy. She puts on a brave face but I know deep down she's hurting and seemed like she was on the verge of doing something quite drastic. She doesn't answer, instead, her phone goes straight to answerphone but I don't leave a message. I pour myself a gentle G&T and sit down to read a couple of chapters of *Pet Sematary*. To be honest, I can't see it helping with my night fear but Janey wanted to read it and I want to do it for her. As I'm getting to the bottom of the first page of the day, my phone pings.

I'm bored. Jimmy away (AGAIN), kids in bed. What are you ladies doing?

She's doing that thing again, where she tries to put on a brave face but I'm not going to say anything on an app.

147

Same. Been a week of work and chores. Saw Edward today. Lost cat. Long story.

Ooh, anything interesting happen?

We just talked. He's a lovely guy.

With Jimmy being away so much, I have to live my romantic life vicariously through the lives of others but you're no fun. She adds a winky face.

Anyway, what did you do today?

Seren was at gymnastics this afternoon so I sat around there for an hour and a half.

Oh fun!

To be honest, the eye candy isn't so bad. I mean, is it wrong to feel jealous of my kid being manhandled into backflips by all those fit, burly men?

I chuckle and reach for my gin but it's empty. I type:

I think it's frowned upon.

Then add:

How did your chat with Jimmy go?

I know I said I wouldn't but I don't know when I'll next see her and I'm conscious that we talk about me far too much.

Fine. As expected … I'll fill you in when I see you.

That doesn't sound good. As I walk back to the kitchen I type a quick reply.

Well let's make it soon!

When I'm back in the lounge, it says that Amanda is typing something.

That awful woman next door is having a party and it's so loud I can't hear myself think.

By next door, she means part of her garden wall borders part of the garden wall of the neighbour's house. Before anyone has the chance to reply, she adds:

Would it be terrible of me to climb over the wall and help myself to a G&T from one of the handsome waiters?

148

How the hell do you know the waiters are handsome? Janey replies quickly.

I might have used the binoculars George got a few Christmases ago.

That's spying! I reply with a laughing emoji at the end. It's nice to see Amanda coming out of her shell a bit.

No, it isn't. I'm on the neighbourhood watch committee.

My phone is alive all night and when I finally drag myself up to brush my teeth I notice I'm smiling. I think a meaningful friendship is starting to develop between the three of us, that's more than just a book club. It's three people with completely different lives providing laughter and comfort for one another. Whatever happens tomorrow, these ladies will be here to help me pick up the pieces.

Chapter 27

Despite only having two gin and tonics (one gentle, one not so) I wake up feeling like I necked a pint of sand. I go downstairs, let Otis out and fill a glass with water before popping two Alka-Seltzers in. Once I've drunk that, I have a cup of tea and get dressed. The kids are due back any time now and since I haven't heard a thing from them, I have no idea what to expect.

When the doorbell rings, I leap to my feet and dart down the hallway.

'Hey, everyone.' I plaster a huge smile on my face.

'Mummy!' Ava hugs me as Ralph barges past and stomps up to his room. I look at Mike who gives a little shake of his head.

'How was it, Ava?' I ask, kneeling down. Mike carries Henry through to the lounge.

'It was fun. Met Daddy's new friend, Kate. She was nice.' She's sporting two of those chunky braids in her hair, the kind that are trendy at the minute. I can't do them and there's no way Mike could have.

I ignore the fireball of bile in my stomach. 'That's good, sweetie. Did Kate do your hair too?'

'Yes.' She beams. 'I want it like this every day.'

'Well, it looks lovely. Can you take your bag up to your room please?'

She bounces up the stairs and I head to where Mike is playing with Henry.

'So, what happened? I've been worried sick.'

'Everything was fine like normal. We went to the park. Ralph was chatting away about a school football match he's got coming up and Ava was singing a song she'd learnt in assembly. Then I sat them down and told them I wanted them to meet someone. Ava was really excited but Ralph wouldn't say a word. He hasn't spoken since.'

'Oh God, do you think he's okay?' I ask.

'I'm sure he will be. It was a shock that's all. Kate tried with him and we had a load of chocolate and fizzy pop in to cheer them up.'

I tilt my head to the side. 'I don't think fizzy pop makes up for something like this.'

'I know. I just wanted them to feel welcome.'

Something inside me softens. 'Fair enough. So what now?'

'Kate and I had a chat and she said she doesn't want to move in until the kids have gotten to know her better. She thinks it's too much for them all at once.'

I can't believe I'm saying this. 'She talks sense.'

'Yeah, they need time to get used to her.'

I nod. Mike stands up and takes out his car keys. 'What's happened to your head?'

I raise my hand to the steri-strip. 'Oh, that. It's nothing. Just a bit of an altercation with a cat.'

Mike gives a small smile. It's actually quite nice having him care this much. He's not the sort to wear his heart on his sleeve.

'Ralph will come around you know,' I say, softly.

Mike purses his lips. He's out of his comfort zone. Fun and games he can do, but feeling sad emotions, not so much. 'I might head up and say bye to Ava … I'll pop in and try and chat to Ralph too.'

'Good idea,' I say, scooping Henry up off the floor. He always looks like he's grown a little when he's been with his dad. It's only ever a subtle change, but there's always something about him that's never quite the same as it was and it makes me feel sad.

Mike comes down about five minutes later. 'Still no joy with Ralph. I'm thinking that a new computer game might cheer him up, what do you reckon?'

'I think no. Not a chance. His dad has a new girlfriend, it's okay for him to be upset or angry and he needs time to process that. You can't buy his acceptance, Mike. Just be there for him and give him some time.'

Mike sighs. 'You're right. Maybe I could pick him up from school one night next week and take him for tea, just the two of us.'

'That's a much better idea.' For once, I think Mike might actually be getting the hang of this dad business, ten years in.

Chapter 28

As I'm struggling to get the buggy down the front steps, Janey calls me from across the street.

'Are you walking them today?'

'Yes,' I shout back, still struggling.

'All right, I'm only here.' She picks up the front of the buggy and grins. Only a superhuman could have crossed the road so fast. 'What's happened to your face?'

I sigh. 'Mrs Pearson's silly cat.'

Janey frowns but then a look of realisation crosses her face as the penny drops.

'How did it go with whatsherface?' she whispers, gesturing to the kids.

'Ava seemed fine about it but Ralph is upset.'

'Ahh, it's a big change for them,' she says sympathetically and we set off walking towards the school.

'Yup.'

'How about you? How are you doing?'

I shrug. 'As fine as I can be really. I don't feel much as an ex-wife, more as a mother who wants to make sure her kids are okay. It's a weird situation; trying to convince your kids that it's okay for their dad to have a girlfriend and that they should be happy for him. The whole thing makes me a bit squeamish. It's made me realise how I don't want to put them through this again any time soon so dating is one hundred per cent off the table for me.'

'How is that fair? Mike leaves you because he can't cope with the pressures of having to always think of others then *he* meets someone first, now you can't? Talk about having his cake and eating it.'

'I know how it looks and he didn't just leave because of that. We rowed a lot but listen, the Kate thing, I'm fine with it, really. I just want to make sure the kids are okay.'

'So no dishy boss then?'

'No.' I roll my eyes. 'You know he's seeing someone anyway.' I notice Ava running towards the road ahead. 'Ava, stop right there. Ralph, grab her hand.'

When I'm satisfied they're both safe, I continue. 'Tell me about you. I know you've got something going on and I feel dreadful that all the focus has been on me lately.'

We near the road and once we've ensured everyone has safely reached the other side, we let the kids go on ahead before picking up the conversation. 'I gave Jimmy the ultimatum.'

I expected she would have, but all the deflection makes me think the outcome wasn't what she'd hoped. 'And?'

She draws a deep breath.

'Oh, God, Janey. I'm sorry.'

'He said I was being ridiculous.' Her voice falters so I reach out to rub the top of her arm. 'It will be okay.'

'He said he puts food on the table and a roof over our heads so we should count ourselves lucky. I stood my ground.'

I didn't doubt it. 'And what? He just wasn't prepared to try?'

'In short, no. My job is to keep the house going and his is to bring the money in. In his words, we shouldn't expect to be "going at it like teenagers anymore".'

'God. What about his needs and stuff?'

'Well, it gets worse than that.'

'Oh no. How?'

'Mummy, Mummy?' Ava comes running towards me. 'Ralph told me to shut up and then he pushed me.'

I glance at Janey and mouth: 'I'm sorry.' She gestures for me to go on ahead.

'Do you mind if I walk with Ralph for a bit?'

She puts her hand on mine. 'Let me push Henry for you and I'll watch Ava for the rest of the way. You go and talk to him, love.'

I thank her, hand the pushchair over and speed up my pace.

Normally, I'd be furious with him but today he has his reasons so I take a softer approach. 'Ralph,' I say as I get closer. He pulls the hood of his coat up and I can't help but feel this could be an early glimpse into his teenage years.

'Ralph,' I say again but softer this time. Sadly, it's not a tone I use on my kids often and the unusualness of it prompts him to look up. I falter. I hadn't actually thought about what to say or how to broach the whole business with his dad. 'Are you doing okay, darling?'

His eyes drop back to the pavement and he shrugs. I get a pang through my core. He feels like his world has been ripped apart for a second time. I know only too well what having your family destroyed as a kid feels like but I never had anyone to talk about it with. I won't let that be the case for Ralph.

'It's okay to be upset about your dad and Kate; angry even.'

Silence.

'You can be happy about it too. Whatever you're feeling is normal and okay.'

All of a sudden, he stops walking and looks at me. 'How do *you* feel about it?'

I stop walking too. That wasn't what I was expecting. Ralph turns to me. 'If he wanted to be with someone, why didn't he come back to us?'

'Ralph, it's complicated. Your dad and I are friends now but we don't want to be a couple anymore. We'll always be glad of our marriage because we have you, Ava and Henry. We'll always be your mum and dad and we'll always be there for you. We just don't get along when we live together.'

'Are you sad that Dad has a girlfriend?'

I pause. Ralph is growing up and deserves an honest answer. 'Perhaps a little bit but it's normal and I think it's just a little weird for me more than anything. It will take a little bit of getting used to but as long as she treats you three with kindness, I'll be fine.'

'She did seem kind,' he says, kicking at a stone.

'Good. Ava seemed to like her and Henry doesn't understand what's going on so it's just you that I'm worried about.'

He looks up at me with the big blue eyes that I adore. 'I'm fine … if you are.'

'I'm more than fine. I'm actually really happy. I've got my book club now and two new friends, plus I love my job.'

'Okay, Mum.' With that, he runs back to catch up with Janey's son Tom.

'He's brightened up,' Janey says as she approaches me.

'Yeah. I think he was worried about me more than anything else.'

'Oh, that's sweet. I doubt Tom would give a monkey's about me if I were in your position. He'd just be panicking about who buys the Xbox games.'

I laugh softly. 'I didn't expect it from Ralph to be fair. Maybe *he's* hankering after an Xbox game.'

After we drop the children off, I take Henry to the childminder and head to work.

'No Mrs Pearson today?' I joke to Carly as it's usually a Monday when Ruby starts to feel unwell, hence Edward's Yorkshire pudding dig a few weeks ago.

'No, perhaps she's actually sticking to cat food. We've got a snake in later though.' She shudders.

'Not a fan?' I ask and she shakes her head dramatically.

I head to the small kitchen to put the kettle on and the door chime tinkles, followed by a loud and cheerful female voice.

'Where is he then, the handsome devil?' I presume she's talking about Edward and to my shame, I take a step closer to the door and strain my ears.

'Oh, he's such a hardworking man. Such old-fashioned values.' The voice coos. Carly must reply in a way that's not audible to me; I imagine her glancing up from her computer wearily and nodding.

The kettle boils and I have no choice but to move away from the door and finish my tea. As I leave the kitchen, the chatter continues and when I near the waiting-room door, I recognise the voice. Stacy. She's talking about some celebrity who was pictured in a magazine flashing her bum as she got out of a car at some red-carpet event. I pity the celebrity whoever she is. A woman should be able to get out of a car without a photograph ending up splashed over the front page of some glossy magazine. I step into the doorway and glance at Carly who rolls her eyes while Stacy dips into her bag for something. In the time it takes for me to reach my desk, she's moved on from bum-flashing to this week's *Britain's Got Talent*.

As she talks I notice it's not a bag in her lap, it's a white fluffy rabbit wearing a pink harness and lead, and for a moment I contemplate buying one for Henry now he's on the move.

'I think we met at the weekend,' I say, to halt her incessant nattering more than anything else.

She crumples her face in thought. 'Oh yes. You were looking for that lady's cat. Did you find it?'

'Yes, eventually.'

'Is that how you hurt your head?'

I wish people would stop asking me about that. 'Yes.'

'Bloody cats. I had one once …'

Then she's off again regaling us with tales of her sofa-scratching cat that eventually vanished. I can't help wondering if it ran away in desperate hope of some peace and quiet.

The examination-room door opens and she finally stops talking. My ears have a faint ring in them.

'Ms Dalton.' Edward smiles as Stacy jumps to her feet and almost runs over to him.

'You don't have to be all formal wi' me, mister.' She stuffs the rabbit under one arm and pats his chest firmly with her free hand. She reminds me of one of those kids' bubble machines just pop, pop, popping an endless assault of words, fluffiness and pink. Edward stands there for a moment, shell-shocked before ushering her into the examination room.

'That poor rabbit,' Carly says but my thoughts are more along the lines of poor Edward.

'What's up with it?'

'Oh, nothing probably. I just mean having to wear that awful rabbit-shaming harness and being constantly bothered by that woman.'

I stifle a giggle. As I return to my tea and work, I am a bit ashamed of myself. I've taken a dislike to Stacy even though she's very sweet and I doubt she has a bad word to say about anyone. It's irrational to dislike someone who is, for all intents and purposes, quite lovely and well meaning. She's full-on, I concede eventually, and I'm allowed to be irritated by that. It has nothing to do with her relationship with Edward and I'm not at all jealous – I'm an adult with no time to befriend the green-eyed monster. That being said, when the door swings back open, my eyes dart to look at it.

'So, I don't think Snuggles is depressed. Just give her plenty of time outside and some of her favourite fresh carrots and I'm sure she'll perk up a bit.'

'So she doesn't need a companion?' She winks animatedly.

'I think she'll be fine,' Edward says, standing up straighter.

'You know us girls love a man around.' She tugs Edward's tie with so much force, his head jolts forward enough that she can plant a big smacker of a kiss right on his lips.

With that, she giggles and walks towards the door and Edward vanishes back into the examination room.

Now *I'm* shell-shocked. There's obviously a lot more going on there than a few drinks at the pub but why would Edward be so guarded about it?

When I glance at my screen, her account is open. 'She left without paying.'

'Special privileges,' Carly says drily.

'Really? Does Edward know?'

Carly shrugs.

'If Edward offered her a discount, it would be on the system. Crookney Farm has a ten per cent discount applied – Edward told me about it when I set the accounts up. It's something to do with honouring a long-standing agreement his father made with the farm owner. If Stacy has a discount, even one hundred per cent, he'd have said because it would need to be applied to her account.'

Carly starts filing her nails. 'I don't think I've ever seen her pay. Just assumed—'

'I'm going after her,' I say. Carly's jaw drops but I don't have time to reconsider. People need to stop assuming and start finding out facts. If there's one thing I hate it's messy accounts that don't add up and right now, the deficit on her account is the only thing not tied up neatly. I'm new(ish). I can get away with this.

As I fly through the door, I spot her heading down the high street in the direction of the bakery. There's no mistaking her pink jacket and the fluffy white tail of her rabbit poking out from under her armpit – if the Barbie Dreamhouse had a beacon, she'd be it.

'Ms Dalton?' I shout as I get close enough. She turns around and her head jerks back in surprise. It's a moment before she plasters on her huge trademark smile.

'Everything all right?' She tucks the rabbit tighter underneath her arm and I wonder if she thinks I've come to steal it.

'Er, yes.' I smile broadly. 'I just realised after you left, that I forgot to charge you for the appointment.' I flick my hand in the air in an attempt to seem ditsy.

Her body stiffens. 'Oh, love, you're new so Eddy probably hasn't told you about me. We're an item.'

I frown. I'd gathered they were more than just friends, but *an item*? It's not the impression I'd got but I suppose Edward's private life is just that, and if he doesn't want to share details with his bookkeeper, that's perfectly fine. 'Ahh, okay. So Edward doesn't charge you?'

She giggles. 'I pay in other ways if you know what I mean.'

Oh, God. I didn't need to know that. Those words are now etched in my mind where they'll stay for all eternity. 'Oh ... that's fine. I'm sorry. I just didn't want to get into any trouble for forgetting to charge a client.' My voice is at least an octave higher than normal and my temples are pulsating.

'If that's everything, I've got to go. I want to get some cream buns from the bakery before they sell out. You can have a lot of fun with a cream bun if you catch my drift?' She winks and then she's off.

My 'too much information' sensor is on red alert and I'm not sure where to file the mental images currently assaulting me. I'm going to need a course of hypnotherapy to forget all that. Perhaps it would have been cheaper just covering her bill for her.

Chapter 29

'Cream cake, anyone?' Janey chirps.

I stare at the three cream horns on the kitchen table and almost retch.

'Don't you like them?' Janey frowns.

All I can see is the image of Stacy licking one seductively as she holds them in front of her chest à la Madonna circa 1990 whilst Edward looks on and ... just ... no. 'Think I'm in the mood for something savoury. Thank you though – I'll have mine later.'

Janey shrugs and she and Amanda each take one. The kids are in bed and we've met to talk about *Pet Sematary*. As they bite into their horns, thick cream oozes out.

'I think I heard Henry cry out. I'll just go and check on him,' I say and run upstairs to the bathroom where I stand staring at myself in the mirror.

'Get a grip, you silly woman,' I say to my reflection. I look older than I picture myself looking. My eye bags are puffier than they feel like they should be and the fine lines on my forehead now cease to disappear when I relax my muscles. It's funny how your brain doesn't seem to age at the same rate as your skin and hair.

'It's just a bloody cream cake,' I say, remembering I've come in here to pull myself together. What two grown people do with their baked goods is none of my business. I check on the kids who are all fast asleep and then go back downstairs. Janey and Amanda have cracked open a bottle of grapefruit-flavoured gin and Amanda is just adding the tonic. I'm pleased to see their cream horns have been reduced to just a few meagre crumbs.

'Everything okay?' Janey asks, popping some ice from the tray and dropping it into the three highball tumblers she's lined up.

'Yes. False alarm.'

'Get this down your neck,' Janey says.

We start discussing the book and whilst Janey and Amanda agree it wasn't as scary as they thought, I remain silent.

'Creepy yes, atmospheric, certainly but scary? Nah. I never once looked at my kids warily,' Janey says.

'I must admit, I enjoyed it far more than I thought I would,' Amanda replies. 'What about you, Stephanie?'

I start to feel quite hot. 'I don't know where to start,' I say, not sure how to confess I didn't read it.

'Did you like the writing?' Amanda prompts.

'Well, it *is* King.' I laugh but I can tell by how hot my face is that it must be bright red. 'Listen. There's something I have to tell you both.'

'You didn't read it?' Janey rolls her eyes.

'No, but … I couldn't.'

Janey's eyes travel to the side table, where my copy of the book is. She frowns.

'I couldn't *bring* myself to, I mean.' My hands ball up in my lap, each word on the tip of my tongue a circus clown; ridiculous and silly. 'I'm terrified of the night.'

Amanda and Janey don't say anything. I'm not sure how much time passes before Janey speaks up. 'Oh, Steph? Why didn't you say you didn't want to read it? You must know we'd understand.'

I shrug. 'I suppose I wanted to give it a go. I only got to the bit where the college guy died at the beginning and had to put it down. The truth is, I sleep with the light on, if I can sleep at all, and it takes a lot for me to go outside when it is dark.'

I go on to explain about my mum and how it's affected me. Before long I find myself in floods of tears telling them all about how I've always wanted the family I never had.

When I finish, I realise I haven't been able to look at either of them. When I do, their tears surprise me. Amanda has a tissue pressed to her face and Janey's mascara has smudged beneath her eyes.

'I can't believe you never told us any of this before,' Janey says moving to my side.

'It's not something I share often.' The words come out tight. My insides feel bound and coiled. 'My family were the sort who didn't discuss anything negative. It was all bottled up or swept under the carpet.'

'Oh, love. Have you ever had any sort of professional help?' Janey asks softly.

I shake my head. 'It wasn't so bad when Mike was here. It just happened every now and again but since being the only adult in the house, things have got worse.'

'I must admit, I've never been through anything quite like you have, Stephanie, but since George passed, I often feel a bit uneasy at night. You must call me if you ever feel on edge, no matter what the time.'

I tell her I will. The warmth that spreads through me now is quite unlike the prickly heat that seared me earlier. It's comforting and laced with a feeling of acceptance. It's no longer something to be ashamed of.

'Anyway. The book, you two should carry on talking about it,' I say, uncomfortable with the attention.

Janey stares into her gin. 'I have something to tell you both.'

I get a pang of guilt for not speaking to her sooner. Every time

I asked about her and Jimmy, she brushed me off or we were interrupted but I should have tried harder.

'I think my marriage is over.' Her hands tighten around the glass but she doesn't cry.

'Janey,' Amanda says in a tone that speaks so many words.

'Yeah …' Janey tails off. 'I told you how he wasn't interested in me or the kids? Well, I tried to involve him, I tried letting him know how I felt, telling him what I wanted from him and all of that. I asked him out to dinner and … nothing. It didn't make any sense to me.'

I give her a look of sympathy but I don't have any words that can make her feel better.

'Anyway, it seemed odd. Even the most slovenly man on the planet would make an effort for their wife if they gave them an ultimatum, wouldn't they?' she continues. 'So when the kids were at school last week, I followed him. He had a job in Manchester with his new apprentice, Alex, and I thought I'd just go and see what has him behaving this way. I get that fitting carpets and running a business is hard graft and tiring so … I don't know, I guess I wanted to see for myself and try to understand his day.'

My stomach tightens; I have a bad feeling about this.

'Anyway that's when I saw him and Alex kissing outside the shop they were working on.'

'Jimmy is gay?' I blurt then instantly regret missing the real point; he's having an affair.

Janey frowns. 'Oh, no. Alex is a girl. A very young, very pretty *female* carpet fitter.'

'Jesus,' I whisper.

'Janey, I'm so sorry.'

'So I confronted him and he swore it was a one-off. He said they'd had a bit of a laugh together and one thing led to another but it was a mistake.' She clenches her jaw but it isn't enough to stop the tell-tale wobble of her chin.

'Oh, Janey, honey. What do you think you're going to do about it?' Amanda soothes.

She shrugs but it's far from nonchalant. Her whole body sort of caves in on itself before breaking into heaving sobs.

'You don't need to decide now. You need time to think.' I rub her back and, admittedly, I'm struggling to control my own emotions. How dare he treat her this way!

She wipes her face with her sleeve and forces a smile. 'Let's not waste our girls' night talking about him.' Then, she claps her hands together like she's drawn a line under it but another tear rolls down her cheek.

'That bastard, making you feel like a needy wife when all this time ...' I don't even finish. What good is it? 'Well, you have us now.'

With that, she smiles. 'I do. And that's all I need.'

We spend some time comforting Janey, talking her through the logistics and we work on a plan of what and how to tell the children. By the time we've finished, she seems her strong, determined self again, evidenced by the fact she's asked us to move to the kitchen so there's easier access to food and gin.

'Right, so what are we reading next, ladies? I need to know more than ever that we'll be meeting up next month to discuss a book and a reading commitment will distract me.'

Amanda presses her palms together and shuffles forward. 'I think we need something with strong women who overcome struggles; women who don't want to fit stereotypes; women who are genuine and open.'

'That's quite the intro, Amanda,' Janey teases.

'I know you're not a fan of classics, Janey, but I'm thinking *Little Women*.' A huge smile breaks out across Amanda's face. 'We can even watch the film *after* we've read the book, which means we get a movie night to look forward to as well.'

'How about we *just* watch the film?' Janey replies. She's rifling through my cupboards chucking the kids' snacks left and right.

'No! We're reading it,' I say and Amanda agrees. 'Hungry?' I ask when Janey's rifling continues.

'Starving! Must be the gin,' she says shoving aside a pack of Sour Cream and Onion Pringles.

'What's wrong with those?' I ask, knowing full well they're the best my cupboards have to offer.

'Pairing is important,' she says, still rummaging. She takes out a tin of golden syrup that's so old, the tin has started to rust. 'Bin?' she asks and I nod.

'Pairing is a bit posh for us isn't it?' I ask, sipping my gin. 'We're happy with a packet of Walkers and a bottle of Blossom Hill normally.'

'Grapefruit gin – delicious. Grapefruit gin paired with Sour Cream and Onion Pringles – notes of cowpat. You mark my words. Try it if you don't believe me.'

By now I'm intrigued. Janey isn't one to let things go easily but I've never seen her so hell-bent on finding the right snack and drink combination. 'All right.'

I sip my gin, eat a few crisps and sip a bit more, then breathe out through my nose. 'Dear God it does.' It's a sticky, thick after-taste with definite undertones of farmers' fields.

'I need to see for myself,' Amanda says reaching across the table for the packet. 'That's so peculiar. Definite notes of manure coming through.'

Janey folds her arms smugly. 'See.'

'Is it just the Whitley and Neill gin or does it happen with any grapefruit gin?' Amanda asks apparently more intrigued than she should be.

'Not sure. I stumbled across the anomaly last Christmas.'

'You sort of get used to it,' I say, taking another crisp. 'It's testament to how addictive these things are.'

'Anyway. How's everything at work this week? Edward still handsome is he?' Janey asks.

'Why are you bringing him up?'

166

'Because your little face lights up whenever you hear his name and I like seeing that happen.'

I narrow my eyes. 'I will admit there's something about him.'

Both Amanda and Janey shuffle forward on their chairs.

'That's it. There's something about him.'

'And?' Amanda asks.

'And he's my boss and he's seeing someone. To be honest, I've enjoyed his company and he's easy on the eyes but the best thing about any attraction I've felt is that it's nothing more than a distraction for the everyday shit show that is my life. I'm actually glad that nothing can come of it because it would just complicate things even more and I've only just found my new normal.'

'Spoilsport,' Janey says.

'If my bakery visits and cat-hunting exploits are the only excitement in your life, you already have nothing,' I tease.

'Touché.'

'I need to see this Edward guy. I've always taken my dog to a vet near Manchester so I think I'm the only person around here who hasn't seen this dreamboat?' Amanda's use of the word dreamboat raises eyebrows from both me and Janey.

'There are a few pictures on Facebook. Hang on.' I grab my phone off the side and start searching through the photographs on the vet's page. I find the one Stacy liked all that time ago – the one with the spaniel and his easy smile. The skin around his eyes is crinkled and his teeth shine a clean white. He looks good in the pictures. 'Here.'

Amanda takes the phone and studies the image for a moment. 'Okay, things make sense now and in completely unrelated news, I'm getting a new vet.' Janey and I laugh softly and, as I take the phone back, I can't resist a second glance.

'How serious is this relationship he's in?' Amanda asks.

I fiddle with the empty Pringles container. 'Not sure. He doesn't talk much about his private life but she was pretty clear about it being quite serious.' That gets me thinking. She was happy to tell me, a virtual stranger, all about hers and Edward's naughty sex life but he's not at all like that. I think he'd be horrified to discover what she told me. The whole thing with them seems so odd but each to their own I guess.

When I've tidied the kitchen and got myself ready for bed I get beneath the covers and sip a cup of tea. Absent-mindedly, I open the Facebook app and the photo of Edward stares back at me. Before I know what I'm doing I brush my thumb gently over his face. It's ridiculous. *I'm* ridiculous. Stacy isn't right for him and I'm sure he's only with her out of convenience but I have no right to be analysing their relationship. Do I think I'm better than Stacy? No, of course not. Do I think Edward deserves better? How the hell do I know?

Am I jealous?

Chapter 30

Edward has asked me to go back into work after closing time to go over the accounts for the year-end. We might have to work quite late but at least he's promised a takeaway. Mike was surprisingly happy to be called over at the last minute. Perhaps it was the stress of having a secret girlfriend that was making him behave like an utter twat after all. I change into jeans and a thin grey jumper for comfort and freshen up a bit before heading back to work. When I get there Edward is sitting behind the reception desk staring at the computer screen. His jacket is slung over the back of the wheelie chair and he's loosened off his tie. He doesn't acknowledge me when I walk in, which is unlike him.

'Hi,' I say, tentatively.

'Steph.' He looks startled. 'Sorry, I was miles away. Accounts and I do not mix.'

I give him a warm smile and head over to the chair next to him. 'That's why I'm here.'

'I haven't even managed to log in,' he says gesturing to the screen.

'Don't be too hard on yourself. You performed emergency surgery on a dog today and saved his life and I couldn't even hold Ruby the cat still whilst you felt her tummy. We all have our skills.' I lean across him and enter the password.

'How long do we have until we need to send these over to your accountant?'

'A few weeks.'

'That's plenty of time.'

'I know but they always come back with a million queries that I can't usually answer and then I ended up having to pay someone to come in and tidy everything up.'

'You have me now.' I catch his eye and he holds my gaze for a minute before nodding in acceptance. To be needed in this way gives me quite the thrill.

I look at the current overview. 'I think we should take a look at the debtors and try to chase payments to reduce our bad debt.'

'We have bad debt?' Edward frowns.

'Not much and it's not necessarily *bad* bad. Some patients haven't completed their treatment and want to pay at the end. Some emergency cases turn up and the owner doesn't have their wallet and then there are patients with discounts that haven't been applied to the system.'

'Discounts?' Edward frowns again. 'The only discount I give is to Crookney Farm and we spoke about that when we implemented the system.'

'Yes, I know. Ten per cent.'

Edward nods. 'I don't give anyone else any discounts.'

I shuffle awkwardly and turn to face him. 'Ms Dalton said she doesn't pay for treatment.'

Edward purses his lips. 'I never said that to her.'

'I'm sorry, Carly and I didn't know what to do and you were busy and—'

'Steph,' he says gently. I look into his soft eyes. 'It isn't your fault. Stacy, Ms Dalton, seems to have many different ways to get what she wants.'

I open up her account and glance at the screen. There was

neutering, a few vaccinations and some other treatments over the past two years. 'It isn't a huge amount. There's only so much you can spend on a rabbit, but it's enough.'

Edward squints at the screen. 'It's the principle though. She lied.'

I take a deep breath. We're venturing into *not my business* territory and whatever is going on here has nothing to do with me.

'Are there any other accounts like this?' he asks.

'No, as I said, there are a few people who probably need a quick call to remind them of money outstanding but that's all.'

'Okay, can you do that tomorrow?'

I nod. 'It's already in hand and, moving forward, I'll do it in the last week of each month anyway.'

'Great.' He seems distracted.

'Do you want me to contact Ms Dalton?'

Edward rakes his hands through his hair. I can tell it's a conversation he doesn't want to have. 'No, I should deal with Ms Dalton.'

'I actually chased her down the street.' I laugh. 'Most people come straight to reception when they come out of the examination room but she just walked out with her rabbit under her arm. I went after her and made out the whole thing was my mistake for forgetting to charge her. She said she doesn't pay and then started talking about cream cakes and fun and ...' I stop talking when I notice Edward's face flush crimson. 'Sorry, perhaps oversharing is infectious.'

Before I can dig my hole any deeper, the door swings open. The takeaway is here. When I look, I notice that the natural daylight has started to dim and the little lamp on the desk has taken over, its small single bulb fighting to keep things visible, offering a warm yet close glow around us. If I wasn't doing accounts with my boss, it would be quite romantic.

'I'd ordered Chinese food – a bit of everything – if that's okay?'

'Perfect,' I say. My voice is a croak.

171

Edward pays the delivery guy and heads to the kitchen for plates and cutlery as I unpack the food and lay it out on the desk. It smells amazing.

'Found these.' He holds up a six-pack of funny-named ales. 'They were a Christmas gift from a client and I forgot to take them home. Fancy one?'

I nod, glad of anything to take the edge off the awkward conversation. We charge our plates with food and move some paperwork aside so we have more room.

As Edward raises a forkful of noodles to his lips, he pauses. 'It's complicated with Stacy.'

My insides freeze. This has nothing to do with me and I should really say something non-intrusive that moves the subject on but I don't because no matter how little this should concern me, I'm compelled and intrigued by Edward and frankly mystified by his attraction to Stacy. Instead, I ask, 'How so?'

'When I said she knows how to get what she wants, I wasn't exaggerating. She has the confidence of Jordan Belfort when he's high.'

'The Wolf of Wall Street?' I stifle a grin. She might be a bit brassy but I can't see her swindling millions of dollars out of people through pump and dump fraud.

'She's one of those people who wants something you're adamant you don't want to give and somehow she ends up making you give it to her willingly.'

Cream-cake sex springs to mind yet I'm too invested to shut this down, so I glug my beer.

'So she's manipulative,' I say diplomatically.

'Sort of, but she's very nice about it – you don't even realise it's happening. Shutting her down would be like euthanising a puppy.'

I put down my fork and twist to face him. 'Edward, are you in a relationship with Stacy?'

He shakes his head. 'I don't think so.'

I splutter my beer. 'How do you not know?'

'She's a very sweet, very lonely lady who has taken a bit of a shine to me.' His eyes drop to his plate and I notice some red blotches appear on his neck. 'She seemed really down and asked if I fancied a drink after work and I said yes. I had nothing else to do and wanted to cheer her up. She'd been bringing her rabbit in regularly with mystery illnesses that I couldn't detect, never mind treat. I knew she just needed a friend; a bit like Mrs Pearson.'

'Well, that's very kind of you. I think.'

'I thought so. We were two adults providing each other with a bit of company. Our weekly drink became a weekly meal and we'd chat about normal stuff – the news – the weather. Certainly nothing that would indicate we were anything more than just friends.'

'Okay, so what changed?'

'Rumours. People started to refer to us as a couple.'

'Because they'd seen you together?'

'Yes, and because she'd told people.'

'Eeek, that's awkward. So did you ask her about it?'

'Well, it's only just catching up with me. I went to talk to her last night in fact.'

My cream-cake alert is at disaster level. Do I put my fingers in my ears? Nope, I'm still too invested.

'I think she knew I was going to cool things off and … oh God …'

'What happened?' Oh, come on! I know what happened.

'I turned up and she'd cooked. There were candles and every-thing. I knew it was way more romantic than we'd ever been. She gave me a shoulder rub then moved on to my feet … Sorry, you really shouldn't have to listen to this. I'm your boss.'

I must have weird voyeuristic tendencies because as much as I don't want to hear about Edward and Stacy's romantic connec-tion, I have some sort of morbid curiosity. 'It's fine. You obviously need to talk to someone about this and you've spent plenty of time listening to my problems. Besides that, I'm a good listener.'

'You are,' he says, taking me by surprise. Heat floods my cheeks – now it's my turn to blush. 'Anyway. I hadn't even noticed she was wearing this wrap dress. It was pink as usual so it hadn't stood out. She went into the kitchen to get dessert and came out with these cream cakes. Only she'd …'

My cream cake-dar is on form. It is, however, the most useless superpower known to man.

'She'd unwrapped the dress and it hung loosely and … well there was a lot of pink lace. Her intentions were very clear.'

'So what did you do?' Every cell in my body is praying he put an end to proceedings.

'I told her I'd overeaten and had a stomach ache.'

'Edward!' I say, both inappropriately relieved and incredulous.

'I know. I'm a terrible wet rag of a human who hates confrontation.'

'You said it,' I say.

'Now she wants to make things up to me with a "night of fun" and I don't know what to do.'

'Sometimes trying to please people just ends up causing more hurt and pisses people off.'

He turns to look at me.

'Sorry for saying pisses … Twice. But it's true. Over promising and always trying to be kind will catch up with you one day when you can't deliver. One day Mrs Pearson's cat will have to be put to sleep and you won't be able to play the affable vet who jests about Yorkshire pudding. You don't have to be liked by everyone.'

He rests his elbows on the table and puts his head in his hands. 'Those are wise words, Steph.'

Words I've used on Ralph before now.

'You're right. Honesty is better than people-pleasing.'

I nod. 'You are a good vet and people trust you. They love you around here, but you have to make some tough decisions that people won't always like.'

'I know and I do that. I just feel terrible about it for weeks.'

'Because you're kind and you have a good heart.'

He pops the lid off another beer and offers it to me. I have my car here and shouldn't drink another but I'm enjoying this somewhat taboo evening and I suppose I could treat myself to a taxi home.

'Cheers to the end-of-year accounts,' I say, accepting it.

'Thanks for this, Steph. I know you have the kids at home and it's outside of hours but I really have no clue as to what I'm doing. That's why I hired someone.'

'It's okay, Edward. Honestly, anyone who works in accounts knows there's always a few extra hours to put in at year-end or when filing is due.'

'Filing? What's that then?' he says. It's a second or two before it registers that he's trying to be funny.

'You are definitely not a tax dodger. You can barely dodge a cream-cake-wielding admirer and that *doesn't* carry a hefty fine and possible prison sentence.' I cringe as soon as I say it. Did I really just call my boss a tax dodger? I've been out of work for so long any form of etiquette has gone out the window.

'That's true.' He laughs softly, putting me at ease.

'If you're not attracted to her you need to say. You'll humiliate her if you keep making excuses because a part of her will always cling on to the notion you feel something for her, even if she suspects you're brushing her off.'

'Jesus, I thought you were good at accounts but it turns out you're also good at making me feel like an absolute idiot too.'

I freeze. I really have crossed the line now. It's the beer and the proximity and the fact he's so bloody easy to talk to. Actually, it's the subject matter to blame and I never brought the whole Stacy thing up. I dare to look at him. His features are relaxed and he wears an easy smile.

I grin and push my luck further. 'Don't act like one then.'

I reach for a prawn cracker smugly and he does too at the

exact same time. His hand brushes mine. Instead of moving it away and apologising like I expect him to, he lets it linger and instead of flinching, I enjoy the rush of warmth that spreads through my body.

'I could tell her I'm attracted to someone else,' he says with a whisper. His breath sends a shiver down my spine.

I swallow hard. 'Don't make up a reason, just be honest.'

'What if I *am* being honest?' Eventually, he moves his hand away.

My body and everything in it sags with the weight of my illicit disappointment. I shouldn't have cared about his relationship with Stacy and I shouldn't care about whoever it is he fancies.

'Then you should be honest with that person too,' I say, adding a shrug for nonchalance. I pick up my beer and go to take a sip but Edward places his warm hand on mine, gently guiding it back to the table.

'Steph.' He turns my chair so I'm facing him. 'I know I'm probably breaking several employment laws and codes of conduct in the workplace here but a wise woman told me very recently that I had to be honest.'

My heart leaps and I'm scared to take a breath in case I spoil the fragility of this moment.

'Okay,' I whisper.

'Since the day you walked through that door with your out-of-date bookkeeping knowledge I've seen something in you. You have a light … an energy …' He rakes his hands through his hair. 'Sorry, this all sounded better in my head. There's something about you I admire. You've had this incredibly tough life and yet you get up every morning and carry on.'

'I just do what everyone does.' I feel seen, for the first time in a long time. The swell of emotion threatens to choke me.

'But you always do it smiling, Steph. You have a kindness that radiates from you. The way you are with your children and others, even Stacy – you blamed yourself for her not paying – you are wonderful.'

The back of my neck tingles and I rub it to try and make it stop. I don't believe it. I mess up, I muddle through, I get my shit together only to find the bag for life I've piled it into has holes in. How can he see something in me that I don't?

'You are beautiful inside and out.'

There's a golf ball wedged in my throat. I swallow hard.

'Enough about me. Who is it you're attracted to?' I blurt. I mean it to be funny because I don't know what else to say but the words land like a feather on a snow-covered rooftop. Sort of silent but lingering.

He tilts his head and his eyes drop to the floor. 'I know you probably don't feel the same way and that's fine. I won't mention it again and things don't need to be awkward between us.'

It's now or never. I either (very quickly) admit to myself and then him that I fancy the tweed pants off him or I pretend his attraction is one-sided, move on and regret it forever. I look at his beautifully perfect face. The sexy way his brown hair is ruffled from his hands raking through it in frustration; the depth of blue to his eyes and the light stubble I want so desperately to touch. Would admitting I too have feelings be so bad? He picks at the label on his beer bottle with his nimble, life-saving fingers. They're big, safe hands and I'm desperate to feel them on me.

'I feel the same about you.' My voice is a petrified whisper. I've never done this before. I snogged Mike in a nightclub and he texted me the next day asking to meet up. We met, snogged again and that kept happening and a few years later we were married. We never talked about feelings. The only time he ever said 'I love you' was after sex. In hindsight it was outrageously blatant foreshadowing.

Edward's eyes widen. 'You do?'

For a second, I'm frozen but I manage a small nod. He brushes my hair off my face and gently traces the cut on my head then moves his hand down the side of my neck. Our eyes lock and a magnetic pull brings us closer together. He moves his head towards me and the warmth of his breath caresses my face.

'Can I kiss you now?' he whispers.

Without replying, I move my mouth to his. My lips are cold from the beer bottle and his are hot and full. Our mouths work in rhythm together and his tongue slips tenderly in. Mine responds eagerly. My hands find his biceps and work down his back and I have to stop myself from pushing my entire body into his.

He's my boss. I banish the thought. This is too good to resist. He's so unassumingly sexy and kind. I want to devour him. *He's my boss.* I want to take his shirt off. My fingers tangle in its hem, pulling it from his trousers as we kiss. Now is not the time to get involved with someone. Suddenly, all I can see is Ralph's face. Hurt and disappointed that his only constant has let him down.

I pull away. 'I'm sorry,' I pant. 'I can't do this. I shouldn't have let it happen.' I stand up and gather my bag and cardigan.

'Steph, I'm sorry if I went too far. I thought you wanted it too.'

'I did. I do, but things at home are complicated right now. I'm sorry.'

Only half of Edward's face is visible in the lamplight but I can tell the sparkle seems to have gone from his eyes. He nods slowly in acknowledgement.

'I'll sort the rest of the accounts on Friday. I can run off some reports and things; it shouldn't take me long. Thanks for the takeaway.'

When I step into the darkness I realise I can't drive home. I'm completely sober now but it would be stupid to drive after two beers. Torn between the embarrassment of going back inside and the uninviting darkness, I start to walk towards the pub where I'll call a cab. As I'm walking, the familiar sensation comes back to me. My heart rate picks up, my scalp starts to prickle and goose bumps pop on my arms. Every sound makes me jump and my eyes dart around searching for a potential attacker. The fear is different this time though. My mind is distracted. I replay the kiss in my mind and my lower abdomen flutters. When I picture the hurt in Edward's eyes as I was leaving it makes me want to cry. How did I make such a mess of everything? I was happy admiring him from the wings and now this casts a shadow over everything. It's one thing longing for someone you can't have, but longing for someone you *can* have but *shouldn't have* is painful.

When I reach the pub, my tension eases. I call a cab and sit down on the wall. A few drunken couples stagger out. I freeze each time until I notice they're either hand in hand or arm in arm, kissing or laughing. As they pass and everything falls silent again, I can't help but wonder if Edward has come after me. I chance a look down the street but I can't see a soul beneath the white glow of the streetlamp. My organs weigh heavily inside me. Of course he wouldn't come after me – he's respecting my wishes.

I never thought it possible to resent your own wishes.

Chapter 31

The next morning I wake up feeling surprisingly chirpy. Then I remember last night and it weighs down on me all over again. When I got home, a million emotions hit me all at once. Regret for kissing Edward, regret for running away, embarrassment and frustration. It must have shown on my face because even Mike asked if I was okay. Mike who has never in our history registered any of my subtle hints or signals. I check the time and I'm fifteen minutes late. Then I remember my car. I turn off my bedside lamp and dive out of bed – if we have to walk to school, I'm actually half an hour late. I run to Henry's room whilst yelling at Ralph and Ava to get up and get dressed.

We practically fall out of the front door in a flurry of coats, bags and lunchboxes.

'Everything all right?' Janey is already crossing the road towards us.

'I overslept,' I say. Janey regards me curiously.

'Where's your car?'

I glance at the gaping hole by the side of the pavement where it's usually parked. 'Work.'

'Was Mike here last night? I thought I saw his car,' she asks, automatically taking the pushchair off me so I can put my coat on.

'Yes, he babysat whilst I went into work for a bit. We had the end-of-year accounts to sort.'

'And by *we*, you mean you and Carly?' she says with a smirk.

I sigh. 'No, you know I mean Edward. It was work.'

'That doesn't explain the car,' she says, pulling down the handles of the pushchair so she can jimmy it down the kerb.

'And who are you? A CSI?'

'Okay, I'm pulling your leg but now I know there's more to this than a flat battery or something. Got time for a coffee?'

'Edward gave me the day off because we worked late last night. I wasn't going to take him up on it but do you know what? I think I will. Fancy a change of scenery?'

The Broadly Country Park is one of my favourite places. Vast green fields, woodland walks and a tearoom with cakes that would make Juliet Sear book herself onto a baking course. Janey drove since my car is still at work and we dropped Henry off at the childminder on the way so it's just the two of us. As the tyres of Janey's car crunch across the grey gravel of the car park, I feel a bit naughty, like I'm wagging it. As she's getting her coat out of the boot, I go and pay for a ticket.

'Walk first and reward cake later?' she asks as I hand her the window sticker.

'Sounds like a plan.'

We take a path that leads down to a small lake. It's a pleasantly mild day. The sun reflects off the water, which is framed by long grass and reeds. A heron swoops down and catches a fish – it all happens in a second.

'If only if was that easy to catch a man.' Janey laughs to herself. 'Although I'd rather have the fish if I'm honest.'

'Does this mean you've made a decision?' I ask.

She sighs. 'Not yet. He's been super-helpful with the kids and lots more attentive with me. Perhaps this could do us some good.'

'Do you think?' It's none of my business but I don't think

Jimmy made a mistake. I hardly know him but I know men and how the heck is he going to distance himself from this Alex if she works for him? He can't sack her because he can't keep his hands to himself.

'I don't know. We'll see. So come on then. Your car? What's it doing at the vet's?' It's typical of Janey to want to talk about my problems. I've come to realise she's not comfortable talking about her own.

I stop walking and turn to look out across the lake. 'We were doing the accounts and Edward ordered a takeaway because we were working through the evening. He had some beers in the kitchen and we drank a few.' I reach down, pick up a pebble off the path, and try to skim it. It sinks straight to the bottom. 'We got talking about that Stacy woman, who he isn't seeing by the way.'

'Oh?'

I shake my head. 'She sounds a little bit obsessed with Edward and he doesn't want to hurt her feelings. Anyway, he said he was attracted to someone and ...'

'And that someone is you?' Janey prompts in an excited high-pitched screech.

I drop my head.

Janey cranes her neck to try and look me in the eyes. 'What's the matter with that?'

I throw my hands in the air. 'I like him, Janey, and when he kissed me—'

She gasps.

'Sorry, I haven't covered that bit yet, have I?'

She shakes her head.

'We kissed and it felt so good. I've never had a connection like that before. I mean, perhaps I once felt like that when Mike kissed me in the early days but it's not a feeling I remember. It was like a movie kiss. I could have been on the top of the Empire State Building at the end of *Sleepless in Seattle* it was so good.'

Janey's forehead is as crumpled as a discarded chip wrapper.

'Okay, that was over the top.'

'No, no, no it's not that. I've just never seen the film.'

I cock my head to the side. 'Really?'

'No, not really. I'm joking. It's the fact that it all sounds so perfect and yet you're about to tell me there's some sort of problem.'

My shoulders sag. 'There *is* a problem. Ralph is still getting used to the idea Mike has a girlfriend. I'm his only constant at the minute and if I change things, I'm scared he'll be mentally scarred for life.'

'Okay, two things. Firstly, why should Mike be the only one allowed to meet someone new?'

'He's not. He just happens to be the first.'

'Secondly, you don't have to tell the kids straight away. See how it goes first.'

'I know that but what if Ralph never accepts Kate? What if he feels worse about it over time rather than better? What if he resents his dad and refuses to go and spend time with him?'

'And what if the international space station crash-lands on you whilst you're wallowing in a self-pitying purgatory?'

'I'm not wa—'

'Look, I'm not going to be one of those friends who tells you what you should do. Crikey, we're old and battle-scarred enough to make our own decisions. Date him or don't date him. I just want you to make sure you consider all the options before you dive headfirst into a current that takes you in a different direction to the one you wanted to go in.'

'Thank you. I have. I just need to make sure these big changes are introduced slowly and sensitively.'

'Consider yourself in this, though.'

We continue to walk around the lake in companionable silence. My mind is on last night but I've no idea where Janey's is.

'You know, after everything I went through as a kid, all I ever wanted was a *normal* family.'

'What is a normal family these days? Clinging on to an unhappy marriage isn't.'

'I know. I don't have any regrets about the divorce ... I just wish we could have been happy, that's all.'

'This is my point. You *can* be happy.'

'I know. I think I'm ready to make some positive changes in my life, but not a man, just some "me" time. Some pampering or the odd night out would do,' I say, stopping as we complete the loop around the lake. 'How about that cake now?'

We make our way to the tearoom and I insist on getting the treats whilst Janey finds a table. Since it's a nice day, she chooses one in the small cobbled courtyard outside. I get us both a scone with the works and a cup of tea.

'Ooh, this looks amazing,' Janey says, building up layers of jam and clotted cream with complete disregard of the 'what goes on first' argument – I doubt she'd be welcome in Devon *or* Cornwall for treating a scone that way.

As I'm about to cut my own in half, my phone buzzes. 'Sorry,' I say reaching in my bag for it. Janey waves her hand.

The name on the screen jolts me.

'What's wrong?' Janey asks. Evidently, my face wears the shock like a mask.

I shake my head. 'It's an old friend: Emily. Someone I haven't spoken to since ...' The memory comes back. 'Since the day I met you.'

'One of those bitches who ditched you when you and Mike broke up?'

I clutch the phone to my chest. 'I don't want to open it. It's a WhatsApp message; if I open it she'll know I've seen it.'

'Can't you read some of it off the notification on your home screen?'

'No, ever since you, me and Amanda set up our group, I turned off the message display in case one of the kids saw something inappropriate pop up.'

184

'You're going to have to open it. It could be something important. Why would she contact you out of the blue?'

'I have no idea, but I'm eating my scone first.'

The scone is delicious. The cool, fresh, clotted cream sits beautifully atop some homemade jam with big chunks of strawberry in. The tea cuts through the sweetness perfectly.

'That was to die for.' Janey leans back in her chair with a groan.

'It was. Who needs lunch anyway?'

Janey gestures to my phone. 'You going to see what she wants then?'

I sigh and pick it up.

Hi Stephanie, I hope you are keeping well. I know it's been a long time since we caught up and wondered if you might be free tomorrow for a drink and a bit of a chinwag? xxx

Whatever I was expecting, it wasn't that. 'It doesn't say anything. Just that she wants to meet up.'

'What? She ignores you for the best part of a year, leaving you to hit rock bottom by yourself and *now* wants to meet up? What a charmer.'

Janey is right to think she's taking the biscuit, but I'd be fibbing if I said part of me wasn't intrigued. 'Perhaps she wants to apologise. I just don't know if I can imagine myself sitting in a bar with her.'

Janey shrugs. 'If you're not comfortable, don't do it.'

'But on the other hand, what if it's something important?'

'Just put the phone away and think about it. You don't have to reply this minute.'

'She'll know I read the message.'

'So, let her stew.'

The usual after-school chaos sees that I forget all about Emily's message and it isn't until I've sat down in front of the TV with a KitKat and a cuppa that it buzzes again, jolting my memory. It's her again.

Stephanie, I'm sorry about the supermarket encounter a few months back. I wasn't myself. It's part of what I wanted to see you about actually. Please message me back xxx

I'm torn between wanting to throw my phone at the wall and feeling compelled to agree to her demand. I watch an episode of *Schitt's Creek* and muster the energy to reply.

Hi Emily, it's been a while. What is it?

To the point, a little sharp, but what the heck? For a moment, I think she might get the hint and stop bothering me but the little dots appear, indicating that she's typing something.

It's a really long story. It would be better to meet face-to-face. Does tomorrow at seven work? xxx

My fingers are nimbly typing 'okay' before I've even thought about it. God she's good at this.

Chapter 32

Work is like Victoria station and Edward hasn't had a second to himself. I make some tea for everyone and pretend to forget to take Edward's through to the examination room, so Carly does it instead. I'm not avoiding him as such, but I am trying to remain focused.

He emerges for a late lunch in his blue scrubs. He's just done a surgery that went well and as such, probably needs to refuel.

'Hi,' he says with the briefest glance at reception. Is it me or is there an atmosphere?

'He's not his usual chirpy self,' Carly says when he's gone. Not just me then.

A little while later, when Carly is on her five hundred and seventy-fifth cigarette break, he comes back out. I shrink into my seat and try to look busy.

'Steph,' he says, running both hands through his hair.

'Hmm?' I type gobbledegook and delete it several times whilst furrowing my brow intently. Despite my best efforts to look incredibly busy, he lingers at the desk.

'About the other night. I wasn't intending to say ... or do anything so unprofessional and didn't mean to make things awkward between us. We'd been talking about honesty and I guess

I got caught up in the moment. Can we forget I said anything at all?'

How do I forget something like that? The GB gymnastic team had an all-night celebration in my stomach. 'Of course.'

His body relaxes. 'Thank you, and I'm sorry to have complicated things. You're so good at your job, I'd hate to make you feel uncomfortable, and ... you know. Strictly professional from now on. Sorry. Again.'

The notion gives me a sinking feeling. 'You don't need to apologise. We can still be friends.'

He gives a wan smile and nods before disappearing again.

I know it's for the best and is exactly what I wanted but my whole body is laden with disappointment.

It's been almost a year since I wore my 'drinks-with-friends' clothes. I've had drinks with Janey and Amanda of course, but jeans and a T-shirt cuts it just fine. Amanda is a fan of a blouse and long skirt but she doesn't make me feel like *I* should dress that way. Emily on the other hand is a different matter. Style and class radiate from her, luring in those similar and warning off those who aren't. I put on my uncomfortable dark-blue skinny jeans and team them with a cream satin blouse and gold necklace with two interlinking circles that Mike bought me for our first wedding anniversary. Before I apply my make-up, I slowly peel off the steri-strip that Edward placed there what now seems like forever ago. The cut has healed nicely – you can barely see it. I wonder if it would have left a scar if he hadn't patched me up so well. Throwing the grubby little strip away feels like I'm ridding myself of the last bit of Edward's tenderness and it doesn't feel anywhere near as good as it should. I push thoughts of Edward aside and put on some court-heeled pumps, brush my hair and I'm ready to go.

I contemplate the drive into Manchester but it's likely I'm going to need a drink, so I take the tram instead. She wants to meet in a pretentious new bar just off Deansgate so I have to walk for ten minutes whilst following a map on my phone. I have butterflies the whole way and when I get there, I can't even remember why I agreed to come. Every molecule in my body experiences a magnetic push away from the entrance. I force myself in. Being a Thursday teatime, it's quiet so I spot her straight away in a cream leather-look booth. Coiffured golden waves, a contoured face and an elegant floor-length silk shirtdress nipped in at the waist with a tie belt give her the 'Emily' signature look.

'Hi,' I say, approaching her.

She smiles sheepishly. 'Hi, Stephanie – I've got the drinks in.'

There's a bottle of Veuve Clicquot sitting in an ice bucket on a stand next to the table. She's already poured herself a glass and starts to fill the second flute for me.

I slide in next to her.

'So, it's been such a long time.' She puts her arm around me and pulls me close in an awkward hug.

'Not through any fault of mine,' I say. I'm no longer scared of losing her friendship like I was in the early days of the divorce. I don't owe her any pleasantries.

She lowers her head. 'I know and I'm ashamed of how I … how we … the girls anyway, treated you. You have to understand that it was very difficult to pick a side.'

Rage fires up inside of me so I take a sip of champagne to settle any shaking that might erupt in defiance of my strong persona. I don't want to look weak.

'Why was it difficult? Why couldn't you call and see if I was okay and do the same for Mike? Neither of us would have asked you to choose a side.'

She presses the tips of her fingers to her forehead; it's a small movement that she manages to make look dramatic. 'We were wrong.'

'So where are the others? Lucinda? Patricia?'

She gives a small shake of her head and whispers, 'It's just me.'

'Oh. Why did you ask me here?' I say, softening my tone.

'Bradley has filed for divorce.' She bends down to search for something before pulling out a tissue that looks like it's one nose-blow past its limit.

I grab a packet from my own bag and pull out a fresh one before handing it to her. 'Here, I'm never without.'

She thanks me before blowing her nose.

'What happened?' I ask.

'He's been shagging his tart of a secretary. Original isn't he? All that effort I put into finding an ugly nanny when the kids were younger too.' She waves her glass as she speaks but somehow manages not to spill a drop.

'I'm sorry,' I say. There must be something in the water.

She waves her hand dismissively. 'I saw it coming and I'll do okay out of the divorce. What I didn't realise was how bad it would make me feel about ... how did you put it? Ghosting you.'

'It was a terrible thing to do but I've made some new friends and I'm working now. I'm okay.'

'Oh,' she says reaching for her flute. I notice her hand has a slight tremor and I find myself feeling a little bit sorry for her. 'Have Lucinda and Patricia cut you off now?'

She nods. 'Yes. I get it. The boys' club is the glue that keeps everything together. We women are peripherals. Marianne will slot right in where I left off.'

I frown. 'Marianne?'

'The secretary.'

'Ahh.'

'She'll be going to the Regency Health Spa this weekend instead of me.'

I remember those pompous getaways. The men would golf while the little ladies got facials and mud baths. There would always be a dinner in the evening where the men, usually Bradley, would regale us with tales of his super-rich friends. It used to annoy me how Mike would try and keep up with them. I'd wince with each bottle of champers he'd charge to our room and despise the others who knew we weren't as well off as they were yet insisted we always had the most expensive bottle on offer. I wonder if Kate is going to this health spa? Mike hasn't asked me to have the kids but he's with them this evening and had them the night I worked late – perhaps he's after brownie points.

'Look, Emily, Lucinda and Patricia are not your real friends. You must have some other friends.'

She looks at me with wide eyes. 'Did you?'

I shake my head. 'No. When we moved to Milden, neither of us knew anyone. That's why Mike's friends are all from the firm and you three were my only friends.'

'I know Mike has met someone,' she says.

'It is what it is,' I say drily.

'Have you met her?' Emily asks.

I shake my head.

'She's not a patch on you.'

I don't for a minute believe her but the sentiment is sweet.

'We were awful to you, weren't we?'

'Yes,' I say. 'But I've moved on and you will too.'

'I guess we just thought it was the boys' work gang and you had other friends.'

'Now you know. Anyway, it's in the past now – I've made some great friends now and you will too.'

'Yes,' she whispers then recharges the glasses. 'So, your new friends, what are they like?'

'Janey is a bit brassy but her heart is in the right place. Amanda is more reserved but very sweet and considerate. It all came about because of a book club, would you believe?'

'A book club?'

'Yes,' I say with a small laugh. 'It's not a proper club that's open to members or anything, just three friends who get together to discuss a book every few weeks and usually our problems.

It's not something I'd ever thought of doing before but it's been great fun.'

'It does sound like fun. I love reading.' There's a sadness to Emily's tone that I instinctively want to ignore, but I'm not the sort of person who can and before I even consider what Janey might have to say about it, I invite Emily to our next meeting.

'Are you sure?'

'Yes. You're more than welcome.'

I fill her in on how it works and she says she's already read *Little Women* recently and loved it. She can't wait to discuss it. We talk about our children (Emily has two teenaged girls in private school, one doing GCSEs and the other doing her A levels) and life after husbands. To be honest, she seems more concerned with the divorce settlement than losing her soulmate of twenty years to a younger woman, but who am I to judge?

Chapter 33

To my surprise, Mike does turn up on Saturday to pick the kids up. Ralph seems in better spirits about going because Mike has promised that Henry and Ava can spend the afternoon with Kate, whilst he and Ralph head over to the go-karting place. I'm glad they'll get to spend some time together. Ralph really needs it and I'm hoping he'll talk to Mike about how he's feeling about the whole Kate thing.

'I must admit, I didn't expect you to come today – I thought you'd cancel.'

Mike's fighting with folding Henry's pushchair but looks up to frown. 'Why?'

'It's the boys' club trip to the golf club and spa this weekend.'

'Ah yes. That. How do you know?'

'I saw Emily the other day.'

'Oh. Wait, how did *she* know?'

'She knew because she was supposed to be going before her husband switched her out for a slutty secretary.'

Mike's jaw slackens. I don't think he's ever heard me speak that way before. 'Look, Stephanie, the thing with me and Kate is nothing like what Bradley has done.'

My stomach curls. 'Oh God, I know. I'm not saying *you* did

193

that. Just that Bradley is a twat – I've always thought so. I thought maybe you weren't going on principle.'

He rubs his jaw. 'No, well, Kate doesn't really like any of them. She thinks the women are stuck-up and shallow and the men are all tossers.'

'And she's right. I'm beginning to like her.' Ava runs through the hallway and smashes right into my torso. She shouts sorry before darting up the stairs.

'Stop running, Ava,' I call after her. She's looking for a teddy she's desperate to show Kate.

'Kate will come around. They're my friends; I can't avoid them forever.'

'I don't even get why you want to be friends with them. They're all making three times the salary you are and they'll never promote you to board level if that's what you're still hoping for. Not unless one of them dies. I think you're wasting your time trying to keep up.'

'Why do you care?'

As I stumble for an answer, Ralph comes down the stairs. 'Have you got everything you need, love?' I ask him, grateful for the distraction. He nods sullenly.

'Great, well, let's get you all in the car,' I say, clapping my hands together.

Janey calls over in the afternoon unexpectedly. When I open the front door I can tell she's been crying. 'Oh, love, what is it?'

She walks in and heads straight to the kitchen. 'It's Jimmy. After everything he said about the kiss being an accident.' She covers her face with her hands and sobs softly into them.

'Oh no, what happened?'

Removing her hands from her face, she takes a breath. 'He's been on his phone a lot, texting. He's always on there. Usually he's looking at stupid sports cars on Instagram but I could tell something was off by all the typing. Anyway, I'm not proud of this but I snatched his phone off him in anger. He was on the loo but hadn't locked the door. I walked in by accident and saw him tap, tap, tapping away. I saw red and just grabbed it.'

'And he was texting Alex?'

She nods before erupting into heaving sobs. 'Sexting, to be precise.'

'How could he do that to you?' I reach out to comfort her.

'He's not going to treat me like that.' She rubs her sleeve across her cheeks. 'One chance. That's what he had and he's blown it.'

'Good for you. You deserve better, so do the kids.'

'I've given him until next week to find somewhere to live. We'll tell the kids next weekend.' She starts pacing up and down.

'They're stronger than you think.'

'Then there's the financial stuff. I have some inheritance money but I'll have to get a job.'

'You can do that. I'll help.'

'The house? What if I have to move?'

'Take it one step at a time.'

Eventually, she stops and takes a breath. 'I can do this, can't I?'

'Amanda and I will make sure of it.'

She smiles through watery eyes and I pull her into a tight hug. When I feel like she's calmed down, I make some tea and dig out the Mr Kipling cakes from the high cupboard where I hide treats from the kids. We talk about the logistics and eventually she starts joking about being the next Mrs Gosling.

'Anyway,' she says, much chirpier, 'how did those drinks with Emily go?'

'I invited her to join our book club,' I say, braced for incoming.

Her eyes pop. 'You did what?'

'I suppose I felt sorry for her. She's in the same position as I was when you found me sobbing in the supermarket.'

Janey sighs. 'Yes, but you're not an awful human.'

'She showed remorse for that.'

'Fine, well if she has time to squeeze in *Little Women* before next Thursday night so be it. Listen, I have to go. The kids will be back from their clubs soon but if you're bored later, text me.'

After spending the day cleaning the house and weeding the garden, I'm as bored as I am knackered by six o'clock. I'll never for the life of me understand why people like Mrs Hinch and Charlie Dimmock love this stuff! Give me a G&T and a muscly gardener to watch any day of the week. Not one to pass on a good idea, I make myself a G&T and sit out on the patio after showering off the dirt of the day. As I'm admiring my handiwork, my phone buzzes.

The woman next door is having a huge party again! There must be two hundred people there – there are cars parked all the way down the lane.

Before I've even read it, I can see Janey is typing a reply.

That's it. We're going this time.

I key out a reply as quickly as I can.

No! We can't do that.

Janey replies a few seconds later.

Oh, come on, Stephanie, I need this and you were saying the other day that you wanted some excitement in your life. Well, here it is.

Isn't it trespassing? I write.

If someone has a party that size, don't you think they have a moral duty to invite the neighbours? It's common courtesy! Janey adds.

I don't think it is. I type. According to WhatsApp, Amanda is typing a message – good – she'll put an end to this ridiculous idea.

I think we should get our glad rags on and do it!

I have to read the message twice.

Noreen barely knows what day of the week it is. She's

**practically powered by gin. Come on, get ready and be at my
house asap. If she says anything I'll just tell her she invited
me and told me to bring a friend or two.**

I have to double-check but those words definitely came from
Amanda.

Are you both out of your minds? I type.

**I will be if I stay in any longer. Jimmy is here and I need to
get away from him.** Janey writes.

Fine! I type. Hopefully, by the time we get to Amanda's, they'll
have both realised what a terrible idea this is.

When Janey and I arrive at Amanda's, she answers the door
with a giddy 'Come in' and an inner light in her eyes I've never
seen before.

'Okay, I've poured us a glass of Prosecco for Dutch courage.
After that, we'll climb over the wall and slip into the party like
we were meant to be there.'

I accept the drink and guzzle half of the flute before saying
anything. 'Do you think we're dressed for wall climbing?' Amanda
has on a pencil skirt for goodness' sake. I'm wearing a calf-length
sundress and Janey has a floaty maxi-dress on. Thankfully we're
all in flat sandals.

'Oh nonsense, it's part of the fun,' Amanda says, sloshing her
glass around as she does. I can't tell if she's tipsy or giddy with
excitement.

'Can't we just walk up the driveway like the other guests? I mean,
if you're going to tell Noreen that she invited us anyway ...'

Amanda almost reels. 'That's a last-resort plan, Stephanie. I
don't want to lie to Noreen's face. What kind of person do you
think I am?'

I shake my head. I have plenty of new ideas but I don't reply.

'Come on, Stephanie, it'll be a laugh.'

'Fine, let's gate-crash some poor sod's party.'

Twenty minutes later we're standing by the garden wall.

'It's eight feet of solid red brick.' I knew it was high but I didn't quite realise it was this high. It's very pretty in a rustic way. The bricks are all different shades and textures after a hundred years or so of weathering and there's an ivy plant covering part of it. Admiration aside, I can't fathom how we'll climb the damn thing.

'Right, I have this.' Amanda comes struggling across the lawn with a stepladder. 'It's the gardener's. We can use it to climb up and then drop down the other side. It's not as high Noreen's side because of the hill.'

I sigh. 'After you.'

Amanda takes the lead. The ladder creaks and wobbles as she climbs it and Janey holds it to keep it steady. When she's at the top, Amanda hitches up her skirt so she can climb from the ladder to the wall, then swings her body around and slides off. It's all rather seamless.

'There's nobody around this area,' Amanda shout-whispers from the other side.

'I'll go,' Janey says, already ascending the ladder. It wobbles and I grab it.

'Thanks,' she whispers.

'Hang on,' I say as she's climbing across to the wall. 'Who's going to hold the ladder for me?'

Janey doesn't hear me as she's already flung herself over to the other side. A rational person would, at this point, go home. There is so much emphasis on peer pressure among teens but nobody ever talks about peer pressure in book club circles. Granted, the number of affected victims could probably fit on a unicycle, but still, we exist and we matter.

'Come on,' one of them shouts in a hushed tone from the other side.

I don't want to do this. I really don't but I know I'm about to. 'All right, I'm coming.'

I reposition the ladder and give it a shake. It seems sturdy enough. I reach halfway without incident but as I step on the higher rungs (or are they called steps on a stepladder? It seems like they should be) it starts to wobble. It's the kind of wobble that could gain momentum if I'm not careful, so I stop still and wait for it to die down. When it's steady again, I breathe a sigh of relief and climb to the top platform as carefully as possible. There's only a foot or so between the ladder and the wall – thanks to a well-stocked flowerbed it can't be put right next to the wall. I stretch my left leg across the gap and my left arm and start to shift my weight over with my limbs. As I do so, the ladder wobbles and that momentum I was talking about kicks in. It does a couple of violent sways from left to right and falls. My body crashes into the wall and I'm left clinging on with my arm and leg like a demented koala bear whilst my face grazes the bricks. Somehow, I manage to clutch the top with my right arm too and pull myself up so I'm lying flat, face-down, atop – clinging on for dear life.

'What happened?' Janey asks.

'The ladder fell.'

'Are you all right?' Amanda asks.

'I think so. A few cuts and bruises perhaps.'

'Come on, you just need to drop down now,' Janey says.

The fall is only about five feet on Noreen's side but it's surprising how high it looks from here. 'Okay, I'm coming.'

I force both legs over and drop down with a thud before standing up and dusting my dress down.

'Oh God,' Janey says catching sight of me.

I frown. 'What?'

'Your face! Here.' She passes me her small compact mirror. I take a look – there's a dirty graze on my cheek.

'Dab it with this.' She passes me a wet wipe. 'Then cover it with this.' Then a concealer.

'Anything else in there, Mary Poppins?' I ask.

'As a matter of fact, yes, Alka-Seltzer so be nice because you might need one later.'

There's some kind of chirpy quartet music coming from around the other side of the house and the sound of chatter and laughter carries over it. Where we are is a grassy area with lots of mature trees dotted about. It's a bit like an orchard.

'Come on, the party is in the main garden around the other side,' Amanda says.

'How the other half live,' I whisper to Janey.

'I know – *main* garden? I barely even have a subsidiary garden.'

As we round the corner of the big house, we all stop dead. The sight is quite something and brazenly walking over to join in is wrong on so many levels. There are fire-eaters, unicyclists, waiters carrying posh nibbles and flutes of fizz. On the far side, there's a marquee where the music is coming from and amidst it all there are a few hundred people.

'She might be bonkers but Noreen knows how to throw a garden party,' Amanda says. 'Come on, let's grab a drink.'

Before I can stop her, she's making a beeline for the nearest waiter and Janey isn't far behind. I have no choice but to follow suit.

'Cheers, ladies.' Amanda raises her glass and Janey and I clink against it. We find an elegantly decorated table to sit at and as we do, a waiter offers us each a mini Welsh rarebit. It's divine.

'See, this is better than sipping gin on your own and eating some sort of freezer surprise,' Janey says, and I have to agree.

By the time we're on our third glass of champers, I've completely forgotten that we're not supposed to be here and have had a dance with an old fellow and a chat to someone's aunty. It's like being at a wedding – you don't know half the people there either. As I'm tucking into some sort of mini cheesecake, someone starts vigorously banging a metal spoon against a glass. It's Noreen. I freeze.

'I just wanted to say a few words. I want to thank you all for being here at my fifty-fifth birthday bash. I know some of you were lucky enough to attend my party a few weeks ago to celebrate the launch of my new business, "Fat Melt". She cups her hand to her mouth in an over-animated way. 'See me later if you want to know more. It's just a few fat-dissolving injections to have you looking your best.' Noreen does a twirl and gestures to her stick-thin self.

'Eugh, she looks unhappy,' Janey says. 'I quite like my wobbly bits.'

I smile. It's one of the reasons I've come to love her.

'I know, I know, I look amazing but my years of personal trainers, yoga and diets just weren't enough. Fat Melt is what's given me this body. Anyway, we're not here to talk business.' She cups her mouth again. 'But seriously, ladies, see me later.' Then she winks. 'We're here to celebrate my fifty-five years young.'

There are warm ahh sounds from the crowd. 'Thank you all for your gifts – I hope they're good as I'm really spoiling you all tonight.' She winks. 'Anyway, I'm sure you could listen to me all night but I need a drink so have fun.'

Janey fakes vomiting. 'If I lived next door to her, I'd nuke my own house just to ensure she was collateral damage.'

Amanda snorts with laughter. 'She's not a bad person, just very self-centred.'

'Now I see why she drinks so much gin. Imagine waking up tomorrow morning realising you'd said all that bollocks to all these people?' Janey says.

'I must admit, I feel better about gate-crashing her party now I know what kind of person she is,' I concede. 'Now, where's the hot waiter with the mini cheese-on-toasts?'

As the daylight fades and the fairy lights begin to twinkle, the evening is one of dancing, laughter and carefree fun. Janey doesn't tell Amanda about the whole Jimmy situation and I sense it's because she just wants a night of carefree fun with her friends – Amanda must too as she doesn't ask. We leave via the driveway and Noreen is too busy talking about her size 6 wardrobe to pay anyone the blindest bit of attention, so our little appearance goes unnoticed.

I'm so buzzed when we leave that I hardly notice how dark it's got.

A little bit of excitement wasn't so bad after all.

Chapter 34

After the party, the week that followed was fairly uneventful and Saturday comes around again quite quickly. Mike and Ralph seemed to bond over the go-karts so Mike has decided to take him again this weekend and meet Kate, Ava and Henry at Pizza Hut for tea. Ralph is still quiet about the whole thing but he hasn't complained either. Maybe he is coming around. With very little to do, I grab Otis and decide to go for a long walk.

We walk down to the river. The grassy banks are overgrown and it's an effort to stomp along. I keep going though as the exercise won't do me any harm. Before I know how far I've walked, I find myself at the pub at Crinkly. I get a brief flashback to sitting there with Edward a few weeks ago and it seems a lifetime ago now. My stomach rumbles in protest at the lack of sustenance so I decide to treat myself to a steak pasty from the bakery. I cross the road from the river and tie Otis to a lamppost outside before joining the queue. I'm so hungry, I ask for a vanilla slice and a coffee too. As I'm crossing back towards the river, a familiar voice calls my name. Despite the warm sunny day, I get a shiver down my spine. For a moment, I consider carrying on and pretending I didn't hear but that would be too obvious so I turn around.

'Hi,' I say. Edward is wearing slim, fitted black jeans with brown leather boots and a white All Saints T-shirt. His hair isn't styled in its usual full-bodied side-parted way but rather rumpled and natural. It's always weird seeing him in his non-vet clothes and it does something peculiar to my lower abdomen. It's like he's two different people, in the same way Superman was never recognised as being Clark Kent. Or was he? I haven't watched it since the Eighties. I suppose what I'm trying to say is, he's hot in the tweed, but even hotter without it.

'Picnic for one?' he asks pointing to my bakery spoils.

I smile sheepishly. 'You caught me. I was walking by the river and didn't realise I'd got all the way to Crinkly.'

'It's a nice day for it. I was just going to treat myself to a chicken salad sandwich but that pasty smells so good.'

'Eyes off!' I pretend to hide it away and he laughs. I'm glad we're able to talk normally again after the awkward incident last week. 'I'm going to eat this on the riverbank if you want to join me?'

'I've just been in the practice but have finished now and was going to eat mine walking home but I prefer your idea. I'll meet you over there in a minute.'

I go and sit down whilst Edward heads into the bakery. It seems natural to sit here and have lunch with him and I can't deny I enjoy his company. As long as nobody mentions feelings or kissing or attraction, it will be fine.

'I'll have to live in scrubs if I keep going in that bakery as nothing else will fit me.'

'It will be worth it,' I say, biting into the flaky pastry and tender steak chunks in a scrumptiously rich gravy.

He asks about the kids, particularly Ralph, which I think is sweet because he knows how worried I've been and as I fill him in, he reassures me that I'm doing a good job. I'm glad we can still talk this way.

'Did you sort your Stacy problem out?' I thought it was polite to ask but the question sounds loaded when it comes out.

He nods until he finishes chewing. 'Yes. I have no idea if she took any of it in. I told her I didn't see her in a romantic way but valued her friendship.'

'That's good. Why don't you think she accepted it?'

'Because her reply was, and I quote, "We'll see about that".'

I laugh. She's a woman who knows what she wants. 'What about the unpaid vet's bills?'

'I've left it. It's my own fault for not being more on the ball. Charging thirty quid as and when she uses the service is one thing, but she owes a few hundred now and I can't do that to her. From now on though, we charge her and I'll make sure she's clear on it before I even look at her devitalised rabbit.'

I splutter my coffee. 'Devitalised rabbit? That sounds like a terrible euphemism.'

'Does it? Oh Jesus, thanks for that mental image.' He puts his head in his hands.

'Sorry. Throwback from an Ann Summers party in the early Noughties where the host had run out of batteries.'

Edward is taking a sip of coffee and splutters. I don't apologise because it isn't just me blurring the lines.

A family of ducks swim past. One little yellow duckling at the back keeps going off course and the mother has to keep nudging it back into line.

I point to them. 'Growing up, all I ever wanted was the perfect family. A mum, a dad and a brother or sister. Look how happy those ducks are – they have everything I ever wanted.'

'I'm sorry. Obviously I know about your mum but didn't know you didn't have all the rest.'

I draw a breath. Explaining this will go some way towards explaining why I am the way I am. 'Obviously, you know my mum died when I was very young. She and Dad hadn't gotten around to having any more children so after she'd gone, it was just me and him. Dad was a long-distance lorry driver and so he was on the road a lot, which meant I spent a lot of time with my gran. She was lovely and sweet but it was lonely there, just her and me. I grew up wanting a bigger family for myself, hence the three children, and for a while, I had it. My marriage ending wasn't a surprise – there was no romance, no spark – but we were a family unit and I'd wanted that my whole life.'

'I'm sorry, Steph,' he says sombrely. 'The divorce must have been tough.'

'It was but my biggest fear is my kids growing up feeling like I did, with something missing from their lives. Now Mike has moved on, I need to be *the* family unit.'

Edward tilts his head to the side and the sun catches his face, illuminating his Mediterranean blue eyes. 'Ahh ... I see where this is going.'

'It's not that I didn't want to kiss you.' I look down and fiddle with my coffee cup. 'Or that I'm not attracted to you. It's that I have to put my kids first.'

'I understand.' He leans in a little closer so his cool breath brushes my neck. 'But you can't do that forever.'

'I know. Maybe if I knew it was serious, I'd take a risk but I can't upset them over someone I hardly know.'

'So, how about we spend more time getting to know one another?'

That doesn't sound like a bad idea. I can't deny that I want to spend time with Edward.

'What about the other problem? The *you're my boss* problem?'

'I think the solution is the same.'

I ponder this. Is it the same? If we're not meant to be, can we go back to the way things were? If we are meant to be, can we work together? I guess there's only one way to find out. 'Okay, what do you have in mind?'

'Maybe a few dates. We could do it when the kids are with Mike so they don't wonder where you're going and you don't have to tell them. If we decide we don't want to carry on, no harm done but if we really like spending time together, we reassess the situation.' He lies back on the grass and rests his head on his arms whilst I think about it for a minute. His long body stretches the width of the broad grassy bank. His T-shirt has ridden up a little, revealing a small sprinkling of dark hair from his navel to his waistband and beyond. For a second, I imagine what it would be like to run my hand along his taut abdomen.

'Okay, what do you have in mind?'

'There's a pop-up cinema experience going on in Manchester. It's a seaside theme and you sit in deckchairs and eat cockles with a toothpick plus there will be doughnuts and sticks of rock. I think the movie is *Jaws*. How about that?'

'It sounds perfect! I love the cinema and haven't seen *Jaws* since I was a kid and it terrified me.'

'Great, I'll get us some tickets for next Saturday.'

'Will you be able to take the time off from being on call?'

'I'll make a special effort to book the whole day off.'

My insides clench with excitement.

Chapter 35

Monday and Tuesday pass without a hitch. Everyone is breakfasted and deposited at their relevant institutions in good time. I even manage to make myself a healthy packed lunch on both days and Mike reckoned that he made some good progress with Ralph – apparently, he let Kate take him to the arcade. Life is generally as it should be.

'You're in a good mood today,' Carly says. I realise I've been whistling the theme song from *The Greatest Showman* for the best part of five minutes.

'The sun is shining; Mrs Pearson left some oat and raisin cookies in the kitchen. What's not to be happy about?'

Carly shrugs and gets back to whatever she's doing. Obviously, I've told nobody about the date Edward and I have planned. I haven't even told Janey or Amanda. Until I know what's going on between us, I don't want it to be a thing I have to explain to anyone, or actively have to hide from the children.

As I bite into my second cookie, the door jingles open and a kaleidoscope of pink enters. It's Stacy in all her salmon-flushed glory. I'm in no doubt that her skin-tight, low-cut dress is intended to impress and her pink strappy heels could probably pass for beginner stilts. I can't imagine going to all that effort to traipse around Crinkly on a Wednesday lunchtime. Each to their own I suppose.

'Ms Dalton?' I say, scanning the appointments diary.

She leans over the desk. 'Oh, don't worry about that. I don't have an appointment.'

'Ahh,' I say. This is awkward. 'Dr Prescott is fully booked today. I can look through his availability for tomorrow if you'd like?'

She laughs as if I've done something really silly. Whatever the joke was, I missed it.

'I'm here to have lunch with Eddy. I know he always breaks off around this time for something to eat. He's a creature of habit that one. Anyway, I've brought him some quiche from the bakery. Could you fetch him?'

'Carly, do you mind popping in to ask Dr Prescott if he's okay to step out? I need to make a call.' I don't want to get in the middle of this and I pick up the phone before giving her a pointed look. She raises her eyebrows at my newfound and very misplaced sense of authority but she'll get over it.

A few moments later, Edward emerges in a clean set of scrubs. When he spots Stacy, his body stiffens. 'Is everything all right with Fluffy?'

Fluffy?

Stacy waves a dismissive hand. 'Oh, she's fine. I've brought you some lunch – a hardworking man like you has to eat. And that's what friends do for one another.' She winks animatedly. I drop my head and pretend to work on something engaging but Carly can't help herself – she might as well grab a tub of popcorn.

'I, er, Stacy, that's very thoughtful of you but you know how my job is really important, like, life-or-death important?'

She nods.

'Well …' He gestures to his scrubs. 'I'm in the middle of one of those life-or-death problems.'

I glance at the diary. He has a dachshund in for a jab – it's hardly a grand-finale-Turner-and-Hooch situation.

'I love what you do,' she gushes as she places a picnic basket on the counter. 'I'm going to leave this here so you can eat when you're ready but I will need my hamper back. Drop it off when you get a break from saving the world one doggy at a time.'

She doesn't even wait for a reply before gliding out the door.

'I'll pop this in the fridge,' Carly says, taking the hamper to the kitchen.

'She's good,' I say once Carly is out of earshot.

'What do I do?' he says with a forced laugh. 'If I don't laugh, I'll cry!'

I shrug. 'I don't know. She's got more balls than Lancelot the lottery draw machine.'

'Seriously help me!'

'You could just marry her and have done with it,' I say.

'Oh don't.' His eyes sparkle with mirth despite his predicament. 'Just talk to her again.'

'Do you really think she'll listen?'

I don't need to ponder this. 'No. You could try being less Mr Nice Guy and more direct. Be firm.'

He leans on the counter and taps his forehead against it.

'Maybe she needs a new focus. A new object of her affections, so to speak,' I say.

'I'm listening, tell me more.'

'Well, no offence, but I don't think it's you she necessarily wants. I think she's lonely and you're the most eligible bachelor in the village.'

'You've got a funny way of saying I'm handsome and charming.'

I roll my eyes. 'Modest too.'

'Jokes aside, you might be on to something. She's already been after the village doctor and dentist but now they've settled down and married, they're out of the picture.' He pauses. 'Hang on, that means I'm her third choice. I have a good mind to keep that hamper as compensation.'

'Oh come off it. You're not seriously insulted – you don't wear nearly enough pink to grab a top spot on Stacy's list. Come on – who are the eligible bachelors of the village?'

'Eligible bachelors? For you?' Carly appears in the doorway.

'Oh no, for Stacy, not me,' I say a little too quickly.

'I've heard that Dave the pub landlord signed up for online dating. He must be over his wife leaving him now, it has been a good three years now,' Carly says with a shrug.

'Dave's all right looking,' Edward says earning himself two pairs of jack-in-a-box eyebrows. 'I can notice these things.'

'He's not exactly the qualified professional she normally goes for, but it could work,' I say.

'She's always flirting with him in the pub,' Edward adds.

I think we need to plant some seeds.

Chapter 36

On Thursday lunchtime, Edward announces he has to pop down to Crookney Farm and asks if I'd like to go. He said it would be good to put the clients' faces and names together to have a better relationship. I thought it was a little odd but Carly didn't bat an eyelid.

When we arrive, I'm utterly charmed. The large, rustic, red-brick house stands proud in the endless, flat fields around. There are several outbuildings built from either brick, wood or corrugated steel. Black and white cows graze lazily in the field to my right whilst the other fields beyond are filled with crops of some description. We drive past the house and pull up by a wooden stable.

'I need to look in on one of the horses. She had an op recently and I said I'd check her over.'

I nod but stay seated. I might as well wait in the warm.

That idea is short-lived when Edward swings my door open. 'Well? Are you coming?'

I follow him into the barn. The smell of hay and horse manure is strong and I cover my nose.

Edward laughs. 'That's the smell of the countryside.'

The farmer greets us. He's a ruddy-looking man who evidently spends much of his time outdoors. He's to the point but polite with it. 'So, what do you think, Doc? Glue factory?'

'Oh no. She's got plenty of mileage in her yet,' Edward replies, patting the brown mare on the side of her face.

'You going for a ride?' the farmer asks. I expect Edward to politely decline so when he says we'd love to, my jaw hits the floor.

'Edward, I can't ride,' I say nervously.

'I can.' He winks. The farmer brings out a white horse and sorts out the tack before placing a little stool by the side of her.

'You can ride with me,' Edward says, shrugging off his jacket and climbing on.

Oh God. 'I don't know about this.'

'Come on. If you hate it, I'll let you get off.'

Something about the idea of clinging to his firm body for dear life entices me.

'Okay. I'll do it.' The farmer helps me on. Even with the foot-stool and the farmer's burly strength, I struggle but once I'm up there and my arms are around Edward's strong torso, I feel safe.

The hind of the horse sways from side to side as Edward guides her towards the bridle path that cuts through the farm. The fresh scent of his aftershave lingers on the breeze. I pull myself in towards him and I'm not sure if it's purely for safety or to inhale the scent of him.

'Edward?' I ask after a while. 'What are we doing?'

His shoulders vibrate gently with soft laughter. 'If I said horse riding, you'd think I was a sarcastic idiot wouldn't you?'

'Yes.'

'Okay, what about if I said I couldn't wait until Saturday to spend time with you?'

My insides squeeze pleasantly. 'Then that would be okay.'

The path leads us to a small brook and Edward pulls the horse to a stop. 'Where did you learn to ride?'

'My mum signed me up for lessons when I was a kid. I don't

do it much anymore but Kev, the farmer, likes me to ride Orla here because it's his wife's horse and she has health issues and can't always get out on her.'

'There you go again, always doing things for others.'

'I think most people would if they had the time. I don't have much else going on aside from work. Let's take a walk. I'll keep her steady whilst you climb down.' He gives me some instructions about using the stirrup but when I kick my leg around the back the momentum is too much and I find myself sliding off.

'Edward!' I scream, trying to grab a hold of the seat but my fingers can't get purchase and instead, I find myself in a heap on the ground.

'Steph? Are you okay?' Edward is off the horse and by my side in a flash. I can't help giggling. Yes, giggling like a fifteen-year-old who's just found out the school heartthrob scribbled her name in a love heart on the toilet wall.

He tethers the horse to a tree and she starts grazing on the grass. As we walk along the uneven ground by the brook, the warm early-summer sun beats down on us. The metallic smell of the brook and the fresh grassy scent is as wonderful as the cool breeze. Suddenly, Edward stops.

'I wanted to bring you here, to my favourite spot. Look at how the land stretches on for miles until it meets those hills in the distance. On a day like today, where the sky is an uninterrupted blue and you can see such a distance it gives me space to breathe if you know what I mean.'

Perhaps this is Edward's version of me hiding in the loo for some peace and quiet. 'Yes.'

Golden beams of sunlight streak across the hills, coating the trees and everything else in their path. It's a lovely spot. We sit down and just take it in for a while. The breeze plays with the ends of my hair, eventually lifting the strands and pulling them across my face. Before I react, Edward reaches up and tucks it behind my ear. I get a pleasant fizz in my stomach and then, gently, he turns my head to face him and moves an inch closer. The warm air is thick with tension. I respond, closing the distance and our lips touch, hot and wanting.

My phone buzzes in my pocket with violent impatience.

'Oh no. I'm sorry.' I pull away, breathy, and check my phone.

'It's Mike?' I give Edward an apologetic glance but he gestures for me to answer.

'Stephanie, Ava had an accident at school. I'm on my way to get her. The school office said she's okay but may need to go to A & E. I don't have any other details but you need to get to us sharpish.'

'Oh God. Of course. I'll see you at the hospital.'

When I hang up, Edward is already pulling me back towards the horse.

When I get to A & E, Mike is in the waiting room with a blood-soaked Ava.

'Oh, my darling girl, what happened?' I fall to my knees in front of her.

'I was playing tig and jumped on the wall near the fence to try and get away from Jordon Fray but my foot slipped and I banged my face.'

I take her face in my hands and inspect the damage. Her lip is split and there is a deep wound above her eyebrow but otherwise, she seems okay. I hug her and slide into the seat next to Mike.

'Thank you for being there,' I whisper.

'No problem. The school said they called you first but it went straight to your answerphone.'

I swallow. Never has a ball of guilt felt so big. 'I … er went out to a farm. It's one of our clients. The phone reception was hit and miss.'

Mike accepts that but for the rest of the evening, I feel terrible. The hospital glue Ava's wounds and give her a teddy sporting the same dressings as the ones they put on her. She can't wait to tell her friends all about her drama tomorrow.

All I can think of is how stupid I was. Out there living so carefree when my daughter needed me. I knew getting involved with Edward was a bad idea.

Chapter 37

When Saturday comes I wave the kids off with Mike and spend the next few hours on the verge of hyperventilation. I'd tried (pathetically) to cancel the date but every time I typed the excuse-riddled message, I deleted it. Deep down I must really want to go. Besides, I know the kids are safe today; they're with their dad. After much toing and froing, I concluded that I should go on the date. Edward is so easy to be around, I don't know why I'm almost rigid with fear at the thought of going to watch a film with him. Granted, I haven't really dated. Being a Nineties teen growing up around Manchester, I never met the sort of boys who 'took you out' on a date. It was more group nights out with friends I got invited along to and by the time Mike and I went on our first dinner out together, we were already an item.

Don't get me wrong, I love the concept. It's romantic and a great way to see if someone is a noisy eater before your heart gets the better of you; however, in this case, I'm scared witless. I can't even enlist the moral support of Janey and her no-nonsense approach to getting on with it because I still don't want anyone to know. I've told her I'm meeting Emily again tonight. I feel terrible for lying but it's temporary and I'll come clean. Eventually.

In order to make an effort, I even put on some fake tan – the sort you sleep in and wash off the next day – but to be honest I wish I hadn't. Despite a good scrub in the shower, I still look and smell like a Wotsit. I lather on some perfumed body lotion to mask it and settle on wearing a strappy linen sundress. It's white with small, red polka dots on and comes just past the knee. It's cute without looking like I'm making too much of an effort. I panic-bought it off Facebook of all places as soon as the date was agreed and it arrived just in the nick of time.

I've used an old wand to wave my hair and now the curls have cooled, I'm running my fingers through to create a looser wave. Once my light make-up is done, I try on some heels, but my feet hurt as soon as I step into them so I settle for some light-tan leather sandals that are flat and much more comfortable.

I'm meeting Edward in the city centre. He had some things to sort out with his day off and I'm going on the tram and meeting him at Victoria station. People swarm the concourse. I fight my way through the throngs of shoppers, concert fans, theatregoers and early revellers. It's a ten-minute walk down Deansgate and a right turn before I'm at the place we'd agreed to meet outside but I can't see him. I glance at my watch. He must be running late. I lean against the wall and watch other people – couples, groups of friends and so on – pour inside. After ten minutes, I spot Edward approaching. It's busy and he hasn't noticed me yet so I let my eyes linger and drink in the sight of him a moment. He's wearing navy chino shorts and a white linen shirt with brown loafers. Seeing him in his casual clothes never fails to take my breath away but I like the tweed too.

'Hi,' I say coyly once he's close enough.

'Steph, you look …' he gives me the once-over with his eyes '… beautiful.'

'Thanks.' Heat rises up the back of my neck. 'You don't look too bad yourself.'

'I'm so sorry I'm late. Mrs Pearson rang and I had to check in on Ruby on my way.'

I wave my hand dismissively. 'It's not a problem. The film hasn't even started yet.'

'Shall we?' He places his hand on the small of my back and guides me towards the door. My skin tingles deliciously beneath his touch. The building is an old hall of some sort. A large open space with a balcony around the edge and a stage at the front. It's painted in a rich, deep red, and ornate gold patterns punctuate the cream woodwork. The floor space has been filled with sand and colourful striped deckchairs are lined up in rows facing a large projector screen that covers the stage. It's showing the promo poster for *Jaws*. We get a pint of lager from the 'beach bar' at the back of the hall and go to find our seats.

'It still terrifies me even now,' I say, pointing at the poster as we shuffle down the row and take our deckchairs.

'Tell me about it. I was scared to get into a swimming pool for years after seeing this. I'm hoping my adult rationale will stand me in good stead today.'

An usher comes around handing out pots of cockles. 'I haven't had these for years.' They're very moreish. As we tuck in, the opening credits start and the room falls dark and silent. I'm trying to concentrate on the film, really I am, but I'm so aware of Edward's body just a few inches away. I want an excuse to touch him but juggling the cockles and beer makes it (thankfully) impossible.

As the city officials refuse to close the beach and Sheriff Brody is patrolling, the movie stops and the lights come on. A fifteen-minute interval is announced.

'Fancy an ice cream?' Edward asks.

'It would be rude not to.'

There's a vintage ice-cream van parked in the back corner that I hadn't noticed when we came in. There's even a fish and chips stand, a counter selling sticks of rock and a couple of those coconut shy stalls.

'I'll get the next round in and see you back at the seats,' I say leaving Edward at the ice-cream van.

He returns carrying two cones with raspberry sauce drizzled on.

'Yum. Gimme.' I make grabby hands. 'This is perfect, thank you, Edward.'

'It's perfect because you're here,' he says with intent. My chest feels light with giddiness. There's a gentle buzz of excited chatter in the air and the beer has given me a heady feeling but even now, here with Edward, everything is underpinned by a feeling that we're complicating things beyond our means. He cups my face with his free hand and kisses me on the cheek.

The feeling lingers even after he pulls away. Before I have chance to respond, the lights fade and the music starts to play. The deckchairs don't make it easy to hold hands or anything like that but they're close enough I can rest my head on Edward's shoulder. I'm not sure if it's a bit much for a first date but the beer gives me a boldness I don't usually have. I hold my breath as I do so and exhale softly when Edward rests his head on mine. For the next hour, I stay in the same position, not daring enough to move. It's the first affectionate contact I've had in a long time and I don't want it to end. By the time the film finishes, my entire right-hand side is as numb as a block of wood.

As the lights come on, it's Edward who shifts gently. He slides his shoulder from under my head and turns to face me. 'This has been great fun but I don't feel like we got to spend much time together and it is our first official date. How about a drink? If it's still nice out I know a great bar with loads of outside seating.'

I fizz with excitement because I don't want the night to end yet either. 'Sounds wonderful.'

It's a short walk under the early evening sun. As our arms swing in time with our steps, Edward's fingers graze mine. It happens a few times until he takes hold of my hand. Now we're walking hand in hand like it's the most natural thing in the world if you ignore the crazy stomach-fluttering I have going on.

'We're here,' he says, gesturing to the bar. He wasn't kidding about the large outdoor seating area. There's an energetic buzz of chatter and it sort of looks like Oktoberfest but with less lederhosen and dirndls and more Abercrombie and Fitch.

I order a glass of rosé because I've reached 'peak beer'. If I have any more I'll be effervescent, to say the least. The tables are all long wooden benches with tall stools. I manage to find two stools next to one another so climb onto one and put my bag on the other. It's a squeeze but it doesn't matter. I check my phone and there's just a message from Janey asking if my drinks with Emily are going okay. I get a pang of guilt over lying to her but I'm not ready to talk about this yet. It's too new; too fragile.

'I got you a large because the bar was four people deep.' Edward has a bag of dry-roasted peanuts in his mouth so his words are all through gritted teeth.

'Okay.' I clench my own teeth and mimic him.

'Hey, if you carry on you're not getting your hands on my nuts!' He says it so loud a few people turn.

'Edward!' I hiss, as my cheeks flush.

'It's okay, there's not a bloke here who doesn't want his nuts handling.'

'Right! That's enough.' I give him a mock-stern glare.

'Sorry, you started it. Anyway, would you like a *peanut*?'

'I would, thank you.' I tear open the bag and split the side so we can share easily.

There's a vibrating sound and Edward takes his phone out of his pocket and glances at the screen before shoving it back in his pocket.

'You can answer it. I don't mind.'

'*I* mind. It's Stacy. She's already sent me three text messages asking if I want to meet up. She's exhausted the meal, drinks, walk scenarios so she's probably ringing to suggest a joint bungee jump or something.'

'That could be fun,' I say diplomatically.

Edward rolls his eyes. 'Don't encourage this; in fact … I'm going to tell her I'm on a date.'

I freeze. 'Don't tell her who you're with. Please.'

'All right. I'm not that embarrassing, am I?' He laughs but I want to make sure I haven't hurt his feelings.

'I just haven't told anyone about this. Not until I know what we're doing.'

He nods in agreement. 'That's fair.'

'And besides that, I've seen *Fatal Attraction* and Stacy has a rabbit and … I just don't know what she's capable of.'

'Hmm, well …' He laughs. 'No, she's a sweet person really. A salt-of-the-earth type who's probably just too big a character for the village of Crinkly so people don't understand her.'

I sip my wine to swallow down the guilt I'm feeling. 'Ahh, you're right. I feel awful now – I was only joking about the *Fatal Attraction* thing.'

'I know. Don't feel bad. I'm the one who should feel bad. I thought I was helping by spending time with her. I gave her a space to be herself when the village wrote her off as "wacky"; now she's developed this misplaced crush on me or whatever.' Edward's cheeks colour. He's practically squirming at the discomfort of someone liking him. It makes me all the more attracted to him.

'That's a really sweet thing to have done,' I say, covering his hand with mine. 'I can see why she likes you so much.'

'Yeah, well … I put a word in with Dave at the bar and he's thinking of asking her out. I can tell she likes him and it turns out he's had a massive crush on her for a while so perhaps I've been standing in the way of them all this time.' His eyes crinkle at the corners as he laughs softly.

'You're a good man.'

He looks me in the eyes and leans towards me, slowly, his face stopping inches away from mine. The fresh scent of the aftershave on his skin hits me as I close the distance, pressing my lips against his. They're cool from the beer glass.

'I could do that all day,' Edward says, resting his forehead on mine. 'It's even better when you don't run away after.'

I bat him playfully on the leg. 'Hey, I wore flat shoes for a reason.'

'Please don't leave me here. That big bloke over there keeps looking at me.'

I glance around to humour him. I thought Edward was joking but there's a redheaded mountain of a man on the next table who is, in fact, staring at Edward.

'What did you do, put his iguana to sleep? He looks like he wants to kill you.'

'I know. I think I knocked into him at the bar – I said sorry. Can we go?' There's humour in his tone still but I can sense an underlying nervousness and nod.

'Drink up then.' It's starting to spit with rain anyway. The evening is still warm and most punters are undeterred but this is Manchester – a downpour could be imminent.

A few minutes later and right on cue, there's a roar of thunder and the heavens open but even this doesn't deter the look of hate from Edward's new enemy. We make a speedy exit running hand in hand whilst I hold my cardigan above my head. When we're out of the bar's outdoor seating area Edward stops and starts laughing. 'God, I've never felt so uncomfortable.'

He pulls me into his body. His shirt is cold and wet from the rain; every nerve ending under my warm skin reacts individually. Gently, he runs his hand through my soggy hair, tucking it behind my ear, then places his finger beneath my chin, tilting my head gently so that my mouth meets his. We fall into a blissful rhythm, exploring each other's mouths. He runs his hands down the skin of my arms as raindrops continue to pelt us. After a few moments, he pulls away, popping our little private bubble.

'You're freezing! I'm a terrible date – I don't even have a jacket to give you. Come on, I'll get you home.'

To be honest, I could have withstood the cold, as the heat raging through the inside of my body kept the cold on the surface of my skin. Now we've stopped kissing, it's seeping in and I start to shiver. I let Edward lead me to the road where some black taxis are lined up and I think he's going to ask for the station but instead he gives an address in Crinkly. I look at him, surprised.

He holds his hands up. 'Only if you want to? It's still early and I thought we could have a warm drink and dry off. I can drop you home if you prefer?'

I shake my head. Seeing Edward's house is strangely appealing. Despite all the time we've spent together, he is still an enigma to me and I definitely don't want this night to end.

Chapter 38

The cab pulls up outside a gorgeous rust-brick cottage. In the dusky light, I can just about make out that there's nothing but open fields and the odd tree around. A low, brick wall wraps the front garden and there's a green wooden gate leading to a path that cuts across the large front lawn and leads up to the front door. He pays the cab driver and opens the door, holding out a hand to help me out.

'Is this your house?' I ask, not even trying to conceal my awe. Houses aren't exactly cheap in this part of Cheshire and without stereotyping, I'd guessed by his battered old Ford Focus and the dated décor at the vet's that the practice wasn't as lucrative as one might expect.

'No, I just thought we'd try the door and see if we can sneak in.'

'Funny,' I say drily.

'Sorry. Yes, it's mine – it was my mum and dad's house. I grew up here but Mum died and then it was just me and Dad for some time. I did live in a rental for a while but when Dad died I inherited this place. I've not done much to it.' He unlocks the door, which is painted the same green as the gate, and gestures for me to go in.

The hallway is cream with an oak floor. There are oak doors leading off in three directions: left, right and straight ahead.

'Head straight down the hall to the kitchen,' he says. His fingers work the buttons on his shirt and I can't help but let my eyes linger a tiny bit too long. His torso is pale and firm-looking with a fine sprinkling of hair, darkening towards his navel. He glances up and catches me looking and I turn my head away so fast I crick my neck but not before I notice the smile playing on his lips.

'Shall I make us a drink?' I ask, making my way to the kitchen.

'Please, I'll have a coffee – everything you need is near the kettle.'

The kitchen is a country-style. The solid wooden cupboards and marble counters look built to last. The entire kitchen is spotless and he doesn't even have a pile of pots in the sink or on the drainer. There are three labelled jars by the kettle; one each for sugar, tea and coffee. I fill the kettle and wait for it to boil. The room is a large space with a slate-grey tiled floor, an island in the centre and a big wooden kitchen table on the other side. There's an oversized clock on the wall by the table and double French doors to the right leading into the night.

'I brought you some dry clothes if you want them.' Edward is leaning in the doorway. He's towel-dried his wet hair and it's darting off in all directions. He's thrown on black joggers and a plain white T-shirt; in his hand are some novelty Christmas pyjamas.

'Sorry, I'm not being presumptuous,' he says. 'Your dress is wet. I mean, you're welcome to stay over. I have a guest room but I'm happy to call you a cab if that's what you want.'

'The pyjamas are great, thank you.' I walk over and take them from him and kiss him gently on the cheek. He points me in the direction of the downstairs loo, just off the hallway. As I'm heading there, I pause.

'Edward, there's something I've not told you about me.' I glance down at my hands, clutching the pyjamas tightly.

He frowns in a way that makes him look worried.

'It's embarrassing more than anything.'

'You can tell me anything.' He walks over and places his hands on my shoulders.

I pause. There's no easy way to tell someone something like this. I glance at the French doors – the blackness intensifying. The thought of having to make my way home now it's so dark makes me feel faint. When I look back at Edward, he's waiting with patience. 'I …' I get no further. He doesn't prompt me; instead his eyes search mine with imploring sincerity, putting me at ease. 'Okay. The thing is, ever since I lost my mum, I've been scared of going out in the dark.'

His Adam's apple bobs and he squeezes my shoulders gently. 'That's nothing to be embarrassed of. You'd been through unimaginable trauma.'

'I know. But still.' I swallow back rising emotion. 'It's consuming sometimes, the fear I mean. I carry a personal alarm with me everywhere I go. I can just about cope with a taxi ride home from Manchester if it's not too late and roads are busy but the thought of getting a cab home from this house in the middle of nowhere at this time terrifies me.'

He hugs me tight against his body. 'Oh, Steph. Stay the night. I won't try any funny business and I'll drop you off home in the morning or I'll take a cab with you and come home. Whatever you want to do is fine with me. I want you to feel safe.'

I stare into his eyes and I believe him. I do feel safe.

It's a relief to peel off the soggy dress in the cramped down-stairs toilet. The linen has gone stiff with damp and it's shrink-wrapped itself to my body. My carefully teased waves have frizzed up too, but fortunately I have one of Ava's hair ties in my handbag. Her blonde hairs are tangled around it and I get a pang of guilt as I gather my hair up and scrape it back. The pyjamas are Christmas Batman-themed and they're huge. The waist tie pulls tight enough that the bottoms shouldn't be subject to an embarrassing wardrobe malfunction of any sort. When I'm ready, I head back to the kitchen.

Edward is adding milk to the coffees and when he looks up his eyes fall over me. 'God, you look good even in Batman pyjamas.'

I walk over to the island and sit on a stool to mask any visible signs of discomfort and he slides my coffee across.

'You don't like compliments, do you?' His eyes are intent on mine, zapping me with their weird magnetic energy.

I look down at the counter, tracing the veins in the marble with my index finger. 'I suppose I'm not used to them. I see myself as a frumpy mum so I guess the few I've ever had have never felt justified.'

He walks around the island and stands next to me. Then, gently tilts my head upwards, forcing our eyes to meet. 'You're far from frumpy. I wish you could see yourself as others do or at least as I do. You're beautiful.'

He puts his soft lips on mine and electricity runs through the entire length of my body. I pull him closer, wanting more, and before I know it his warm hands are sliding up my Batman top. He pauses.

'Is this okay?'

There's no coming back from this. No light-hearted brush-offs. If we do this it will change what we are forever.

I nod, not needing to give it a second thought.

Chapter 39

'Anyway, you're full of the joys of spring. What are you so chirpy about?' Janey asks. She popped in to borrow my carpet cleaner but that was an hour and twenty minutes ago and she's still here drinking tea. She and Jimmy told the children about the break-up yesterday and whilst it went as well as it possibly could have, I get the impression she's after a distraction. She's explained how it went and stated quite clearly that she doesn't want to talk about it anymore. Jimmy is taking the kids to pick out furniture for his new flat today so they feel involved and I think she's starting to feel the magnitude of it all.

'Nothing.' I can't help the grin that breaks on my face. It's reminiscent of two tectonic plates pulling apart and you can probably see it from space.

'Okay, well it's clear there's something you're not telling me and I'm not buying the whole drinks with Emily line. You saw her last week and she's coming to the book club meeting tonight so I just have this to say: whatever you're up to, be careful and use a condom.' She sips her tea, peering at me comically from above the rim of her cup.

'Hey!' I chuck a tea towel at her but she bats it away and it falls to the floor pathetically.

'Okay, I've hit a nerve and you'll tell me when you're good and ready but know this: I'm on the neighbourhood watch and I did see you come home in a cab this morning. As a concerned neighbour, I couldn't help but notice you had a nice dress on. It wasn't your usual attire.'

'Fine, Miss Marple. Something happened but I'm not ready to talk about it.'

'That's fine.' She breaks into an excited grin. 'Was he any good?'

'Where's that bloody tea towel when I need it?'

'Oh come on. It's only me.'

I go to open my mouth but the doorbell rings and I wink instead.

Janey lets out a puff of air. 'I suppose I'd better go and clean the carpets. I'll see you later for the book club.'

'See you later. Oh, and Janey, please can we keep this conversation between us?'

She laughs. 'I wouldn't know what to tell anyone anyway.'

As I answer the door, Janey slips past the throng of Mike, Ralph, Ava and Henry and there's an exchange of pleasantries. As Mike and the kids burst in, I feel a giddy light-headedness.

'Who fancies pancakes?' I ask. Ralph raises his eyebrows in surprise. Pancakes are usually reserved for special occasions such as Christmas and birthdays or a royal visit but today I'm in the mood to do something nice.

As I gather flour and eggs, I turn to Mike. 'Fancy staying for some pancakes? I have maple syrup – the proper one not the "maple-syrup flavoured" stuff.'

He checks his watch and for a moment, I think he's going to say no. 'Yes, that sounds good.'

I decide to make the thick, fluffy American kind so when it comes to flipping they're less of a challenge. Ralph flips his successfully and we all cheer. Then Ava has a turn and hers barely leaves the pan and lands the same way up so we try again. This time she cracks it and we all cheer again.

'Your turn,' I say to Mike.

'Easy,' he says, taking the handle of my non-stick frying pan. 'One, two, three.'

He flips it so hard it hits the ceiling and bounces off, hitting the floor. We all burst out laughing. When the laughter dies down, I pour some more batter in and he has another try.

'How about you give it a bit less welly this time, Dad,' Ralph says.

Mike and I look at one another and Mike mouths 'Dad?'

'I know,' I whisper, widening my eyes in shock. 'Our big boy is growing up.'

When the pancakes have gone and five bellies are groaning, I make some fresh coffee. I offer Mike one, sure he'll say he has to dash off but to my surprise, he says he'd love to stay. The kids suggest a game of hide-and-seek and Mike is designated 'seeker'. As the house fills with the sound of stomping feet and shrieks of laughter, it dawns on me that whilst it isn't exactly what I'd planned, perhaps I do have my dream family after all.

Janey and Amanda arrive early for our book club meeting. 'We thought you might be nervous, what with Emma coming.'

'Emily,' I correct. 'And no, I'm not.'

'We are,' Amanda says. 'I'm not good with new people and I haven't heard great things about Emily.'

'That's because everything you know about her came from Janey.' I shoot Janey a look. 'Let's just be nice and see how it goes.'

I pour us each a glass of Pinot Grigio and put some nibbles out on the coffee table.

As Janey and Amanda go to sit down, the doorbell rings. 'Okay, best behaviour.'

Janey makes a scout's honour gesture and Amanda gives a small, reassuring smile.

'Hi, Emily,' I say, swinging the door open.

'Hi, Stephanie.' She looks frailer than usual. I'm sure the divorce is taking its toll. A copy of *Little Women* is tucked under her arm and she's holding a bottle of Prosecco in her free hand.

'Come in,' I say beckoning her with a friendly smile. 'The others are in the lounge.'

She steps in timidly. After an awkward introduction, we have a slightly laboured discussion of the book. Amanda saves the conversation with her in-depth analysis of the women's struggle between family obligation and personal growth.

Emily adds something about Jo and the danger of gender stereotyping, which is interesting. I'm listening but mostly I'm sitting on eggshells just hoping the new dynamic works.

Janey clears her throat and everyone looks at her. 'What really stuck out for me was the theme of honesty and the importance of being genuine. When Amy turns down Fred's offer of marriage it struck a chord with me because ...' Her voice wobbles and she looks at me. I give her a nod of encouragement but don't want to take over.

'Even though Fred is rich and he can give her a good life, she says no because she doesn't love him. Well, Jimmy isn't rich ...' Amanda and Emily both look confused. 'But staying with him was an easier option. We could share the bills and coast along but I realised that I wasn't being honest with myself. Our relationship wasn't genuine. How could it be when he cheated on me? I don't want the children to think a marriage like ours is normal.'

'Are you saying you've left Jimmy?' Amanda asks. Janey nods and starts to cry gentle sobs. Amanda embraces her whilst Emily sips her drink awkwardly. After some comforting, Janey dries her eyes and we spend some time talking through the logistics of separation. Amanda's experience of sudden loss is surprisingly useful and she has plenty of practical advice to offer. Emily chips in now and then with a few comments but I think she senses how different her life is to Janey's.

'We should call ourselves The Book Club of Waifs and

Strays,' I joke when we're washing the glasses in the kitchen a little later.

'How about The Single Mums' Book Club? Seriously,' Janey replies. 'Now we're bigger, we should have a name.'

I laugh. 'Does this mean you think Emily is all right?'

'I actually felt a bit sorry for her. She seems so lost.'

'She's spent the last twenty years not wanting for anything. Her house had staff for goodness' sake. She's probably had to venture into the kitchen for the first time in forever – that's why she's lost – probably never been in there before.'

Janey raises her eyebrows. 'That sounds like something I'd say.'

'I'm sorry. I do feel sorry for her but I just got a little pang of the pain I felt when they all ditched me.'

Janey pulls me into a hug. 'But you found me.'

'I did.' I rest my head on her shoulder. 'And I'm not the same as they are. I can rise above it and be kind.'

'Good for you. A shag really has done you the world of good.'

'I didn't *shag* anyone … we just … Being around him may have put me in good spirits.' I smile and nudge her with my hip before heading back through to the lounge. As I walk in, Emily is standing up and gathering her things.

'I'm going to set off but thank you so much for inviting me.' She shuffles her weight from foot to foot.

'Are you sure you want to go? I've just opened the bottle of Prosecco you brought.'

Her eyes fall to the tray of flutes I'm holding.

'Yes, stay,' Amanda adds, probably glad of someone to raise the level of book-related conversation.

Emily clutches the strap on her handbag tighter and looks down at the coffee table. Her lips twitch as though she wants to say something but doesn't quite know how.

'Is everything all right?' I ask as Janey comes in wittering something about Amazon's top one hundred books chart.

'I …' Emily glances at Janey and back to me with glossy eyes.

'I was going to the loo and overheard something about the book club for waifs and strays and I think I've overstayed my welcome.'

'Oh shit.' I throw my head in my hands. 'We didn't mean you. We were talking about all of us. Janey was up to the eyeballs with her kids and found me blubbering in the supermarket one day; now she's going through a break-up. A week or two after Janey found me, Amanda approached me in the café, hunting for new friends because she was lonely.' Amanda's eyes widen. 'Well, it's true and I'm so glad you did. What we meant is that, somehow, we were all at a bit of a loss and the book club has been an excuse to come together for a laugh and some companionship. We're not the best book club in the world and sometimes we don't even read the books but we always show up and we're always here for one another.'

'So have you named the club that?' Emily asks, shifting uncomfortably.

I shake my head. 'In the end, we decided we should be called The Single Mums' Book Club because that's what we are and we shouldn't be ashamed of that fact.'

Emily sits down, slumping back into the soft cushions of the sofa, and fixes her eyes on the white marble fireplace.

'You're not a pity case,' I continue then sigh, sitting on the arm of the sofa next to her. 'Actually, you are a little bit, but the truth is we all are. That's the point. If it's high-brow discussions of literary fiction you're after, we are not the club for you. But, if you like a book that Richard and Judy might pick and you want some company, some fun and plenty of wine, then I think we might be perfect.'

She manages a weak smile. 'Thank you, I think I'm going to quite like this book club.'

Chapter 40

Waking up early on a Monday morning is never fun. Waking up early on a Monday morning after sharing a few bottles of wine and tipsy tears is hell. I can categorically confirm this because it's the exact scenario I've found myself in this morning.

'Mummy,' Ava shouts. 'My cardigan has sauce on it.'

I bury my head in my pillow and groan. You know those posts on Facebook that say things like: 'I'm not adulting today.' Why isn't that a thing? We get work holidays by law because it's too stressful to work every single day of the year. It's about time that the powers that be realised that parenting should come with the same entitlement.

'There's a clean one in the utility room. Just brush your teeth.' My phone's alarm clock starts going off. Each high-pitched beat is a bubble of annoyance pricking at me. I lean over to turn it off and notice a message.

I didn't want to send a message yesterday as I knew you'd be spending time with your family but I can't stop thinking about you. E xxx

My stomach flips as I read the message again.

'Mummy.' Ava runs in and dives on top of me. There's a dull thud as she knocks the air out of my lungs.

'Ava, what have I told you about that? You're too big to be chucking yourself around – you'll hurt someone.' She ignores me and picks up my phone.

'Oh, a message. Who's it from?' she asks, frowning at the screen. 'I d-i-d.'

I snatch the phone back. 'Nobody. Go and brush your teeth like I asked you to ten minutes ago.'

She sulks off towards the bathroom and I lock the phone and place it screen down on the side whilst I go and have a quick shower.

When I get to work, I have a few knots of apprehension about seeing Edward. I convince myself it's normal to feel this way and force myself through the door. Carly shouts a cheerful 'morning' as I head straight to the kitchen in search of coffee. Thankfully, there's a fresh pot brewed.

'Morning, Steph.' I turn to see Edward in the doorway, his tall frame filling the space. He's in maroon scrubs today and they really bring out the dark depth of colour in his brown hair. I must admit, as smart as the tweed looks, I'm a sucker for the scrubs. 'I hope the text message this morning wasn't too much. I'm a bit hopeless at these things.'

'No.' I soften my features. 'It was actually really nice to get a message like that. I couldn't reply because Ava grabbed my phone and started to try and read the message. Fortunately, she's barely grasped phonics.' Am I seriously saying I'm thankful my child can't read? I'll have to process that later – probably whilst I'm panic-buying early reading books on Amazon.

'Oh, Steph, I'm so sorry. I didn't think. I thought so carefully about not causing any trouble on Sunday – I didn't consider anything past that.'

I smile softly and take a step closer. 'The fact that you thought at all means a lot. Dealing with the logistics of this is more something I need to get used to.'

'So ...' He traces his finger up my arm, leaving a tingling sensation in its wake. 'Logistically, can we see each other again on Saturday?'

'How about fish and chips in the park on Friday?'

He frowns. 'Okay.'

I smile. 'I know it's not the most exciting of dates, but I was thinking I could bring the kids along. They already know you as my boss, but perhaps if they get to know you as my friend ... and get to like you ...'

He kisses me softly, sparing me the awkwardness of the conversation. 'I would love to but perhaps we could go one better.'

I frown. 'Bring them into the practice. They can meet some animals, see what it's like to be a vet and then we'll get something to eat after.'

'Are you sure?'

'Of course I am.'

My insides are light and fluttery as I bite down a smile. 'Then on Saturday, it can be my treat. How about I cook for you at my place? I do mean chicken nuggets, chips and beans.'

The corners of his mouth twitch. 'If you have Heinz ketchup, you're on!'

'Is someone getting the bacon butties in?' Carly puts her hands on Edward's arms and moves him out of the way before squeezing past.

'Er ...' It takes me a second to catch up. She must have heard the ketchup comment. Great, now I'll have to do a bacon sandwich run.

'Yes, I think we all deserve a treat,' Edward says. 'I've got a gap between clients and thought I'd pop to the sandwich shop.'

'Brilliant!' Carly grins like the Cheshire cat. Who'd have thought that all this time, it would be processed meat that put a smile on her face.

'Thank you,' I mouth to Edward when Carly's head is buried in the fridge. She pours herself a cup of coffee, adds some milk and then disappears, completely oblivious to the ten-quid dent she's just made in Edward's wallet.

'So, Saturday,' he says.

'Come about sixish and since you're treating us to bacon butties, I might even go above and beyond chicken nuggets.' I tap my chin in thought. 'Although Iceland do have a deal on.'

'I don't care if you serve me Otis's discarded marrow bone in an old boot as long as you're there.' He glances backwards. Satisfied the coast is clear, he takes a step closer and kisses the tip of my nose. I close my eyes as his lips linger there for a moment.

I can't keep it quiet anymore. It's been three days of sneaky kisses and stolen glances. Edward keeps buying baked goods for everyone in the practice, which must be his way of coping with all the secrecy, and if it carries on for much longer, none of my clothes will fit. So, I grabbed Janey after school and we've brought the kids to a god-awful, giant play gym that has the aroma of sweaty feet and bad coffee. There's a cacophony of squeals, crying and slide-squeaks; which, on a normal day would be headache-inducing, but today it provides the perfect cover for me to spill my burning secret.

'I got you a fruit tea. It's powdered milk so I thought we'd best avoid a milky beverage,' Janey says, placing the tray of teas and Fruit Shoots down on the sticky coffee table in front of me.

'I thought you hated play gyms,' she says, sitting on the brown pleather sofa opposite.

'I do. I wanted to talk to you about something?'

'Oh?' No genuine surprise registers on her face.

'You know what I'm about to tell you.' I draw a breath. 'Yes, Edward and I went on a date.'

'You're dating?'

'Date, singular so far but for want of a better word, yes. We went out last Saturday and it was perfect.' I hug my warm cup close to my chest.

'If that smile on your face is anything to go by, I can tell. Where did he take you?'

'It was an indoor seaside-themed pop-up cinema thing. It was wonderful. We watched—'

'Hang on. You didn't get home until Sunday morning! You're telling me you slept over after the first date? You dirty dog!'

'It wasn't like that. We just stayed up for hours and it got so late it seemed a bit silly to get a taxi home in the early hours when he has four bedrooms. We talked. A lot. There was kissing, and cuddling.'

'Oh, God! You've got it bad.'

I rub my cheeks where the muscles ache from smiling. 'It's very new and obviously, the kids don't know anything about it. I want to see where this goes before I even think about introducing Edward to them as anything other than my boss.'

'Fair enough. I'm proud of you though. Stepping out of your comfort zone like that can't have been easy.'

'It wasn't, but Edward sort of *makes* it easy. I don't need to try and be anything but myself. After years of pretence keeping up with Emily and her friends, I'm done with that way of life. Maybe I'm getting older and wiser in my three decades—'

Janey raises her eyebrows.

'Okay, nearly four decades. What I'm trying to say is that I'm done with the nonsense. I don't care who went to the Maldives over Christmas, or whose BMW has the biggest engine, or who saw Tiger Woods at some exclusive golf resort in Hawaii. I care about the people who will pop the kettle on when I have tonsillitis and the kids are driving me mad; the people who will listen if I need to vent; the people who can see me at my worst and come to help rather than climbing over each other to get away. I care about the people I can talk to without judgement. People like you and Amanda. Edward too, but I have to be careful with him. I have to be certain that things are serious.'

'It makes sense. You do what's best for you and I'm here to help in any way I can.'

'Thank you,' I stand up and hug her.

'Now, I want to know everything. Is he a good kisser?'

Chapter 41

My leg jiggles as my foot rests in the footwell. I've collected the children from school and nursery and now I'm stuck at traffic lights on my way back to the vet's. I haven't had much chance to talk to Edward about the kids but if this thing between us starts to turn into something, it's quite a big deal for all of us.

'Hello, small folk.' Edward greets the children with a wide smile. Ava steps backwards whilst Ralph rolls his eyes without looking up from his DS.

'I'll take that, thank you,' I say, snatching it from him and stuffing it into my bag.

'Too much?' Edward whispers to me whilst the children head over to the dog toys we sell.

'A little.' I nod. 'Just be yourself. They'll love you.'

'Mummy, can I have one of these? It shows the little boy putting biscuits inside.' Ava holds up one of those Kong toys.

'No, sweetheart, that's for dogs. Otis has one similar, remember.'

'I want a toy with biscuits in.'

'We can sort that,' Edward says disappearing into the kitchen. He comes back with a small bag of biscuits, the little mini Cadbury ones, and opens it. He takes one out and tries to wedge it in the open end of the toy. It fits.

'Why should dogs have all the fun? I've washed the Kong so you're good to go.' Edward hands it over to a delighted Ava. 'Now, who wants to see some rabbits?'

The three rabbits were in a box dumped on the doorstep of the practice a couple of days ago. They're too young to be away from their mother so Edward has been hand-rearing them.

'They're ready for weaning now. See how they have fur and their eyes are open? That's how we know they're old enough.'

'How old are they?' Ralph asks. He's leaning on the table peering into the cage.

'About eleven days.'

'Eleven *days*?' Ralph says. 'I thought they'd be a few months.'

Edward nods. 'They grow pretty fast. I'm going to take them to my house this weekend as they need some grass to run around on now.'

'Cool,' Ralph says.

'Mummy, can we take one home?'

'No, sweetheart. Edward should do it because he's a vet. They need to be looked after in a certain way.'

'They need an experienced handler, but you're welcome to visit them at any time.'

I flash Edward a look of gratitude.

'Can we, Mummy?'

'Of course we can.'

Whilst Edward closes the shutter over the door, Ava comes and hugs me tightly. She's still clutching the biscuit-filled Kong toy. 'Your work is the best place. I want to work here when I grow up.'

I smile. 'It's not just eating biscuits and stroking rabbits,' I say. 'I do a lot of boring stuff too.'

'Can we get some food now?' Ralph says, obviously much less impressed with Mummy's work than Ava.

'I hope so,' Edward says. 'I'm starving.'

Ralph gives him a sideways glance and nods in approval. Throughout it all, Henry has been fast asleep in my arms but he's starting to stir. 'I think your brother is hungry too. What is it with you boys? You're like bottomless pits!'

We carry our steaming carrier bags to the park. The fish and chips smell so good I have to use every ounce of my willpower not to tear into them before we reach the bench. We sit down. I'm not as relaxed as I was last time we were here but I suppose the dynamic has changed a lot. Edward was the boss I secretly admired back then. Now he's the boss who I'm kissing and I'm seeking the kids' approval.

'I got you a large portion,' Edward says, tossing a paper package to Ralph.

'Cool.' Ralph smiles a half-smile at Edward and I think that might just have done it. Edward asks Ralph about school and his hobbies and after struggling to find some middle ground, they eventually discover a shared love of Formula One racing. As Ralph lists his top-three racing drivers with enthusiasm, I give Henry a piece of fish to be chewing on, which he takes greedily.

'So, Ava, did you like the rabbits?' Edward asks.

'Mmm,' she replies through a mouthful of food. 'Will they die?'

Edward puts his little plastic fork down. 'Someday, when they're older, but not any time soon, I hope. I'll make sure they'll be okay.'

'I want to make sure animals are okay when I grow up,' Ava says. Edward flashes me a smile.

'It's a great job.'

'Can I feed the ducks?' Ava asks, holding up a piece of batter off her fish.

'Yes, but over the wall of the playground. You can't go to the riverbank,' I say.

'Hang on.' Edward pulls a brown paper bag out of his pocket. 'I came prepared. Batter isn't great for ducks so I've brought some duck food.'

Ava takes the bag from him and peers inside. 'Yuck. It looks like Mummy's breakfast.'

'Hey, my muesli is delicious, you cheeky monkey!'

She and Ralph go to the drystone wall at the edge of the park and lean over. Soon they're throwing handfuls of feed over whilst laughing.

'They're great kids,' Edward says, watching them.

Now is my chance to bring up the topic that's been gnawing away at me. Taking on a divorcee with three kids is a big step. He's been great with the kids so far but if this were to go anywhere, he'll be in their lives properly. I need to know he understands that and he's not just tolerating them for my sake. I lean across the table a little, bringing my face closer to his.

'It's a lot to think about though. If things did get serious between us.'

'Steph, honestly it doesn't worry me in the slightest.'

'Three kids though? It worries me every bloody day.' I laugh and he does too.

He starts to pick at the corner of the chip paper. 'You know I wanted a family and the truth is, I'm pushing forty and I sort of came to terms with the fact it might not happen for me. Being around Ava, Ralph and this little guy' – he tickles Henry under the chin – 'is definitely no hardship. I'm more worried about them resenting me.'

I exhale. I'd been on tenterhooks, dreading him saying they'd be the next best thing, like they were some sort of booby prize. I do moan about my kids a bit but they will never be anyone's second best. Him not saying that, makes me like him more.

Ava comes running over. 'Edward, can you push me on the swing?'

'Go on then.' He gets up and sighs, pretending he doesn't want to but I can tell he's thrilled to be asked. I jiggle Henry on my lap and get him some sliced grapes out of my bag. Watching Edward and Ava laughing together should feel so weird but it doesn't. It feels right.

Chapter 42

It's been ages since I've made anything 'proper' and today I'm braving beef wellington. I splashed out on a fillet of beef from the butcher in the village and I've made my own pastry; all being well, I'll avoid the curse of the soggy bottom or a disastrous duxelles. I'm doing triple-cooked chips on the side and the bloke in the wine shop recommended the perfect red. The doorbell rings as I'm straining the red wine sauce.

'Something smells delicious,' Edward says as soon as he steps through the door.

'Let's hope it tastes that way,' I say, heading back towards the kitchen.

'I meant you. Come here.' He spins me around and brushes the hair off my face before kissing me on the lips and causing my stomach to somersault in the process. 'Mmm yes, you taste good too,' he says.

'Funny,' I say rolling my eyes. 'The wine is breathing; pour yourself a glass whilst I get this in the oven.'

I take the meticulously prepared beef wellington out of the fridge and unwrap the Clingfilm before popping it in the oven. The cooled chips are on the side waiting to go into the deep fat fryer and remarkably, everything seems to be under control.

'I brought you these.' He pulls a bunch of pink peonies out of a canvas shopping bag. 'I also brought dessert although the Co-op's own-brand cheesecake seems a bit naff now I've seen what you've cooked.'

'Don't be silly,' I say, setting two plates out on the kitchen table. 'Can you put the knives and forks out?'

We move around the kitchen in unison, never colliding, never duplicating. It's effortless. When the table is set, Edward takes charge of the wine whilst I dish up. As I turn around with the two plates of well-presented (even if I do say so myself) wellington, I notice Edward has found some old candles. He must have been in the cupboard under the sink and found several too-good-to-throw-out but not-nice-enough-for-guests candle dregs. Lit, they give the kitchen a soft, romantic glow.

'This smells amazing,' Edward says, inhaling the delicious scent of meat and pastry. He reaches for the bottle of red he'd been allowing to breathe and pours us both a glass.

'Cheers,' he says.

'To us.' As I say the words and clink my glass against his, I can barely meet his eye. It's all so new to me. I'm in that strange place in a new relationship where I'm elated and excited but also scared witless. A new relationship is a fragile thing. It isn't robust like a solid marriage and even those fall apart. It's like a breath too deep or a joke too far could be all it takes for this to crumble. There's so much anxiety and dread inside me, I'm too full to eat.

'Are you okay?' Edward wipes his mouth on his napkin and places his knife and fork down. I notice he's already halfway through his meal.

'I am. It's just … I …' Air rushes out of my lungs. 'I'm happy.'

He smiles and covers my hand with his and whispers, 'I'm scared too.'

He leans towards me and kisses me gently on the lips, causing a surge of electricity through my body. 'I'm terrified there could be a time you won't want me to do that.'

The comforting warmth of his vulnerability smothers the unbearable tension that has been mounting up since he arrived. He understands me and for the first time since Janey found me in the supermarket, I am seen.

'Me too.' It comes out as a whisper. 'Do you think it's so scary because it feels so right?'

He nods with deep certainty in his eyes. 'Probably that and because we've both been hurt before. How about we stop worrying and start enjoying? Starting with this wonderful food!'

'Sounds like a plan.' Tentatively, I try the beef wellington. 'Bloody hell, that's good,' I say and Edward laughs.

'Just wait until you try my cheesecake.'

We chat about normal stuff through the rest of the meal. Places we'd love to travel to, embarrassing fashion faux pas in our teenager years and where we saw ourselves as adults versus where we are now.

By the time we've eaten Edward's cheesecake, we're both feeling the effects of the wine and he suggests we sit out in the garden for some fresh air. The sky is a clear, sooty black and the moon bright white against its canvas, illuminating the trees and grass, giving them a navy-blue colour. The air is a bit chillier than it has been so I pop back inside for a blanket and we snuggle up on the swinging sofa, rocking to and fro under the moonlight.

'How do you feel being out here? In the dark I mean.'

'Surprisingly okay.' Perhaps it's the wine or the company but I'm more relaxed than ever. I used to sit out here with Mike, but after he left, the fear got worse and I haven't sat out on my own at night since.

After a while of sitting in companionable silence, listening to nothing but the gentle sound of the river, Edward shuffles a little in his seat.

'Can I say something?' The warmth of his breath caresses my scalp.

'Of course.'

247

'I know we've not been doing this for very long and we haven't known one another for much time at all really but being here with you like this feels so right.' He kisses me tenderly on my forehead. It's a small gesture that sends my body into hyper-awareness like every nerve end is on speed. I don't know if it's the wine but I'm overcome with the urge for something more passionate. I stretch my neck so my lips reach his and our mouths work slowly in unison. His tongue probes deeply. Wanting more I climb onto his lap and run my hands through his hair, pulling his head even closer as the swing rocks us gently to and fro.

His hands rest on the outside of my thighs, which tingle with warmth as he glides them slowly upwards, lifting the hem of my dress.

'Is this okay?' he asks in a breathy voice.

I nod, my open mouth still pressed against his.

The next morning I wake up to bright sunlight streaming through the window. In the heat of the moment, we obviously forgot to close the curtains. Edward is still in a restful sleep. I lay my head on his chest. The gentle rise and fall of it is somewhat comforting.

'Morning, beautiful,' he says after a while. His voice is thick with sleep.

'Morning,' I reply, kissing the fine hair on his chest then inhaling the scent of him. He wraps his thick arms around me and squeezes me tightly. I could stay here forever. But I can't. It's Sunday and the kids will be home in a few hours.

'Let me cook you breakfast,' Edward says, kissing my hair. 'You can stay in bed if you like.'

Reluctantly, I let him slide out from beneath my head. I watch as he pulls his jeans on over his naked bum. 'Wait.' He had pants on last night. I panic. 'Where are your boxers?'

He grins devilishly. 'Either in the garden, in the kitchen or on the stairs.'

'Oh, God. Please find them.' I bury my face in my pillow.

I rest my head back down, after a while, relishing in the sense of calm that a full night's sleep has brought. I haven't slept that well since Mike left. I think I doze back off because I wake up to the sound of sizzling and the whiff of bacon. I pull on my dressing gown and head downstairs.

'Something smells good. Did you find your pants?'

'Scrambled eggs, bacon and grilled tomato.' He pulls out a chair. 'Sit down and I'll get you some coffee and yes, my pants are safely on my person.'

'I could get used to this.'

'It's nice to have someone to do it for.'

Just as we finish eating, the telephone rings.

'You answer that; I'll clear up,' Edward says.

'Seriously.' I kiss him on his light stubble. 'I could get used to this.'

There's a definite spring in my step as I head to answer the phone. Whenever the landline rings, I normally ignore it but today I'm in such good spirits, I want to answer it. I want the person on the other end to hear how happy I am.

'Hello?' I chirp.

'Stephanie?'

'Is that you, Mike?' He sounds so serious. My heart pounds my sternum. 'Is everything okay? Are the children all right?'

'Yes, they're fine. Sorry, I didn't mean to panic you.'

'What is it? Why are you calling? You're coming over in a couple of hours.'

'I just wanted to know if you're free today. There's something I want to talk to you about.'

'Yes, I'm free but can't you just say whatever it is now? You're worrying me.'

He exhales a long, deep breath then he shouts the kids' names. 'Okay, they're out of earshot. I want to talk about us. I know we already spoke about it and decided we shouldn't get back together but I think we may have made a terribly rash decision and the divorce and everything could have been a mistake.'

'What the …? Are you saying you want me back?'

'I think it's something we should talk about.'

I'm dumbfounded. I can't keep going over this. It's not enough to get my team back; for the kids to get their dad back. Like Janey said, I don't want my children to think marriage is about being miserable. We were terrible together and things are better between us now. Things with Edward are going well. I like him so much and what's more, he seems to like me.

'Mike.' My voice is a whisper. I hold the phone to my chest and glance towards the kitchen. It's silent in there. 'Mike, I can't talk about this now. Not over the phone.'

'That's why I want to know if you're free. I thought we could stick a film on for the kids and sit out in the garden and talk.'

The garden. Oh God. The things Edward and I did in that garden. I rub my face with my hands. 'Come over and we'll talk.'

'Great. We're just having breakfast and then we'll set off.' As Mike finishes his sentence, the front door closes. Edward?

'Okay. See you later.' I hang up the phone and dart down the hall. As I swing open the door I'm just in time to see Edward's car turning at the bottom of the street.

Oh God, what a mess.

Chapter 43

Even though I know Edward has gone, I go into the kitchen hoping for some trace of him. The dishes from breakfast are clean, he's wiped down the table and everything has been put away. The only reminders of the time we spent together are two plates, two cups and two sets of cutlery draining by the sink. My phone sits still on the side. I pick it up. Nothing.

By the time Mike's car pulls up outside, I've paced the house approximately one thousand times. I even check the carpet to see if I've worn a rut in it. When I open the door, the kids burst in. There is a flurry of hugs, kisses and hellos and they head to the lounge.

'Dad bought us the new *Toy Story* DVD,' Ralph says.

'And popcorn,' adds Ava.

'Brilliant,' I say, smiling brightly. 'Go and stick it on then.'

It isn't until now that I actually look at Mike. He needs a haircut and his face is thinner – the skin sort of hangs loose, grazing the structure of his cheekbones.

'Come on through to the kitchen, I'll make you a cup of tea.'

When the tea is brewed and poured Mike opens the back door and goes into the garden. He takes the double swing chair and I sit on one of the green plastic patio chairs opposite.

'I used to love sitting here,' he says. It is quite a spectacular view. The never-ending green fields beyond are still covered with a layer of low morning mist even though it's almost lunchtime.

'What's happened, Mike?'

'Nothing.'

'What's brought on all this "trying again" business?'

'I miss you, Stephanie. I miss *us*.'

That word hits me like an arrow. *Us*. For so long all I wanted was *us*. The imperfect, miserable version we'd become. I sip my tea to hide any emotion that may have manifested on my face. 'What about Kate?'

'She's great but I miss our family. I miss the way we were, Stephanie. We had a great life.'

I lean forward and look him in the eyes. 'Mike, what's brought this on?'

'You. Ever since that night you told me you wanted to try again, I've been thinking about it. The more I do, the more it makes sense.'

'No. No it didn't make sense – we both agreed on that. Besides, it was months ago. You're supposed to be moving in with Kate.'

'I know but once that happens, that's it.'

'What do you mean that's it? Once you move in with her you're stuck with her?' Poor Kate!

He sighs. 'No, I don't mean that. I just want to be sure I've thought about it and all I can think about right now is you and the old life we had.'

'Mike,' I say softly but I don't follow it with anything. He's offering me what I've always wanted. The family unit back together. The kids would be ecstatic – it's what Ava asked Santa for last Christmas. My eyes fix on the swinging chair. The memories of last night pelt me like little balls of hailstone. Mike is offering me a safe, familiar route to the dream I've always had. He's offering me something comfortable. Dare I want more than that? Dare I want some desire? Some passion? Dare I want more than Mike? Dare I do something just for me?

'Stephanie?' Mike asks. My forehead is tense so I try to relax it.

'Why are you here, Mike? Why aren't you with Kate?'

'I … you know why.'

'Where is Kate?'

'She's at the flat.'

'Blissfully unaware you're here asking your ex-wife for a reconciliation, I'm willing to bet?'

'Well, I didn't tell her—'

'You're just scared. It's new. You have to find your rhythm again when you move in with Kate and that's okay. The kids have just got used to the idea of her. You can't keep flitting and changing your mind. It's not fair to them.'

'I know. But I thought *you* wanted to try again.'

I go and sit beside him on the swing. I brush my hand over the floral print fabric and my lower abdomen clenches inappropriately at the memory of last night.

'I was wrong. We went over this. We were a dull couple without a spark. I think we found safety in one another early on and just fell into a relationship. Don't you want more? Don't you want passion and excitement?'

He shrugs. Mike isn't the passion and excitement sort so it surprises me when he says: 'I suppose so.'

'Have you got that with Kate?'

'Yes, I guess so. She's different to you though. She's driven by her career and her friends. She's not a homemaker like you.'

I raise my eyebrows and he shrugs apologetically.

'And that's exactly why she's good for you. She keeps you on your toes and she gets out of your hair a few times a week. Perhaps we were just too lazy together. We didn't challenge one another and in the end; we just bickered over whose turn it was to take Ralph to football or Ava to ballet. We became like—'

'A couple of moody teens?' Mike cuts me off.

I laugh softly. 'Exactly.'

We swing back and forth for a moment, listening to the birds chirp.

'I do love you and I always will,' I say. Mike takes my hand in his and squeezes it.

'Me too.'

'Don't be afraid of moving in with Kate. Yes, she probably will make you cook a few times a week and pick up your own socks off the bedroom floor, but it will be good for you.'

'Hey, I pick up my own socks and cook for myself now, thank you very much.'

'Then you're already a better partner to her than you were to me.'

'Was I really that bad?'

'I think we both were.'

'What about you? Are you okay?'

I think about Edward and how he left without saying goodbye this morning. I might have some explaining to do but I know what I want now. 'I think so.'

Come evening time, I've still not heard from Edward. My stomach has been off all day and I haven't eaten since the breakfast he made me. I should text him. I can't blame him for not getting in touch, he obviously overheard me on the phone and wanted to give me space. He'll be waiting for a text from me, I'm sure.

I key out a few different messages ranging from a lengthy explanation to a brief message saying Mike and I sorted things out. The thing is, I don't know how much of the conversation he caught. He may have just heard it was Mike, realised the time and left because he thought the kids were nearly home or he could have heard the lot. Explaining over text could be complicated so I just settle on:

Thanks for breakfast and a great night. Hope you're okay xxx

When I press send, I clutch the phone, waiting for the buzz of a reply. After ten minutes, there's nothing so I force myself to get ready for bed. I brush my teeth; nothing. I put my pyjamas on; nothing. I climb under the covers; nothing.

In the end, I put my phone by my lamp and snuggle into the duvet. The fresh scent of Edward's aftershave combined with his natural musky scent lingers in the fibres. I'm so dopey with sleep, it feels like he's here in bed with me. As I'm drifting off, my phone buzzes violently on the hard wood of the bedside table. I peel my eyes open and glance at the bright screen through blurry eyes. It's Edward but only the first few lines are visible. I sit up to read it.

I'm so sorry I left without saying goodbye.

The anxiety I've had all day melts away. He's sorry. Things are fine between us. I open the full message.

I'm so sorry I left without saying goodbye. I really didn't mean to eavesdrop on your conversation but the sound just carried. I heard what Mike was calling you for and I suppose I just panicked and left. I was frightened of hearing you say you wanted to call things off between us and you were going to try again with Mike. It's silly because I already knew that's what was happening. I suppose I just wanted to relish in the good feelings of last night for a little bit longer. You're probably really confused now. Maybe you've already decided to be with Mike, maybe you haven't. I can't be a factor in your decision. What we have is new and new relationships are exciting but we have no idea what lies ahead. I know that your family is the most important thing in your life and I don't want to confuse matters. We should cool things off between us so you have time to think and process everything. I want you to do what's best for you and the kids. xxx

I throw my head back too quickly and it cracks the headboard.

'Ouch.' I rub the back and there's already a lump forming. I need to explain everything to Edward. He needs to know that I don't want to fall back into a rut with Mike. My fingers start tapping my phone frantically.

Edward, Mike was just confused. We're not getting back together. Can we talk tomorrow? xxx

After five minutes, I check to see if the message has been read. It hasn't even been delivered. He must have turned his phone off.

Chapter 44

When I pull into the small car park at work, I'm relieved that Edward's car isn't here. He must be on a call-out which is good. He still hasn't received the WhatsApp message I sent last night so he has no idea Mike and I aren't getting back together and I can't exactly explain it to him here. I grab my bag and head in. As I open the door, the phone starts ringing. Carly is on a call and Helen, the nurse, is running around the bulky reception desk to answer the second line. Both women look flustered.

'What's going on?' I ask Carly when she's hung up.

'Edward—' The phone starts to ring again and she shakes her head. Edward? What about Edward? My heart starts to race and even though I know he's not here, I go and look for him in the kitchen and then the examination room. When I get back to the reception area, Carly is just putting the phone down.

'He's off sick,' she says, just before it rings again.

'Edward's never off sick,' Helen says when she's finished her call. 'For some reason everyone has picked today as the best day to need a vet. We've had three emergency calls already this morning and it's only five past ten.'

I get a heaviness inside. Is Edward off because of me? 'What about the animals? What happens now?'

257

'We've been sending them over to Johnson's.'

'But that's miles away,' I say. Animals could die and it will be all my fault. 'I'm going to go and see him.'

Carly looks up in surprise. She's on a call so can't say anything but I can tell she thinks it weird and probably, from the outside, it is a little but I'm committed to the idea now and I don't have time to fill in the gaps.

'Do you think you should be bothering him?' Helen asks. 'As I said, he's never off sick so it must be bad. I'm not sure if going to see him is a bit over the line.'

'Exactly, it must be bad and he has nobody to help out. I'm a mother of three – there are few illnesses I don't have a remedy for.' That's a lie I use Calpol for everything but she doesn't know that.

'Fine. Just don't tell him how chaotic things have been here. The last thing we want is for him to rush back and infect us all,' Helen says.

'I'm just checking on him. I'll make up my hours later.' I pick up my bag and head to my car.

This is good. I'd been dreading facing him at work. This way, I can explain that whatever it was he'd overheard was just a misunderstanding. Hopefully, then we can go back to how things were between us. I call at the sandwich shop on the way and pick up some chicken soup. I don't for a second believe he is actually ill but on the off-chance he does have a fever or whatever, at least I'll be prepared.

As I take the winding road through the endless green fields, I play over what I'm going to say. It should be easy since all I have to do is tell him the truth but every time I play it over in my head, I try to imagine what he'd think in response. What if he doesn't believe me? What if he thinks I'll change my mind a few months down the line and run back to Mike? Actions speak louder than words I suppose – I'll have to show him. As I turn the sharp bend before his house, I think I have the words figured out but as the property comes in to view there's a pink Mini parked in the driveway. My heart plummets to the pit of my stomach. Stacy.

I slow down. She's there, on the doorstep. Before I get too close to Edward's house, I pull over and watch her as she knocks on the door. She has a little brown paper bag in her hand and a bunch of flowers. She didn't waste any time. I chew my fingernails while I wait. A minute or so later, the door opens and Edward steps out. He's wearing the festive Batman pyjamas I'd worn a few weeks back. They're talking. She laughs and throws back her head then hands him the flowers. As he takes them, she touches his bicep. My whole body stiffens. I shouldn't be watching this but I can hardly drive away now. They'll see me. I could always look at something else but I can't seem to tear my eyes away.

Stacy hands the brown paper bag to Edward. He peers inside. They chat about something and Edward smiles. If he is ill, he doesn't look it from where I'm sitting. Then he leans in and hugs her. 'Okay, lady, you've given him the flowers and the bag; now get back in your car.'

They carry on talking. I let out a big puff of air. I'm getting impatient now. If I don't get back to work soon, I won't be able to stay long enough to make up the time. Stacy takes a step backwards. Surely this is it – she must be going now. As they talk some more she kinks her knee coquettishly. I squint – did I really just see that? Then Edward points his thumb over his shoulder and towards his door and Stacy walks in. A coldness runs through my core.

I'm already too late.

Chapter 45

When I get back to work, things seem to have settled down a bit. The morning rush is over and Carly is filing her nails at the reception desk.

'Where's Helen?'

'She went home. There was nothing for her to do,' Carly replies. 'How was Edward?'

'Hmm?' I say, pretending to be distracted in the hope she'll carry on with her manicure.

'Edward?' She rolls her eyes. 'How was he? Will he be in tomorrow?'

I throw my hands up in the air. 'Dunno. When I got there Stacy had just arrived so I didn't want to pile on him too. I just left without speaking to him.'

'Oh,' Carly says sullenly. 'I hoped you might get some answers out of him. If he's off tomorrow I don't know what we'll do. We have a few big procedures booked in and I don't want to cancel them last minute.'

'Sorry, I didn't know. I just went to check on him to make sure he was okay. I wasn't even planning on asking him about work.'

'Oh, don't worry. It's my fault Stacy went over.'

I try to act casual. 'How so?'

'She was in this morning with that rabbit again and I told her he was sick. She said he shouldn't be alone and something about needing someone to take good care of him. To be honest, I just wanted her to leave because the phones were on fire and she kept talking to me.'

I force a smile. 'I'm sure Edward is glad of the company. Perhaps you could call him just before you leave tonight and see if he thinks he'll be well enough to come in tomorrow. If we leave it as late as possible he'll have a better idea.'

As the kids tuck into their pasta, I stand at the sink staring at the swinging chair in the garden.

'Where's your tea, Mum?' Ava asks.

I turn around and smile at her. 'I'm not hungry yet, love. I'll eat later.'

She tucks back into her food and I steal a glance at my phone. Still nothing. I think about sending another message but what good would that do if he's not opening them anyway? I could text him or get in touch via Facebook Messenger but I think that just pushes me into stalker territory. Instead, I text Janey.

Are you free to come over for a brew tonight?

She replies a little later on as I'm bathing Henry.

Will pop in when kids are in bed xx

By the time she knocks on the door, I've spent so long stewing that I've decided I don't need advice. Why would I need advice? It's not my choice. If Edward has decided he doesn't even want to hear me out, there's nothing I can do. I can't force him.

'What is it? What's going on?' Janey holds up a bottle of wine and a tub of ice cream. 'Wasn't sure what kind of chat it was going to be.' I take the tub of ice cream off her and walk into the kitchen.

'Things between Edward and me took a bit of a turn.'

Janey raises her eyebrows. 'Oh?'

'We're going to need two spoons.'

As Janey prises the lid off the Ben & Jerry's, I try to calculate how up to date she is and realise she doesn't really know how *together* we were. 'Things were going well. Really well, in fact. We were going on dates; he came here and I cooked for him.' I shake my head. 'It doesn't sound like much but we had this connection that I can't explain. When I was near him, I never wanted to leave and when we weren't together, all I could think about was him.'

'Sounds like you've got it bad.'

'Yes,' I say quietly.

'Then why are you talking like it's all over?'

'On Saturday, Edward stayed the night. It was the perfect evening; I cooked, we drank and sat beneath the stars. In the morning, he cooked bacon and eggs and it was terrific. Then Mike called.'

'Mike?'

I nod, not wanting to break my train of thought. 'He was having some sort of wobble about moving in with Kate and his way of fixing that was to ask if I wanted to get back together with him.'

Janey's eyes pop. 'What?'

'I know. It's typical Mike to have a massive overreaction when things get a bit tricky. Anyway, Edward overheard part of the conversation and left before I started to talk Mike down. I haven't been able to get hold of him since and he was off work today.'

'It's just a misunderstanding though; you can explain he didn't hear the whole story.'

'He's not opening his messages.'

'Go and see him?'

'I did. This is where it gets worse. As I got to his house, I saw Stacy going in.'

Janey digs her spoon in the ice cream and takes a mouthful. 'Shit.'

'Indeed.'

'Maybe he just wanted to talk to someone.'

'Or maybe he realised Stacy can offer him something much less complicated.'

'I thought she was seeing that pub landlord.'

'Given half the chance I think she'd run back to Edward and there he was on a self-pitying platter.' I plunge my own spoon into the now softening cookie dough ice cream.

'I don't get it. If things were so good, why has he run away at the first hurdle? It seems a bit pathetic to me.'

'The thing is, I understand where he's coming from. I have a lot of baggage – excess baggage at that. I don't just come with a bit of history, I come with three kids and an ex-husband who may or may not want me back at sporadic and ill-timed intervals.'

'So what? At our age, wouldn't it be weirder if we didn't have baggage? Even Edward has an ex-wife doesn't he?'

'Apparently so, but she's long gone and with no kids to tie them together, she's no reason to come back to him.'

'What do you want to do?'

I draw a deep breath. 'Eat more ice cream.'

Janey nudges me. 'And *then*?' She gestures to the almost empty tub. 'This isn't going to stand the test of time.'

I sigh. 'Then I draw a line under it and move on.'

Chapter 46

Except I can't move on. I can't because I think about Edward every waking minute; his kind, calm manner, his warm lips, the softness of the hair on his chest, his delicious scent and the intensity of his blue eyes when they're on me. I'm hollow without him. When I've dropped the kids off at school the next day, I head to work determined to sort this mess out once and for all.

When I walk in, the scene is much worse than yesterday. A woman is standing by the desk holding a tiny, limp black puppy in her arms, jiggling it gently like you would a colicky baby. Her eyes are red-rimmed and puffy. I glance at reception where Carly and Helen are manning the buzzing phone lines again and get a heavy, sinking feeling. Edward must be off again. Bubbles of anger build inside of me. It surprises me at first but once it's there, I go with it. Upset or confused he may be, but this is his job and he can't avoid coming in because he doesn't want to see me – this is exactly what I didn't want to happen. That puppy doesn't look like it will make it if Edward doesn't get here soon. When Helen hangs up the phone I march over and take it from her.

I dial Edward's number. It goes straight to answerphone so I slam it back on the receiver. 'Damn it.'

Everyone looks at me but nobody speaks. 'I'm just going to …' I point towards the kitchen.

Once I'm in there, I dial Edward again, from my own phone this time. When the answerphone picks up I speak.

'Edward, I don't have time to talk about Sunday but you need to get your backside back into work. People need you and there's a puppy here that won't survive if you don't get here quickly. I know you don't want to see me right now and I'm going to go home so you can come in and do your job. I know you're not ill. I saw—'

It's probably for the best that the beep cuts me off there. I type a much briefer version up on my phone and send it by email and text in the hope he'll get just one of the messages.

I tell Carly and Helen that I'm going to take the rest of the week off but I hope Edward will be in soon to deal with emergencies. I don't wait for them to say anything, I just leave.

I think I go through a mini-state of hysteria. I clean, by choice, and enjoy it for once, and when I think about the whole Edward thing, I laugh. I laugh so hard my abdominal muscles think I've done fifty sit-ups (or maybe ten sit-ups – it's been a while). It's ridiculous when I think of it. Me, dating. Me, swept up in a romance with my boss of all people. It's bonkers. I don't even know how it happened when I think about it. When the house is sparkling, I sit down with the local newspaper and as I'm flicking through, notice an ad for a bookkeeping job in the city. It's an outsourcing company so basically, I'd be working in an office for an accountancy firm doing the books for small businesses who outsource their books and payroll. I'd only have to meet the business owners a couple of times a year, if at all and now I'm more up to date, I stand a chance at getting it. I run upstairs for my laptop, tweak my CV and fire it off before I think better of it.

This is what I need. It's good that I'm putting myself out there. Driving some distance between Edward and me is the best thing to do for both our sakes. A year from now, I'll look back and this will just be a tiny bump in the road.

Chapter 47

'You got the job!' Janey beams. It's Saturday and we're waiting for Emily and Amanda to arrive for tonight's book club gathering.

'No,' I say, 'I got an interview but three positions are going because they're expanding, so I think my odds will be good. I'll have to go into their office in Manchester a few times a week but otherwise, I can work from home. It's a few more hours and a bit more money than I'm getting at Prescott's too.'

'It's great,' Janey says with little enthusiasm.

'What's the matter?'

She twists the corner of her mouth. 'Nothing, it really does sound great. I suppose I just saw you patching things up with Edward and staying at the vet's.'

I shrug. 'The vet's wasn't meant to be.'

'But you were so happy there. You shouldn't have to leave because you fell out with your boss.'

'This is why you shouldn't mix business and pleasure. Look, Edward hasn't asked me to leave. It's just better that I do.'

'You should at least look into constructive dismissal.' She presses her lips into a hard line.

I laugh softly. 'Nobody has done anything wrong other than fall in—'

Janey's eyes bulge. 'I didn't know—'

'I didn't mean that. I just meant it was a mutual thing and nobody breached any contract or broke any employment laws.'

Janey draws a breath and her lips part like she's about to speak.

'End of story,' I add before she gets the chance. 'Now, let's get the nibbles ready.'

The doorbell rings shortly after and it's Amanda. Emily arrives a few minutes later in a flurry of wine, chocolates and flowers.

'You don't have to bring anything,' I say, kissing her on the cheek.

'I know. I just want to show how grateful I am to be a part of the group.'

'Ahh, well that's very sweet.' I lean in for a hug.

'Get a room, you two.' Janey barges past with a tray of wine glasses and Emily laughs softly.

'Right,' I say once everyone is sitting down. 'I have a bit of a confession to make.'

Three pairs of eyes are upon me. I take a breath. 'Okay, I didn't read the book. Truth be told, I can't even remember what book we were supposed to be reading. It's been a bit of a … hectic month.'

'I didn't read it either,' Janey says. 'I started it but I'm only about halfway through. I came here tonight hoping to wing it through the discussions. Sorry.'

'I just had the ending left to read,' Emily says, hunching her shoulders.

Amanda folds her arms and sighs. 'So I am the only person who read the book?' The three of us nod sheepishly as Amanda looks at us. There's a moment of tension before her face cracks into a smile. 'It wasn't that great anyway. How about we head into Manchester for some cocktails?'

We glance at one another. None of us are really dressed for the occasion.

'Can we go and get changed first?' Janey asks.

'It's eight o'clock now. I think if we're going we just do it,' Emily says. She looks great anyway. She's one of those people who always wears something casual enough for the daytime but smart enough to wear to a bar. She just has that whole office-to-club vibe permanently. Not that she's ever stepped foot in an office. Anyway, I digress.

'Emily is right. Let's go,' I say.

Even when we do wild and spontaneous, we're reserved. I laugh to myself.

Thirty minutes later, we're standing outside some swanky new cocktail bar that Emily suggested. A few people are queuing to get in but the doormen are letting people in quickly. I get a shiver and wish I'd put my coat on. Although it's still light, the temperature has dropped with the dipping sun.

As we go to walk in, one of the door attendants sticks his arm out. 'Sorry, love. No tracksuit bottoms.'

We all glance at Janey's bottom half. She shrugs. 'It's loungewear and it's comfy. I did ask if I could get changed but you lot wanted to be spontaneous.'

'Come on. This isn't going to ruin our night – I know a place,' I say. It's only a five-minute walk. On our way, we pass the beautiful, cylindrical library. My eyes are drawn to it, like it's taunting me for being the world's worst book club member.

'Benny's Beer Keg?' Three voices whine in protest at the budget pub chain.

'It's a nice one and they do cocktails. Come on, it's either this or we head back to my house.'

Five minutes later we're sitting on battered sofas drinking gin and tonics.

'Ladies, I want to say something.' Amanda puts down her empty glass. 'For months now, I've enjoyed our gatherings. My house is very empty and being alone so much can feel suffocating so I wanted to thank you again for taking me in.'

'You don't need to thank us,' Janey says. 'We love you.'

Amanda smiles. 'Well, I love you too but what I want to say is you've helped me more than you know. I was in quite a dark place and if I'd have sunk any deeper, I don't know if I would have ever re-emerged. Watching you all cope with your break-ups has given me strength. Janey, you choosing to be honest with yourself and, Stephanie, you moving on and giving in to your desires has really pushed me to do more for myself. So …'

We all stare at her, desperate to know what's coming. 'I've joined a dating site for mature adults and I have a date next weekend.' She squeals at the end and we join in.

'That calls for another round,' Janey says already heading to the bar.

All the commotion seems to attract some attention. There's a small group of men nearby. They're loud but in very high spirits. When we're on our second round of G&Ts one of them comes over.

'Hi, ladies. I'm on my mate's stag do but I've had enough of them.' He perches on the arm of our sofa next to Amanda who squirms with discomfort. He's quite handsome with a rugged, yet affable face. His eyes are punctuated with fine lines and there's a sprinkling of grey in his light-brown hair.

'Why?' Emily asks, sitting forward. His eyes light up when they catch sight of her and soon, the two of them move to a table and begin chatting away.

'He looks a few million quid short of her usual type,' Janey says.

'Maybe her usual type is the wrong type.' I shrug, glancing over at the two of them. Despite being middle-aged, she's laughing and twirling her hair like a crush-ridden teen and I'm pleased for her. Seeing her so happy reminds me of being with Edward and that comment Amanda made about giving in to my desires was a little too much. I get a pang so sharp, it's like my insides have been sucked out by a Dyson vac.

'I think I'm going to go home,' I say feeling like the world's biggest party pooper.

'What? Now? It's so early,' Janey says.

I tilt my head to the side. 'It's eleven o'clock,' I say, like it's some magnificent feat.

Janey puts her hand on mine. 'Let me finish my gin and I'll come with you,' she says.

'No,' I say sharply. This night out is a blue moon event for all of us.

'What about your, you know?' She gives me a knowing look. 'I'm coming.'

'You stay here. I'll be fine. Track me on Uber.'

I say my goodbyes and step out into the cool summer's evening. The doormen are chatting and there are a few people milling about. I feel okay. I feel safe. I try to order an Uber but for some reason the app keeps freezing. I don't know if it's my signal or what but I have no choice but to walk to get a cab. The streets near the taxi rank are quiet for a Saturday night. I wrap my arms around myself and walk as quickly as I can. A group of men nearby start laughing loudly and my throat starts to constrict. I look up and see the stars. It reminds me of being under the night sky with Edward last weekend and it calms me a little. As I walk, I take deep, slow breaths and try to imagine he's here, beside me.

Chapter 48

I find a taxi straight away and climbing inside offers me some relief. There is a bang on the window as we pull away from the kerb and I jump. It's a young guy. Drunk. Probably showing off to his mates. I hug my handbag to my body. I just want to get home. As we leave the built-up city centre and course the country lanes I get that ball of apprehension again. On the back of the driver's seat is a 'cash only' sign. I check my purse. I only have thirty quid left. Because I'd planned on getting an Uber, I hadn't thought about drawing any cash out and the only cash machine in Milton is inside the Co-op, which is shut now. The meter is on twenty-five pounds already and at the rate the numbers are whizzing by, I'm not sure I'll make it home.

When the meter gets to twenty-six pounds, I draw a breath. I need to stop him now. Sometimes, at night, taxi drivers press a magic meter button that adds an extra few quid on. I can't take the risk of being short. We're so close to streets with houses that I risk a few more moments of taxi-roulette. When the meter hits twenty-seven, I can't take it anymore.

'Just here will do.'

From my position, I make out the side of the driver's face crumple into a frown as he realises we've not quite reached the address he'd tapped into Google maps on his phone. I squint at the map. It says five minutes driving left. What's that? About a fifteen-minute walk? I can cope with that.

'Are you sure?'

'Yes. I need some air.'

'Okay then.' He presses his magic meter buttons and to my relief it only jumps by one pound thirty.

'Keep the change,' I say automatically, handing my thirty quid over. I can't help but wonder if that one pound seventy tip would have seen me home.

The streets are deathly quiet. Some of the houses are in darkness but the odd one has a light on or the bluish tinge of a television screen glowing through the net curtains. I'm perfectly safe but my heart doesn't know it. My heart thinks it's joined a jungle-trance band as the lead percussionist. A loud rustling noise coming from a front garden across the road makes me turn with a start. In my haste, I twist my foot and a snapping sound echoes in the darkness. I go to step forwards but my foot falls clumsily. It's the heel of my shoe – it's snapped off completely.

'Brilliant.' A fox darts out from between some rubbish bags and runs across the road into some other poor bugger's garden to terrorise their bins no doubt. I pick up my hobbled pace. Only a few more streets left to go. There is a small park to pass but there are houses all around it. As I near the park, my palms start to sweat. I clench my fists and relax them again for no reason other than to distract myself. The houses stop like a void of coal-black darkness has swallowed them up. I stop for a moment. If I cut across the park it will save me some time. With my heel broken it's going to be a struggle to walk all the way around. I draw a breath and set off. There's a path that winds through the expanse of grass. I know it like the back of my hand because I bring the kids here all the time during the day. At night, it's different. I hate feeling like this.

An owl hoots and wind rustles the dry leaves on the trees. I hold my bag tight to my body and allow my eyes to dart around the pitch-black as I pick up my pace. The sparsely dotted trees thicken up towards the end of the path, blocking any moonlight that broke through the navy clouds. I slow down and strain my ears for voices. Silence. Heart racing, I carry on. In just a few minutes, I'll be through the park and back under the comfort of the streetlamps. As I near the gate, I get a whiff of something familiar. Marijuana. Then, a noise. The low murmur of voices. My blood runs cold through my veins. I contemplate turning back but that means walking all the way through the park and I'm so close to home. Just a street away. It's probably just a few teenagers enjoying a spliff. It doesn't mean they ... I can't bring myself to think the words.

I slide my hand in my bag and wrap my fingers around my personal alarm. As I near the exit, I can make out the outline of two figures leaning at either side of the opening in the iron fence. Their silhouettes illuminated by the orange glow of the lamppost. There are houses just a few metres away, across the road. Surely, if I were to scream or use my alarm, someone would come?

I glance behind me. The memory of that tall, scrawny teen coming up behind me and Mum floods back to me. My mouth is dry and blood thumps my eardrums. There's nothing there but darkness. Holding my alarm in one hand and my door keys in the other, I walk towards the men.

My senses are heightened as I approach them quietly. If they don't know I'm coming, they can't plan anything and by the time they see me, I'll be on a residential street. As I put down my foot with the broken shoe, it slips. It must be wet leaves or something on the path but whatever it is, I can't get purchase and the stubby nail where my heel used to be scrapes along the ground loudly.

'Fuck was that?' one of the voices says.

Shit. Shit. Shit. What do I do now? Running back towards the woods is a bad idea. I force myself to keep walking.

'Some pissed bird,' the other one says. My heart is hammering

274

so hard it might break out of my ribcage. I'm close now. Close enough to take in their laid-back postures. Perhaps they are just having a smoke and a chat.

As I pass them, my legs start to tremble. My fingers are poised and ready to pull the pin out of my alarm. I fix my eyes on the houses ahead that are just a few metres away.

'You all right, love?' one of the blokes asks. I glance at him. A thick beanstalk of fear has climbed my throat and entwined itself around my vocal cords, rendering them useless. I slip again on my stupid shoe and a hand grabs my elbow firmly. My body convulses and my legs give way. Another hand grabs me from the other side and I yank the pin out of my alarm.

'What the ...'

'Easy, love. Just trying to help.'

I can only just hear them over the ear-piercing screech of the alarm. A few windows illuminate in the houses across the way. A front door opens and the hands slide away. The two men run off.

'Is everything all right?' the man in the house shouts. With trembling fingers, it takes a couple of tries to put the pin back in the alarm and silence the thing. My ears still ring the same pitch as the alarm.

'Yes. Sorry. It was a misunderstanding.'

He eyes me for a second then nods. As he closes the door, I carry on walking home. My whole body is shaking, but it's no longer the violent shakes of fear, it's the jelly-like wobble of shock and humiliation. Warm moisture seeps from my eyes and rolls down my cheeks. So much emotion hits me all at once. I'm embarrassed, incompetent, damaged ... I can't go on like this and the one person who makes me feel complete and sane and normal and all the things I want to be has gone. The tears turn into heaving sobs. I must look a right state stumbling home like this.

My house is visible now. Just a few more metres and this will all be over, for now. My keys are still in my hand so as I climb the steps, I don't pause to find them. As I near the top step, someone steps out of the shadows.

'Steph?'

I jump out of my skin.

Chapter 49

'Steph, it's just me, Edward. Your friend Janey rang the out-of-hours number and said you might need me.'

I look up and I can just about make out the comforting familiarity of his eyes.

'What's happened to you?' He places two firm hands on my shoulders and I can't help it, I collapse into him and sob softly. Gently, he unfurls my fingers from my keys and manoeuvres me so he can reach the door to open it. Then, he scoops me up into his arms and carries me inside. I let my head fall to his shoulder. His familiar scent washes away all the anxiety and trauma from my walk home.

'Are you hurt?' His eyebrows press together as he looks me over. I shake my head.

'I'm going to run you a bath,' he says, climbing the stairs two at a time. I haven't spoken a word since I got home and when I whisper a quiet thank you, it sounds louder and sharper than it should. He lays me on the bed and goes into the bathroom. The sound of water streaming from the taps soon follows. I sit up to slide off my dress. My reflection stares back at me from the mirrored wardrobe door and it's as bad as I expected. Black streaks have cut trails through my foundation and blusher, smudged lipstick and wild hair make me look almost as bad as I feel. I peel off my clothes and put on my bathrobe. I'm securing the belt as Edward knocks softly on the door.

'You can come in,' I say.

'Your bath is ready. I'll go and make some tea.' When his footsteps reach the bottom of the stairs, I lower myself into the steaming water. It's hot and my skin reddens but I quite enjoy the feeling. He's put some sort of bubble bath in, probably an old Christmas gift he found in the cupboard. I rarely take a bath – you don't get a chance with three kids dictating your every minute – but I could get used to this. For a few moments, I can forget about what a tit I made of myself in the park. I rest my head back and close my eyes.

I don't know how much time passes but there's a knock on the door. The water is suddenly tepid. I glance down at myself and there are still enough bubbles to cover me. 'Come in.'

'I wasn't sure if you might want your tea in the bath,' Edward says. He's holding a cup in one hand and is shielding his eyes with the other.

'Thank you.'

'I'll just leave it …' He trails off.

'It's okay. The bubbles are shielding my modesty. You don't need to cover your eyes,' I say.

Tentatively, he lowers his hand. He still won't look at me but he does spot the windowsill next to the bath and sets the tea down there. Then he turns to leave.

'Can you stay?' I ask.

'Yes, I was going to wait downstairs.'

'No. I mean can you stay here with me now.'

His Adam's apple rises and falls as he thinks for a moment and I instantly want to take the words back. If he says no it will be awkward. I'll feel like some sort of crap temptress.

Eventually, he nods and my tense body relaxes. He closes the toilet lid and sits down on it then crosses his legs before uncrossing them straight away.

'What happened tonight?' he asks.

'Nothing,' I say honestly.

'Nothing doesn't have you running home in floods of tears in a broken shoe.' The muscles in his jaw flex.

'I mean it was *over* nothing. I ran out of money for a cab and had to walk part of the way home. It was dark and my imagination got the better of me. There were two men in the park smoking weed and I panicked – the smell brings back memories of …'

He crouches at the side of the bath and strokes my face. 'Oh, Steph. *You* should have called me.'

'You were ignoring my calls and messages and emails, remember.'

'I'm sorry,' he says quietly, resuming his seat on the toilet lid.

'Why did you come?' I ask. I'd been so grateful to see him there when I got home, that I didn't think to ask.

He's looking down at his lap where his resting hands are intertwined. 'I checked my emails.'

My mind races backwards through the week. The only email I sent was the one telling him to get his butt back to work. I'm not sure that warranted a late-night visit.

'I know you've been applying for new jobs. I had a reference request through.'

Oh. That. 'I panicked. What was I supposed to think when you disappeared at the first sign of trouble? A dog almost died.' Thankfully, Carly told me that Edward came and saved the day but not before almost giving me a heart attack.

He drops his head in his hands. 'I know. What I did was stupid. I know Mike wanted you back and I just wanted to give you space. I wanted you to make a decision without me influencing any part of it.'

'Mike didn't want that,' I say in a frustrated tone. I'm fed up with the conversation.

'I know. I read your message this evening.'

'And how about Stacy? I saw her at your house with flowers. You invited her in. Are you back together?'

He furrows his brow and then understanding registers. 'No. Not at all. She came to get her picnic basket. I invited her in because I knew I'd have to root around in the pantry to find it and didn't want to leave her standing outside. She'd brought flowers to thank me for setting her up with Dave. The two of them really hit it off. She'd also brought soup because she knew I was ill.'

From what little I know of her, it sounds plausible.

'So what now?' I ask. How can Edward and I go back to what we had when the first bump in the road sends him flying off course like a kite in a hurricane?

'I suppose I need to apologise. I'm sorry. My behaviour was inexcusable. I just didn't want to be the guy who begs you to choose him. I knew I couldn't offer you your perfect family like Mike could and I was coming to terms with that.'

I give my head a little shake. 'I'm not really sure what this means for us if pets have to almost die every time we have a row.'

He tilts his head to the side. 'It wasn't a row, Steph. This was the father of your three children saying he wants to start again.'

I glance at the thinning bubbles and reposition them with my hands. 'I suppose I can see why you were upset.'

'I could have handled it better and I shouldn't have taken time off work. I've never done anything like that before. If any creature had died because I wasn't there, I'd never have forgiven myself.'

'No harm done in the end.'

A few moments pass. 'I don't want you to leave the practice. No matter what happens between us, I love the team we've got.'

I swirl the water with my hand and notice the bubbles are dissolving at a rapid rate. 'I think I'd better get out.' Edward's eyes widen. 'Of the bath, I mean.'

He rises to his feet. 'I'll let you get dressed.'

'Will you be here when I come down?'

He gives a small smile. 'If you want me to be?'

I nod. 'I do.'

Chapter 50

I towel-dry my hair and wrap my dressing gown around me before heading downstairs. As I near the bottom, I slow down. It's so quiet, I wonder if he's had second thoughts and gone again. The lounge light is off, so I head towards the kitchen clutching my dressing gown tightly as I walk in. To my relief, he's still here, sitting at the table reading a newspaper. The teapot sits in the centre with a reassuring ribbon of steam travelling out of its spout. I grab a cup and sit down.

'I feel better for that,' I say to break the silence.

'I'm glad I was here, you seemed so upset.' Edward lowers his paper and folds it, placing it down on the table. He adjusts the position so its corner is square to the table edge.

'I'm glad you were here too.' Although in hindsight, I'm embarrassed about the state he saw me in. I can't believe I set off my alarm. I'm such a fool but I am glad Edward was here. I can't imagine wanting any other person here comforting me and the thought of coming home and being alone is unbearable.

Edward covers my hand with his. 'Listen, I don't want you to leave the practice but it was wrong of me to ask you to stay. You should do what feels right for you and the kids.'

'I don't want to leave either,' I whisper. I've come to love my job. I love being around the people there and I love the clients, especially the furry ones, which surprises me. Most of all, I know how unbearable it will be not seeing Edward every day. Whatever happens.

'Then don't.' His eyes are so intent on mine the intangible contact makes my body tingle. It's so intense, I want to look away because the feeling is unbearable, but at the same time, I can't because I don't want to break the spell. It feels like we're talking about more than the job now.

'I've missed you this week,' I say.

'I've missed you too. It's been hell.'

'Can we sit outside?'

He looks surprised but doesn't say anything. He stands up and holds out his hand for me and when I take it, he leads me out to the swinging chair. We sit down and, as he puts an arm over my shoulder, I snuggle into the nook of his armpit. The sky is an intense navy and the moon is full and bright. It's beautiful.

'Are you okay out here?' he asks.

'Yes. Strangely, I was just thinking about how pretty the night sky is. Is it weird to admire and fear something at the same time?'

'Not at all.'

'I lost my mum on a night like this, but sitting here now doesn't make me sad anymore. I like to think of her up there somewhere.'

'Perhaps she is.'

I tilt my head a little so I can just about see Edward's face. 'I might be afraid of the dark when I'm outside and all alone but that's nothing compared to the darkness that consumed me all the time when you weren't around. That terrified me.'

He sweeps the hair from my face and kisses my forehead and whispers, 'I want to be here for you. Always. If you'll have me of course.'

I'm light-headed and dizzy. My brain seems to have forgotten how to function. All I know is that I want Edward in my life more than anything and I'm willing to take a chance on him. He sets parts of my body alight that I thought died years ago. He's kind and thoughtful and he always puts me first, no matter what. I'm ready to bring him into all of our lives, slowly of course, with plenty of tact and love. The kids accepted Kate pretty quickly. Perhaps I feared for them much more than they ever feared for themselves. I think now Mike and I are in a good place; in time, we could be some sort of big happy family. I do need some reassurances though.

'Mike is always going to be in my life. Some, albeit small,' and very much above the waistline, 'part of me will always love him. Can you promise that you won't have a huge wobble and disappear again? The kids can't have that kind of instability in their lives. Heck, I can't have that kind of instability in my life.'

He stands up, takes me by the hand, and leads me to the fence at the end of the garden. The river bubbles lightly and a gentle breeze toys with the leaves in the nearby white willow trees. I can just make out their dark outline against the inky sky. Edward pulls my hands in close so we're facing one another.

'I promise it wasn't a wobble. I really did just want to give you space. I switched my phone off because I knew if I spoke to you I wouldn't be able to help myself in telling you how I felt and it wasn't about me. I'm not going to pretend it wasn't killing me staying away from you.' He pulls me closer. 'Not knowing whether you and Mike were trying again was hell but I was doing it with good intentions. In hindsight, I should have spoken to you first. I acted like an idiot and I'm really not that guy.'

'I know you're not.' I rest my forehead on his chest. He steps in, closing the last few inches between us so the length of my torso is touching his, then cups my face in his hands. I get that weird magnetism again when our eyes meet. The ripples of anticipation ride through me, and my knees weaken as if they might give way. He brushes his tongue over his lips. Cupping my face with both his hands, he brings his lips to mine. Warm and moist they glide smoothly across mine, falling in sync instantaneously.

The kiss is intense, breathy and hot. I pull his T-shirt wanting his body even closer although it's not physically possible. I wrap my leg around his waist and he lifts me up so I can wrap the other one around too. My fingers knot in his hair now and I run them down the sides of his face through his soft stubble as he carries me to the bedroom.

Chapter 51

I run my hand over the fine hair on Edward's warm chest and snuggle into the nook of his arm. Waking up next to Edward is like sleeping on silk sheets after having a full body wax. It's delicious. Everything about his smell and the warmth of his body is a comfort to me. It's more than that – I want to drink him in and inhale him at the same time. Any worries I had seem to have vanished like they've been hit with an Oxy-Action spray. I think if we can move past this bump in the road we'll be stronger. We've learnt early on that we have to be open and honest. If we start in such a healthy way, we'll be building on strong foundations. It's so right. Every molecule in my body is tuned into it and it's so powerful. More so than when Mike and I were together.

Perhaps I just wanted a protector all those years ago. I was never scared to be out at night with Mike by my side and maybe I mistook safety for something more in the early days. With Edward it's different. It's a raw and unfiltered kind of love that grew from physical and mental attraction. I'm no expert but I think that's how it's supposed to be. It's why I've decided to see someone about my fears. I don't want Edward to be my crutch; I want him as my equal.

Edward buries his face in my hair and inhales, breaking my train of thought. 'Morning.'

'Morning, sleepy,' I reply. I've not decided how to tell the kids yet but I'm ready to do it. They might not be happy about it at first but they do like Edward and they have a sort of respect for him that they didn't get a chance to build with Kate before they knew she was their dad's girlfriend. I'm hoping it helps but if it doesn't, time certainly will and Edward won't stop trying with them.

'What will you do if my kids really hate you?'

He wraps both arms around me and squeezes me. 'I'll just keep trying to win them over. I'll talk to them, spend time with them doing activities and things. I'll tell them jokes—'

I crane my neck so he can see my raised-eyebrow expression.

'Okay, perhaps I won't tell jokes. You did say win them over and not send them running off into oncoming traffic, didn't you?'

'Exhibit A, your honour.'

He laughs a soft, easy laugh. 'So, you're telling the jokes now, hmm?'

'What if that stuff doesn't work?'

He kisses the side of my neck. 'It will eventually. I'm impossible to hate long term, I promise.'

'I don't know about that, mister,' I tease.

'Remember that time we didn't talk and it caused a lorry-load of problems?'

'You mean this past week?'

His head moves up and down, sweeping stubble across my chin. 'Well, the solution was to talk. We'll talk to them as a team or individuals, whatever the issue calls for, and we'll listen to their concerns and treat them with respect.'

'It's like you've done this parent thing before,' I say.

'It's dealing with awkward clients 101.'

I elbow him gently. 'What you're saying makes sense.'

'They're vulnerable little people who think they know all they need in the world because they're not aware of adult life yet. They do know all they need for now but this is something that connects their world to the adult world so there are elements of what's happening here that are incomprehensible to them.'

'You've hit the nail on the head and you're right. We'll respect them, we'll listen, we'll explain and we'll give them time.'

'And we don't have to do anything until you're ready.'

I don't need to think about it any longer. I want to be with Edward; he's the one for me, for us. 'Let's have a few more family dates and in a few weeks, we'll find a way to tell them.'

'Whatever you want.'

Chapter 52

It's been six weeks since Edward and I decided we were going to be together. We've eaten lunch together each day, had sleepovers every Saturday and lots of 'play dates' with the kids. All three of them love 'Mummy's boss friend'. I think Ralph suspects there's something else going on. I've noticed the odd 'look' when I've mentioned Edward's name. When we're all together though, he never acts out. He's chatty and always wants to show Edward anything he's been working on, be that a painting, a story he's written or a computer game. I'm not sure if this is Ralph's way of giving his silent approval or if I'm reading too much into things. Either way, I'm about to find out.

'Go to the man for your life jacket,' I say, gently shoving the children in the direction of the boat rental person.

'Did you decide to tell the kids about us on a narrowboat so they can't run away?' Edward whispers when they're out of earshot.

'Not at all. I thought it would be a nice day out.'

Edward raises two disbelieving eyebrows.

The guide escorts us to our vessel for the day and stands at the side ready to help us aboard.

'It's okay, I've got this,' Edward says, scooping Ava in the air and dumping her on board. Ralph jumps across unaided and Edward helps me step aboard whilst I'm balancing a rather weighty Henry on my hip. Otis is spending the day with Janey, who's hoping he'll help tire her kids out.

Once the rental guy has been through the controls and canal rules, we're handed the keys and given free rein over the waterways of Cheshire.

'Mummy, are we going under that bridge?' Ava asks.

'I don't know, honey. We're just looking at the map now,' I say. Edward unfolds the map and lays it out on the bench seating.

'We can head north to Walton Gardens or south to Anderton, where we might get to see the big boat lift.'

'Gardens are boring. I vote we head south.' Ralph's response comes as no surprise.

'Ava, do you mind which way we go?' Edward asks.

She's playing with the hair on her Barbie and gives a shake of her head.

'South it is then,' Edward says. Carrying Henry, I follow him up the wooden steps, which lead out of the back of the boat and he starts the engine. I hand Henry to Edward and jump across to the bank, untether us and jump back aboard, then Edward hands Henry back, pushes the thrust (if that's the right word) and off we go. We're working in sync without even thinking about it and I like it.

The boat turns sharply towards the opposite bank, so Edward yanks the tiller the other way and the bow starts heading towards the other bank. 'Careful,' I scream as we continue zigzagging across the canal.

Edward laughs. 'I just need to get a feel for it.'

'Can you get a feel for it quicker?' I say, not trying to hide my unease.

'It's harder than it looks,' he replies, frowning.

'Remember, the guide said less is more with the steering.'

'Mum, what's going on?' Ralph says, peeking out through the little door down to the tiny galley.

'Edward is just getting a feel for things,' I say, with underlying mirth in my tone. Ralph does that 'cool' thing where he sort of raises his eyebrows and nods his approval at the same time.

'Are we going to crash, Mummy?' Ava shouts from inside.

'No, everything is fine.'

Once Edward has 'a feel for things', we're soon navigating the waterway like pros, waving at other boating folk as they pass and walkers on the banks who are almost keeping pace.

'This is nice,' Edward says, giving me a smile with depth. 'I wish I could wrap my arms around you and kiss you right now.'

My insides clench. 'Me too. But we might have to settle for a cuppa for now.'

I take Henry inside and check on the kids. Ralph is on his DS and Ava is colouring. 'Come on, you guys, let's go out front.'

I shepherd the children out and we sit on the wooden benching that fills the bow. The sun is just starting to warm the morning air and the canal water is a deep green beneath the blue sky. A family of ducks look as though they're about to swim into our path and Ava gasps. We miss them, or they miss us. Probably the latter.

'I have some duck food in my bag.' It's left over from when I took the children to the practice and we had fish and chips but I'm sure it's still okay. When I hand it over, both Ava and Ralph start throwing it in. The ducks keep up with the boat and Ava laughs with glee when they stay with us a while. I give Henry a handful of food and he chucks it randomly. Half of it hits me in the face so he giggles and so do I.

Later, when I remember, I make some tea. After sorting some snacks out for the kids, I head out the back to Edward.

'Are you okay out here by yourself?'

He smiles. 'Yes. I've been lost in my thoughts – it's quite therapeutic.'

'I didn't realise that we'd probably struggle to talk to the children if one of us has to drive the boat at all times.'

'We can moor up, but I've been thinking. Perhaps it would be better if you spoke to the children alone. Telling them together might make them uncomfortable and feel like they can't ask any questions.'

I think for a moment. We had planned to sit them down and tell them together so we could both offer reassurance and the kids could ask us both anything they wanted but perhaps Edward is right. If I take them to the front of the boat and talk to them, they might open up a bit more. Edward is still here if they want to talk to him too and when we stop for lunch later, he can talk to them then.

'I knew there was a reason I liked you,' I say, winking. 'I'm going to do it now. Wish me luck.'

As I head down the steps and think about how to start the conversation, I get a dryness in my mouth. Part of me believes they'll be fine but the other part thinks they've been through so much that it's unfair to burden them with any more change that will upset them.

'Kids, can I talk to you?' I say before I have a chance to change my mind. Ralph shrugs and Ava says 'yes' brightly.

'Let's go back outside. It's lovely and sunny.' I'm not sure how effective vitamin D will be in such a situation but experts do say it helps lift your mood.

Once we're outside and I'm seated with Henry on my knee I can't seem to find the words. As Ava and Ralph stare at me with wide, expectant eyes, it's like the words have fallen out of my head.

'What is it, Mum?' Ralph asks. He doesn't seem impatient; he seems worried. Oh God, I need to just say it.

'Well.' I swallow. 'The thing is …'

'What is the thing, Mum?' Ralph lets out an exasperated breath. Perhaps he *is* impatient this time.

'It's Edward. And me.' Ava's brow crumples in confusion whereas realisation starts to register on Ralph's features. Before Ralph can respond in words or expression, I carry on.

'I love you three more than anything in the world, you know that don't you?' Ava nods. 'But Mummy misses having a grown-up around to watch films with when you're in bed. I'd like someone to chat with and help with the cooking and things like that.' I'm aware that I'm waffling but the children are still listening intently. 'Edward and I would like to be a couple. We really enjoy spending time together and he makes me happy but he's not moving in or anything like that; he'll just be spending more time with us … if that's okay with you guys.'

Ralph sits in stone-faced silence. The only sound for the agonising few moments that follow is the bow gently slicing through the water.

'I like Edward, Mummy, and I don't mind if he is your boyfriend,' Ava says, eventually.

I smile warmly. 'That's great to hear, sweetheart.'

Henry wraps his sticky fingers in my hair and looks at the passing trees obliviously.

'Edward's cool,' Ralph says eventually, shattering the tension that had built up in my chest.

Those two words mean and say so much more. I don't want to ruin the moment with a big gush of emotion, so instead, I just say: 'Good, I'm glad.'

I stand up and hug Ralph, then Ava. 'I love you both so much and you can talk to me about anything that makes you unhappy. You will do that, won't you?' They nod. 'Okay, I'm going to give you some space and you can come and ask us anything you want when you've had a think. Ava, do not lean over the side of the boat.'

'I won't, Mummy.'

I head back through the cabin to the back and climb out.

Edward is still standing at the tiller, gently manoeuvring it from side to side. Somehow, it keeps us going in a straight line.

'You look like you've been through a tumble dryer,' he says, eyes dancing mischievously.

I smooth my hair over and roll my eyes. 'Henry.'

'How did it go?' he asks, with more sympathy in his tone.

'Okay, I think. They didn't have much to say. I gave them some space to mull things over.'

All of a sudden, there is a scream then a splash. My eyes dart to Edward's. A split second later, I hear Ralph screech Ava's name.

Chapter 53

I freeze. My heart has stopped, I'm sure of it.

'Stop the boat,' I scream at Edward but he's already done it. He quickly kicks off his shoes and starts walking around the gunwale. Another boat passes us and the ripples cause ours to bob about, just adding to the jelly wobble of my legs.

'Stay there, Ava. Don't panic,' Edward shouts. He's almost reached the front. I lean over and see her blonde hair. Her head is well above water thanks to the mandatory orange lifejacket. As Edward nears, he jumps in.

'Stay there, darling,' I yell.

The water reaches the Ralph Lauren logo on Edward's shirt as he wades through the murky water. It isn't until she's safely in his arms that I realise I'm holding my breath.

'I'm going to take her to the bank,' Edward shouts. 'The boat is too high to climb back onto.'

I watch with relief as he makes it to dry land and sits Ava on the stone side before hauling himself out of the water. They both look cold and mucky.

'I'll try and get the boat over. Hang on.'

Trying to remember the tutorial, I turn the ignition with shaky hands and push the thruster gently so the boat starts to move. I ease the tiller away from the bank and the bow starts to go towards the bank so I pull it back. Somehow, I manage to have the boat parallel to the bank after a couple of tries. Edward comes running over and I toss him the rope, which he secures to a mooring post. He runs to the front and Ralph tosses him the rope from the bow. As Edward helps Ralph jump across, I head down to get Henry, and the bag of blankets I brought in case it got chilly. I grab the bag with our picnic in too because I've brought a flask of hot chocolate for the kids.

As I step over to the bank, another narrowboat comes past. 'Are you all okay? We saw what happened,' a lady at the helm shouts.

'Yes, thank you. I think we are.'

'We have towels and things if you need. It's happened to us before now. Bet the little one is wide awake now.' She smiles and somehow, I'm glad at that bit of reassurance that I'm not the worst parent in the world. I thank her again and tell her we're okay and she sails off.

'I thought we might as well have a break,' I say, laying down the picnic blanket and plonking Henry in the centre with his favourite teddy. We sit down and I take out the other blankets and pass one to Edward, who is shivering now, then wrap the other around Ava before scooping her up onto my knee. Her hair is sticky-wet and she smells like stagnant pond water. Ralph pours hot chocolate into the plastic picnic cups I brought and hands Edward the first one. I tense up, waiting for some kind of snarky comment but he just hands him the drink.

'Mum, I was going to jump in after her but I panicked,' Ralph says.

'Oh, honey, I wouldn't have wanted you to. I should have been the one to jump in but I think I panicked too, love.'

The corner of Ralph's mouth twists a little then he turns to Edward. 'Thanks for saving Ava.'

'It was nothing. I just acted on instinct.'

'Yes, I second that, Edward. I can't thank you enough,' I say.

'Honestly, please, it was nothing. I would never have let anything happen to Ava. Or Henry or Ralph for that matter.' He sips his hot chocolate as though what he's just said was nothing but those words mean the world to me. The fact he'd risk his life, or perhaps not his life but some very expensive-looking clothes, for my children shows he cares for them and that's all I want. Perhaps Ava wasn't really in peril. She was bobbing about quite safely in her life jacket, and in fairness we could have probably scooped her out with the big wooden pole thing on the roof of the boat. But Edward jumped right in without a second thought. Even now, he's sipping his hot chocolate and playing with Henry and not complaining about his soggy clothes.

Ava wraps her little hands around the warm plastic cup that Ralph has just passed to her and takes a sip before making a sound of approval. She then shuffles into a more comfortable position in my lap. 'Edward,' she says, 'Mummy said that you're her boyfriend because you can help do some of the cooking.'

Edward laughs and glances at me with one eyebrow raised. 'Oh, did she now?'

'Yes, so I want to know what sorts of things you cook?'

The corner of his mouth twitches. 'Well, my favourite thing to cook is chicken nuggets, chips and beans but there has to be plenty of ketchup.'

Ava gasps. 'That's my favourite thing to eat.'

'Really?' Edward rubs the stubble on his chin. 'Does that mean it would be okay for me to spend more time at your house?'

Ava shrugs. 'Yes.'

'How about you, Ralph? What do you think?' Edward asks.

'I'm okay with it,' he says. Most people would leave it at that because it's what they want to hear, but Edward presses further.

'It's going to feel different for a while and it's okay to not be okay if you know what I mean,' Edward says as Ralph stares into his cup. 'You might want time alone with your mum or you might want to hang out without me there or maybe we could do some things together. I don't know how this will work for us all as individuals but I want you to know you can be honest. If you need a break from me being there I can give you space. Whatever you need, just say.'

My body tenses up again and I have butterflies. I'm not sure why this is so nerve-racking. I suppose it's because I don't have the magic formula to make this work. If I want it to and Edward wants it to, I'm sure we can, in time, all be happy.

'There is one thing that's bugging me,' Ralph says. Edward casts me a look before turning to Ralph.

'Okay? You can say or ask anything.'

'Will I still get to see my dad?'

'Of course you will. I'm not coming in to try and take his place. Think of me as an extra grown-up around the place,' Edward says, looking to me for backup.

'Ralph,' – I reach over and stroke his knee – 'your dad will always be in your life. He loves you all so much and nothing will ever change that.'

Ralph nods. 'Then I suppose I'm okay with this.' He points, moving his finger between Edward and me.

'And if ever you're not, you talk to us,' I say.

'Okay. Can I have a fairy cake now?' he asks and Edward and I laugh.

'Eat up. We still have that boat lift to go and see before dark.'

'Dark? It's not even lunchtime,' Ralph says.

'Have you seen how fast that thing goes?' Edward points to the boat and Ralph laughs.

As the children tuck into their cakes, Edward reaches across the picnic blanket and covers my hand with his, squeezing gently as he does. My chest swells with a fizzy warmth and I give him a reassuring smile. I think we're going to be okay and I'm sure he knows it too.

Chapter 54

It's dark when we get home. We raided an outlet store for dry clothes and stopped at a pub for dinner and the kids fell asleep in the car. Edward carries Ava upstairs and I wake Ralph and take Henry. As I'm undressing Henry, Ava stirs and asks Edward to read her a story in her dozy, sleep-thickened voice. When I hear him start to read *Room on the Broom*, I smile. He won't know but it's her favourite. I put Henry in his cot then go to make sure Ralph has brushed his teeth but he's already conked out in his bed fully clothed. I sit beside him and just look at him for a moment. It's hard to imagine he was a squidgy baby once. He's so tall and lean now and he's at that funny age where his teeth look too big for his face. He's perfect; they all are. I lean over and kiss him on his forehead and he stirs a little.

'Shh,' I say, stroking his face. 'Go to sleep.'

'Mum,' he croaks.

'Yes, honey?'

'I do like Edward you know.'

I lean over and kiss him again. 'I'm glad. Get some sleep.'

As I tiptoe downstairs, Edward is just finishing off the story.

'I like your reading voice,' Ava says. I smile.

Leaving him to it, I sneak outside. The sky is a clear black and the air is cool. I tilt my face to the stars and inhale three times. It's something I've been working on and I'm getting there. After speaking to a therapist, I called my dad too and he's coming up in a few weeks to talk about Mum. I think it will bring me some much-needed closure.

When I head inside, Edward is just coming down. He looks shattered. His new outdoor wear is brightly coloured and not at all *him* and his hair is pointing in all sorts of directions. Somehow, he still manages to look sexy as hell.

'Come here you,' I say, pulling him by his clothes.

He steps towards me and wraps his arms around my waist.

'I don't know about you, but I've had a wonderful day.'

I search his eyes for some hint of sarcasm and see nothing but honesty. 'I think if you can cope with jumping into a canal, then you're quite well cut out for spending time with me and my brood.'

'I'd love nothing more,' he whispers, resting his forehead on mine. 'Right now though, I'd like to spend a bit of time doing this.' He places his lips on mine. Our mouths are starting to fit together like a jigsaw puzzle if a jigsaw puzzle came with a little firework kit that you swallow since little explosions of delight have filled my body.

I know the road ahead won't be smooth. This is real life. We'll have work to do and challenges to face, but right now in this moment I have all I ever wanted.

Epilogue

'I don't know why you waited a whole year to move in,' Ralph says as he carries one of Edward's boxes in from the car.

'Your mum and I wanted to make sure it was right for all of us, especially you, Ava and Henry.'

'Well, I've done sex education this week and you should know that I'll be hitting puberty soon,' Ralph says without a hint of embarrassment. 'All I'm saying is you would have probably got a decent run of my good nature before I turn all grumpy and hormonal.' Edward's cheeks flush and I raise my hand to my mouth to hide my smirk.

'He's got this newfound, unfiltered confidence all of a sudden,' I whisper to Edward when Ralph disappears inside.

'It's, er, good that he can talk about this stuff, isn't it?'

I smile. 'Yes, I suppose so. It's taking some getting used to though.'

'Oh, before I forget. I think I left my jacket at Mike and Kate's when we went over last weekend. Can you ask them to bring it round later?' Edward's brow crumples.

'Already done. They're coming earlier to help with the food. In fact, they'll be here any …' Mike's car pulls up. 'Speak of the devils.'

'Hi, you two,' Kate says, kissing Edward and me on our cheeks. When I first met Kate, I wasn't sure what to make of her. She's younger than me but it isn't a case of swapping me for a younger model. She and Mike are genuinely in love. Kate and I are like chalk and cheese but she's got this infectious friendliness about her that makes it impossible to dislike her. Moreover, she keeps Mike in line. I ended up inviting her to join the book club. We're still meeting every month or so and most of the time we do read the books. Amanda ended up putting a notice in the village library inviting people to join. Quite a few did so now we have to meet in the pub where the landlord reserves a special area for us. Although our official name is The Milden Book Club, to me, Janey, Amanda and Emily, we will always be The Single Mums' Book Club. We didn't realise how much we needed it at the time, but it plucked each one of us from a dark place and helped us live again.

'Hiya, pal,' Mike says shaking Edward's hand. 'Hello, love.' He hugs me.

'Kids are inside. Help yourselves to drinks and I'll be in shortly.'

As Kate and Mike go inside, the kids squeal in excitement. 'Come on, we'd better get the last of your stuff in. There's a party happening soon.'

'Ahh yes, my moving-in party,' Edward says with a twinkle in his eyes.

'It's not your moving-in party. Just a celebration of …' Oh, I don't know. Who am I kidding? It's our first family barbecue and I've invited everyone. Janey, Amanda, Emily and Stacy are coming, as well as Carly and Helen from the practice. Obviously, Mike and Kate are here too and my dad is coming up. We've met twice in the past twelve months and although things were a bit awkward at first, he's really trying – we both are. I'm not sure how everyone will fit in but if the rain holds off and we can stay outside, we'll be okay.

As Edward heads inside, I spot Janey and her two heading

over. She has some kind of large flan in her hand and the children are carrying crisps and fairy buns. 'Told you I didn't need a man,' she whispers in my ear as she kisses my cheek.

'I never doubted it.'

Tom hands me a bag of Doritos and darts inside.

'I'd better get the fancy serving dish out for those bad boys,' I say, winking at Janey.

'Don't start – I've had the day from hell,' she says. 'This is my second attempt at this bloody flan and it still doesn't look right.'

'It looks good to me. Anyway, you didn't need to bring any—'

Janey holds up a finger. If I finish the sentence I don't know what she'll do after all the effort she's put in so I let the words dissolve into a puff of air. 'Edward has set a bar up in the garden.'

'Now you're talking,' she says, heading in.

Edward helps me get the food ready and we decide to be brave and set it up outside. The rest of the guests arrive and I head inside to get more tonic. As I look out of the window and see Edward and Mike chatting, I get a rush of love. When I longed for a family, I longed for the nuclear type that I had for five short years. I suppose I wanted it, not because it was right, but because it was ripped away from me so cruelly and I always felt like something in my life was missing. What I have now is so much more. I know not all divorces work out this way and no part of me takes it for granted. I'm lucky and what I have is a special sort of perfect. Mike has even started saying no to treats and telling the kids off a bit when they play up. He's still a big softy but at least he has some boundaries now.

The doorbell rings. 'I'll get it.'

I walk down the hallway with a happy buzz. 'Hi, Amanda.'

'Hi, Stephanie, this is my *boyfriend*, Steve.' There's a wicked glint in her eye. Their romance has been a slow burn but they clicked on their first date and I've never seen her happier.

'Nice to meet you, Steve.'

Edward pops his head from out of the kitchen. 'Ahh, the elusive Steve! Come and get a beer, pal.'

'He's handsome.' I raise my eyebrow.

'I know.' Amanda winks and heads towards the kitchen whilst I let my bemusement settle. My phone buzzes. It's Stacy.

Me and Dave are on our way. Got stuck at the pub. Long story. Found a great book for our next book club read. I'll let Amanda know because she'll want to send us out her discussion points. See you and Eddy soon xxx

I smile and tuck my phone back in my pocket as I head through to the garden. Amanda now sends us key points to discuss before every meeting because she got so fed up with us talking about everything but the books. Once the discussion points have been covered, the conversation can move on to anything we want. We mock her for it but the notes have given our club more structure. We have so many members now, we need it.

Somehow, the kids have found water pistols and a code red is now in place for my pretty (paper) gingham tablecloths. I'm about to give them all a rollicking but something stops me. Ralph's mischievous smile as he blasts Seren with a super soaker? Ava's scream of laughter as a jet of water just misses her? Screw the tablecloths. Edward hands me a glass of wine but doesn't speak. He knows what I'm looking at and I think he knows why. These kids have been through a lot but they're happy. To see them now living as kids should, I know they'll be all right. Edward wraps his arm around me and I turn my head to kiss him.

'What was that for?'

I smile. 'I feel complete.'

Acknowledgements

As always, this book would not have been possible without the safety net of so many people. Firstly, I'd like to thank HQ Digital, for making my writing dreams come true and publishing all seven of my books. I'd also like to thank my wonderful editor, Belinda Toor, for her honest and supportive feedback and little comments that made me smile. On that note, I'd like to express huge thanks to Helena Newton for spotting all of my instances of repetition. I think after spending the past twelve months constantly repeating myself to get the children to listen to my home-schooling, it had become somewhat ingrained in me.

The writing community is incredibly supportive and I'd like to say a massive thanks to the following writers, Rachel Burton, Rachel Dove, Maxine Morrey, Sarah Bennett and Jenny O'Brien for always being there to offer support, lift spirits, provide a few laughs or give advice.

Rachel Gilby at Rachel's Random Resources, thank you so much for all your support with marketing and blog tours over the past few years and for your own wonderful reviews. They mean the world to me. On a similar note, I'd like to say a massive thank you to all the bloggers who take part in tours and shout about my books. There are too many to name individually but

I'll be sharing all of your wonderful reviews so do tag me in.

The Chicklit and Prosecco chat group is a great place for readers and writers who love this genre to connect. Anita Faulkner deserves a huge thank you for setting the group up. In a similar vein, ChicklitChatHQ on Facebook is a wonderful place full of supportive authors and bloggers. Lucy from the Book Club Bitches – thank you for making me laugh and supporting my books.

Last but certainly not least, I'd like to thank my readers who make this all possible.

Keep reading for an excerpt from
Sun, Sea and Sangria …

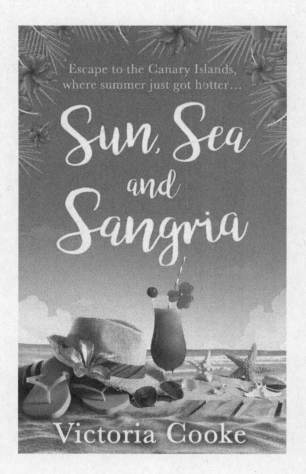

Andrea's Sunny Sangria Recipe

One bottle of your favourite Rioja
(I like to have an extra one so I can have a glass
whilst chopping fruit)
An orange
A lemon
An apple
A few strawberries
2–3 tablespoons of sugar
A dash of banana liqueur or brandy/rum/gin or
whatever you have left over from Christmas
(choose one of these – not all)
A cup of orange juice
Ginger ale, soda water or lemonade to taste
A few frozen raspberries

1. Chop the fruit and squeeze a little of the juice from the lemon and orange pieces into the pitcher then toss the rest of the fruit in.
2. Add the sugar and pour in the full bottle of wine.
3. Add the dash of dusty-shelf booze and chill until you're ready to serve.
4. Before serving, add ginger ale, orange juice, frozen berries and ice, then give it a stir.

Chapter 1

'Where the hell is the dry oil spray?' My chest is tightening. 'We're on in ten and Sammy needs to be glistening like an Adonis and smelling of coconut in five.'

'I've got some olive oil from the restaurant,' Ant pipes up. 'That's what I've used.'

'Yes, well you look like a deep-fried sausage and don't smell much better. Grab a towel and rub it off. It's the twenty-first century, for goodness' sake, and nobody here is auditioning for *The Full Monty.*'

'Yes, Kat,' a few voices mumble. I don't have the time to think about who they belong to, but I do spot one or two other super-greasy torsos.

'Seven minutes to go. Come on!' I'm rummaging through my bag, throwing things left and right in a fit of panic. 'Here.' I produce an old bottle of Skin So Soft from Avon, which I've been using as a mozzie repellent since my mum gave me a bottle in 1997.

'I want you all shimmering seductively and smelling nose-twitchingly floral in three minutes tops.' I toss the spray to my lead dancer, Marcus. 'Go!'

Through the fog and nose-tingling scent of dry oil mist, I

check myself in the mirror. My stage make-up looks like Mary Berry has daubed it on with a silicone spatula, but this glam look is for my bold stage persona. It helps me get into the character of a strong, confident woman who knows what she wants. It should look natural under the lights. Anyway, it's the guys who need to look good out there, not me.

'Okay, huddle up.' The guys gather dutifully around me. 'Right, remember that Sammy has pulled his shoulder, so when you all go into the backflips segment, he will be stage left, grinding. Don't wait for him. Also, Marcus, that thing you did with the eye contact and the winking last night – the audience loved it. I want to see more. Remember, the crowd loves you. Do your best and let's blow this thing up.'

There are some whoops from the audience as the amplified beats of 50 Cent's 'Candy Shop' start. I'm up. I wiggle my curvy hips as I saunter onto the stage and pump the mic above my head in time to the music. The crowd whoop and cheer and the excitement is tangible. Under the glare of the bright white spotlights, I can barely make out the hundreds of people who've come to see the show, but the energy is electric.

'Ladies … and gentlemen,' because there are always a few blokes in the crowd, 'welcome to the Grand Canarian resort complex where we are going to Blow. Your. Mind! There won't be a fire hose or PVC thong in sight, because tonight we're giving you your dream man. Think gorgeous Adonises who can satisfy your deepest desires. Think dreamboat pick 'n' mix. Ladies and gents, think the Heavenly Hunks …'

As the crowd goes wild, my five men come out dressed in distressed blue jeans and T-shirts that struggle to contain their abs. Marcus and Ant lift me into the air and turn me around as 'I Want It That Way' by the Backstreet Boys kicks in and the boys start to dance. It's the same routine we do every night, but each show feels a little different depending on where we're performing. As the boys move to the front, I slip back into the shadows.

'They always bring the crowds,' a male voice with a thick Spanish accent says. Gaël, the hotel manager, has appeared in the wings beside me.

I smile. It's taken a while to get to this point. When we first started up here, there was just me, Marcus, Hugo and Pauw trying to get gigs (Pauw's real name is Paul but everyone loves to make fun of the fact that despite living in East London his whole life, he doesn't have a cockney accent – it's incredibly hard to just call him Paul now). Most of the big hotels wanted tribute acts or magicians and we just about scraped by in seedy bars.

Things changed when Gaël booked us a couple of years ago for his huge, fancy hotel, on a whim, after a spate of complaining Brits rightfully whinged about a geriatric gymnast who took five minutes and two helpers to do a cartwheel and called it a show. After that, people couldn't get enough of the Heavenly Hunks. The *Canaries Today* called us 'The Chippendales for the Modern Woman'. We're probably piggy-backing off the success of *Magic Mike* a bit, but I don't think their lawyers are worried.

'My favourite part.' Gaël nudges me. He's a skinny, six-foot, heterosexual guy but even he can't help but glue his eyes to the backflips and breakdancing. Pauw does his run of six consecutive backflips as Ant, who's a trained ballet dancer, leaps across the stage in mid-air splits, his long brown hair billowing behind him. The crowd can't get enough of his porcelain skin.

The music slows down and the intro to Ed Sheeran's 'I'm a Mess' kicks in. Marcus appears in an open dark denim shirt that reveals enough of his smooth, toned chest to drive the audience wild. The shirt is paired with fitted, dark jeans and chunky boots. His short dark hair and light-brown skin look beautiful under the light, and the whole ensemble is one of my finest pieces of work, even if I do say so myself. He sits on the edge of the stage, making eye contact with as many lucky audience members as he can manage, whilst his silky voice gives its pitch-perfect rendition of the song. I still get chills watching him and I've seen this act a billion times.

'Even *I* am almost falling in love,' Gaël jokes.

'See, that's the point, Gaël. Women don't want cheesy hosepipe-stroking and pant-dropping to the beat of "Hot Stuff". We don't even want to see any naked bottoms.' Gaël shifts uncomfortably, but I'm proud of the act I've put together so I carry on regardless. 'Women want sexy all-rounders. Men with talent. Half the time, the Heavenlies are fully clothed, yet you can practically hear the ladies' ovaries scream.'

'I admire what you've done. You know, if you ever get fed up of managing the Heavenly Hunks, there would be a job here as my entertainment director. I'm terrible at it.' He laughs.

'Thanks, Gaël, though I can't see that happening any time soon.'

I switch my mic back on and step back into the spotlight. 'I don't know about you but I've come over all hot and bothered,' I say over the screaming cheers. 'We've had a hard day today, haven't we, ladies? I mean, I bet some of you even had to fetch your own cocktails from the pool bar, didn't you? Well, we're going to slow things down and treat as many of you as possible to your own *heavenly* massage whilst our talented Hugo plays the piano, just for you.'

The spotlight switches to Hugo, who starts playing 'All of Me'. As dry ice fills the stage, the rest of the guys filter through the audience giving shoulder rubs to as many audience members as possible. Those not having their shoulders rubbed are fixated on Hugo. His black hair shines under the light and his muscles ripple beneath his tanned skin as he hits the keys, his eyes intent on the sheet music. A ripple of excitement washes over me. We put on a bloody good show even if I do say so myself.

As the song finishes, it's time for our pièce de résistance, and okay, the song is nicked from *Magic Mike* but we did our own choreography and I doubt Mike cares. The beat starts and the guys bound across the stage from behind the curtain as 'Pony' kicks in at the chorus, and the crowd are up, out of their seats, singing and going wild. Under the blue-white spotlight, with the rising dry ice, they look like mythical beings.

'That was awesome, guys. The manager is really pleased with us and has booked us in for an extra show next month when we're back from Gran Canaria, as well as the bookings we'd already secured for early next year.' The guys cheer and there's a bit of back-slapping. 'We have the show over in Playa de las Americas tomorrow, which is going to be huge, and there's a British newspaper doing a piece on the resort – they want to include a short review of our show, so I want you all bright-eyed and bushy-tailed for the rehearsal tomorrow. That means one drink tops in the bar tonight then bed, okay?'

I glare pointedly at Ant and Hugo. Ant looks sheepish and Hugo looks downright confused. He speaks English fairly well, but he doesn't always catch what I'm saying if I go off on a rant and sometimes I wonder if it's 'selective' understanding. I'm hoping a stern glance in his direction is enough to stop him going home with an audience member or two, tonight at least.

'Love you, Kat.' Pauw leans in for a hug.

'You too. Make sure you get yourself to the doctor's tomorrow and have that mole on your back checked,' I say, unhappy with the raised appearance it's taken on recently. He gives me a salute and blows me a kiss. I shake my head as he walks away.

'Marcus, you left your driver's licence in the dressing area,' I sigh, holding it out to him between my fingers.

'What would I do without you, Kat?'

'I honestly have no idea,' I say drily as he wanders off.

Hugo gives me a sheepish look and waves goodbye as the rest of the guys give me hugs and disperse. When I'm alone, I take a deep breath, gather my things and walk out through the hotel's reception on a high.

Chapter 2

As I walk out into the crisp silence of the early hours, my skin bristles. I feel on edge. A man is loitering across the street. He has a messy bun and a giant camouflage-print Puffa jacket on. Granted, it can get chilly here at night in September but it's hardly the Arctic Circle. My body is tense with apprehension; each nerve ending senses danger. He's watching me whilst sipping something from a bottle. I tuck my bag under my arm and walk briskly past. It isn't until I'm much closer that I realise he's sipping some kind of smoothie drink. I relax a little, as though it's a given that muggers don't really worry about their vitamin intake or care much for liquefied kale. It's silly how our perception of people works sometimes, but right now it's making me feel safe.

Something grabs my shoulder, and my heart catapults out of my chest. I spin, fists clenched, ready to pound seven bells out of Smoothie Man or whoever it is.

When my eyes focus on the person in front of me, I get quite the surprise.

It isn't the camouflaged man-bun man I was expecting. It's a dark-haired man I don't recognise. Something about his soft brown eyes, fixed with concern on my clenched fists, stifles my alarm.

'Sorry, I'm so sorry.' He holds his hands in the air. 'Just realised how bad it was to touch your shoulder. I didn't want to just shout a random "excuse me" down the street at half twelve.'

'But grabbing a lady on a dark, lonely street at half twelve is okay?'

'Like I said, I'm sorry. I didn't think it through, I just really wanted to talk to you and you left the hotel before I got a chance. Can we start again?' He grins a wide smile and two small dimples form either side. He may have terrible etiquette but he *is* handsome. That thought is quickly overshadowed. What could he possibly want to talk to me about at this hour? I'd send him away but I'm too intrigued.

'What is it?'

'I saw your show tonight and thought it was great ...' He runs a hand through his hair, messing up the longer-on-top side-parting thing that seems trendy these days. 'Anyway, I think I have what it takes and I wondered if you might have an opening for another dancer? I've just moved out here and I'm looking for work. I think it would suit me.'

I get a pang in my stomach. He certainly looks the part despite perhaps seeming a little older than the others, but that's not a problem. The age range of our audience is eighteen to anything goes. I just can't take someone on at the moment. 'Look ...' I look pointedly at him, hoping he'll furnish me with a name.

'Jay,' he says, taking the cue.

'Jay. It's not that I'm trying to brush you off. You certainly *look* the part and if you can dance I'd definitely audition you if I had space ... The thing is, our profit margins are small and I'd not budgeted for taking on another dancer this year. I'm sorry.'

'No, I'm sorry. I shouldn't have hijacked your evening. It was just an idea. I've just got out here and I'm looking for work. It looked like fun, that's all.' He drops his head and turns to leave.

I feel really bad, not that he's my responsibility or anything, but when I first arrived out here, desperate, I was given a chance and it indirectly kick-started the Hunks. Perhaps I'm just shattered after back-to-back gigs but I want to throw him a lifeline. I'm sure we probably *could* afford another body on stage and it will give us an excuse to update our posters and fliers.

'I'll tell you what, why don't you come along to a short audition tomorrow and I can keep you in mind.'

The dimples reappear. 'Yes, great. Tell me when and where you want me.'

I shiver. Must be the arctic conditions. I rummage in my bag and pull out a tatty old business card for the bar we rehearse in. 'We practise at three so come at two. Prepare a routine to "Pony" and we'll take it from there.'

'Okay, I'll be there …' He gestures to me with an open hand.

'Kat,' I say and take his hand in mine sealing the arrangement with a firm shake.

'Nice to meet you, Kat.'

A Letter From Victoria.

Dear reader,

I just wanted to say a huge thank you for taking the time to read *The Single Mums' Book Club*. The inspiration for this book came through the lockdown of 2020 when I had the pleasure of spending months on end with my family. To hit pause and just enjoy the spring and summer together was a real blessing even through the tough times.

In this book, it was nice to revisit my roots and head back to Manchester, where I spent my first 22 years as a human. If you've read *The Secret To Falling in Love* or *Who Needs Men Anyway?* you might have gathered it's one of my favourite cities in the world.

Reviews long and short, good or bad are incredibly valuable to authors. They let us know how we're doing, how we can improve and give us warm fuzzy feelings when people like our work. If you can spare a few minutes to leave one on your chosen retailer's website, I do read them and would love to hear your feedback. I also love to hear from you directly through either my website, Facebook, Instagram or Twitter where you can usually find me procrastinating like a champ!

Finally, thank you again for your support in purchasing this book and, if you liked it, please check out my others.

Best Wishes,

Victoria Cooke

Dear Reader,

We hope you enjoyed reading this book. If you did, we'd be so appreciative if you left a review. It really helps us and the author to bring more books like this to you.

Here at HQ Digital we are dedicated to publishing fiction that will keep you turning the pages into the early hours. Don't want to miss a thing? To find out more about our books, promotions, discover exclusive content and enter competitions you can keep in touch in the following ways:

JOIN OUR COMMUNITY:
Sign up to our new email newsletter: http://smarturl.it/SignUpHQ

Read our new blog www.hqstories.co.uk

🐦 : https://twitter.com/HQStories

f : www.facebook.com/HQStories

BUDDING WRITER?
We're also looking for authors to join the HQ Digital family!

Find out more here:

https://www.hqstories.co.uk/want-to-write-for-us/

Thanks for reading, from the HQ Digital team

If you enjoyed *The Single Mums' Book Club*, then why not try another delightfully uplifting romance from HQ Digital?